MURDERED BY THE MOB

SEAN CAMPBELL

PARTNERS IN CRIME

Murdered by the Mob

First published in Great Britain by Partners in Crime 2023.

Cover design by www.nickcastledesign.com

10 9 8 7 6 5 4 3 2 1

PROLOGUE: DEAD LOYAL

IN HIS USUAL BROKEN ENGLISH, Tank had explained Russian roulette.

He was older than me and knew what it meant. One gun, one bullet in the chamber. Spin and shoot.

'It fine,' he'd said earlier, 'she probably live, *tak*.'

But this wasn't Russian roulette.

This was Tiny's version. He called it Ukrainian roulette and said it was a game to test if I was loyal or not. To know I'd put them before blood. Tiny handed me the gun.

'This is a Rossi 32,' he said with a grin. 'Hold it nice and tight 'cause it'll give off a hell of a kick when you fire it. It's no Smith & Wesson... but that won't make anyone any less dead. Now, you know what to do...'

He looked at me expectantly. Ukrainian roulette was the same as Russian roulette except for one thing.

It wasn't my head I had to point the gun at.

It was my mum's.

Around me, the boys jeered from the shadows. They'd been here before. Everyone had to do it.

I looked for Tank, but he wouldn't look back at me. His head was in his hands. The other boys lined up around the warehouse, blocking every exit. I couldn't see everyone in the dark, but in the front row Tiny stood between his big brothers Nico and Pavel, all three of them grinning.

Only Mum and I were lit up by a big lamp overhead.

Mum stared up at me. She knew what I had to do. She'd been here before. The last time, it was my brother's turn.

The gun was heavy even holding it in both hands.

Tank's voice echoed in my mind. 'Auggie, just do it.'

I didn't want to.

But I had no choice. The brothers were watching me for any sign of weakness.

If I didn't shoot her, *they* would. Then they'd shoot me too.

We'd wind up at the bottom of the Thames. Like the others who hadn't done it right.

I tried to say sorry but I couldn't. There was a lump in my throat. My lip began to quiver. I hoped Tiny couldn't see.

Mum nodded as if to say it was okay.

Five in six.

My hands started to shake. If Tiny saw, I'd get us *both* killed.

It was now or never.

I pulled the trigger.

PREDICTABILITY KILLS

Twenty-five years later...

HIS ROUTINE WAS SO PREDICTABLE. Walk the dog, buy a coffee, and head home for a late breakfast.

We looped around the cul-de-sac and parked up outside his house with the rear doors of the van as close to the front door as we could get.

'This is it, Tank,' I said. 'House number forty-three.'

From the road, we couldn't see the front door as a hedge blocked our view, but the GPS never lies.

Tank got out of the van just before I did, leading the way through the gate and up to the front door. A tall, dark-haired man answered. He looked down at us, his forehead creasing up. Had he recognised me? It had been well over a decade and we'd only met in passing. Besides, I didn't look anything like I used to. If he somehow did recognise me, we'd have to change our plan and rush the job.

'Parcel for Zholnovych,' I said. A neutral, London accent. One I'd spent the last few years perfecting. With a bit of luck that, plus the courier uniforms and clipboard, would throw him off.

He looked confused, glancing from Tank to me and back again. My heart began to race. Finally, he gave a little shrug.

'No order anything,' he said grumpily.

'Must be a gift then,' I said, holding out my clipboard officiously. 'See, *GIFT ORDER for ZHOLNOVYCH. Deliver to LOUNGE.*'

He held out his hand for the clipboard, took it, and screwed up his face as he read the delivery manifest that I'd knocked up in Word last night. Then he handed it back and shrugged.

'We'll be right back. It's in the truck.'

Tank followed me back to the van. We quickly fetched the parcel. Tank did the heavy lifting, like always. At six foot four, he was almost as tall as the parcel was long. Not only that, but the box was several feet deep, almost as wide, and heavy with it; the inside was reinforced to take the weight. On one side, there were pictures of a surround-sound speaker system. We made sure to have that side facing the door as we walked back up the path.

When Zholnovych saw it, his eyebrows shot up and then he cracked a smile.

'Big parcel!' I said cheerfully. 'You must be a lucky man. Keep clear and we'll bring it through. Which way's the living room?'

'Straight ahead.'

The hallway was nice and wide, so it was an easy job. A little huffing and puffing later, we laid the parcel on his living room floor, but not before he'd spread out a bedsheet to protect his carpet.

'Sign here please, mate,' I said, 'to confirm you've checked it all and it's in good condition.'

'I no check!' Zholnovych said.

'Fine. You'd best take a look then, hadn't you?' I held out my Stanley knife. 'For the tape. It's thick stuff.'

For the next minute, the only sound was that of the knife ripping cleanly through the tape as Zholnovych cut the thick layers of it off of his gift. Finally, he began to unfold the top layers of cardboard.

'What fuck? Is all cardboard?'

'Nah,' I said more confidently than I felt. 'Must be something inside it – keep going, yeah?'

Zholnovych looked sceptical. His grip on the knife tightened. For a minute, I thought we might have trouble. Holding my knife gave him a false sense of security.

He opened the box and leant forward, eager to see what was inside. It was dark enough that we had a few seconds before he realised it was empty.

Before he did, I slowly pulled out my weapon from my jacket pocket, took aim, and fired.

One shot at point blank range, straight into his back. Despite only using compressed air, the pop reverberated around the room.

He tumbled forward, unsteady on his feet, his hands desperately trying to pull the dart out of his back. I saw his shoulders tense, desperation mixed with adrenaline letting him fight through the effects of the tranquilliser.

'Tank!'

As Zholnovych struggled, Tank leapt forward to grab hold of his arms and yanked them behind his back with a sickening crack. He tried to scream as Tank manhandled him into the box, pinning his face against the liner to muffle the noise.

No sooner had Tank pinned him down, Zholnovych lashed out with his foot, connecting with Tank's groin.

As Tank yelped, he let go of Zholnovych's arms just long enough for him to flail around, his hands scrabbling around, snatching at Tank's head. The big man roared again. Tiny droplets of blood flew through the air like confetti. Tank clutched his ear: Zholnovych had torn his diamond stud out. Shit. I'd have to get my hands dirty. As Tank backed away in pain, I leapt in to take his place, pinning Zholnovych down with all my weight. I eyed his feet warily as he struggled. This was *supposed* to be Tank's job. Finally, he stopped struggling. He'd passed out.

'Help me fold his legs in!'

Once Tank had found his diamond stud, he slipped it, blood and all, into his pocket, and then came to help deal with our unconscious friend. We folded his arms in so he lay flat in the box, checked the floor to make sure we hadn't lost anything else, washed our hands in the kitchen sink, and then, slowly, we did everything in reverse. We folded the box back down and replaced the tape with new.

And then, all three of us left, Zholnovych concealed in the nice, neat parcel that Tank and I carried back to the van.

On the doorstep, I paused.

'One sec,' I said to Tank. 'We've got to take the bedsheet.'

Tank and I put the box down for a moment so I could nip back in and get rid of the last piece of evidence. While I was in there, I grabbed the laptop and phone from the coffee table too. They might have something useful on them. I made sure they were both off so the Rozzers couldn't track us using 'em.

When I came back out, a neighbour was in his front garden. He looked at us curiously.

'Return to sender,' I explained cheerfully.

2

MISSING, PRESUMED DEAD

THE BOSS HAD *LOST IT.*

Now, Rafferty had to clear up his mess. Again.

She found herself in Balham, south London where a man had gone missing. A neighbour had called it in and now Rafferty was going door-to-door around the cul-de-sac to see what, if anything, each neighbour had seen. The woman hadn't invited her in.

'I told your colleague everythin', didn't I?' she said, her exasperated tone matched by the tapping of her foot. She looked around anxiously as if worried someone might see her talking to the police. While Balham had made great strides since it's nineties and noughties heyday as a drug-fuelled cesspit, gentrification wasn't yet complete despite the hefty price tags of the two-up two-down mews houses.

'I'm aware of that,' Rafferty said, 'but if it's not *too* much trouble, can you tell me what you saw?'

The woman chewed her lip, clearly tempted to tell Rafferty to sling her hook. She was a strange one, clearly younger than Rafferty, and yet dressed in a thick-knit, Angora jumper befitting someone in their dotage. Her hair was likewise coiffed into a bun that sat sternly atop her head. If Rafferty had to guess, she'd have said retired school mistress.

Except the woman wasn't anywhere near old enough, and a schoolteacher's salary wouldn't be enough to live here. Her house was at the end of the cul-de-sac, well away from the traffic of Balham High Road, the hum of which was barely audible.

'Didn't see much, my love,' the woman said. 'I was on the Peloton, sweatin' buckets – been a bit warm lately, ain't it? – and then, I heard a van. I'd been expecting a delivery so I looked out, but it was outside number forty-three where that 'andsome chap lives. I do like me a tall, dark, broody one. Ya know, 'e barely said a word. My perfect fella.'

The woman pointed across the road. She needn't have bothered. The front gate to number forty-three was already bedecked with blue-and-white crime scene tape which read *Police Line Do Not Cross*. Someone had got a bit enthusiastic. The cordon had gone up long before Detective Inspector Rafferty had arrived on-scene. Thankfully, no crowds had gathered to watch proceedings. Rafferty supposed that crime happened far too much for a bit of tape to spark interest. She glanced out of the window. From here, the spectacle was limited to a couple of forensics vans and her own car. If the woman's timing were perfect, she would've seen the delivery as well as Purcell and his white-boiler-suited team heading in earlier today.

'What were you expecting?' Rafferty asked. 'To be delivered that is.'

It had to be something important. Else why would the woman be looking out for it?

She turned beetroot red and muttered, 'None of your business.'

'It is, I'm afraid, Mrs...?'

'Miss,' she corrected. 'Miss Rosie Bray.'

She even sounded like a schoolteacher. 'Miss Bray, your neighbour is missing so I need to know what you saw not what you didn't, and I need to know why you were paying so much attention to the road.'

'I wasn't payin' attention, was I? I just looked out while on my bike 'n' saw a van pull up. Two blokes got out and then disappeared behind the hedge. A few seconds later, they were back, pulling some god-awful box out of the back of the van. It was bloody huge. That's when I realised it wasn't my delivery and I stopped paying much attention.'

She still hadn't said what she was waiting for. 'Then what happened?'

'Then they came back out. Same box, same blokes. They looked a bit tired, as if the contents were really heavy, but I didn't think much of it. Had to be summat like furniture, right? White glove service, ya know? The kind where they put the thing in place for ya and take away the old one. Can't blame 'em for lookin' knackered. I would be too if I had to cart a dirty great box in and out, especially with just two of 'em.'

'Could you describe them?'

'Both were white, 'bout your age, I'd say, late forties-'

'I'm thirty-six!' Rafferty protested before she could stop herself.

Bray ignored her, '...and the other one was average build, tall-ish height wise, maybe six foot... Like I said, I didn't see much.'

In Rafferty's experience, every man was "about six foot tall". Just like on dating sites. Though if Bray's guess about height was as accurate as her ideas about Rafferty's age, she'd be worse than useless as a witness.

'Would you be willing to sit down with a sketch artist?' Rafferty asked through gritted teeth. The Met didn't pay her enough to be this polite all the time.

'Only if you're paying me for it. Hundred quid an hour. Plus me travel costs.'

'We don't do that.'

'I know ya don't, love. But I ain't taking time off work for no good reason. Was there anything else? Or can I get back to my Netflix show?'

Rafferty looked back at the house across the street. From Rosie Bray's doorstep, the view was dreadful. It was almost sixty feet, the angle wasn't great, and a wall of leylandii meant that all she could really see was the gate and the road in front. Hardly ideal.

'How well do you know the man who lives there? You said he's handsome, right?'

Bray shrugged. 'Not at all. He keeps himself to himself and I do the same. Not that I haven't tried. He is – was,' she corrected herself, 'a bloody nice-lookin' fella. Muscled, only a touch of grey hair, always well-groomed. My kinda man. Not many eligible bachelors around here, not without kids or an ex-wife in tow.'

'Was?' Rafferty echoed.

'He's dead, innee?' Bray said. 'You lot wouldn't send out a dozen blues 'n' twos, an Armed Response Vehicle, the dog unit, a forensics van, and an unmarked car for nought now, would you?'

Yet again, Rafferty was struck by Bray's brash manner. The woman was clearly exaggerating. There was no denying that there were coppers in the cul-de-sac but it was just her, Mayberry, a few uniforms and the forensics team on-site. They hadn't even had to call out a pathologist. With no body to recover, Dr Chiswick had no work to do.

'At the present time this is a missing persons inquiry.'

'Sure, sure. So what Fred told me about a body being carried out of the house, was that him spouting bollocks as usual?'

Crap. Rumours had already spread. That meant they were behind the curve. Neighbours on all sides were talking and not just to the police. One, Fred Albright, had called in for a welfare check. Rafferty hadn't spoken to him yet but she soon would. Another had seen a big box on the doorstep. Presumably that was where the body-in-a-box rumour had started.

Ayala – or rather, Detective Chief Inspector Ayala to give him his new, official rank – ought to have treated it as a murder from the get-go, kept the neighbours apart long enough to get independent stories rather than Chinese whispers, and then they'd be on top of the investigation by now. It was serious enough to merit forensics and the search team being called out but not enough for the new boss to lock everything down so Rafferty could do her job properly.

It didn't help that he was already chasing her to get back to work on the other cases on her desk.

Now she was chasing her own tail, trying to sort the fact from the fiction. There was only one thing for it: to head inside and look at the crime scene itself.

Rafferty handed Bray one of her business cards.

'Call me if you remember anything else.'

3

DEAD EASY

THE PORTLY PORTENT OF MURDER, as Rafferty called him, was on the doorstep when she approached the house. His overalls were so old that they were emblazoned with "Chief Scene of Crime Officer", the old title for his job and a reminder of just how long he'd been in forensics.

His clothes were looser on him than normal as if he'd lost weight, a rarity for a man seldom seen further than ten feet from a box of Krispy Kreme doughnuts. His skin was sallower too, greying like his hair, and he had an air of sadness about him that Rafferty couldn't help but notice.

As she watched, he bellowed orders at a young, black man that she didn't know. Then he disappeared inside, his footsteps heavy on the boards his team had laid down to protect the crime scene.

'What was Purcell having a barney about?' Rafferty asked.

The new guy looked at her and gave a casual shrug. The bollocking had rolled right off him.

'Blood spatter,' he said.

'Too much?' She hadn't imagined the inside would be a blood bath. Not without a body. Masses of blood might be gory, but it made it much easier to get Ayala to sign off on a formal murder investigation. If there was so much blood the victim couldn't survive, Ayala would have no choice but to stump up the resources to investigate properly.

'Not enough. There's a void, Inspector...?'

'Rafferty.'

'Kflom,' the man said. 'I'd shake your hand if we weren't wearing plastic. Want me to walk you through the scene? The PolSA is around upstairs somewhere, but I don't think she's found much.'

He pronounced his name like "Kerflum". Presumably it was a surname. Rafferty made a mental note to Google it later. No doubt the poor bloke got asked where he was from all the time. His accent wasn't much of a clue either. She'd have sworn he was English born and bred if it weren't for the way he'd pronounced "shake" and "scene" emphasising the "s" as its own syllable so that they became "es-hake" and "es-sheen". That was vaguely Spanish but he didn't look like any Spaniard she'd ever met. If she had to guess, she'd have guessed East African. He was tall, black, with the sort of hair most British barbers wouldn't know what to do with. Sharp cheekbones contrasted against rounded designer glasses. Nerdy but cute.

'Please.' She motioned for him to lead on. As soon as she was inside, she could see Purcell's team had worked their usual magic. Boards were everywhere. Juniors were dusting every surface, collecting samples, and snapping the photographs that would all wind up on the HOLMES 2 database.

'The lounge at the back of the house is the primary scene. From what we know so far, the killer, or killers, probably entered through the front door, traipsed down the hallway, and had an altercation with Mr Zholnovych in the living room.'

'What evidence is there for that?'

Kflom stood aside when he reached the door to the lounge. 'See for yourself.'

Inside, Rafferty could see an immaculate, if somewhat empty, living room. One large, patchwork leather L-shaped sofa ran to her left and along the near wall. It looked older than she was. On the other side of the room was an enormous, ultra-modern television hanging in the middle of the wall. It had to be pushing six feet wide and looked twice as big this close up. All around it were shelves filled to the brim with 4K Ultra HD Blu-rays. The contrast was obvious. Rental property, maybe? Land-lords were notorious for keeping furniture long past its useful lifetime after all so the well-worn sofa was no surprise, but even the nicest of landlords wouldn't be providing a cinema-sized telly to their tenant.

But it was what was missing that struck her the most: the absence of any furniture in the middle of the room, and, more strikingly, the near-complete absence of blood.

'Told you there wasn't much. Look closer.'

Rafferty did. There was a huge rectangle where the carpet wasn't flecked with blood. Around the edge, there were a few drips that spread out from near the void in the direction of the door to the hallway. If Kflom hadn't pointed it out, she'd have missed it entirely.

'Look at how it's spread. I'd bet my last penny there was a shooting in here,' Kflom added as he crouched next to her to point out the direction the spatter had travelled. 'Low-calibre, point-blank range, I'd say.'

'Where from?' Rafferty asked. The thud of heavy boots on wood echoed down the hallway as she spoke.

Kflom straightened up. He looked around the room and then pointed at a spot behind Rafferty, near to the door.

'I think,' he said hesitantly, 'the shooter would've been about there. The victim would've been roughly where you are.'

Just as Rafferty shuffled around, Purcell whipped his head around the door. 'For Christ's sake, Kflom! I've told you already. Evidence, evidence, evidence. I could hear your speculation from the other end of the house. Don't go jumping to conclusions when the facts aren't in yet.'

Kflom looked at him sheepishly. 'Yes, boss.'

'No more, okay? Wait for the lab to confirm GSR before we mention gunshots. We test the blood – and check it's the same bloody DNA as the toothbrush in the bathroom so we know it's the victim's – before we announce that a misper is a murder victim. Evidence, not theories.'

The difference between a misper and a murder investigation was stark. The former would be kicked to a different team, one with thousands of cases on their books, while the latter would become Rafferty's fifteenth open case.

Purcell shook his head and turned to Rafferty before continuing in a much softer tone. 'Sorry, Ash. He's new. At a scene yesterday, he was convinced there had been a murder – until I pointed out it was the owner's cat that had knocked over a vase. We've all been there but fuck me I didn't realise how annoying it was.'

Blimey. First, he looked like shit. Then he actually swore. What happened to the happy, doughnut-loving Purcell?

Rafferty forced herself to laugh, waved off his apology and he retreated back to carry on doing whatever he'd been up to out in the hallway. When he'd gone, Rafferty turned back to Kflom and lowered her voice.

'And the big bit without any blood on. What was there?'

Kflom grinned. 'Like I said, it's just a void. Something was there. Now it's not. Can't really guess what though.'

That explained why there was a large, rectangular patch of clean carpet. There wasn't much of an indent so it couldn't have been there long. In Rafferty's experience, heavy furniture tended to leave a visible impression, especially in cheap, made-for-rental-property carpet like this.

Someone had been shot in here and then whatever had been in the middle of the room had been removed. A lightbulb went off immediately. It had to be the box that the weirdo neighbour, Rosie Bray, had seen being removed from the house.

The size of the void lined up.

'What about DNA? From the killer, obviously.'

The victim's DNA would be everywhere. It was his house and, presumably, his blood.

'We're looking, of course. But Purcell's not hopeful.'

Rafferty cracked a half-smile. 'When is he ever?'

Purcell's pessimism was a running joke in the department. Or it used to be. Morton used to be responsible for the wise-cracks, but he'd been "retired" for a few months. That was Superintendent Silverman's doing, with some assistance from now-DCI Ayala. It was to the Met's detriment as they were quickly realising.

'Looks like a professional job to me,' Kflom volunteered.

'You're a detective now, too, eh?' Rafferty teased. 'Where have the Met been hiding you all this time?'

Privately, she agreed with him. This had career criminal written all over it. The killer, or, if Bray was right about two delivery men, killers, had been in and out in minutes and left nothing behind them. It was what the profilers would call a sophisticated, forensically aware crime.

He cracked a grin. It was the sort of cheeky chappy smile that you couldn't be angry with. 'Nah, I'm not, but how hard can it be?'

Cheeky bastard.

She was saved from having to invent a quip by the arrival of DS Mayberry. 'Finished talking to the PolSA?'

The Police Search Advisor was responsible for co-ordi-
nating the search.

'Y-yup,' he said. 'N-not much to log. L-looks like a rental. A
few c-c-clothes in the wardrobe. No phone or laptop.'

Poor Mayberry's stutter wasn't getting any better. Years ago,
he'd suffered an on-the-job injury resulting in aphasia. It was a
wonder he hadn't been let go on medical grounds.

'Are they still here?'

'G-gone.'

Lucky so-and-so. This was a dream job for a search advisor,
short and sweet. Utterly useless for the enquiry, but with no
evidence found, there wouldn't be much paperwork to
complete. Nor would there be any follow-up work to crack the
victim's mobile. For a brief moment, she wondered how anyone
could exist without a phone or laptop. Hers were constantly
binging and beeping as all and sundry tried to get a hold of her.
Maybe that was it. Someone trying to disconnect from an
increasingly digital world. She put the thought from her mind
and concentrated on the evidence they did have to work with.
No doubt one of Purcell's staff would bag the clothes to look for
stray DNA.

'So why the long face?'

'It's Be-Be-Bertram.'

Mayberry was one of the few who still called him Bertram.
When she'd joined the team, she'd been told in no uncertain
circumstances that her colleagues were Mayberry and Ayala,
not Roger and Bertram. At first, it struck her as a bit weird and
archaic and then she'd realised why Morton had insisted
upon it.

It wasn't for his sake or hers. Nor was it some throwback to
the good old days. Calling Ayala and Mayberry by their
surnames was an act of mercy. To avoid upsetting the applecart,
everyone got treated the same and the barrister-style naming

convention stuck in the office. Now it would be weird to even
think of them by their first names. Except when she wanted to
royally piss off old "Bertie".

'What's our beloved overlord done now?'

Mayberry winced. Bugger. She shouldn't have said that.
God knew why, but the two of them got on well. They'd been
on the team before Rafferty had joined so perhaps it was just
down to the passage of time. Their personalities were chalk and
cheese: where Mayberry was thoughtful, conscientious and
quiet, Ayala was quick to take credit for everything and responsibility for nothing.

'He w-w-wants to k-kick this over to M-M-MisPers.'

Seriously? She'd been expecting it ever since he'd tried to
chivvy her back to the rest of her caseload. But now they'd seen
the evidence, a misper was mental. They had an eyewitness, a
void the size of a body, and blood spatter suggesting someone
had been shot. If Morton were still around, he'd have declared a
major incident within minutes of the shout coming in.
Unluckily for Rafferty, her old boss had been replaced by the
man who'd sabotaged his career.

'That's mental,' Rafferty said flatly.

'N-n-no body, no murder, he says.'

Ridiculous. It was about as logical as the time Silverman
told the world the Met "didn't investigate retrospective crimes"
when one of her friends was under investigation. She'd even had
the gall to suggest that the police couldn't investigate because
they had no evidence. Hello? Who the hell did she think was
going to collect that evidence?

No wonder she'd promoted Ayala.

'So Zholnovych's death gets a misper budget instead of a
murder enquiry. That'll go bloody nowhere.'

Mayberry shrugged. It was out of his hands. No point
yelling at a colleague when Ayala was to blame.

'Can you and Purcell handle things here?'
He nodded.
'Good. Because I need to have a word with Ayala.'

4

TRIAGE

SHE FOUND His Royal Highness hiding away in his office. Just because it annoyed him, she opened the door as soon as she knocked, forcing him to hastily drop his copy of The Impartial.

'What is it now?' he asked tersely, nostrils flaring as if he were right to be annoyed at the interruption of a murder investigation. Never mind that the great DCI Bertram Ayala now headed up London's most prestigious murder investigation team. Talk about rising to the level of one's incompetence.

'Elijah Zholnovych.'

As if it could be anything else.

'I told you, pass it off to MisPers to deal with.'

Rafferty put her hands on her hips, biting back the urge to address him by his first name in her best parent voice. He hated that too. Come to think of it, Ayala hated a lot of things.

'He's dead, Ayala. If we kick it to MisPers, they'll kick it right back to us in a few days and we'll have lost so much time that it'll be impossible to find his killer.'

He leant back in his chair. 'And your evidence for that is...?'

'For one, there's blood in the living room.'

'I've seen Purcell's preliminary findings. He said it's millilitres. That's not proof of loss of life.'

'Then there's the gunshot.'

An arched eyebrow met her statement. 'What gunshot?'

'Kflom said-'

'Kflom is a recent graduate,' Ayala said coldly. 'He ought to know better than to make definitive statements before the labs come back.'

'And you ought to know better than to stall out an investigation waiting on a gunshot residue test that we both know is going to prove Kflom right. How else can you explain the blood?'

'I don't have to explain it. Even if you're right and someone was shot, there's no guarantee that the victim is Elijah Zholnovych nor is there any proof he's dead.'

'DNA.'

'Also not back yet. Try again.'

Rafferty swore under her breath. 'Nobody's seen him.'

'That, my dear Ashley, is par for the course with a missing person. The clue is in the name. We've got a dead simple case. A man didn't walk his neighbour's dog. Big deal. The neighbour found the place empty when he went poking around the back. This should've been a simple welfare check. What a waste of bloody resources. A grown man doesn't need to tell his damned neighbours if he's going away.'

She glared. 'Or answer worried phone calls? We're lucky the neighbour did call it in otherwise we'd never have found the blood spatter.'

'That could've been there for months,' Ayala said. 'If it even is blood.'

Rafferty clenched her jaw. Why wasn't Ayala getting it? This wasn't a misper. Zholnovych hadn't just gone out and left his entire life behind without a trace. If he wasn't dead, Rafferty was a traffic cop.

'You might have the swanky office now you're a DCI, but that doesn't mean you need to be a dick.'

'Detective Inspector Rafferty, if you ever speak to me like that again, you'll be fired on the spot. Do I make myself clear?'

Against her better judgement, she nodded. She'd have to call him a dick behind his back from now on.

His expression softened a fraction. 'Look, Ash, it's not that I'm unsympathetic. We've got dozens of open cases right now and I don't have the resources to fully investigate every one. We've got no body, no witnesses, and no forensics.'

'Yet,' Rafferty objected.

Ayala ignored her, though his nostrils flared angrily. 'If I allocate cash to investigating Zholnovych's disappearance, another investigation draws the short straw. I can't spend money on him when we've got three dead children, fourteen dead adults, and several mispers with blood loss consistent with loss of life. And that's not even counting the cold cases. Forget Zholnovych. He's a middle-aged loner who, for all we know, could've fucked off to Butlins for the weekend. You're clutching at straws. Until and unless you've got something concrete to work with, pass the investigation over to MisPers and get the hell out of my office.'

5

IGNORING HIM

ALMOST AS SOON AS she'd left his office, she ignored Ayala's orders. Rather than hand everything over to Missing Persons, she'd called Mayberry. Luckily, he was still in Balham. Something about the place called to her. It was too spartan, too utilitarian. Not at all messy or lived in. Unlike her own home. Someone had taken the decision, rightly in her opinion, to step up resources to deal with Zholnovych's disappearance. The fact that the shout had escalated as far as Purcell and Ayala meant there was something going on that she was missing. Perhaps Bray had been exaggerating when she'd described so many units on the scene but even so, it was clear that other people agreed with her: this wasn't a middle-aged bloke having an unexpected weekend by the seaside.

By the time she was back in the cul-de-sac, Mayberry was waiting on the doorstep. A light rain had begun to drizzle down so he was huddled under a plain black umbrella. She joined him underneath it.

'I've l-l-locked up,' he said, jangling the keys. 'Just g-got to wait for M-M-MisPers.'

Thinking quickly, Rafferty extended her hand palm up. 'Tell you what, I'll hang around for them. Gimme the keys and you can get off home.'

When Mayberry hesitated, she added: 'I'm sure your missus will appreciate seeing you home early for a change.'

For a moment, it looked like he was going to insist on doing things by the book. Just like Ayala would have. Then he handed her the keys and headed for his car, shaking and then folding his umbrella as he went.

The keys were nondescript. One Chubb-branded key and one generic mortice lock key, both of them attached to a simple metal ring. No keyrings. If the victim had dropped them on the floor, it would've been impossible to get them back to him.

She waited until the sound of Mayberry's engine reverberated around the quiet cul-de-sac. Then, when she saw the rearview lights of his Vauxhall Corsa disappearing in the direction of Balham High Road, she put the key into the lock.

The generic key undid the bottom lock with a click. A second turn with the Chubb key and the door swung open. Finally, she could nose around in peace.

Once inside, she could see right down the long corridor to the lounge at the back. Now that the crime scene investigator's boards were gone, the carpet underneath was in full view: beige, scrupulously clean, and short enough to last a decade even with heavy footfall. It was the kind of carpet landlords all around the capital loved.

Glancing right, she could see there was a small study. She headed inside. An oversized IKEA desk and mismatched armchair dominated the room, immediately giving Rafferty student vibes. On closer inspection, she saw an assortment of international newspapers on the table: The Moscow Times, Kyiv Post, and, from right here in London, The Impartial. A little book of Sudoku sat atop the pile, a biro tucked within its ring-binding. She flipped it open at random. Neat, tiny numbers were scrawled within. Despite being the more difficult kind of Sudoku, the kind where one wrong guess could mess the whole thing up, the puzzles had been completed in ink rather than pencil. A man after her own heart. An interesting titbit but not a particularly useful one.

Dangling wires in Rafferty's peripheral vision drew her attention. A four-way extension socket ran from the far wall to underneath the desk. A couple of chargers were plugged into it without any devices attached.

Defeated, she returned to the hallway and peered through the door on the opposite side. It was the tiniest of bathrooms with a toilet, sink, and an under-basin cabinet. Nothing of interest in there either, just a bottle of Domestos toilet cleaner, a refill for the Carex bottle by the sink, and a half-finished nine-pack of Andrex toilet rolls. Damn. All branded goods. If there had been supermarket own-brand goods, she'd have been able to work out where he did his weekly shop. From the posh newspapers and Sudoku, she had him pegged as a Sainsbury's or Ocado kind of guy. Nothing too expensive, just the usual trappings of a firmly middle-class life.

The lounge yielded nothing she hadn't learned earlier and so she traipsed upstairs.

Yet more beige carpets paired with off-white walls. If there were more natural light, the glare would have been painful, but with just one tiny window at the rear of the landing, it was bathed in darkness.

The bedroom at the back of the house wasn't much better. She flicked on the light switch, casting a pallid yellow glow over the room. There was a low, single metal bed with a bare mattress on it. Next to it was a small wardrobe. Empty. Perhaps it was a guest room.

One room left to look at. Perhaps coming back had been a

waste of time. No doubt the PolSA had already thoroughly checked everything. What was it she was hoping to find? A missed blackmail note? A "here are my enemies" list?

No such luck.

The master was almost as barren as the guest bedroom except in here the bed was made with military precision. Mr Zholnovych was plainly a fan of ironed sheets. She glanced at the manufacturer's tag: Marks and Spencer.

Another generic brand. It fitted with her Sainsbury's theory. Zholnovych was wealthy enough to live alone but he had none of the trappings of a rich existence. With the exception of the man's Blu-ray collection downstairs and his love of Sudoku, he had no knickknacks or keepsakes. There wasn't a photo frame with a picture of a wife, a child or even a pet.

In fact, the room was totally devoid of any clutter. It was like a freshly made hotel room. Everything was pristine, with clothes folded and tidied away in a large pine dresser. No doubt that was IKEA too. Surely, he could have afforded proper furniture? Even Rafferty had some nice antique G-Plan she'd picked up for a song from a neighbour who'd left the country. It was so cheap that she didn't even get mad when her cat Swain sank her claws into it.

The disconnect was obvious. Middle-class tastes, cheap, disposable furniture. It *had* to be a rental. If Zholnovych owned the place, he'd have bought furniture to match the fancy tech, wouldn't he? Unless, she mused, he'd spent all his money on the big OLED telly and had nothing left in the piggybank for home furnishings.

She made a mental note to check with the land registry to see who owned the place and then headed towards the wardrobe. Surely in there, at least, there ought to be some sign of personality?

Again, she was disappointed. Zholnovych's wardrobe had

his laundry hamper hidden inside occupying the left-hand side. One peek inside confirmed it was almost empty, his only dirty clothes were a pair of tighty-whities that weren't so white and equally filthy socks. On the right-hand side of the wardrobe hung cookie-cutter shirts that were so similar, she might have thought they belonged to Homer Simpson. She looked closer. Hanger after hanger was laden down with button-down shirts in white, blue, and, for added variety, blue-and-white. Each had a tie loosely hung around the collar, all solid colours. All of it was yet again from M&S. Did Zholnovych work for them or something?

Their stuff wasn't bad. Most Brits probably had something from them in their drawers, but it seemed that Zholnovych thought there was only one shop on the whole of the high street. Perhaps that was it. Convenience. Middle-aged dude moves to a new area, nips into the nearest clothing shop that's in budget and carries his size. That was plausible enough. At least he hadn't gone to the dreaded *Primarini*. He was much too classy for that.

Wait a second. Was there even an M&S nearby?

Quick as a flash, she whipped out her mobile phone and Googled it. The search results flashed up in an instant.

There was one on Balham High Road, but it was the "Simply Food" kind without a clothes department. He hadn't simply gone to the nearest shop then. Maybe he worked near one. Or maybe he just really loved their clothing. Odd thing to be fanatical about but it took all sorts.

Whatever.

There was nothing to see here. Not one piece of evidence.

As far as Rafferty could tell, Zholnovych was a loner with no hobbies other than watching action movies and playing Sudoku. He didn't own books or art. His shelves were piled with the most generic of brand name goods. Even his clothes were nondescript. His white goods and furniture likewise.

He didn't have any sort of electronics beyond the big screen telly.

How the hell did he cope with modern living without a phone or a laptop? She hadn't noticed a pile of letters or a folder full of bank statements anywhere, so he wasn't doing everything old school either. There definitely wasn't a landline phone plugged in. That would've stood out like a sore thumb.

Cables.

She'd seen cables, hadn't she? Weren't there a couple dangling loosely under the desk downstairs?

Quickly, Rafferty backtracked downstairs. She found the cables. One was clearly an Apple charger, the kind with a Lightning port. That screamed iPhone. The other cable looked more generic; a power plug plus brick kind of affair, the sort used for a laptop. She picked it up, turning the brick over as she did so. On the bottom was a label that read "Dell Latitude".

So he *did* have a laptop.

Where the hell was it? Surely the PolSA would've flagged something like that?

One way to find out. HOLMES 2. The police database was where *everything* was catalogued. Every stray fibre, every item collected, every phone call and text logged, and every crime scene photo uploaded. It hooked into a myriad of other databases so detectives like Rafferty could cross-reference modus operandi against past cases, look for DNA hits including familial hits – more than a few gangsters had been caught out by their uncle or brother being in the database – and even compare bone measurements against standardised tables to work out if a skeleton were male or female, young or old, black or white.

A modern miracle.

When it worked.

Today, it was slow as hell.

Rafferty's gaze flicked to the top left of her phone screen. 3G. Not 5G. Not even 4G. She didn't know the technical limits of each of the radio frequencies, but she knew the higher the number, the faster her phone's access to the internet. She held it up, walking around the downstairs until the little number flickered.

5G. Now, she found herself in the kitchen. It too was bland as all hell. The view out to the little garden revealed an empty strip of Astroturf without plants or decoration. Awful. It was so unlike her own little balcony packed full of her favourite flowers: the kind she couldn't easily kill.

Her phone vibrated as HOLMES conjured up the evidence log for Zholnovych's case. The list was already several dozen items long: fibre samples, DNA from his toothbrush, fingerprints from the doorknobs. All the basics.

What Rafferty couldn't see was a list of the usual chattels seized, things like cash, hard drives, USB keys, and any personal electronics. Nothing was listed.

No phone.

No laptop.

No electronics of any kind.

Maybe it hadn't been logged yet?

The name of the PolSA – the Police Search Advisor – who was responsible for the case was listed on every line item: Lesley Rea.

Man? Woman? Something in the back of Rafferty's mind said there was a rule about -ey and -ie... but she couldn't for the life of her remember it.

She cracked a smile. When she'd first met Morton and the team, they'd assumed that Ashley was a man, not a leggy brunette.

The first rule of policing: assume nothing.

Barely a ring went by before Lesley Rea picked up.

'Hello?'

A clipped, woman's voice. Slightly nasal perhaps. Rafferty would've guessed that Rea was a little older than her, perhaps in her mid-to-late-fifties.

'Lesley Rea?' Rafferty said. 'It's Detective Inspector Rafferty. I'm calling about the Zholnovych crime scene.'

'Okay...?'

'Your evidence log doesn't mention a laptop or mobile phone.'

Rea's voice dripped with venom as if she'd been accused of missing key evidence. 'That, Ms Rafferty, would be because there wasn't a mobile phone or laptop at the crime scene.'

'Right, right. I thought as much, but I wanted to confirm that the log was right. I found a charger for a Dell Latitude and another for an Apple iPhone in the study.'

'Those, Ms Rafferty, *are* on the log and you'd have seen them if you'd bothered to look at the crime scene photographs.'

Whoops. She'd not thought to check the photos before heading back to the house. Just as well, she could easily have missed them.

'Then it would be fair to assume the victim had those devices, but no longer does.'

'You're the detective.'

That one stung. 'Thanks for your time – and thorough log – Ms Rea.'

The PolSA hung up before Rafferty could.

What a strange woman.

But now she knew the victim wasn't as disconnected from the world as he'd looked.

He'd had a phone and laptop.

And someone had taken them.

COMING UP BLANK

TANK HAD COCKED UP.

Twice.

I hadn't hesitated in letting him know either. Not only did he fuck up pinning down our vic, he left his DNA behind to boot.

And the gear was a load of shit. We bought it from this Russian guy, Ivor, that Tank used to know. I should've known there was no such thing as a good drug dealer.

Ivor had lied to my face. He'd promised it would knock a man out in 15 seconds flat. No muss, no fuss. Knock him out, throw him in the box, take him out. Easy peasy.

Except the gear hadn't worked. Russian nerve agent my arse. We'd probably paid five Gs for bloody ketamine.

Zholnovych had been awake for *minutes*. Pinning him down while Tank arsed about finding his bloody earring – and making a pig's ear of the damned box in the process, not to mention the carpet – meant our simple, in and out job was damned impossible.

We didn't even know how long he'd be out for. If Zholnovych had woken up before we'd got him to the safe house and tied the bastard up, we'd have been fucked. At least that didn't happen.

But something worse did.

While we were "extracting" information, the bastard had a heart attack. Coward hadn't even lasted for twenty minutes. Maybe Tank had worked him over a little too hard. Wouldn't surprise me. Tank wasn't himself during the job. I usually call him out on it. But extracting information is a dirty business and if Tank needs a little something to get through it... Well, I can't blame him for that. If I had to do my own dirty work, I'd want to forget it afterwards too.

In the end, we only got one bit of information out of Zholnovych: the name of the man who'd hidden Tiny's so-called "bolt fund", the money he had stashed away in case of a rainy day, was a weasel called Nathan Linden.

I knew him. Back in the day, the Collector, as we'd called him, was Tiny's go-to fence for moving high-value jewellery, watches, and the like. Pretty good at it too as I recall. He'd worked with his brother back then but he was long dead.

Sod's law, the bastard also turned Queen's. No doubt he's in the programme too. It took months to find Zholnovych. Now, we have to repeat the miracle. And I don't have another decade to waste.

But first, we have to get rid of the evidence.

Getting rid of the body was the easy part.

We'd dumped it with the others. I figured if they hadn't found the bodies that Tiny had us dump down there, they wouldn't find this one either. Sorted.

The next job's going to be a bit harder: dealing with Zholnovych's phone and laptop. I could just ditch 'em, but I have to get in first, just in case Zholnovych didn't tell us everything. He and Tiny were tight and I wouldn't be surprised to learn they were still in contact.

Not exactly my skillset breaking into electronics. I had a guy who knew his way around a laptop, but he's in the clink. Useless prick got himself caught.

Can't ask the old boys either. Everyone's disappeared. Some are in prison. No biggie. Most of us have done a stretch.

Criminal training college. Do a bit locked up and you can learn all sorts: forgery, lock picking, the best ways to break into places. Got to take that with a pinch of salt, though. After all, only those who get caught end up inside so it's more a case of learning from what they did wrong, not what they did right.

My stretch in Cookham Wood was a breeze. Easier than growing up in Ilford anyhow. Miles more likely to get shivved wandering around town than in juvie. I'd gone in a cocky teenager and come out far wiser. Never been back since either. The records were sealed on account of my age so as far as the world knows, I'm a respectable man.

Maybe it isn't so easy these days now the boys haven't got the Bakowski name to throw around. People used to be scared of us. Terrified even.

Can't say I blame them.

Cross any one of us and the whole damned Syndicate would be out gunning for you. Fucking NATO for gangbangers. More than a few of the guys found that out the hard way. The lucky ones are buried in a proper cemetery.

The unlucky ones are bunking with Zholnovych. Fuck knows how many bodies are down there now. If the police ever find it, they'll have a bloody field day. Half their historical crimes will be solved overnight. The final legacy of the Bakowski Syndicate.

Not everyone's dead mind you. A few of the old-timers managed to fuck off to the Costa del Crime. That's what I should've done: fled. I could've gone and got myself a year-round tan in Benalmadena. Maybe even started a bar. Tank could've been security. Girls, beer, sunshine, it would've been a heck of a retirement.

But I can't take the easy route. Not yet. Got a job to do first. Revenge. Tiny's gotta pay. I need to find him. Easier said than done. The police have been looking for years. He's right up there on Interpol's Most Wanted List.

First, I've got to find the turncoats, the snitches who turned Queen's. Got themselves nice, cushty new names. Like "Zholnovych". Obviously named after the politician. Someone being cute.

Bet he thought he was safe, hiding in South London, watchin' his Blu-rays, getting fucking Sainsbury's deliveries, and letting the days tick by. Suppose eight years and change ain't a bad stretch in police protection.

It was his missus that got him killed.

Wasylyna. Waxy we called her on account of... well, that doesn't matter.

Bloody gorgeous she was. I'd pretend I don't know how she ended up with a boring git like Zholnovych, but I know exactly how. She didn't have shit all choice in the matter. What Tiny said went. He passed women around like a blunt.

Can't blame her for ditching the old codger. He should've seen it coming. Without Tiny's say so, it was dead obvious she'd ditch him soon after they went into witness protection.

And when she did, she went right back to Ilford. Home sweet home.

Not the smartest move.

Or maybe it was.

Maybe she *wanted* me to find him. She told everyone she'd been "abroad". Didn't take a genius to realise that was a lie. Her bastard of a husband was one of the traitors. The pair of 'em holed up in Balham, less than ten miles away, but another gang's territory. The Fitzgerald crew ran the place. No love lost there.

They split and she came right back into the fold. Silly broad never could keep a secret. No sooner had she come back, she was back on the pole, selling herself for a few quid and using coke to numb the pain. She'd sold her "wasband" out for less than a gram.

Zholnovych was a fucking moron. If he'd thought ahead, he'd have realised what life as a snitch would've meant: hiding forever, watching his damned movies, forever looking over his shoulder knowing that one day we'd find him.

But he relaxed. Thought he got away with it. Silly bastard didn't even recognise us.

That was part of the con. He saw the box and the clipboard. Didn't realise I'm losing my hair and that I'm four stone lighter than I used to be. Few people do.

The moment he'd unlatched the door, he'd guaranteed his fate.

Had to be done.

He was a means to an end.

Or was supposed to be.

The Collector was a start. But another man in bloody witness protection is a shot in the dark.

Now his laptop is the best chance I've got of finding Tiny.

If I can get into the damned thing.

7

_____

FOOTPRINTS

THE CASE WAS NOW with MisPers. Officially anyway. Unofficially, Rafferty had exaggerated the amount of paperwork she had to get done for other cases so she had an excuse to hide away and investigate. Not that Ayala cared much what she did. So long as she sat in the open plan part of the office, right where he could see her whenever he deigned to nip out of his corner office to go and grab yet another coffee.

That gave her ample opportunity to look up Elijah Zholnovych.

Or try to.

As far as Google could tell, Mr Zholnovych didn't exist. No Facebook profile. No Twitter account. He wasn't even on LinkedIn. Who didn't have a web presence of any kind?

Was he unemployed? That struck Rafferty as unlikely. Who could afford the latest OLED telly on Job Seeker's Allowance? Seventy-seven quid a week wouldn't touch the sides.

Could he have inherited money?

That was plausible. A quick probate search took a sledgehammer to that theory. There was no mention of him in any probated will. Then again, it wasn't totally impossible. He wouldn't be the first to keep quiet about an inheritance and fail to give Her Majesty's Revenue and Customs their fair share.

Public records then. If Google couldn't find Elijah Zholnovych, surely officialdom would.

Rafferty pulled up the roll, officially the Electoral Register, the local government's list of who lived where. Technically, everyone had to register if they were eligible to. But prosecuting those who didn't tell the local government they existed would always prove a challenge.

Thankfully, Zholnovych *was* on the roll. He'd been living at the house in Balham for a little over two years.

Two years? And his place still looked like a show-home? No junk, no personal belongings. From the cheap and cheerful furnishings and the instant Marks & Spencer's wardrobe, it looked like he'd only just moved in.

What else was there to check? Utilities? Tax filings? Stuff like that would need a court order. Without Ayala's say-so, that was never going to happen.

She stifled a yawn. Her amateur digital sleuthing wasn't going to get her very far. What she needed was a nerd. Luckily, she knew there was one downstairs.

Five minutes later, she stepped out of the lift and into the Met's digital forensics department. Entry was guarded by a secure door and so, after explaining what she needed over the intercom, she stood tapping her feet impatiently until the solid-metal door swung open to reveal the nerd in question.

Brodie wasn't the stereotypical nerd. He was built like a rugby player, tall and broad with bright ginger hair which had grown since Rafferty had last seen him. It was tied back in a dodgy ponytail.

'Nice do,' she said by way of greeting.

'Ta,' Brodie said, his thick Scottish brogue discernible from just one syllable. 'Saw it in *Vogue*.'

'I can tell.'

He chuckled and beckoned her to follow him down the corridor. There were dozens of steel doors, each with its own number-coded lock. It was a far cry from the first time she'd been down here. Back then, it had been an open plan office, the many techies beavering away in the harsh light of over-sized monitors, their fingers dancing over mechanical keyboards that sounded a bit like old-fashioned typewriters.

Brodie stopped by one of the doors. Apart from the "3B" stencilled above it, it looked just like the others.

'Mind looking away, lassie? Sorry, security's been tightened up since you know what.'

She didn't know but she looked away anyway.

Once they were inside, Brodie took up residence in a huge gaming chair behind two enormous screens which were affixed to his desk with lever arms that looked as if they could hold up a small car. With a heave, he pushed the two monitors. They swung to one side so that she could see him once again.

'Nifty,' she said enviously. The tech down here was, as perhaps she ought to have expected, much nicer than anything the detectives upstairs were given access to. Glowing LEDs in a dazzling rainbow of colours lit up the mice and keyboards. On Brodie's desk there was an Ember mug keeping his coffee at the perfect temperature.

'What is it ya need, lassie?'

She hesitated. Could she trust Brodie not to tell Ayala? She knew that Brodie and Mayberry were tight... and the latter got on with Ayala. It wasn't hard to imagine that the Chinese whispers would get back to the boss. She decided to risk it.

'Background,' she said. 'I'm tying up some loose ends. We got a shout about a possible murder vic. Weird case. A guy called Elijah Zholnovych. He lives down in Balham. Seems to

keep himself to himself except for one thing: he walks his neighbour's dog twice a day come rain or shine.'

'Okay... and?'

'And when he didn't turn up, the neighbour got suspicious
and called in a welfare check. Officers went out, found the place
empty. No signs of a struggle except for a tiny bit of blood on the
carpet. Lab results aren't back yet, but the new CSI, Ka... Kaff
Lum? You met him yet?'

'Kflom,' Brodie said. 'Aye, he's awrite wit' me. Though he
still owes me forty quid.'

He looked at her expectantly, daring her to ask what for.
She did.

'Beat 'em in the ruggers. The Crooked Hookers 42, CSI
Guys 26. Not the same without Morton as our fly-half mind
you.'

Morton used to play for the Met's rugby team? She hadn't
figured her old boss was the type to go sprinting up and down a
rugby field. Come to think of it, she'd never seen him voluntarily
run after anyone. Sure, he'd disappeared down to the staff gym
once in a blue moon but she'd assumed that was for a few
minutes' peace or a chit-chat with the real gym rat in the force,
Xander Thompson of the Serious Organised Crime Agency.
Maybe Morton wasn't faking it after all. Had he been a regular
Johnny Wilkinson all along?

'How so? Was he that good a fly-half?'

'Well, without him, we win more,' Brodie said before
promptly laughing at his own joke.

Men.

'Right,' Rafferty said, trying to steer the conversation back to
the Zholnovych case. 'Kflom reckons the blood on the floor is
high-velocity spatter.'

'Yer man was shot?'

Rafferty nodded.

Brodie swung one of the monitors back into place and began to type at lightning speed. She could see the light of the monitor reflected in his eyes as he pulled up HOLMES and scanned the case file.

He grinned. 'Says this one's been passed over to MisPers. Assigned to a case manager by the name of Joe Singleton. You changed your name by deed poll on the down-low, Ash?'

'Like I said, I'm tying up loose ends.'

'Don't take me fer a bampot.'

'Sorry,' she mumbled. 'Something's not right with this.'

Her gut feeling lined up with Kflom's assessment: Zholnovych was dead.

'S'alreet wit' me if you're ignoring the bawbag upstairs.'

Relief flooded through her. She returned his grin. 'Not just me that thinks Ayala's a tit then.'

'Nae. Power's gone to his wee head.'

Too damned true. 'His Highness doesn't want the inconvenience of a murder investigation without a body.'

'Then you'd best find him one, hadn't ye, lassie?'

'I need to know who this guy was first. He's a ghost. Nothing on Google.'

Brodie's brow furrowed in disbelief. 'With a name like Zholnovych? That's mad.'

He began to type once again. As he did, Rafferty leant forward and craned her neck to look at his screen. He took the hint and angled it so she could just about follow along with what he was doing.

'What sort of digital footprints would you expect someone to have?'

Brodie pulled a face. 'Bank accounts, tax records, credit cards, credit history like loans and mortgages, loyalty cards, social media accounts, a website, at least one email address, usernames, app data like geolocation, biometric info if yer daft enough to share it, voice notes, right through to cringeworthy photos, old school text messages, voicemail. Everyone leaves a footprint somewhere.'

'Even if you're trying to stay under the radar?'

'Aye, whether you put it out there or not, someone's scraping data on you. Facebook even build shadow profiles for people that haven't joined yet. If people you know are on there, they can make a lot of educated guesses.'

Exactly as Rafferty had suspected. It only made the whole thing more confusing.

'Then why can't I find anything about Zholnovych online?'

'Normally, I'd say you're not looking in the right place,' he said with a shrug. 'But when I can't find *anything*... now that's weird. Yer boy's been living off-grid.'

'Apart from being on the roll?'

'Bloody weird,' Brodie muttered.

With anyone else, Rafferty would think saying that was the height of arrogance, but she'd seen Brodie work time and time again. He was the best the Met had to offer, and the Met wasn't short on talent.

'He had a phone and a laptop,' Rafferty said. 'Or chargers for them were in his house anyhow. Same thing, right? He's not gone Amish.'

The Scot stroked his beard. 'Get me the laptop and the phone and I'll crack 'em faster than Ayala demands his half-caf caramel macchiato on a Monday morning.'

'I'm trying. Anything you can do before then?'

'Mebbe. I'll keep lookin'. But no promises.'

8

DISAPPOINTMENT

WORTHLESS.

There was shit all on the laptop or the phone that I didn't already know.

And it had cost me a fortune to get someone to crack into them to boot.

Turns out, Zholnovych really had cut himself off from the old crowd. Cold turkey by the looks of things. There wasn't a single name in his address book that sounded vaguely like it could lead me to the big boss, the *shef*. Tiny Bakowski himself. The man the Italians would've called *il capo*.

I should've known Zholnovych had gone straight. The moment he'd turned Queen's Evidence, he'd given up everything the Syndicate – we – had ever known. Mr Fucking Boring. Suppose I can't blame him. Boring doesn't get you killed.

My next victim on the other hand was never called boring. Nathan Linden, or the Collector as we used to call him, was a first-rate fence. He'd sold everything from powdered ivory, which he convinced his punters was a world-class aphrodisiac, to rare parrots, heroin and diamonds. And he liked his own product.

He'd sold us all out too. One of the first actually. The moment the police busted his front door, he'd started singing. We know that from our man inside. He'd been put in protective custody, the wing where the nonces, the traitors, and the former cops got locked up. It was a dead giveaway that he'd betrayed the Syndicate.

But, unlike Zholnovych, the Collector wouldn't have gone straight. No matter how cushty the life the government offered him, he'd have started moving stolen goods the moment their back was turned. He couldn't help it. A life of sitting at home, watching movies, and having groceries delivered would never scratch the Collector's itch. He'd be flogging whatever he could find to feed the beast.

That has to be my way in. Find whatever he's flogging now. Follow the breadcrumbs, find the Collector.

And find out whatever he knows.

9

CANVASSING BALHAM

WITHOUT THE PRIORITY – and budget – of the murder investigation team behind her, Rafferty was forced to rely on the old standby: dogged police work and a little luck. And none of it on the clock either.

Luck was in short supply. Despite Brodie's help, the digital breadcrumb trail was as cold as a body in a morgue. It was as if Zholnovych had popped into existence a little over two years ago, a fully formed middle-aged loner, one who had never before set foot on planet Earth.

How the hell did that happen?

Everything was online. Right now, Rafferty's Apple Watch was recording her heart rate as she traipsed around Balham High Road showing random strangers Elijah Zholnovych's photograph. Nobody recognised him, not even in the little independent film and music store on the high street. He must've bought his enormous film collection online.

With what though? Nothing in his house suggested he worked. No suits, no smart shoes, no briefcase. The man lived in those boring blue-and-white shirts. Perhaps it was a time-saver: Zholnovych never had to decide what to wear in the morning.

Thanks to a little off-the-record searching, Brodie had "found" Zholnovych's tax returns, a resource they couldn't normally access without a subpoena. Zholnovych filed as an IR35 contractor, just once and only for the previous tax year. On it, he'd vaguely described himself as a "consultant" which was code for God-knew-what.

The house wasn't much help either. A Land Registry search showed that it was owned by a company, not a real person. Yet another dead end.

Apart from his name, she knew nothing. No known acquaintances, no job, no way to find how he'd paid his bills, or even talk to his landlord to see what references he'd given.

Then it hit her. The neighbour who'd reported him missing. He was the only known connection to the community, the only clue they had as to who the hell Zholnovych was and what he did all day.

Stopping on the corner of Ravenstone Street, she folded up the ten by eight photo print and tucked it into her handbag before retrieving her phone. Half a dozen button presses and a secure thumb-print authentication later, she pulled up Zholnovych's file on HOLMES.

The case file was thin. Two neighbours had spoken to the police. One was Rosie Bray, the Peloton-loving woman that Rafferty herself had interviewed. The other chatty Cathy was Fred Albright. He lived right next door to Zholnovych. What he'd said had been roughly transcribed by the first officer to respond:

Usually, Eli walks Champers [Albright's poodle] twice a day, first thing in the morning, then again in the evening. He's never missed a walk once. I think he gets lonely. So when he missed Monday evening's walk, I thought he must be ill. I knocked on the door, no answer. I didn't want to push too much – he's doing me a favour ya know? – so I left it there.

But then he didn't come around the next day either. I knocked again. No answer. I tried ringing his mobile. Nothing. It was off. When I got home, I looked out the window and I could see there was a light spilling out into the garden like the curtains were wide open. Eli always pulls them shut. He's damned paranoid about that. Thinks someone's watching him. So I knew something was up.

I told my wife I was going to check. Walked around the side gate and let myself into his garden. The lights were on. Couldn't see nobody though. I thought about calling the cops there and then, but what was I supposed to say, that my neighbour left his lights on and his curtains open?

So I went home, asked my wife. She thought I should leave it well alone, let the man be. He might've gone off on a date, she said. Unlikely, I thought. Not much of a Casanova was Eli. We compromised – if he didn't come around to walk Champers in the morning, I'd call then. He didn't turn up. Three days in a row without answering his phone? That was beyond weird. I called for a welfare check, and, well, here you are. Wait until my wife hears I was right. I'll never hear the end of it!

Despite the situation, Rafferty laughed, drawing funny looks from passersby on Balham High Road.

That explained how the investigation got started. The lights were easy to explain: Purcell's team had found a timer, an old school one that went on and off at set times. If the lights had kicked in while the curtains were wide open, it was no wonder that Albright had thought something was amiss.

What Albright hadn't said was anything about Zholnovych's personality. Apart from a non-existent love life and a fondness for poodles, Zholnovych was as much a mystery as ever.

There was one pertinent titbit: Zholnovych did have a mobile as Rafferty had expected.

And now she knew the man who had his number.

10

THE PHONE

'YER KIDDING, LASSIE?'

'Pretty please,' Rafferty said. 'I wouldn't ask if it weren't important.' *And you've already been looking at his tax records for me*, Rafferty thought but didn't dare say.

'I wish I could. But the boss man's been down in person.'

Ayala got to Brodie?

'When?'

'Last night. Told me in no uncertain terms that you're not on the case and that if you came to ask a favour that you're – and I'm quoting here, so don't yell at me, okay lassie? – "a stubborn goat who needs to learn to listen to her superiors".'

Why the hell was Ayala so hell-bent on stopping Rafferty from investigating Zholnovych's disappearance? It couldn't just be money, surely?

'Since when was Bertram Ayala the boss of you?'

Brodie surveyed her over his cup of tea. 'Since Morton retired, lassie. Did ye not see the fancy new office he's got? Think he's got his own parking space too now.'

'Suppose I deserved that. Look, I need to find this guy. He's gone, so has his phone and his laptop. I've got his number. Surely there's a way of seeing if his phone is active?'

He put his mug down. 'There is, lassie. Convince Ayala, get a warrant, and then we can find out which phone mast he last connected to.'

'We both know it could be too late by then.'

'It already is. I'm on yer side, ye know. But if he's dead, his killer's hardly goin' ta be wandering around Oxford Circus playing Pokémon Go on a dead man's iPhone now, is he?'

She glared at him. 'They took the phone for a reason.'

'Aye,' Brodie conceded. 'They've probably sold it. Easy few hundred quid even if the IMEI gets blacklisted. Just ship it out of the UK et voila. The laptop is even easier to flog.'

He had a point. But there was no way she was going to concede that easily. 'Then why not take anything else?'

'Ye don't know what they took. Unless ye found a nice, neat inventory of the fella's home. From what I read you didn't find much stuff. No cash on the inventory either. Who doesn't have a few quid tucked away for emergencies?'

Rafferty blushed. She didn't. Ever since contactless payments had come out, she'd done away with carrying actual notes.

'Ye don't know what ye don't know, Ash. And yer assuming he's dead. What if he's not?'

'But the blood-'

He held his hands up in surrender. 'I agree with ye, lassie. But it ain't me you need to convince, is it? When're the results due back on the blood spatter analysis and the like?'

'Monday.' She'd been chasing Kflom about it non-stop. 'At a push. Could be longer if a priority case comes in, mind.'

Anything officially designated a murder would go straight to the front of the queue. Rafferty had seen it all before: low-level cases got bumped all the time. A middle-aged misper would never be a high priority.

'Then go home, get some rest, and forget about Elijah Zholnovych. He might even turn up over the weekend. Stranger things have happened.'

Rafferty shook her head.

Like hell Zholnovych was going to turn up.

Not alive at any rate.

11

OUTSIDE THE BOX

NADA.

Nathan fucking Linden went straight too.

As if.

I'd sooner believe the Collector dead than out of the game.

We'd spent the day knocking on doors, talking to old friends, anyone who might've spoken to the Collector. Now, we were driving home, this time in a Ford we'd "borrowed" so nobody could trace our movements on ANPR.

We'd hit up every major fence, every runner, every dealer we'd ever heard of. They were the guys running the major ports – Liverpool, Newcastle, Southampton, even bloody Brighton. Nothing of note came in or out without them knowing. We'd bribed, blackmailed, threatened and cajoled, searching for one tiny crumb that might help us find the Collector.

Nor did anyone admit to selling him drugs, though I hadn't expected them to. There were a few dozen big fences, but thousands of small-time dealers. Buying heroin was as easy as picking up milk from the corner shop.

Not one of them admitted to talking to the Collector aka Nathan Linden since he'd turned Queen's. If he is still in the game, he isn't the hot shot he used to be. To fly under the radar, he'll have to be moving just small, meaningless stuff – pickpocketed iPhones, knocker boy's tat pilfered from old folks and the like. That's not the Linden I used to know.

Then again, he could be dead. Wouldn't have put it past Tiny to have disappeared him if he could.

But Tiny couldn't play puppet-master in hiding, could he? Back in the day, we were all terrified. He said jump, we asked off which bloody cliff. If we didn't, he'd have us thrown over the edge. Now, it's just two of us. I've known Tank longer than anyone else in my life. He's a few years older than me and more of a brother to me than my actual brother ever was. He's the one person I know I can trust.

I glanced over at him in the passenger seat. He looked as exhausted as I felt. His eyes were bloodshot, his skin haggard, and his hands were trembling. I knew what that meant.

'You alright, Tank?' I asked as we drove home.

He ignored me, staring at the dashboard as if it were bloody fascinating.

Tank changed the subject. 'What now?'

So we're ignoring it then. Fine. Unless Tank asked for help, he wouldn't take it. He's stubborn like that.

I gave a confident shrug. 'We'll find him.'

'How though? If he really is in witness protection...'

He has a point. Finding Zholnovych had taken *years*. And we'd only found him by sheer luck. I can't wait that long to find Linden.

'Have I ever let you down?' I asked.

'No...' His voice trailed off.

He was about to say "not yet", but caught himself just in time.

'I will find the Collector,' I said, much more confidently than I felt. 'And then I'll find Tiny Bakowski. And end him.'

Or die trying.

12

UNDERFUNDED

THE OFFICE of the Missing Persons Unit looked just like theirs: row after row of desks, Herman Miller Aeron chairs tucked neatly behind each one, a Dell monitor atop the desk next to a laptop dock. Just as it was in Rafferty's office, staff were hot-desking. In theory that meant anyone could grab any available space. In reality, she found most people quickly settled on "their" desk and guarded it jealously.

The man she was here to see was the only one who did have his own desk, one made just for him complete with adjustable height mechanism, ergonomic keyboard, and a vertical mouse.

It would have been easy to assume that he was the boss, flaunting his status by marking his desk out as special.

But Joe Singleton wasn't the boss.

He looked up as she approached, flashing a broad smile. 'Ashley Rafferty, I presume?'

'For my sins,' Rafferty said. 'Thanks for seeing me at such short notice.'

'Well,' Joe said with a grin, 'I was going to go for a quick run before lunch, but you caught me just in time.'

He chuckled at his own joke and leant back in his wheelchair.

There was a northern twang to his accent. It wasn't strong enough to be from Yorkshire. His enunciation was more pronounced. Rafferty would've guessed at a Lancastrian accent.

'Good job I brought lunch then.' She set a bag containing two cardboard bowls of curry on the desk, took one for herself, and put the other in front of Joe. She pulled up a chair and began fishing in the bag for the disposable cutlery that she was sure she'd remembered to ask for. She found it and handed one set over.

He gave an exaggerated sniff. 'That's not a Wigan Kebab.'

'As if anywhere around here is going to dare stick a meat pie in a bap.'

She knew her northern food. As soon as he realised she wasn't one of those southerners who hadn't been north of Watford, his expression softened. At least, she thought it did.

'How'd you know Wasabi chicken curry was my second choice?'

'Lucky guess,' Rafferty said. It hadn't been. She'd asked a friend who worked alongside him in MisPer how to get on Joe's good side and learned that he ordered in a large chicken Katsu curry every other Thursday.

Without skipping a beat, he tore the lid off, sniffed again, and then snatched up his wooden fork. They ate for a minute or two in silence, Joe eying Rafferty with every forkful as if daring her to explain why she was sitting at his desk.

'So?' he said finally. 'To what do I owe the bribe?'

'I'm looking for someone.'

Joe arched an eyebrow, smirked, and held up his left hand. 'Sorry, love, I'm married. Ta for the curry though.'

Hilarious, Rafferty thought, resisting the urge to roll her eyes. She'd set herself up for that one. 'Elijah Zholnovych,' she said.

'Awfully specific name. Can't imagine you'll find one of those on Bumble.'

He laughed again at his own joke. At Rafferty's rising anger, he held up his hands again, this time in surrender. 'All right, all right, gimme a minute.'

As she watched, he pulled a Brodie, tapping away at his keyboard to pull up Zholnovych's case file. Unlike Brodie, who typed so fast that his fingers became a two-hundred-words-a-minute blur, Joe preferred a torturously slow hunt and peck method that still saw him take three attempts to spell Elijah correctly. Finally, he got there, the familiar HOLMES case summary screen flashing up on his monitor.

Joe scanned it, his eyes traversing left to right as slowly as he'd typed, a reflection of the screen visible in his reading glasses. 'Sorry,' he said finally. 'Can't help you.'

He reached out to grab what was left of his curry, but Rafferty got there first. She put the lid back on to keep it warm.

'Hey!'

'Quid pro quo, Joe.'

He glared at her. 'It's not that I don't want to help. I just can't. Mr Zholnovych's been classified NAR.'

'Fuck,' Rafferty said. Joe was referring to the College of Policing's classification guidelines for missing persons. NAR was short for "No Apparent Risk", the lowest classification possible.

'What happens now then?' she demanded, glaring at him once again.

'Bugger all,' Joe said, glancing back at the HOLMES summary. 'We spoke to your witnesses, the neighbour whose dog wasn't walked. We've agreed to review further in 72 hours if the gent in question doesn't show up.'

It was the standard response: put the case into the so-called missing persons investigation cycle. Investigate, search, locate. Then, once the misper was found, manage their return, engage in harm reduction, and start all over again when they next went missing. It was a strategy dreamt up thinking about kids going AWOL, not a middle-aged man being carried out of his house in a box.

'That's it?'

''fraid so. Budgets are tight, love. He's a middle-aged man who didn't take his neighbour's dog for a walk. We can't spend tens of thousands of pounds investigating that, now, can we?' Joe gestured at a screen at the far end of the room that Rafferty hadn't noticed before. Faces of children, plus their ages and last known location, were running on a slideshow. The implication was obvious: MisPers had more important things to do.

Joe carried on talking: 'Chances are your missing man's gone away for work or gone to visit a friend. We see it all the time.'

Rafferty glared at him. As if she didn't know that MisPers were stretched. Before joining what was then DCI Morton's murder investigation team, she'd worked for what used to be called Sapphire, investigating sexual offences. Apparently, the unit was called that because a victim had proclaimed the team "diamonds in the rough" except working with sex crimes all day had the tendency to break people over time. The kind that could stick it out for more than a year or two were even rarer than diamonds but a bit less durable, thus Sapphire. Whether it was a true story or not was beyond her but the name was gone now. In 2018 it was reinvented as "Sexual Offences Investigation", one of three Safeguarding teams. The rebrand didn't change the reality. Sapphire was where Rafferty saw the worst of humanity first hand. Catching rapists and paedophiles had left her with no tolerance for bullshit and she wasn't going to be fobbed off by a mere desk jockey.

'Do you see high-velocity blood spatter all the time too?' she asked sarcastically. 'Nice, normal marker of a man who's gone off on a jaunt, is it?'

His head whipped back to his screen faster than he'd been shovelling Wasabi into his gob. 'Eh? It doesn't say any of that here, love.'

At her incredulous expression, he turned the monitor towards her. 'Take a look for yourself.'

It was true. Nothing in the case summary mentioned the blood spatter that Kflom had discovered. Nor was the witness statement from the neighbour, Rosie Bray, in the case file. What on earth was going on? They had been there this morning when Rafferty had left the office. All that Joe had on screen was the welfare check that Fred Albright had called in.

'Hang on,' she said. She pulled out her phone, fetched the file from the server herself, and pored over it. Maybe, just maybe, it was a permissions thing and Joe didn't have the proper access. No wonder he'd classified it NAR if all he had to go on was the statement from Albright.

HOLMES slowly loaded. She scanned down.

Nada.

Bray's witness report wasn't there.

Nor was Kflom's request for expert analysis of the high-velocity bloody spatter.

It was as if they'd never been uploaded in the first place. If Rafferty hadn't seen them with her own eyes first thing, she'd have sworn that Joe was right.

It had to be a glitch. A system error, maybe? However it had happened, files had been deleted.

Except... this was the HOLMES database, the pinnacle of digital policing. Everything was supposed to be ultra-secure. It had to be. Virtually every criminal investigation, from petty theft right up to trafficking, was run through it. If there were a glitch in the system, she'd have heard about it by now.

She clicked on case history, the log section of HOLMES. Every interaction with a case report was supposed to be on there, timestamped and with a record of which user had added or amended any record. It was supposed to be foolproof.

Still nothing.

It was as if the files had never been uploaded in the first place. Had she saved a copy on her laptop? She hoped she had.

'Something wrong, love?'

Rafferty shook her head. 'Just a glitch in the system. If you were to take my word for it, and assume there was high-velocity blood spatter, plus possible gunshot residue, what would you say?'

He finished his last forkful of curry before answering. 'I'd say, Inspector Rafferty, that then it would be a case for a murder investigation team, wouldn't it?'

'So what're you going to do about it?'

He smiled.

'Nothing. That's well above my pay grade. But thanks for the curry.'

13

WATCH THIS

GOING into hiding ain't just losing your name. It's losing every-thing. Friends. Family. Even hobbies.

I couldn't do it. Even the threat of death wouldn't keep me away from the woman I loved.

That's what'll break him. The Collector is a bloody magpie. If we can't find him through his habits, we'll find him with the thing that makes him unique, the very thing that earned him his nickname.

'What if we lure him in?' Tank asked. He was sitting on my sofa, his Aviators perched on the bridge of his nose as he stared out the window at the people walking the streets. Living a stone's throw from Barbican doesn't come cheap, but it's worth every damned penny. A bowl of *salo* was on the table besides him, the smell of it strong even from the kitchen. Cured pork fat, thyme, paprika and garlic. I can't stand the stuff but it's Tank's favourite. He piles it high on rye bread and then chases it down with vodka. It's one vice I can forgive.

Luring The Collector out of hiding isn't a bad idea. Even if he ain't dealing, he's not turned into Marie bloody Kondo. Wherever he is, he'll have a pile of old tat to bring him joy.

'What with?' I asked.

'His nickname. How'd he get?'

My mind flashed back to a safe house. Can't remember which one. They all blur together after a while and we used to swap them out to stay one step ahead of the Fuzz. We were on the sofa – Tank, Linden, and Pavel Bakowski. The police had just nailed one of our boys for importing coke hidden inside tins of baby formula coming through Southampton docks so we were all on tenterhooks, wondering if he'd rat anyone out. He didn't in the end. Wise man. Unlike The Collector. He'd earned his nickname by rabbiting on for hours, going on and on about his damned watch collection. Not just any watches either, mind. It had to be *old* watches, the kind that didn't even keep good time. Fucking pointless if you ask me.

'Watches. He used to collect 'em. Hoard 'em even. He was obsessed with one brand. I can't remember which though. Something obscure. Starts with a V?'

Tank looked at me. 'Volvo!'

'Christ almighty, Tank, they make cars. You used to drive one, remember?'

Idiot.

He screwed up his face.

'Vulva?'

I laughed. 'Definitely not.'

Tank held up his hands in surrender. 'Beats me.'

Watches. Watches. The Collector was obsessed with them. Now I wish I'd actually listened to his monologues. The details were fuzzy, hidden somewhere in the back of my mind. Where the hell were they from? Russia maybe? That made sense. His mother was from the Donbas, one of the few Ukrainians who thought of themselves as Russian.

'You know anyone who knows shit about watches?'

He chewed his lip as if thinking.
Then, slowly, he shrugged. 'Google?'
'Fucking ace, Tank, fucking ace.'
As if I hadn't thought of that.

14

WITHOUT A TRACE

IT *WASN'T* A GLITCH.

She didn't need Brodie to tell her that either. Everyone knew HOLMES was heavily logged. Every click, every keystroke, all of it. If a document had been deleted from a case file, it would have been in the logs and someone would have had to fill in a form to say why it had been deleted. Rafferty had filled out a few of those herself, usually when there were duplicate copies of something or someone had accidentally attached the wrong file to the wrong case.

But Ayala would just deny it. No doubt about that. Until a body turned up or the blood spatter analysis came back and confirmed that someone had been shot in Zholnovych's living room, he'd stonewall any attempt at opening a murder investigation.

All of which left Rafferty stumped.

In the old days, she'd have wandered into Morton's office and asked what he thought. The old-timer had seen it all. From the days of no DNA to police corruption right through to the most heinous of serial killers.

Fat lot of good it had been replacing him with Mr

Jobsworth. Ayala should've been shunted sideways into a desk job doing something boring like serious fraud. Investigating the big cases, the criminals smart enough not to lay a trail back to their door, took a certain panache, a creativity, that he sorely lacked.

Nobody had ever attributed such failings to Morton.

Now she had to bribe the old-timer with booze. The offer of a free pint had convinced Morton to join her in the Cask and Glass pub, a brisk, ten-minute walk from her desk: just long enough to clear her head and far away enough that word wouldn't get back to Ayala.

When she arrived, Morton was nowhere to be seen. Unlike the old days, when Morton had always been the first to arrive and the last to leave, he kept her waiting. The great DCI Morton, no longer a stickler for being prompt. What was the world coming to? Had retirement taken the edge off his razor-sharp wit? Was age finally catching up with him? Was he finally dedicating his days to his non-existent talent for romantic poetry?

It didn't look like it. The man who walked in looked somehow younger than the day he'd been forced out of the Met. Gone were the frown lines, the dark circles, the hunched over posture. Instead, a more relaxed Morton sauntered in, nodded to acknowledge her presence, and then made a beeline for the bar.

He sat down opposite and eyed her curiously as he supped his pint. She'd been wrong. Up close, the wrinkles were deeper, the skin more tanned – no doubt the result of his recent purchase of a holiday home in Gibraltar – and he seemed happier as if he were lighter, freer, less laden down with the weight of responsibility that went with being in charge. For a brief moment, she envied him. And then she remembered the adrenaline, the rush, the feeling of victory at catching the worst criminals London had to offer. All that was still in front of her.

'Out with it then,' he demanded between gulps.

She grinned. No need for small talk.

'I've got a weird one.'

'Nothing new then.'

'Really weird,' Rafferty said. She relayed a quick case summary, explaining what Rosie Bray had seen, the blood spatter evidence Kflom had collected, and that Joe had put the misper case on the back burner. Throughout, she tried to be fair to both sides, giving both Ayala's argument – that a man ought to be free to bugger off without telling his neighbours – and her own gut feeling that something was amiss.

'Wait, back up a second,' Morton said. He stared at her for a moment. 'You're overlooking something.'

She stared back. 'Am I?'

Morton-the-teacher was back.

'Think about it. Mobile. Laptop. Both gone.'

'Right...?'

She knew that. She'd told him that.

'And no other devices on the log, right?'

'Nothing. The place was empty. The man didn't own jack.'

Where was Morton going with this?

Morton smirked. 'It's not what you've seen. It what's you didn't see. How did Zholnovych access the internet?'

Damn it. Why hadn't she noticed that before?

No router.

No God-damned router.

Which meant no broadband service.

Who on earth worked from home without an internet connection? She debated pushing back – arguing that he'd used 5G on his mobile instead – but there wasn't any point. Morton knew, just as she did, that the odds of being able to work on such a slow connection were slim to none. London's mobile networks were so congested that even "quick" services like 5G got bogged down with too much traffic. When she'd been at the house, her own signal kept dropping out. She'd barely managed to get a 3G signal in Balham let alone 5G.

It explained the Blu-ray collection too. She'd assumed Zholnovych was old-school, that he just loved having a physical collection, or maybe that he could only get the content he wanted on disc. She hadn't even considered the possibility that he might not use Netflix like everyone else because he didn't have an internet connection.

'It doesn't matter now anyway,' Rafferty said, eager to change the subject. 'It's all gone. Every bit of evidence on HOLMES wiped without a trace.'

Morton's eyebrow lurched upwards. He set the last dregs of his pint down. 'You're sure it's not an IT error.'

It wasn't a question. Morton knew she'd have checked. 'In what circumstances can stuff disappear from a secure system like HOLMES?'

'A glitch-' Morton began.

Rafferty held up a hand to cut him off. 'Nope. No other files affected, no security breaches, nothing.'

That much Brodie had confirmed.

'Then someone with authority... There's only one obvious answer.'

She thought she knew what he was about to say, but she wanted him to be the first to say it.

'National security,' he volunteered.

'Then I'm not going crazy. Thought working for Ayala had driven me to the madhouse.'

Rather than reply, Morton drained his pint and stood up. 'Another?'

She shook her head. 'Don't let me stop you though.'

When he returned from the bar with a fresh beer, he'd clearly been working out what he wanted to say.

'Drop it,' he advised. 'If someone up high has decided that this needs to be deleted as a matter of national security, no good will come of you sticking your oar in.'

'You sound just like Ayala.'

He mock-recoiled as if wounded. 'Don't lump me in with that backstabbing ba-'

'Backstabber?'

'Close,' Morton said with a grin. It was the first time she'd ever heard him openly talk ill of a colleague. Not that she blamed him after what Ayala had done.

'But when would that happen? What sort of national security concern stops a murder investigation dead?'

'You said his name's Zholnovych, right? That sounds Russian to me.' Morton said. 'Sounds like you'd have to ask K.'

Morton really was old. The Director General of MI5 hadn't been known as "K" since the 1940s.

'Like MI5 are going to talk to me.'

'Then you're going to have to drop it, aren't you?'

She smirked. 'Just like you would have.'

As if the great DCI Morton would've given up so easily.

'Not everything is a battle, Ash,' Morton said. His smile was gone now. 'Sometimes, you have to know when to hold 'em and when to fold 'em. If this is just a glitch, you'll get your blood spatter analysis back and then you'll be on your merry way. If it's not – and it turns out that the Security Service really did pull the files – then you'll be glad that you left it all well alone. It'll be one of those things that'll drive you bonkers forevermore, but believe me, they'll never tell you a damned thing. The closest you'll get is a polite "leave it alone" from on high. Like it or not, that's Ayala these days. So, do me a favour, and wait and see.'

She nodded curtly.

For now.

15

OLD FRIENDS

THE SHOP REEKED of burnt tobacco leaves, leather-bound books, and oil. Not the fry-up kind, but the sort used by mechanics.

Except the man we were here to see didn't fix up old cars.

Nikolai Peskov was a watchmaker, the old-fashioned kind who wore a visor with dozens of lenses of varying intensity, and an overall with more pockets than I'd had hot dinners, presumably stuffed with itty-bitty parts ready to fix whatever came across his desk.

He also had a bit of a reputation for selling fake and stolen goods. If the Collector had dodgy cash to spend on old watches, Peskov would've been his go-to seller.

We waited outside until his last customer left; tailgating our way in meant we didn't need an appointment.

'Gentleman,' he said as we approached the desk. He eyed us cautiously. We didn't look like his typical customers. The bloke that had walked out as we'd approached the front door had been dapper, proper suit, tie, the whole shebang. Tank and I were incognito: jeans, Nike's, generic long-sleeved t-shirt. Not that

Tank could ever manage subtle. He was taller than virtually every other man on the street and had more ink than bare skin.

'You in the right place, boys?' Peskov said with a gap-toothed smile. 'Argos is down the street.'

Ha fucking ha. I pulled a wedge of twenties out of my coat pocket, fifty of them neatly wrapped in a Grosvenor Casino wrapper that read £1000.

The watchmaker's hand reached out to pick up the wad. Before he could, Tank snatched at Peskov's wrist, pinning him against his own counter.

'Not so fast, old-timer,' I said. 'You know an old friend of ours. Nathan Linden.'

'Who?'

Tank twisted his arm, smushing his face against the tabletop.

'Nathan Linden,' I repeated clearly. 'Tank, let the man breathe a little.'

He did. Peskov glared up at me. 'Suppose the name *might* ring a bell.'

'I'll bet it does. Word on the street is you were his go-to dealer.'

For a moment, I thought he was gonna bullshit me about client confidentiality. Then Tank flexed his muscles again. I could see the pain on Peskov's face – and the fear. It would be child's play for Tank to break his wrist.

'Alright, alright, leave off! I know Linden. Knew him anyway. What do you care?'

'When was the last time you saw him?'

'Eight... maybe nine years?'

That fitted.

Linden hadn't been back in to buy since he'd gone into witness protection. Wise move.

'What was it he bought?'

Peskov jerked his neck up at Tank. 'Mind telling sasquatch here to let me up?'

I nodded and Tank released him.

'Thank you,' he said, and then rubbed at the back of his neck. 'Didn't have to rough me up you know. This isn't Kaliningrad.'

I smiled but said nothing.

'Right, Linden, Linden. I'm going to reach under my counter, nice and slow. There's a binder under there, okay?'

When I nodded, he slowly reached down. I tensed, half expecting him to pull a gun.

He didn't. Instead, he plonked a great big leather binder on the counter. It was stuffed with yellowed papers bulging out the sides. When Peskov opened it, I saw neat, uppercase Cyrillic writing. Occasionally, an English name jumped out. It had to be his ledger, a record of sales. As we watched, he pored over an indecipherable index, muttering to himself in Russian as he read. There were coloured tabs inserted throughout which made no sense to me, but Peskov knew what he was looking for. He flipped through until he found the right page and then drew a gnarled finger down it, line by line, methodically looking for something.

'Here,' he said. 'The first time he came in was nineteen ninety-nine.'

'What did he buy?'

Peskov turned the binder around with a flourish. 'See for yourself.'

There were several columns on the page. Name, date, value, and a description of the item bought.

VOLNA was written neatly next to the price of sixty pounds. Tank hadn't been too far off with his guesses then. The description field was blank.

The word echoed in my mind. It was Russian.

'Wave?' I guessed.

'You speak Russian?' Peskov asked approvingly. 'You're right. He wanted a *Volna*, a late model one.'

I didn't. Not much anyway.

'You remember selling him it? After all this time?'

It had to have been a special watch for Peskov to remember it.

'No,' the watchmaker said. 'But it's cheap. Sixty pounds. Even back in ninety-nine, that didn't buy you much. The only *Volna* watches I stocked for under a hundred quid were the cheaper, later models. Gateway watches, I call 'em. People come in, try one, like it, and eventually they come back and buy something I can actually make money on.'

Fair enough. That explained the lack of description. Why bother filling in the ledger properly for a sixty quid taster sale?

I nodded. 'Just like Linden did.'

He took the binder once again, riffled through, and nodded. 'Exactly. He came back a lot. Hundreds of times.'

'Did he follow your pattern?'

By now, Peskov seemed to have forgotten both the threat and the stack of cash. This was a man who loved watches. The kind of guy who'd put horologist on his Tinder bio. I'd learnt the word while Googling info on watches last night. There's a bloody word for everything. Is there one for someone who Googles everything? If so, that's me.

'He started with a cheapie like most do. But he didn't follow my usual pattern – clients get older, then they want bigger, blingier watches. Linden wasn't like that. His acquisitions were always Russian, always Soviet, and always the best brands.'

'Like *Volna*?'

'Sort of,' Peskov said. He pointed towards a shelf where dozens of *Volna* watches were lined up. From here, I could see the price tags were all over the place. Everything from £90 at the bottom end up to thousands.

As I looked, Peskov carried on talking: '*Volna* went into production back in '57 and were made through to '64. They churned out millions of 'em in that time.'

Boring. Mass-produced tat. What the hell did Linden see in them? Surely once you've seen one cheaply-made watch, you've seen 'em all? I'd had a cheap Casio once. It still told the damned time.

'They all look pretty similar to me.'

'They're similar,' Peskov conceded. 'All of them employed the Vostok 2809 movement, not quite chronometer grade but good enough. Like most Russian watches, it was based on stolen Swiss tech. Then they switched up the colour, metal, and the like to create hundreds of different versions.'

'And Linden only collected these *Volna*?'

'Anything Russian, I think. I know he had a *Shturmanskie*. That one he wore every time he came in. I didn't sell it to him though. I tried to buy it a few times, but he wasn't having any of it. Must've been sentimental.'

When I look at him perplexed, he continued: 'First watch in space? Don't you kids know anything these days?'

We weren't *that* young. Then again, Peskov was probably old enough to remember the nineteen-fifties. 'So, what did you sell him that wasn't the mass-market crap?'

He walked around his counter, pointing at shelves hidden behind glass. 'Mostly NOS models – New Old Stock – stuff that hasn't been worn but I've had hiding in the back forever and a day.'

From the number of watches on the shelves marked NOS, I knew Peskov was full of shit. Nobody had that much brand-new stock leftover from the nineteen fifties. One or two, I'd buy.

Dozens? Hell no. Especially when the seller had Peskov's reputation.

'Linden fell for that, did he?'

If he had, Linden was even thicker than I thought.

Peskov's grin widened. 'Alright, maybe not *entirely* new...'

'Or entirely Russian,' I finished for him.

The watchmaker carried on yabbering as if I'd said nothing. I let him ramble on about the Chistopol Watch Factory, how it used to be the First Moscow Watch Factory, and even nodded along as he mumbled about twenty-two jewel movements. Part of me wanted to stop him but the idea of tech stolen from the Swiss, a factory moved out of Moscow during the war to get industry away from the front, and Pekov's sheer joy at telling me it all... it was intoxicating. He was a damned good salesman and a crook to boot. Shame we couldn't be friends. He even kept glancing longingly at the thousand pounds on the table. Just like I would have.

'If Linden could have had anything, what would it have been? What was his dream watch?' I asked.

'You're a strange fellow,' Peskov said. 'You bribe me. Then threaten me. But then you listen to me talk. All to find out what a long-gone customer wanted. What's Linden to you?'

I considered telling him the truth. I didn't. 'None of your damned business. But if you'd like to avoid angering my friend, answer the bloody question. What would've been the jewel in Linden's collection? The one that got away?'

'A *Komandirskie* by Vostok. The original Tank, not the Amphibia and not one of the 90s reproductions either.'

Tank grinned at me. As if the watch were named after *him*.

'Nobody ever wants later version,' Peskov continued. 'It has to be one of the first production batch. And it'd have to be in perfect order. As it happens, I've got one in the back – yours for two grand.'

How convenient. Linden's nasal whinge flashed through my mind: *provenance.* That's what he'd have called it. A fancy way of asking someone to prove that what they're selling is genny. If Peskov had had Linden's dream watch, he'd have sold it to him long ago, and for far more than two thousand.

'Not fixed up using those dodgy Chinese parts you mentioned?'

This time, Peskov didn't grin. 'They've *all* got Chinese parts in. A genuine *Komandirskie* from '65 is as rare as hen's teeth. The Chistopol factory only made them to the order of the Defence Department of the Soviet Union. It was a badge of honour to get one of the first batch. Families kept them, treasured them as heirlooms. Linden wanted one for years. But I could never find the right one so there's sod all chance you will. This is as close as you'll get, son.'

'Then we'll take it.'

Peskov grinned at the thought of two thousand pounds. As if I was going to be conned by the likes of him. He motioned towards the register. I motioned towards Tank and then picked up the £1000.

'I didn't say I'd buy it. I said we'll *take* it.'

16

THE ITCH

ALL WEEKEND, she tried to forget. But the more she pushed it out of her mind, the more it drove her mad.

The Met never "lost" data. Even Brodie couldn't find out what had happened and digital forensics were his bread and butter.

Could Morton be right? Were the Security Services involved?

It wasn't something she'd ever come up against before. The idea that an investigation, by one of the Met's busiest murder investigation teams no less, could simply be aborted at the whim of an unseen spy agency. It left a bad taste in her mouth.

She turned over in bed, wrestling with the covers as much as with the idea of MI5 or MI6 kiboshing her investigation. How the hell would that work exactly? Someone in the Met would need to be in the know. Ayala, perhaps? He was a DCI now.

Then again, Morton said he wouldn't have known either. That could have been a lie, of course. But Morton was more apt to say nothing than to lie outright.

Was it Silverman? Had the Met's illustrious Commissioner

of Police of the Metropolis sent word down that the Zholnovych case was to be quietly aborted? Or was it someone in her office? The whole thing was like something out of a bad movie. A man disappears and now the most mundane of evidence – a witness statement from a woman who'd been too busy cycling to even see anything – was gone.

Why delete that? Rosie Bray's statement had been no threat to anyone. She hadn't seen a damned thing, had she?

Enough, Rafferty thought. She wasn't going to get to sleep without doing something – anything – to put the thought to bed. She swung her legs over the side, stood, and groped in the dark for the light switch. Harsh yellow lights assaulted her eyes as the familiar buzz of the LED hummed to life.

Her notebook. Where had she put it?

She fumbled her way through the flat, flipping light switches as she went, until she found her coat on its hook by the front door. Her notebook was tucked safely in the inside pocket, a tiny blue pen in its spiral binding. She took both out on her way into the living room, sat down on the sofa and flicked on her beloved Anglepoise lamp before beginning to read.

ZHOLNOVYCH reported missing by his neighbour Fred Albright (for whom he walks the family dog).

Another neighbour, ROSIE BRAY – lives across the road – saw a delivery van pull up and then leave, apparently unable to deliver. Could suggest ZHOLNOVYCH was gone before this time.

Except for the void in the lounge – size lines up with parcel described by BRAY.

KERFLUM (sp? – new CSI) found what he thought was high-velocity blood spatter consistent with a shooting; not enough to confirm fatality. Carpet sample sent to lab for GRS test. PURCELL warned against jumping the gun.

Rafferty blinked. The lab results. She snatched her phone

off the coffee table, blinked as its OLED screen came to life, and then waited for FaceID to do its thing and unlock the phone. When it did, she thumbed through to the Met's intranet app and went in search of the new CSI's number. When KERFLUM didn't return a result, she took a different tack, looking through Purcell's team.

There he was.

Kflom!

Not Kerflum which was how he'd pronounced it. Now she knew how to spell it, it would be easy enough to remember. There was a work mobile number listed for him. She glanced at the clock on the wall – half past two in the morning. Bit late to be calling. She rang anyway.

It went straight to voicemail: 'You've reached Kflom. Leave a message and I'll get back to you.'

When it beeped, she cleared her throat and spoke: 'Hi, it's Ashley Rafferty. Could you give me a call back at your earliest convenience? Ta.'

Someone might've accidentally deleted a file. She didn't believe it, but it wasn't impossible.

But they couldn't destroy the physical evidence.

17

THE HONEYTRAP

THE WATCH WAS a piece of shit.

Not that I'd expected any better from Peskov. Takes one con man to spot another. I prefer the bigger, more elaborate cons, but I respect the grift. If I'd paid him the two grand, I'd have overpaid by at least eighteen hundred. When I looked at the *Komandirskie* under a magnifying glass in the light of my kitchen, the flaws were way more obvious than they had been in Peskov's shop.

What we'd taken was less Soviet Military and more Fisher-Price. The movement didn't work for more than a couple of hours. The "jewels" in it were glass pebbles. And when I looked real close, I could see the paint was flaking off too.

Doesn't matter though. I don't want to wear it. I don't even want to *sell* it. Not really.

The watch is a lure. The thing Nathan Linden has always coveted. In my experience, greed's the best way to con a mark. For most people, that's money or sex. For Linden, it's his beloved collection, one that would never be complete without the 1965 *Komandirskie* Tank.

Going into witness protection must be hell. One day, you've

got a family, friends, interests. The next you've got none of it. Losing people is one thing – and that was what broke Zholnovych's wife, going home – but losing yourself has to be harder. I'd still like the same shit even if I had to change my name.

That's what I'm banking on. That Nathan Linden could never give up his beloved collection. It was what he'd rabbit on about to anyone who'd listen. Watches were where he spent his ill-gotten gains. No doubt he's still got them, even if they're stashed somewhere well away from prying eyes.

It has the side benefit of being subtle too. Who would expect an eBay listing for a collectable watch to be a honeytrap?

'Uh, boss?' Tank said. He looked at me, his eyes hollowed out and bogged down with dark bags that never go away. With it comes the irritability, the mood swings, and his utter inability to see the bigger picture.

'What?' I snapped.

'I don't get it,' he said. 'How do we know Linden's the one who's going to buy the damned watch?'

We don't. That's the great flaw. It has to be so enticing that Linden will want it, but up for long enough that he'll take the bait. All we can do is try and stop someone else from hitting the buy button.

'We overprice it,' I told him for the nth time. 'That's part of the con. Linden knows these things are valuable. If we sell them too cheap, he'll smell a rat. We need to price high.'

Reassuringly expensive. That's what I always called it. Got counterfeit Luis Vuitton bags to move? Don't stand at Camden Lock and flog 'em for twenty quid a pop. Nobody's going to think they're real, they won't make shit all, and the rozzers will be all over it in an hour. The last time I'd had designer bags to shift, I'd set up a "pop up store" in a fancy shopping arcade. One weekend only, twenty percent off RRP. Cheap enough to be a bargain, reassuringly expensive enough that customers didn't spot the scam.

Rich bitches had lapped it up. In less than 48 hours, I'd sold a couple of hundred fake bags – all from China, just like Peskov's watch parts – and made nearly retail on them to boot. Way more profit, way lower risk.

Just like this.

Linden is going to want the watch. I'll list it high, photograph the damned thing carefully so he can't see the flaws – and photoshop it if we have to – and then sit back and wait. And wait. And wait.

He's been in hiding for over eight years.

I can wait a little longer.

18

LOST

'IT'S GONE,' Kflom said.

He'd called Rafferty back before she'd had a chance to finish her breakfast. The poached eggs, salmon, and sourdough toast she'd made not five minutes earlier were now rapidly cooling on her plate, her fork abandoned. In its place, she clutched her phone to her ear and stared out of the window at the back garden. She could see two foxes, probably the little bastards who'd been making a racket last night. Their blood-curdling mating was enough to keep anyone up at night, and worse, the local vermin were getting more action than she was.

'Come again?'

'Gone,' Kflom repeated. 'Someone lost the samples. All of them – blood, DNA, gunshot residue tests, fibres, an entire bundle gone. Something about a courier mishap.'

Bullshit. She said as much.

'Thought so too,' said Kflom. 'It's the first time I've ever heard of samples going AWOL.'

'In your three weeks of being a fully-fledged CSI you mean,' Rafferty said. 'What's Purcell got to say about it?'

'That it happens and that I should go back and get another sample.'

Finally, someone talking some sense. 'When?'

'I'm heading there now. Should get there by eight.'

Rafferty glanced at her watch. Half seven. 'Can you wait for me? I'll square things up with legal en route, just to make sure we're not crossing any lines. I shouldn't be too far behind you.'

'Sure. See you outside then.'

AFTER A QUICK CALL to a CPS lawyer and then a brief stop at Starbucks, Rafferty made it to Balham just after nine. As soon as she had turned into the cul-de-sac, the business of the high street had given way to an eerie calm.

A bored-looking Kflom was sitting in his car, lost on his phone. Rafferty parked up, made her way over, and rapped smartly on the window. His gaze jolted upwards, a guilty expression on his face. She could see Tinder open on his phone.

'Any luck?' she said as he stepped out of his car.

He shook his head sadly. 'If I see one more woman asking for "*six-figure salary, six-foot tall, six-inch penis*", I'm going to cry.'

She looked him up and down. He was a fraction shorter than her.

'Five foot eleven,' he said with a sad smile. Then he winked. 'But one out of three ain't bad.'

'Blimey,' Rafferty said. 'If I'd known you were that loaded, I wouldn't have bought you a coffee. Even if it is an apology for making you wait.'

She held out his coffee expecting him to take it. He burst out laughing, an infectious grin spreading from high cheekbone to high cheekbone.

'Touché, Ms Rafferty.'

She returned his smile and turned to face the house. The same hedge, the same quiet sense of foreboding. Down to business. When she turned back to Kflom, his Hollywood smile had vanished.

'What's wrong?'

'I think,' Kflom said slowly, 'we may have... a complication.'

He looked over at Zholnovych's home.

'I saw someone going in there, newspaper tucked under his arm. He hasn't come out.'

'Zholnovych?'

He shrugged. 'No idea.'

Could he have come back? Had they imagined it all? Was it, as Joe had all but implied, a simple case of a middle-aged man going away for a mid-week break without telling the neighbour that he wouldn't be able to walk the man's dog?

What an anti-climax that would be. After the missing files, the lost evidence, Ayala's bewildering order to stand down, had Rafferty jumped the gun in assuming foul play?

'I'd best find out then. Wait out here for me.'

He nodded. No point dragging him to the door with her if all she had to do was confirm Zholnovych was safely at home and put the matter to rest. She plodded towards the front door, wondering why on earth she'd lost so much sleep over Zholnovych's disappearance. It wasn't like her to overreact.

Through the gate, and a final glance backwards at Kflom. He was back on his phone, no doubt swiping right like a madman. She could hear music coming from inside the house. Someone was home. It sounded like pop music, Eurovision style, upbeat and not in English.

She knocked on the door. A gruff voice shouted something indecipherable from within.

The door swung open to reveal a man in his late twenties or

early thirties. He was well dressed in an exceptionally well-fitted suit with a bright pink shirt and mauve tie. It wasn't the cookie-cutter Homer Simpson look she'd seen in the wardrobe.

'Elijah Zholnovych?' Rafferty asked.

He looked at her blankly. '*Excusez-moi?*'

A French accent. That didn't fit with what Rafferty knew of Zholnovych.

'Are you,' Rafferty said slowly, her irritation getting the better of her, 'Elijah Zholnovych? I'm with the police.'

'Police?' the man echoed, clearly alarmed. '*Un moment, s'il vous plaît*. Lili! Lili!'

A woman, clearly Lili, trundled out of the living room at the back of the house. She was wearing one of those half-blanket, half-jumper affairs that Rafferty had seen advertised on the telly. A pair of big, fluffy slippers completed the look. It was a far cry from the chic, trendy look Rafferty had expected based on the husband.

'Yes?' she said, her accent not as thick as her husband's but still discernible.

'I'm Detective Inspector Ashley Rafferty, Metropolitan Police. I'm looking for the man who lives here, Elijah Zholnovych.'

She spread her palms wide. '*Non,*' she said firmly. 'There is no Zholnovych here. We are, how you say, new to the area.'

'When did you move in?'

'*Dimanche.*'

Sunday.

Rafferty's mind reeled. It was as if every shred of evidence of Zholnovych's existence was being systematically wiped out.

'How did you rent this place?'

She turned to her husband and a rapid-fire of French followed. Rafferty caught some but not all of it.

'We have an agent.'

That's what they'd been saying: a relocation agent. It wasn't a service Rafferty had ever used. But then she'd never left London.

'Which one?'

Another exchange in French. By now, her husband looked thoroughly confused.

'*Je ne sais pas.* His work – a law firm in Paris – organised it all.'

'Do you have a tenancy agreement?'

'*Bien sûr.*'

Of course.

'Can I see it?'

'*Oui*, come in.'

Rafferty followed Lili inside. The hallway looked largely the same, but with piles of moving boxes visible in the front room. They traipsed through to the lounge where the look and feel had been drastically altered. Gone were the Blu-rays, the over-sized sofa, and the OLED telly. In its place were a chaise longue, a baby's bouncer, and a dozen boxes covered in Sellotape, each marked up with black pen. The smallest was marked SDB, presumably short for *Salle de bain* or bathroom while the next box down in the stack was marked *Chambre d'enfant*, or nursery.

Lili gestured for Rafferty to perch on the chaise longue. She disappeared off for a moment before returning with a battered-looking iPad. She passed it over.

A document was open marked "Assured Shorthold Tenancy". Rafferty scanned through. It was between Lili and her husband Jean and a firm in the Marshall Islands that owned the house.

The Marshall Islands?

She'd missed that little titbit when looking at the Land Registry.

Why on earth did an overseas company own a family home in Balham?

She switched over to Google the company listed as the landlord. Sure enough, it was a trust company in the Marshall Islands. From the furore in the press about the Panama Papers, Rafferty knew it was the sort of set-up used to hide things and evade tax liabilities. But what she didn't know was how common they were. Google's first page was a treasure trove of controversy with articles about fraud, tax avoidance, and the way the rich hid their money. She fought the urge to click through to read more. That would have to wait.

What else did the lease contain? Rafferty flipped back and scanned down further, looking for the signature page. Someone had to have signed the damned thing and that had to have been a real human being, not a company based out of a PO Box.

At the bottom, she found it. Jean had signed for the family. For the landlord, there was an indecipherable scribble. Underneath the firm's name was "SYMMONDS (SYMMONDS & SYMMONDS)".

A law firm, one of the big ones. They'd been part of the Panama Papers scandal so it made sense. Dodgy lawyers, even dodgier jurisdiction. The firm specialised in representing sleazy billionaires looking to avoid paying their fair whack of tax. Rafferty had read all about that too.

Curious.

Who then had cleared out the house? And so quickly?

'Can I take a copy of this?' Rafferty asked.

Lili gave an exaggerated shrug. 'Be my guest.'

'And one more thing, would you mind if I call a colleague in? We'd like to swab your living room carpet.'

The call she'd made to Kieran O'Connor at the CPS was moot at this point. He'd told her it was fine to go back to an active crime scene without having to get a warrant. That wouldn't hold up now someone else lived here.

Rafferty pointed at where the blood spatter had been the last time she'd been in the room. From where she was, she couldn't see it.

'A... swab?' Lili asked.

She obviously didn't understand. What the heck was the French word for it? Sod it. Google Translate would have to do.

'Hey Siri, how do you say forensic swab in French?' Rafferty asked.

'*Un écouvillon forensique*,' Siri answered.

Understanding dawned on Lili. Another shrug, this time accompanied by a nod.

Rafferty set to work. She went out to grab Kflom who she found anxiously standing on the pavement, his kit case in one hand and his phone in another. As soon as he saw her, he quickly thumbed the lock button on his phone but not before she'd spotted that he was still swiping away on Tinder. She pretended not to notice. They returned to the lounge and set to work.

'Psst,' Kflom said.

'What?'

'Come have a closer look.'

Rafferty bent down to examine the carpet. 'I don't see anything.'

'Exactly.'

'But I do smell something.'

It was only a faint whiff but it was unmistakably bleach. If she hadn't leant in to look at the fibres, she'd never have noticed it.

'Someone's bleached the carpet,' Kflom said, unnecessarily, 'so it's a waste of time. Luminol reacts to both blood and bleach – so spraying again won't help.'

'And the GSR?'

Kflom cocked his head to one side as if to consider what bleach would do to a gunshot residue sample.

'It'll be degraded. Probably useless. But I'll take a swab anyway.'

He did.

They soon found themselves on the pavement outside. Rafferty looked at him in disbelief. They'd gone back to a "missing" man's home only to find he didn't live there, and someone had taken the time to deep clean the carpets. Was that just a thorough end-of-tenancy procedure? Had Zholnovych's lease simply run out and he'd moved on without telling the neighbours?

If so, why had his stuff been there last week?

And where was it now?

19

TRUST BUT VERIFY

IT WAS JUST AS WELL that we had plenty of bloody time. Tank was right.

The world's biggest auction house ain't exactly Gumtree or Craigslist. It's much, much more complicated.

First off, we had to make a profile. Simple enough.

Except we had no feedback. No reputation. No list of things we'd bought and sold over the years. Instead, we had a big button that announced to the eBay world that we had just joined. Would've been way too big an ask to expect the Collector to fall for a blank profile, a newbie popping up with the watch of his dreams.

So we started laying the groundwork.

First, I bought tat. Lots of it. DVDs and books for a penny, that sort of thing. Just to have some feedback, any feedback. It came trickling in: *AAA+ great buyer, thanks for the instant payment, best eBayer ever.*

But that hot air wasn't gonna cut it.

What I needed was to sell stuff. So I did. I bought some old watches – not from Peskov, but from charity shops and the like – and sold 'em on. Made a few quid into the bargain.

Slowly, Tank and I built up our reputation.

It took *months*. Buying, selling, shipping, rinse and repeat. I'd send Tank off to buy stuff from the charity shops in the posh parts of town – Oxfam in Chelsea, the British Heart Foundation over in Marylebone and the like. He'd leave with fistfuls of notes and come back with whatever shit he thought might sell. I had to be careful. Too much cash and Tank would be tempted to spend it. It took a tight rein to keep that demon in check. I should know. I resorted to sending him out with fifty or a hundred quid at a time, enough to do the job but not enough to get him in much trouble. Then I checked the receipts to make sure he wasn't skimming off the top.

Trust but verify.

Most of the tat he came back with went in the bin. The good stuff got piled so high on the kitchen table that I couldn't cook a damned thing and we had to resort to buying from our favourite pizza delivery place in Whitecross Street.

Then I listed everything. I'd set up one corner of my living room with a camera on a tripod and a macro lens attached. That had come from one of the charity shops too. Then there were boxes, flat packed and ready to rock, in another corner. The final bit of kit was a printer which churned out my postage labels. Tank was dealing with today's labels, all eighty of them. All legit. I wasn't gonna get nicked for dodgy stamps.

Time and again, I got stupid questions from buyers. Over and over, I got lowball offers. Ten quid for a watch worth three hundred? Sod off. I learned to block those people. Then I set up rules, telling the site that anyone who offered less than half got automatically rejected. I wanted to ape the professional sellers, to look like one of them, to become the Peskov of eBay.

My descriptions got better too. People kept asking about provenance, about repair history, that sort of crap. So I started including it all up front.

Sales soared.

At this rate, I'll have to tell the bloody taxman about it all before PayPal dob me in. I need to find Linden before then.

And hope he knows where the old *shef* has gone to ground.

'Tank,' I said.

He looked up from the printer. 'Yeah?'

'It's time,' I said. 'Get the watch.'

'Which watch?'

'Peskov's watch, you bloody moron. We've got over 10,000 feedback. We're a top-rated seller. It's time to put the bait on the hook.'

He looked at me blankly.

'Just get the damned watch.'

Can't get the help these days.

20

THE WAITING GAME

MONTHS OF CASES, months of investigating. Suicides, cot deaths, even one rather grizzly murder of a judge in a locked courtroom. Thank God that case had ended up with another murder investigation team. No doubt Ayala would've swept it under the carpet too.

But not one could put the Zholnovych case out of Rafferty's mind.

When Kflom had confirmed it was bleach, she'd run the case back up the flagpole.

And been shut down.

Again.

He would, Ayala had claimed, "turn up in time".

Like hell he had.

Of course, she'd investigated. Quietly.

The Marshall Islands address turned out to be a post office where tens of thousands of firms were registered. As expected, a total dead end.

Just like the law firm.

Symmonds & Symmonds had politely told her to fuck off. They'd said they couldn't comment on any of their clients. Nor would they explain, even in general terms, why someone would register a firm in the Marshall Islands.

Kieran O'Connor, the CPS lawyer, hadn't minced his words when she'd called him: 'They're up to no good. Nobody uses an address in the Marshall Islands unless they're criminals, tax evaders, or both.'

'Any way to trace who owns a firm there?' she'd asked.

For a moment, she'd thought she heard a sharp intake of breath. 'Short answer? No. It'll be owned by lawyers or stooges. The real beneficiary will be hidden by so many layers of obfuscation that you'll never find them.'

That wasn't the weirdest part of it all either. When she'd gone back to Balham after work one evening, the neighbour across the street – Rosie Bray – told Rafferty that she'd been on the Peloton early Saturday morning and seen a van arrive a little after five. She'd watched as they'd taken everything out.

'Why didn't you call us?' Rafferty had demanded.

'I did!' Bray had protested. 'Twice. They promised to send someone out if they needed a statement. Nobody came. So I assumed you didn't need me, didn't I?'

The only bright side to her trip south of the river had been that she'd solved the mystery of the missing router: Zholnovych had been sponging off Champers' owner, Fred Albright.

'Quid pro quo,' Albright had explained. 'Elijah walks the dog and I let him cadge our internet. Not like it costs me anything, is it?'

He wasn't wrong. Unlimited bandwidth made it a freebie for Albright and he'd saved a packet on professional dog-walking services twice a day. Rafferty couldn't blame him.

When she'd got back in her car to leave the cul-de-sac, she'd looked back at the house Lili and her husband now lived in.

She'd known she'd be back there one day.

Whenever Zholnovych's body turned up.

21

NIBBLES

TURNS out big pieces move slowly. Even on eBay. In the time it took me to sell my first five-hundred-odd cheap watches, I only got two realistic offers on the *Komandirskie*. Both were from watch dealers looking to flip them. Obviously, we turned them down. One came back with two more counter-offers, both of which would've been tempting if I'd actually had a *Komandirskie* to sell.

I began to think we'd fucked up, that the plan was never gonna work.

Then, finally, a bite.

We could've easily missed it. A simple "question for the seller" message, asking about the provenance of the watch. We knew that Linden – and anyone like him who wanted the real deal – would ask. It's mental how much of a watch's value comes down to paperwork.

Naturally, we faked it.

When Tank had been in Pentonville, he'd bunked with a Hungarian guy. Normally, I don't work with people who've been inside for obvious reasons – Tank's the obvious exception to that – but this guy only got caught because his mother ratted him out.

Talk about bad luck.

His counterfeits were so good that, at one point, nearly five per cent of ten thousand forint notes in circulation were fakes he'd knocked up at home. Obviously, he'd had some help in distributing them, but the man could fake a note – any document really – so well that the Syndicate had come to rely on him for fake passports and the like. Shame he hadn't done one for Tiny Bakowski. That would've made tracking him down much easier.

Tiny was too smart for that. He never used the same counterfeiter as everyone else. He ran the Syndicate like a terrorist organisation, everything broken up into cells so nobody knew everyone or everything. It was probably why he stayed in charge for so long.

Don't think he'd have regretted using the Hungarian. The paperwork on my desk was proof of his skill. One stack was a service history which claimed to trace the watch from the First Moscow Watch Factory through to the late seventies. The second piece of paperwork was an invoice from Christie's auction house which claimed it had been sold at auction in 1990. We'd picked a sale date at random. It was supposed to be old enough that Christie's wouldn't have a digital record of the sale so any buyer would have a hard time checking it with them.

I couldn't see a flaw in either document. The Hungarian had copied real documents from the right time, using the right paper, the right ink, and the same font. He'd used old, slightly yellowed paper for the service records too so even carbon-dating wouldn't catch us out. He'd been insistent on all of that. I'd thought he was just driving up his fee, a whopping ten grand, but now that I've got them in hand, I can see it was well worth it.

The scans are even more convincing. Without inspecting it all in person, a buyer can only go on the scans. After checking out the eBay history of the buyer, I saw he'd been a member for six years. That fitted with when Linden had gone into the programme. He'd turned Queen's against Tiny in a trafficking case, the one which had driven him into hiding, and away from my gunsight.

Now, Tiny's one step closer to being in my grasp.

If, this time, it is Linden. If it isn't... well, I'll just have to wait. And try again. And if all else fails, come up with another way to find the last man to talk to Tiny Bakowski before he disappeared.

I opened my Messages and hit reply, imitating the posh tone I'd seen other luxury watch sellers use in their messages:

Good afternoon. Thank you for your enquiry. Please find attached scans of the relevant paperwork for the Komandirskie. If you have any further questions, please don't hesitate to let me know how I can be of service.

I re-read it. Even for a guy pretending to be a watch seller, it was a bit much. I deleted the last six words. Much better.

I hit send.

Third time's the charm, right?

22

STAKEOUT

THE BUYER'S IN. He wants the *Komandirskie*. Even though I've overpriced it by several grand. Sucker.

His profile checks out too. Lots of positive feedback from other eBayers, all of it glowing. Everything fits.

But now we need to know: is it him? Have we finally found the Collector?

We have a name and an address to work with. As soon as he paid – via PayPal – I sent a note, all nicey-fucking-nice, saying that the watch was stored in a safety deposit box and so it would take a few days to arrange delivery. Like a good little eBayer. The buyer quickly replied to say he had no problem with that. Polite. Too polite for a bloody gangster? Nah. If I can fake it, so can he.

'We've got a week, tops,' I said to Tank. 'If we leave it too long, he'll think it's a con.'

If he works out that we're not on the up and up, he'll open an eBay dispute at best, and cut and run at worst. But it's been the better part of ten years. Surely, he thinks his time with the Syndicate is well behind him by now? It can't be easy constantly looking over your shoulder. Sooner or later, he has to slip, think it's safe, and take off the mask.

'What do we do?' Tank asked.

'Simple. We've got an address – up in Enfield – so let's go stake it out. We'll start there, no need for a van or weapons if it's just a reccy. There's a park across the road and a row of shops. I reckon we take a wander through and see what's up.'

I debated leaving Tank behind. It was less weird if one man hung about outside a flat than two. But in the end, I had to take him with me. Every moment alone is a chance for Tank to fall off the wagon. One slip and I'll lose him. And I need the bastard. Without him, I don't have the muscle for the job and Tank's damned good at pulling fingernails and twisting limbs.

As we drove over, I wondered why the Collector would still be in London. Two people in the programme, both still in London. They could have been hidden anywhere in the country or even in another country so why were they still here?

Maybe it isn't him. Maybe we've got the wrong man. Again. He wasn't the first to enquire about the damned *Komandirskie*.

Then it hit me: it's much easier to hide in a crowd.

Most people can't tell Eastern European accents apart. Polish speakers sound like Germans, Ukrainians like Russians, and forget the nuances of Macedonian, Serbian, Slovak, and Czech. Brits just don't pay attention to that sort of thing.

That has to be it. A Ukrainian, even a half-British one like Linden, would stick out like a sore thumb in the home counties, and even more so somewhere up north. Here in London, the melting pot of the world, it's much easier to hide which suits me and Tank too.

When we arrived, it was even better than I'd expected. The park wasn't big, but the A105 ran down the eastern edge of it so the wall of traffic made covert surveillance a breeze. So long as the Collector didn't stumble across to the park. If he did, well, we'd have to bundle him into the back of the car before he realised what was what. Another good reason to have Tank with me.

I sent Tank to go and grab us some chips from The Happy Plaice. The Collector's flat was right above it so I couldn't go myself. He'd recognise me even after my weight loss. But he didn't know Tank. Few did. Tank's work was the quiet, violent kind, not the white-collar work done by fences and money launderers.

When he came back, the chips smelt heavenly.

'You remember my onion vinegar?'

Tank nodded, handed me a bag, and sat next to me on the bench. Nice part of London, this. Lots of decent-sized houses about. They haven't been divvied up into flats either, unlike those closer to Zone 1.

We watched people milling around as we ate. It wasn't too busy, but we'd run the risk of witnesses around here. The chip shop was doing a good trade, the main road in front of it was busy, and the park was popular too.

I tried the chips. Not half bad. Fluffy on the inside, crunchy outside. No wonder The Happy Plaice had a queue.

'Did you spot the opening times?' I asked Tank.

He nodded, his mouth full of chips. 'Closed on Mondays,' he said.

'Shut your gob when you talk, man.'

At least he'd got the opening times down. Mondays. It made sense. I'd heard someone say once that there were no trawlers out on Sundays so chippies close on Mondays. Maybe that's true. Or maybe they just need a day off and can't afford to skip the weekend. Whatever. Monday's our window. I smiled.

Tank cleared his throat. 'Uh...?'

He looked thoroughly confused. 'What now?' I asked.

'How? Can't see. Is obvious, no?'

Tank had a point. The very road that hid us from The Collector's flat was also hiding him from us. We couldn't loiter too nearby even if the chippy gave us a bit of crowd cover; there were only so many times we could buy chips before it'd be weird. I could send Tank in every night as if he were working construction nearby and needed a meal. I'd buy that schtick, but getting a view of Linden's flat meant staring into an upstairs window.

Maybe we could drive by?

Nah.

The traffic's too quick. We'll only get a fleeting view. Not much cop there.

'I'll think of something,' I said.

23

THE LEFTOVER CLUB

SHE'D LAUGHED, but Kflom wasn't the only one having
trouble with online dating. And she'd tried all the apps: Bumble,
Tinder, HER, Zoe, and Hinge. The only big one she hadn't dare
try was ReviewMyEx.

Unlike Kflom's complaint that he never got any matches,
Rafferty had the opposite problem. She had plenty of matches,
but it was like picking between herpes and gonorrhoea. Men
jumped into her inbox with a simple "hey" or worse, an unso-
licited dick pic. The women weren't much better, though the
problem flipped to mirror Kflom's experience. Instead of a
quality problem, she had a quantity problem. Whoever thought
being bi meant being greedy hadn't tried modern dating apps.

Even being a detective was a double-edged sword. Some
people hated her for being a cop, others fetishized the badge and
ignored the human. In the end, she'd changed her bio to read
"Prison Recruitment Specialist". That way she could tell her
dates in person and see their reaction for herself.

Maybe she should've listened to Mayberry and tried
Uniform Dating. Then again, who wanted to date another cop?
Or, in Mayberry's case, a cop's daughter. The git had married

the former Superintendent's girl, not that he'd ever taken advantage of that.

Dating a colleague wasn't an option. Not after the last time. A fireman or a doctor wouldn't be quite as bad, but two hectic schedules in one relationship was a recipe for failure. They'd be like ships passing in the night.

Especially with how her career was going. Ayala had her running all over the place, tackling the most mundane cases. All she'd had under his leadership were suicides, accidental deaths, and the occasional domestic murder. The husband always did it.

Most days, she felt more like an untrained mental health worker than a detective. It was humanity at its worst with none of the rewards of solving a crime.

The excitement of the job was gone.

Maybe it was time to move on. Could she go back to Sapphire? Dealing with sex crimes had been almost as challenging as murder but like everyone else, she'd burnt out in a matter of years. That door was closed for a reason.

A bing snapped her back to reality. A SuperSwipe.

A photograph flashed up on screen. Three men, all topless. No doubt it was the ugly one on the left, not the ripped guy in the middle. Did men think they were fooling anyone with group photos? What was their genius plan if she actually agreed to meet up with them?

She sighed.

This was as pointless for her as it was for Kflom, maybe even worse.

Life seemed to have a way of either being totally crap with both her career and love life in the toilet or for both to be going swimmingly. This time last year, she'd been investigating a serial killer and dating one of the Met's most eligible men.

It was time to give up for the night. She swiped to close Bumble, then Tinder, and then RateMyEx. Only WhatsApp

remained. She put her iPhone into Airplane mode so she
wouldn't accidentally turn any ticks blue and then had a look.
Three unread messages, all from Kflom.

Any luck? He'd typed. *Me neither...*

24

EYE IN THE SKY

TECH WAS THE SOLUTION.

I couldn't see the flat from the park across the way, but a drone could.

I bought one on Amazon. Same day delivery.

When people think of criminals, they think of hard men. Gym rats with tats and egos to match. Truth is, the best criminals look just like everyone else. They blend in. We blend in. Except Tank. People notice him. He's too tall, too muscled, and too tattooed to ignore. I'd taken a chance and left Tank back at my place. I'd be gone for a few hours. Hopefully, he wouldn't get into trouble without me. It'd be obvious if he'd slipped. I know that sweaty, far-off look he gets when he's high.

Not that I'd been any better. Thank fuck I'd kicked the habit. Now I just look like any normal bloke. Part of me used to hate that.

But when it comes to staying out of sight, out of mind, boring is an asset. I was just another middle-aged, balding bloke with a dad bod out flying his drone.

The buzzing sound was loud enough to hear from a way off, but the busy road to the east of the park masked it. That was good. Couldn't have Linden hearing me and getting spooked.

The damned thing wasn't easy to control. People make it look so bloody easy. Good job my first drone was a cheap one. No sooner had I got it in the air, a gust of wind blew it straight into a tree.

This second one was faring better. I'd gone upmarket, opting for one with a better lens so I could scope out the detail more easily. Where the first was a bit fuzzy, showing a Google Maps-esque aerial shot with little detail, the second was sharp, accurate, and multi-directional. I flew it on the eastern edge of the park at first, testing what I could see in the windows of the houses there. The image was now good enough to read the Countdown conundrum on in an old lady's sitting room. Impressive.

When I spotted a man sitting on a bench, I hovered overhead. From fifty feet up, I couldn't quite make out the text message on the screen, but I could see where he was putting his thumbs. If I'd managed to steer overhead as he'd entered his phone PIN, I reckon I could've recorded him typing and worked it out from his finger placement, so long as he didn't have one of those Android phones that randomised where the numbers appeared.

Once I could fly well enough not to crash, I swapped the battery pack for a fresh one to give me the maximum flying time and avoid another disaster and then swept the camera towards Linden's flat.

There wasn't much to see. The curtains were pulled three quarters of the way shut. Through the crack, I could see a dim yellow glow. The lights were on. The buyer – who I'd started assuming was the Collector – was home.

Now what?

I needed to get a good look at him. To see if the *Komandirskie* buyer was indeed Nathan Linden.

The drone only got me halfway there. Tech alone wouldn't

solve it.

Thinking on my feet, I looked around the park. Two kids were racing up and down on skateboards. The taller of the two stopped about twenty feet away to check his phone.

'Hey, you!'

He looked up, expecting to be bollocked for skating on the footpath.

'Want to make fifty quid?' I said.

No reply. Not straight away anyhow. He eyed me suspiciously. 'What for? I ain't blowing you or nothing.'

Fucking hell. And this was supposed to be a nice part of town.

'Not like that. There's a chippy over there. The door next to it. I want you to go ring the doorbell, then run off. Knockdown ginger like.'

'Knockdown who?'

Now I felt old. What the hell did the kids call it these days?

'Knock-a-doo-run?' I tried.

Still nothing.

'Look, just knock on the door. Run off. Easy.'

'And then I get fifty quid?' the kid asked.

'Only if the guy who lives there comes to the door – but doesn't see you. Got that?'

He nodded. 'I can do that. Half now. Half after.'

I nodded and took out my wallet to give him a twenty.

'That's not half.'

I shrugged. 'I haven't got any fives.'

This time, the kid grinned ear to ear. 'S'alright. I got change.'

Christ. Even kids were on the make. After paying the kid, I got the drone up in the air and watched as he dashed off to tell his mate about his good fortune. Then, just as he'd promised, he went and knocked on the door.

The first time, nobody answered.

The second time, nobody answered.

The third time, an irate man answered the door, craning his neck out to look up and down the pavement.

There's no mistaking it.

The buyer is Nathan Linden.

We've finally found the Collector.

Soon, we'll find Tiny Bakowski too.

25

BODY FOUND

THE SHOUT CAME in on the first Saturday of August. A man's body had been found in a flat above a chippy in Enfield, a stone's throw from Bush Hill Gardens.

It was the stench of decomposition that announced his death. At first, the neighbours had thought The Happy Plaice was frying up something particularly awful. Apparently, it wouldn't have been the first time. No doubt the owners thought that a punny name made up for crap chips. It seemed as if every chippy in London had to get in on the action, competing for the most memorable fish 'n' chip puns: Oh My Cod! on the Caledonian Road, the famous Fishcoteque in Waterloo, and the simple but brilliant Fry Days in Watford.

The Happy Plaice was on a derelict row of shops, next to a long-abandoned launderette.

By the time the first responders were on-scene, the body in the bathtub was a putrid mess, a bag of bones sweltering in melted, fetid flesh, flies buzzing all over, the body a feast for them.

It was the last place that Rafferty wanted to be called on a summer's day when the mercury was set to hit forty degrees.

Not long ago, that would've been a new British record, but now London was at the whim of irregular, unpredictable heatwaves that struck without warning. She'd planned to spend the day prostrate on her bed, surrounded by fans, occasionally venturing out to the local Sainsbury's to visit the cool relief of the freezer aisle.

Instead, she was dressed in the plastic overalls required to visit a crime scene without contaminating it and trying her damndest not to vomit. She made it as far as the hallway at the top of the stairs, pinching her nose shut the entire way.

And promptly ran back the way she came, all the way down the stairs, until she was on the street outside, before losing her breakfast.

Kflom appeared as if by magic to hold back her hair.

'You alright there, Ash?'

He pulled a pack of Kleenex from his pocket and offered her one. 'You've got something... here... there... well, kind of everywhere. There's a staff loo in the chippy.'

She looked in the direction he'd pointed. An image flashed into her mind: a queue of police officers and forensics techs all queuing for the bog. Stifling a laugh, she nodded her thanks and made a beeline for the loo.

When she returned, newly freshened up and only a very light shade of scarlet, Kflom was waiting for her on the pavement.

'I haven't done that before,' she said. 'Honest.'

'You're the third one this morning,' Kflom said. 'A bloater gets people. But hey, you don't have to work out how to get Soupy McMurder Victim to the morgue for an autopsy, once the bloody pathologist gets here to release the body anyway.'

'Maybe the chippy can lend you some takeaway containers.'

She expected him to laugh but he just shook his head sadly. 'That is pretty much how we'll do it. Once the pathologist signs off on it, we'll take the whole bathtub out. Then you lot can check out what's left of the crime scene.'

'Rightio. When's the autopsy going to be?'

'Beats me,' Kflom said. He opened his phone and looked at an app Rafferty didn't recognise. 'Chiswick's not too busy, but we're going to need Autopsy Room 4.'

Autopsy Room 4, colloquially the Bloater Room, was a fully-ventilated negative pressure room, designed to deal with the most badly decomposed bodies. Usually, the poor souls who ended up in there had come out of the Thames, body dumps and accidental deaths alike. Today's body in the bathtub would go the same way.

'Any idea on cause of death?'

'Too early to say,' Kflom said with a shrug. 'I could guess drugs were involved. There's heroin residue everywhere. But overdose victims don't tend to dismember themselves in their own bathtubs, do they?'

As he was speaking, Rafferty spotted Dr Larry Chiswick appear in the hallway. Kflom must've noticed him too as he darted off to greet the pathologist. The pair launched into a technical conversation straight away, something about needing to call in a forensic entomologist. Rafferty knew that meant calling in a bug expert. But the rest of the conversation was beyond her expertise. If it were important, one of them would catch her up later on.

After changing into new plastic booties to avoid contaminating the crime scene, she headed back inside the flat. The parade of shops was laid out with commercial units below and pokey, flat-roofed flats above. At the top of the stairs, there was a thick, wooden security door with locks top, middle and bottom. Talk about paranoid. Then again, perhaps it wasn't paranoia when the occupant appeared to have been murdered and left in his own bathtub.

Inside, three more doors. One to the bathroom. The stench emanated out of there. The second to a bedroom. Unable to face the body just yet, Raffety headed into the bedroom. The smell was still strong, but a window at the back, which overlooked an alleyway, offered a little relief.

The low-rent vibes continued. A soiled, uncovered mattress lay on top of a rickety metal bedframe. Instead of a proper wardrobe, the occupant had an exposed hanging rail bedecked with plastic hangers. It was student-poverty mixed with crack den. Whoever lived here had a serious problem with hygiene. It looked as if they didn't even own a hoover.

The lounge was even worse. Unlike the bedroom, which merely felt neglected, the lounge screamed crime scene. There was blood *everywhere*. Spatter ran up the walls, the sofa, even across the television screen. There was a rusty mark on the coffee table as if there had been an old iron toolbox atop it very recently, leaving no doubt in Raffety's mind what had happened here.

Her stomach churned again. This wasn't just murder. This was pure, unadulterated evil.

While she was staring, Kflom must have appeared in the doorway. 'Ash?' he said. 'Doc wants a word.'

THE DOC WASN'T IMPRESSED. The normally unflappable Chiswick had a peg-like device over his nose as he surveyed the bathtub. A stench rose from it, growing stronger with every step that Raffety took towards the pathologist.

'Don't suppose you've got a spare one of those, Doc?' Raffety said.

He grimaced, shaking his head. When he spoke, his normal

baritone had a squeaky, nasal quality to it, a bit like a bad cold. 'Afraid not.'

'So what did you want to tell me?' Rafferty peered into the bathtub with some trepidation. The water had gone a funny colour and texture. If she hadn't known better, she'd have thought it was the remnants of cooking a gammon from scratch that had been left out on a hot day for far too long, the soupy, salty liquid full of decomposing fat. There were bones visible in the murky depths, all mingled up in a pile in the centre. It wasn't obvious that it was a human body. She'd expected to see a body – or a skeleton at the very least – laid out in the tub. But whoever was in the tub was so far gone that he or she no longer looked human. There were insects buzzing around that Rafferty didn't recognise. Chiswick seemed to be lost in his own thoughts, staring at the same mess.

'He's dead then,' Rafferty said to break the silence.

'And that's about all I can tell you. You'll want a forensic entomologist out here for that.'

A bug man. Or woman. Rafferty had worked with them before. By analysing the life cycle of the insects present, they could narrow down time of death. 'Roger that,' she said. 'What else?'

Chiswick gave a shrug. 'We'll have to get him back to the morgue for any more than that. The bones look to be in a state. Until then, I can't definitively tell you anything.'

'General impressions then?'

'He – and I'm guessing it's a he, we'll need to look at the bones to be sure – has been dead a while.'

'Days? Weeks? Months?'

'Weeks,' Chiswick said. He didn't sound totally convinced by his own conclusion. 'This sort of decomp doesn't happen overnight... but the weather's been unusual.'

'So you'll need to double-check then,' Rafferty parroted back at him.

The pathologist nodded and gestured at the body. 'There's a lot of damage to the body too. Keep an eye out for any tools you find while searching in case we can match up tool marks to the body. While you're doing that, I'll get him bagged – or rather, bucketed – up, and we'll get the remains back to the morgue. We've got a few other cases in the queue so it might be a day or two.'

Typical. Cutbacks everywhere had led to queues for everything. Lab samples were taking longer, or going AWOL, experts were booked out well in advance, and now even the dead had to wait their turn.

'I'll let DCI Ayala know,' Rafferty said.

As Chiswick nodded, he said: 'Still sounds strange, doesn't it? Chief Inspector Ayala?'

'Yep. No more Morton. It's a travesty. The upside is, Ayala doesn't leave his office so I get to run my own crime scenes.'

'And take all the flack when it's not solved in ten minutes. Bet Ayala's got all sorts of KPIs to measure you by now.'

Rafferty grimaced. Chiswick wasn't wrong. Key performance indicators. The bane of middle management. It was the sort of crap that ought to be banished to the private sector. There was no such thing as a "normal" murder. Every case was unique. Setting a timeframe to solve one in, or worse, a maximum budget, made no sense. Except to Ayala.

'Ever since his promotion, he's turned into Mr Spreadsheet,' Rafferty said.

'That's Detective Chief Inspector Spreadsheet to you, young lady,' Chiswick said with a grin. 'And I think you'll find he Excels at the job. Mark my Word.'

Oh God. Not Microsoft puns. 'Right. I'm leaving you to the body before you can crack another one.'

'Back to the Office, eh?'

'Doc! Quit it!'

Chiswick smirked again. 'Alright, alright, I Still Love Vista, Baby.'

As she walked away, she couldn't help but smile. Chiswick was a grumpy old codger, but at least he did crack a joke every now and then. Ayala was so damned serious all the time. Humour was the best way to deal with being around the dead all day.

26

THE 27 CLUB

I'D TAKEN my eye off the ball for five minutes.

It hadn't been just fish and chips that Tank had got at The Happy Plaice, he'd found a baggie full of smack too.

He must've nicked it when we were in Linden's flat.

Cagey bastard. I didn't know he had it in him. Somehow, he'd managed to torture a mobster to death and still found the time to find, and then steal, Linden's stash.

When I found him, he was passed out on my bathroom floor. There was a tourniquet around his arm and a needle sticking out of his arm.

'Fuck!'

For Tank to have passed out he must have taken a shit ton. Between decades of use and his massive bulk, his tolerance was sky high. I've seen him at his worst. Before breakfast, he'd shoot up twenty times more than Tiny had given us as kids and then drive around as if he'd taken paracetamol.

Back then, it was less than a tenth of a gram. Enough to leave us chasing the high forever. Whenever people ask me what it's like, I tell 'em to imagine the hottest, kinkiest sex in the world. Heroin makes that feel like a cardboard cut-out. Afterwards, everything else is washed out. Grey. Lifeless. Soulless. It's not that heroin feels bad. It doesn't. It feels too good. And once you get a taste, you're done for. Most of the time anyway.

I shook Tank as my mind ran. He was breathing. Just.

'Tank! Listen to me. You've got to hold on.'

Last time, it had been me with the tourniquet. After Tiny thought it was funny to give me a massive bloody dose. One I'd have done anything for. We did whatever the hell Tiny wanted because he doled it out. If he told Tank to knife someone, he did. Ask me to steal? No problem. Hell, I'd have sat on a barbed wire dildo to get my fix.

When I woke up after that massive dose, I found my brother leaning against me, slumped over. Heroin was cruel like that. Random even. We'd taken the same shit and fate had decided to flip a coin. I'd lived and he'd died.

That was my turning point. Seeing him keeled over, limp and lifeless, was bad enough. Watching Tank – at Tiny's request – throw my brother's body in with the rest of the gang-bangers – was what did it for me. It was the first time I'd been to the Syndicate's mass grave, an old bunker Tiny had filled with bodies. We'd clambered through a small hatch not much bigger than a manhole, and then gone down a ladder down into the earth where a fetid, sweet smell had hit me. I remember seeing a sign which said something like Royal Observer Corps. And there was a bathroom with bright pink bog rolls. Weird.

The navy must've forgotten about the place. Tiny hadn't. He'd sworn me to secrecy, told me I'd killed my brother and that if I ever ratted the gang out, it would be me that went down for it.

A raspy wheeze brought my attention back to the present.

'C'mon, Tank, breathe!'

I debated calling 999. He'd lost consciousness. His body was limp. I leant in to listen to his breathing. It was shallow and

I could smell stale vomit on him. He'd puked before he'd passed out.

Naloxone!

Why hadn't I thought of that a minute ago?

I ran through to the kitchen and grabbed my first aid kit. As well as the usual crap like plasters and bandages, I had Steri-Strips, field dressings like the army use in combat, and, there, at the bottom, naloxone.

It was a miracle drug, one that would've probably saved my brother's life. If we'd had it. I'd kept several doses in ever since I'd got clean. Just in case. I'd got them from a nurse with her own heroin addiction in return for supplying her. Part of me wondered if naloxone sprays ever went out of date. No use worrying about that now.

'Nurse, eight milligrams, stat!' I muttered to myself, trying to make light of the situation.

The packet said each little nasal spray contained 1.8 milligrams. I put the first dose up against Tank's left nostril and sprayed.

'C'mon,' I muttered.

Nothing. His breathing was getting shallower and shallower. It wasn't working. The pack said to wait two to three minutes and dose him with another spray up the other nostril. I couldn't wait that long.

I unwrapped the next dose, put it against his right nostril, and sprayed.

'Tank, you bastard, don't leave me.'

I leant in, listening to every breath. Each one I counted, timing how long there was between breaths. My hands trembled as I punched in 999. If I lost him...

I pushed that thought from my mind. If I called, it'd be over. He'd be in hospital. I'd probably get nicked. We'd be fucked.

Sod it, I had to do it.

I hit call.

'Operator, what's your emergency?' a voice said.

Then, before I could reply, Tank gave a sharp intake of breath.

It was working!

'Sorry,' I said. 'Pocket dial!'

27

BREADCRUMBS

THIS IS fast turning into some Hansel and Gretel shit.

If he weren't lying to us, Linden hid the Syndicate's money all over the fucking place.

Now I have to find out what happened to it.

Easier said than done. Especially while babysitting Tank. He's back to his old self, constantly begging for another hit. I had to wait until he fell asleep to carry on my search.

Not only is there cash to hunt down, there're Bitcoins, drugs, property, even companies.

Tiny had his fingers in every pie under the sun.

Some of it was easy to discount. The cash he'd buried and left with loyal lieutenants. Linden swore he didn't know who or where. I believed him the first time he said it. Tank had to make sure. No matter what, his story didn't change: bin liners full of pounds, euros and dollars, treble bagged, put inside those big plastic tubs some people keep under their beds, and then left with people or buried all over the show.

The cash is what I'd want if I were on the lam. None of this fancy "property owned by a company" rubbish. A paper trail is a paper trail even if it's complicated. It'll get you caught eventually. Ain't nobody hiding a God-damned house forever.

It's also the easiest to nick. The moment Tiny fled the country – and got himself on the Interpol red list in the bargain – people would have nicked whatever shit they could find. I know because I did. I nicked every damned penny I could get my hands on.

Bitcoin's no good. Tiny had some, of course. But I don't know how to chase that. I know Tiny moved it around. The Met thinks it's trackable. In theory, it kind of is. Every transaction is public. Wallet address, coin value, dates, and metadata. It's all there.

Except when it's not.

See, Tiny was too smart to leave a trail. He knew wallets were trackable. If he sent me money, the police could see the coins leave his wallet and go into mine. But what they couldn't track was if the owner of the wallet changed. So Tiny abused that loophole. He swapped his Bitcoin wallet for someone else's Bitcoin wallet. Or swapped for another cryptocurrency. Or even traded a wallet for hard cash, gold, drugs, guns, whatever. Once we started swapping wallets, it screwed the police over. Anonymous wallets ping-ponging around the globe in return for untraceable assets. Genius. No way I'm keeping up with that.

Property then? Tiny owned stuff all over the place. Some of it was in his name. Some belonged to lieutenants. Some to stooges. Everything Tiny did was about reducing risk. If one part of the Syndicate got shut down, it didn't matter. He was always hands off.

No doubt the police had still seized something. Easy enough to check. I pulled up my laptop and Googled "Tiny Bakowski, Proceeds of Crime Act". If there was one thing we all learned, it was that the police didn't need a conviction to take our ill-gotten gains. Not anymore. The fact Tiny fled looked bad. To bang us up, they'd have to prove our guilt "beyond reasonable doubt". Taking our money on the other hand was "on the balance of probabilities" as the wigs called it. Much easier for them.

Sure enough, lots of news results popped up, I clicked on the first one, a BBC report titled "Proceeds of Crime hearing for Dimitri "Tiny" Bakowski". It was dated for May.

There was a picture of Tiny pulled from The Impartial's fashion supplement. He was wearing a wide-pin suit, crisp white shirt, and natty black shoes. Bloody attention seeker. Image was always Tiny's downfall. He wasn't content to be the *shef*, he had to be *seen* to be the *shef*.

He'd been warned. Attention from the public, or the law, is never a good thing for a criminal. Somehow, he'd always got away with it. Like Teflon, nothing ever stuck to Tiny.

Now he's out of the country and his mugshot has been plastered all over the BBC. Underneath it was the caption: "Bakowski fled Britain ten years ago. He is wanted on a variety of charges including murder, racketeering, blackmail, and fraud."

I'll bloody bet. I know how many bodies we dumped. Gotta be hundreds by now. When Tiny gets caught, the courts will be backlogged for years if they try to nail him for all of it. Not that they'll bother. They'll get him on one or two murders and be done with it. No point throwing time and money at charging someone once they've been given a whole life sentence. It'd be like shooting a corpse.

I carried on reading. The first couple of paragraphs were boring. His brothers – Nico and Pavel were arrested. I knew that. One of them's dead now. Can't remember which. I skipped ahead.

'Tiny Bakowski remains at large. He was last spotted at St Pancras international, travelling under a fake identity.'

Quelle surprise. Of course he'd travelled on a fake passport.

The Syndicate's fakes were so good that they were almost totally indistinguishable from the real thing. It took an expert looking under a microscope to tell them apart. It's harder these days with electronic passports but even those can be faked with enough time and money.

'Police called the Bakowski Crime Syndicate, which Dimitri "Tiny" Bakowski is alleged to have led, an "unprecedented and sophisticated operation which covered every sphere of criminal activity from importing cocaine to manufacturing of so-called soft drugs like Purple Drank".'

I laughed. Purple Drank. As if anyone actually called it that anymore. Lean is what everyone calls it these days: codeine cough syrup, an antihistamine, and cola. Easy to get, cheap to make, highly addictive. The perfect gateway drug, one of dozens that the gang sold. Pavel used to handle everything drugs-related from importing the gear from Amsterdam and Latin America right the way through to street-level distribution. He'd run the doors at nightclubs all over east London, especially around Shoreditch where the Syndicate had a near-monopoly. Once Pavel had paid off the bouncers, he'd send in a dealer, flog a few pills, and then rinse and repeat almost every night. The clubs were a constant source of new customers.

But the Syndicate didn't just get kids addicted to crack. The other brother, Nico, ran the extortion ring or "private security" as he'd called it. Another simple con: pay the younger kids to stone a few houses. Offer security to stop it. Take the money, stop paying the kids. Clients were happy coughing up a few quid a week. Nico had the neighbours robbed instead. Sooner or later, everyone coughed up. Nice little earner.

And Tiny masterminded it all. He set up the cells, ensuring nobody knew everyone. He had me running carousel fraud – a boring gig, running sweet shops up and down Oxford Street – to help launder things.

Then he had guys for everything else. Kidnapping. Trafficking – though that guy got arrested – and even murder-for-hire. One guy, I only knew him as The Frenchman, was absolutely fucking terrifying. He'd be chatting in a room, totally chill, lean over to pick up a drink, and then, ten seconds later, slit someone's throat. Unpredictable, emotionless, ruthlessly efficient. No wonder Tiny liked him. He was just like him.

As I skimmed, paragraphs jumped out at me.

'After a thorough multi-agency investigation, comprised of detectives from the City of London's fraud team, the Met, HMRC investigators, the Serious Organised Crime Agency, and representatives from Interpol, Bakowski was found to have benefitted from his criminal enterprise to the tune of £149,312,990.35. His available assets were valued at £88,540,120, including a penthouse apartment overlooking Hyde Park, a classic car collection, and holdings in numerous British businesses.

Recorder Lynda Checkley QC ordered that Bakowski's assets be seized.'

I laughed. It sounded like a fortune. It was. It is. But Tiny made way more than that. He'd once shipped twenty mil in cocaine from the Cali cartel in one go. We didn't even have to hide it. Pavel had flat out bribed the border guard. Then, a week later, Nico had broken into his house, taken the cash back, and left him for dead. Efficient.

Never trust a Bakowski. While Tiny liked to splash the cash, little and often, around our home turf, he didn't do it out of the goodness of his heart. He bought loyalty and it cost him bugger all. Kid going hungry? Tiny would feed him. Single mother falling behind on her loan payments? He'd cut her some slack.

Tiny always had an angle.

As I'd learned far too late.

28

ANOTHER GHOST

THE MACHINERY of death slowly roared into action. Under Rafferty's watchful guidance, the local area was canvassed for witnesses, Purcell and Kflom set about cataloguing every bit of evidence in the flat, and Brodie began to compile all the digital evidence he could. Automatic number plate recognition, plus local CCTV, would cast a very wide net.

The biggest problem was that the time of death was just as wide. The body had putrefied. It wasn't recent. Most businesses kept their CCTV for a relatively short time so the odds of uncovering the killer that way were slim to none.

Digital records about the victim weren't helping either. The more Rafferty read, the eerier it got. The victim appeared to be one Cem Watzinger, aged 45. He was on the roll as living above The Happy Plaice.

The flat itself was owned by an overseas company, this time a post office in the Cayman Islands. Another dead end.

And, yet again, Cem Watzinger appeared not to have existed prior to 2014. It was as if he'd magicked himself into existence in his late thirties, a fully-formed human who hadn't stepped foot onto planet earth before then.

Just like the Zholnovych case. It was eerie how similar they were.

She said as much to Kflom while on a coffee break. The pair of them leant against the wall besides The Happy Plaice, traffic whizzing by before their eyes. A police cordon separated them from the queue for the chip shop.

'Umm...'

His hesitation made his thoughts obvious.

'You think I'm clutching at straws.'

'Well, yeah. Look at the two scenes. The first was immaculate, almost totally clean, no body, no break in. This one, we've got a mark on the front door – as if the killer stuck his foot inside the door and brute forced his way in – and then we've got blood everywhere. This place is a total dive. And your vic's been cut up and left to stew in a bathtub. I'm not seeing the similarities.'

He wasn't wrong. The physical evidence was diametrically opposed to the Zholnovych scene.

And yet... Rafferty had to trust her gut.

'Ash?' Kflom said, his voice snapping her out of her thoughts. 'I've got to get back to work... but one thing, why are we assuming the body in the tub is the guy who lives here?'

It was a fair question. 'It's the simplest explanation,' Rafferty said. 'But you're right. He could be someone else, maybe even a victim killed by Cem Watzinger. We'll have to wait for DNA results to confirm that. Until then, it's a working hypothesis.'

Presuming, of course, that they could get DNA samples. They'd need one from the body – probably from the teeth as that was the most likely source with the state the body was in – and a second from the home, probably the toothbrush in the bathroom. It wasn't foolproof. A killer could plant a toothbrush at a crime scene, but that took a particularly forensically aware murderer, the kind that probably would've taken the victim with them and disposed of them somewhere they wouldn't have been found. Building sites for skyscrapers were popular as nobody wanted to dig up the Gherkin or the Shard just to check for a body. The Thames was another, especially weighted down with chicken wire or the like. Those were the worst kind of bodies to work with; wet, bloated, and decomposed. Just like this guy.

It was such an arms race. The forensic tech got better and better, but the killers were getting smarter and smarter too, a never-ending arms race between the law and the underworld. All the information needed to circumvent the police was available freely online. Hell, even the college of policing manual for murder, the by-the-book approach to investigating crime, could be found on the net.

'Even then, you don't know that the name on the electoral roll is who really lives here, do you?'

'Well, you're a barrel of optimism today. Another bad Tinder date last night?'

Ribbing him about his Tinder dates would never get old. Not that Rafferty's own adventures had gone much better. Only last night, she'd met a guy who seemed perfectly nice until he'd asked if he could lick her feet.

Kflom glared. 'I don't want to talk about it. Must crack on.'

With that, he stuffed the rest of his Pret sandwich into his gob, chewed, and stomped off towards the bin by the bus stop.

How the hell could he eat and go straight back to work? Rafferty's stomach was churning and the worst was yet to come: she was due to attend the autopsy in an hour's time.

Perhaps Kflom was made of sterner stuff.

29

FOOTSTEPS

AT HALF EIGHT, we arrived at King's Cross Underground Station and headed up to the surface. The two stations on top of the tube, King's Cross and St Pancras, went nearly everywhere. The international trains left from St Pancras.

Recreating Tiny's footsteps is the best plan we have which doesn't give us much to go on. It has one big benefit: travelling with Tank will minimise the odds of him finding a dealer as we'll be together 24/7. I'll add that one to the slate.

We know how Tiny fled the country. He left on the same trainline we're taking, bound for Paris. The callous git was probably the one that tipped off the Met that Nico and Pavel were leaving by boat from Southampton Docks. He let them get caught so he could slip away.

What we don't know is where he fled *to*.

'Needle in a bloody haystack,' I muttered to Tank as we headed through to the Eurostar lounge. People milled about, sitting in low-rise seats, cases, and bags everywhere.

I glanced up at the departures board. The Eurostar runs direct trains to Paris, Lille, Brussels, Rotterdam, and Amsterdam. That's just the direct trains. One onward change and Tiny could've gone anywhere from Strasbourg to Biarritz. Or he could've rented, stolen, or bought a car and driven virtually anywhere on the continent.

'I'd go to Odessa,' Tank replied.

'Yeah, and Interpol would've nabbed you the moment you got there.'

It was too damned obvious. Yes, Tiny could've gone home. He's got friends there, family there, even properties. But the police ain't thick and nor is Tiny. He would've gone to ground somewhere unexpected.

Where else can I discount? Did Eurostar even run to Holland back in 2012? I don't think so. I'm sure I saw adverts pushing it as a new thing a few years ago. Besides, Amsterdam is the drug capital of Europe. Turning up there would be too brazen. Tiny's got balls the size of coconuts, but even he wouldn't dare go there.

France then. It has to be. Not Lille. There's fuck all there. One big Carrefour and that's about it.

We bought tickets to Paris last night. That still seemed liked our best bet. Just as Zholnovych had hidden in a crowd in London, Tiny could hide in Paris. Having a strange accent and not speaking the language is miles easier when everyone else is from some far-flung place too. Ain't the melting pot of life grand?

Then again... would Tiny have *stayed* in Paris? The French are a notoriously "papers, please" society. Sooner or later, he'd have had to change his fake ID to a new one. The police would've found his "travel name" for the Eurostar in ten minutes flat by looking at who'd booked on the outbound trains and eliminating the legitimate people. There's CCTV every-where here.

If I were him, I'd have ditched that identity the moment I got to Gare du Nord. Had Tiny thought about that? Surely he had. But how many identities had he faked? Travelling with multiple passports would've been a huge risk too. If security had stopped him at the border, he'd have wound up in HMP Wakefield in a cell right next to Nico in ten seconds flat. The papers called the place Monster Mansion on account of all the killers locked up there. Tiny would be right at home. Bit weird that the HM now stood for His Majesty. Spending time at His Majesty's Pleasure sounded like getting a bit too close to Prince Andrew.

'Boss?' Tank said. He jerked his head towards the train. 'Time to go, yeah?'

We shuffled along. Security was already out of the way. It's strange having the French running a border in London, but them's the breaks. We'd had to get past the UK Border Patrol too. And a ticket gate. It was like a series of hurdles. Some of it was new. Bloody Brexit. So that didn't help with recreating Tiny's footsteps.

Once we were on the train, it was plain sailing.

Apart from Tank being a bloody coward.

'But, but, but.... It's underwater,' he said, gripping his armrests tighter than he'd held Linden's windpipe.

'And it's never had a safety issue. Calm the fuck down.'

I'd read online that the trains were just the right length to always be besides at least one, if not two, of the emergency side exits. I wasn't going to tell Tank that though. It was far too much fun watching a man who had literally beaten dozens of men to death cower at the thought of going through an underwater tunnel.

On arrival at Gare du Nord, we strolled straight out into the sunset. We'd already cleared customs so it was like getting off any normal train. The stink of piss hit us immediately. The French weren't big on cleaning up public areas. Or public loos.

Come to think of it, I needed to go.

When in Paris...

We wandered for a while, past the restaurants, the high-end fashion boutiques, until the crowds began to thin out. Eventually, I spotted an alleyway. Nobody in sight. Perfect.

'Tank, keep an eye out for the *Gendarmerie*, yeah?'

Once I'd emptied my bladder, we began walking, not in any particular direction. Think like Tiny, think like Tiny, I kept telling myself. If I were on the run, I'd want three things. First, I'd want anonymity. I could see cameras everywhere. Some of them might have gone up since 2012, but like most capital cities, Paris is riddled with CCTV. That means getting out of Paris.

Second, I'd want cash. Tiny would've had a plan. If he had cash stockpiled around the UK, he probably had money stashed around Europe too. He wasn't the kind to wing it. Back in the day, that would've been cash in a Swiss bank. Easy to access, hard to trace. That easy ride was over by the time Tiny fled.

Where would he have kept his cash? A safe house? That would've worked. Keep a small Parisian apartment, stick the lucre in the *cave,* the basement storage most flats have? Or perhaps he had people here.

Or even just Western Union. He could've had one of his people wire cash to virtually any shop in the world. Take the money transfer control number or "MTCN", plus fake ID, and he'd be quids in within minutes of arriving in the city.

Then what?

He'd have to get out of Dodge. That's the third thing I'd need: an escape route, one that couldn't be easily traced. Assuming the police tracked Tiny's train journey, they'd have their French counterparts scouring the capital for him. I suppose he could've gone to ground for a while, holed up in a flat or a hotel that took cash in hand, but that would've been a short-term thing at best.

What if he hadn't been planning to hang Nico and Pavel

out to dry? They'd hoped to take a boat to Bilbao. Would Tiny have arranged to meet them somewhere in Spain? Barcelona maybe? It's an easy trek from here. Another big city to get lost in the crowd.

Nah.

Same problem: CCTV.

Tiny's been on the run for the better part of a decade. That doesn't happen by chance.

It had to be somewhere smaller. Somewhere Tiny had friends or resources.

Then, it hit me.

Málaga.

It's due south from Bilbao, just east of Gibraltar. The Syndicate had operations there: tobacco smuggling from Gib, weed from Morocco, and, more profitably, coke coming in through the port of Algeciras. I don't know who ran the ops, but there would have been several contacts Tiny could've gone to there. And unlike Amsterdam, there were more private places to meet contacts. Málaga was full of private homes spread out over a huge area and the Guardia Civil were known to turn a blind eye to it all.

I pulled out my phone and brought up a map.

'Where're we going?' Tank asked.

'South. Montparnasse.'

He looked at me blankly.

'The railway station.'

'Didn't we just come from...?'

I shook my head. 'More than one, Tank. We arrived at Gare du Nord. To go south, we've gotta go via Montparnasse.'

South to Bordeaux. A mere two hours by TGV. From there, we could change trains or nab a hire car and cross the border into Spain. We can figure that out when we get there. Like Tiny, we have to keep moving.

Except we aren't being chased.

We're doing the chasing.

And we're getting closer.

30

THE BONE DOCTOR

STRANGE, the light outside Autopsy Room 4 was red, code for Do Not Enter.

Rafferty glanced at her Apple Watch, tapping it so the screen lit up with the time. She wasn't late. Why had Chiswick started without her?

Undeterred, she hit the intercom button.

'Doc, it's Inspector Rafferty.'

Chiswick didn't reply over the intercom. Instead, the light turned green very briefly which Rafferty took as a sign that she should go in. After double-checking her gown and plastic booties were in place, the minimum required to prevent contaminating the evidence, she let herself in.

Her stomach churned as the familiar smell from the flat above the chip shop struck her. The sound of fans told her that the negative pressure ventilation system was running as intended and yet the stench was, if anything, even worse as though the body had continued to deteriorate on the journey over. That had to be her imagination.

The pathologist was hunched over the body when she entered. It was only when the doctor stood up and turned towards her that she realised it wasn't Chiswick. Instead, Rafferty was confronted with a short, angry looking woman with stern, high cheekbones, big green eyes hidden behind a magnifying visor that distorted her face and swept-back hair plaited into a braid.

'Am I in the right room?' Rafferty asked. 'Body from the chip shop flat? I was expecting Larry Chiswick.'

'You'd be wasting your time with him,' the woman said. 'Chiswick's a flesh man. What he knows about bones wouldn't fill an evidence bag.'

Charming. 'Then you would be...?'

'Doctor Lucie Fearn-Wright, forensic anthropologist, at your service.'

The name rang a bell. 'Not the Doctor Fearn-Wright who—'

'Excavated the mass graves in Chile in 2010? Gave war victims in northern France back their names after decades? Helped discern the identities of victims of gang violence in Mexico last year?'

'I was going to say who was on Britain's Got Talent. But I guess you're not the one with the dancing Collie.'

Fearn-Wright chuckled. 'No, I'm not. And it was a Sprollie for your information.'

'A what?'

'A Springer Spaniel-Collie cross,' Fearn-Wright said. 'Never mind...'

Ridiculous name. Rafferty nodded as if she cared. 'So, you've taken over from Chiswick on this one.'

'To put it crudely, yes. The bones that were recovered were in a state of disarray, so my assistant and I have spent the last two hours cataloguing and laying them out in the correct anatomical position.'

Rafferty looked past the doctor to where the remains lay on a metal gurney. 'Looks like some of them are missing?'

'We haven't finished.'

That explained the red light.

'The rest of your victim is in the buckets over there.'

Rafferty recognised them as the plastic forensic buckets that Kflom had employed to transport the bath water. It was from them that the smell emanated.

'Should I come back later?'

'No need,' Fearn-Wright said. 'I can give you enough to work with now and send over my full report in due course.'

Rafferty nodded. 'Rightio.'

'First, sex. Take a look here at the Os Coxa.'

'The what?'

'The pelves, Inspector. Do keep up.'

Pelves? It took Rafferty a moment to clock that Fearn-Wright was referring to the pelvis in the plural.

'Note how they're narrow and steep.'

'Right...'

'Rather than shallow and gracile with a broad subpubic angle.'

Layman's terms: women have babies.

'That suggests this skeleton may be male.'

'Suggests? May be?'

'Determining gender isn't a binary yes or no. It's a sliding scale. Take a look at the sciatic notch. That's intermediate, i.e. neither acute nor large, which means it's not definitive so no use in determining gender. Instead, follow the curve.'

As Rafferty watched, the doctor traced a finger along the one edge. 'This,' she said 'is the superior surface of the auricular arch. It's continuous, again suggesting male.'

Rafferty pulled out a notebook to jot down notes and then paused. 'Still only suggesting?'

'There are other factors that suggest the same – some sloping to the back of the skull, a pronounced brow ridge, and the like. More useful, I think, is the victim's height. They would've been approximately six foot four. Very few women are that tall.'

As she spoke, the doctor looked Rafferty up and down.

'I'm six foot tall,' Rafferty said to pre-empt the inevitable question. So the victim was even taller than her. Apart from at international netball matches, which Rafferty had attended a few of in her day, she'd never once seen a woman taller than her out and about in public.

But the bones weren't all there. How could the doctor know that? Rafferty asked her.

'It's an easy enough calculation. We've got a database that contains thousands of records. By comparing the length and thickness of certain bones with that data, we can estimate height with a reasonable degree of accuracy. I will, of course, confirm this in my report once I've finished reassembling the body.'

'Of course,' Rafferty parroted. As she spoke, her phone buzzed in her pocket. She ignored it.

Fearn-Wright looked at her sceptically as if trying to work out if Rafferty were taking the Michael.

'Unlike gender, height is pretty non-contentious,' she said.

'Gender is contentious?'

'There's a whole discipline dedicated to the politics of death, Inspector. Physiology can be changed quite radically by hormones, especially among individuals who have elected to affirm their chosen gender.'

'Transsexuals?'

'Yes, though I wouldn't put it quite so crudely,' Fearn-Wright said. She turned away for a moment and then changed the subject: 'Then there's the most contentious of all – ancestry.'

'Like 22 And Me?'

'Indeed.'

Her tone was scathing. As if she thought all DNA testing were no more than pseudoscience.

'The less said about ancestry the better. I would venture that your victim is likely white, but beyond that he could be anything from Irish to Russian or anything in between.'

Rafferty scribbled that down too. 'Thanks, Doc.'

She turned as if to go.

'Ahem, Inspector?'

'Yes?'

'Don't you want to know what killed him?'

Rafferty glanced at the bones on the table again. 'You've worked that out already?'

From the way the doctor had spoken, Rafferty thought they'd only just started piecing together which bones went where.

'As you know, all the usual rules go out the window when you're dealing with a cadaver like this. We can't look at cooling, decomp, and the like. There's no algor mortis/rigor mortis delineation to tell us the post-mortem interval, so we've got to work with what we've got: bone.'

The phone in Rafferty's pocket buzzed again. A name flashed up on her watch. She glanced at it just in case. Of course, it was Ayala.

'Doc?'

'Yes?'

'Not being rude, but can we cut to the chase? I have a team of thirty-six officers working on this, plus support staff, and my pain-in-the-arse boss is hitting up my inbox demanding an update already.'

'That pain-in-the-arse is a close friend of mine.'

Blood drained from Rafferty's face. 'I, uh, I'm sorry-'

Fearn-Wright burst out laughing. 'You are SO easy to wind up. I don't even know who your boss is. But yes, I'll keep it quick. Your victim has had a hard life. There's a lot of damage to unpack. We've got to separate that out into ante-, peri-, and post-mortem.'

'Before, around the time of, and after death?'

'Exactly. Now, the bones have been in that tub for a while. As you may know, there are two types of bone, cancellous, i.e. porous bone, and compact bone. The latter survives much better than the former.'

'Especially when immersed in a hot bathtub of soup-y flesh?'

'Exactly. We can see lots of healed fractures.'

'They're old.'

'Exactly. Bone takes time to heal. We can safely ignore all the perimortem damage suffered months or years before death. Except, perhaps, in the teeth. Now, I'm not an expert here, but have a look under that microscope there.'

The doc pointed towards a small sample dish with a tooth in the middle. When Rafferty peered through the microscope, she saw the tooth had banding in it.

'What's that mean?'

'Again, this isn't my area of expertise, but banding usually means defective enamel. It's indicative of malnourishment or childhood illness.'

'Tough life indeed,' Rafferty said. Maybe it would be useful in confirming the victim's identity. 'Do we have dental records?'

'Not yet. We do have some, well, odd-looking fillings going on. They're old fashioned, nothing I've seen before, and I'm not entirely sure what I'm looking at. If you've got the budget, I'd suggest they're inspected by a forensic odontologist.'

That was yet another thing she'd have to wheedle out of Ayala. If her experience with the Zholnovych case earlier in the year was anything to go by, he'd expect her to solve this on a shoestring. But if Ayala needed her to grovel, grovel she would.

'On the other hand, post-mortem injuries usually happen as the bone dries. The collagen breaks down, the bones lose elasticity, and we get jagged breaks with an uneven colour. That could be from anything from mechanical damage caused by handling of the body right through to rodent activity. Rats especially love to have a gnaw on bones. None of that is helpful.'

'Then what are we looking for?'

'Perimortem injuries which are smooth-edged, bevelled, and have oblique angles on the fracture margins, and the colour is consistent.'

'All the stuff that happened at the time of death?'

'Around then,' Fearn-Wright cautioned. 'Because of the lag from injury to healing, there's a wide window. These injuries aren't necessarily what happened right before death. What I can tell you is that your victim suffered repeated blunt and sharp force trauma to nearly every part of his body.'

Blunt force trauma was low speed or impacting a large surface area. Punching, kicking, shoving, and the like. Sharp force trauma, which Fearn-Wright had put on the screen as she spoke, showed smoother, shiny edges and small striations as if the bone had been struck by a tool like a crowbar or a knife.

Horror struck Rafferty as she flashed back to the rusty marks on the coffee tables, the rusty old toolbox that was long gone by the time she got there. She imagined them: crow bars, drills, and more. The tools of torture.

Whoever did this to him did it without so much as a hesitation mark. Blow after blow raining down on the victim until he was no more than a bag of flesh, blood leaking everywhere, bones crushed to the point they had impaled his organs. When she regained the ability to speak, her voice came out in a hoarse, barely audible whisper.

'He was tortured.'

Fearn-Wright nodded.

'And then – judging from the crushed hyoid bones – the killer finished him off by strangling him to death.'

After they got what they wanted.

He'd been tortured for a reason.

But what?

31

THE RHINO

THE DRIVE TOOK TWO DAYS. Over 1,200 kilometres winding our way across the border and then down through Donostia-San Sebastián, an hour east of Bilbao. If Tiny had intended to meet up with his brothers, this route, heading through the heart of Spain down to the Costa del Crime made perfect sense. He'd have been able to join up with them anywhere from San Sebastián to Puerto Banús, the tiny town I expect he'd travelled to.

The undisputed capital of the Costa del Crime, Puerto Banús looks out over the Bay of Malaga. It's the meeting hub and home of organised crime bosses from around the world, full of luxury, women, and the big houses. It even has the weather to match. The authorities don't care where the money comes from as long as it's spent in the town.

We'd stopped overnight in Madrid as it was roughly the halfway point on our journey south. If we had actually been on the run, we'd have gone wide and found somewhere less central to stay. Tiny could've stopped anywhere from Toledo to Cuenca. Or taken a more circuitous route entirely. I figured learning his exact route wouldn't help much but if we could confirm he'd gone through Puerto Banús, we might just be able to trace where he'd then moved onto.

By the time we were greeted by the *Rinoceronte vestido con puntillas*, a giant rhino statue at the roundabout on the way into Puerto Banús, we'd been travelling for days and we smelled like it too.

We wouldn't fit in here. Designer shops started to appear and then, as we approached the marina, hundreds of luxury yachts came into view. I wondered which of them were owned by criminals and which, if any, were real businessmen's playthings. The nearest, a huge, modern beauty called the *Gaeltacht*, must've cost a damned fortune. It wasn't exactly subtle.

Suited and booted men milled around. From their tats and shaved heads, it was obvious they were soldiers, underlings to the crime bosses that made the town home. The Costa del Crime is a melting pot of international smugglers, drug dealers, and other criminals. I know why – it used to be impossible to extradite criminals from here. Now, the gangs hide in plain sight, their ill-gotten gains tied up in luxury yachts and mansions nestled in with those of the legitimately wealthy.

What I hadn't expected was to see so many soldiers. This used to be a place for the high-level criminals, the *capos* and the *shefs*. Now it's overrun with kids, high on cocaine, dressed in Gucci and Prada, spoiling for a fight.

'It's no good,' I said to Tank. 'We're going to have to find a place to hole up, get clean, and swap this old banger for something a bit classier.'

And get Tank away from temptation.

We'd rented a hatchback in Bordeaux. At the possibility of legroom, Tank's eyes lit up. His six-foot-four frame didn't fit in the car too easily.

'And dinner?'

Trust Tank to think of his stomach. I nodded, pulled on the steering wheel, and headed back east, past the *Rinoceronte* and toward Málaga. On the way out of town, I saw the burned-out ruins of a hotel, one I'd stayed at the last time I was here. Sisu Boutique. Shame. It was a nice place and reasonably priced too.

I carried on driving and didn't stop 'til we arrived in Benal-madena, a few miles east of Marbella.

It couldn't have a more different vibe. No luxury yachts or mansions here, just low-rent, all-inclusive hotels, the kind British tourists flock to in their droves so they can veg out by the pool with a book by day and drink to karaoke and Abba tribute bands by night.

We drove around until we found a hotel with a car park.

'Wait here, okay?'

Tank looked at me like I'd slapped him in the face.

'You can stretch your legs. Just don't draw attention to yourself, alright?'

And no drugs, I added in my head. Not that he'd have time to find a dealer before I got back.

I left Tank to untangle himself from his seatbelt and headed into reception. A Spanish gentleman flashed me a picture-perfect smile. The moment I asked if he had any rooms, he took a sharp intake of breath. As if they were full during the off-season.

When he'd checked his computer, he gave me a price.

Much too high. I turned to leave.

'But sir,' he said. 'If you wish to book via our website, we have some web-exclusive deals...'

I nodded. Ten minutes later, after doing as he suggested, I strolled into a family room. The equivalent of sixty quid a night bought us one double bed and a sofa bed. Breakfast and dinner were included too.

When we got back to the car, Tank was standing by the boot, ready to unload our bags.

'Not yet, you moron.'

'Huh?'

'We've got to return the car to Hertz. Get back in.'

The nearest drop off point was in Málaga.

Tank would have to suffer cramps a little longer yet.

Just wait until he finds out he's sleeping on the sofa bed.

32

THE BUG LADY

ANOTHER DAY, another expert.

This week, Rafferty had met the new forensic anthropologist, Fearn-Wright, and then been to see a curmudgeonly old stiff called Dirk Raoult. She knew which of the experts she liked more. Raoult extracted DNA from teeth, especially those that were even more ancient than he was. Boring.

Now, worst of all, Rafferty had to deal with an entomologist of all people, one Doctor Cowan. The bug expert had already been to the scene, under Purcell and Kflom's supervision. That had been part one of her work, looking at the crime scene itself. Rafferty imagined her examining the surroundings in which the body had been found, noting down things like the ambient temperature, how much moisture was in the air, and how many points of egress there were. All those things affected the lifecycle of bugs during decomp but as the bathtub was made of relatively inert fibreglass-reinforced polyester rather than layers of nutrient-rich topsoil, it probably wouldn't be all that useful. Especially as the body had long since been sent for autopsy.

Cowan had also been provided with extensive, 360-degree photographs of Cem Watzinger's body in situ and samples of all the bugs collected on the body. That left Rafferty with the easy, less messy part: meeting Cowan at her office in West Kensington to discuss her findings. From Scotland Yard, it was a quick two-mile hop through Belgravia. Once she'd briefed Ayala on the latest comings and goings, she headed down to the car park, and emerged into the rain before fiddling with her Sat Nav.

It was only when she punched the destination postcode in that Rafferty realised that Cowan's office was in the Natural History Museum. What a cool place to work. Ever since she'd been there as a kid on a school field trip, it had been one of her favourite museums. Looking up at Dippy, the gigantic Diplodocus skeleton, was one of her most vivid memories. The museum wasn't quite the same without him.

Naturally, the journey took almost twice as long as it should have. The roads around Kensington were gridlocked right up to the museum. Fortunately, Rafferty was able to drive straight past the enormous line of visitors queuing to get in and head for the staff car park.

'Bay 138,' she muttered to herself.

No sooner had she cleared security and parked the car, a young woman in a long white trench coat appeared holding an umbrella. Rafferty was about to ask if she was there to escort her to Cowan when she read the name badge. Surely not. She didn't look old enough to have a PhD.

'Detective Inspector Rafferty?' Cowan beamed. 'Welcome to the Natural History Museum.'

'Err, thanks.'

Almost immediately Cowan held the umbrella high above her head and shuffled forwards. The height gap between them – which Rafferty would have guessed was at least a foot – made it wholly ineffective. By the time they reached the metal security door that led into the bowels of the museum, poor Cowan was soaked through. She shook off the umbrella and tucked it under one arm before leading the way to her office.

As they bounced down the stairs three at a time, she turned and said over her shoulder: 'I thought we could get a coffee from the staff cafeteria and then review my findings in my office. Of course, I'll give you a tour of my collection too.'

What an offer. Her voice lilted upwards at the end of the sentence as if it were a question. Rafferty put it down to nerves. Sure enough, Cowan's hands were trembling.

'Coffee sounds great,' Rafferty said. 'I'll pass on the bug tour though if that's alright with you.'

Cowan's face fell.

Then, gesturing at Cowan's tremble, she added: 'I don't bite by the way. Don't be fooled by the height.'

'Sorry, this is my first murder investigation.'

That explained the nerves mixed with exuberance.

'Mine too.'

Cowan parked up. 'Really?'

Rafferty laughed. 'No.'

The entomologist didn't see the funny side. Rafferty could've kicked herself. The Met culture was one of dark humour, sarcasm, and banter and it was easy to forget the impact that could have on people outside the force.

The rest of the journey to Cowan's office was made in stony silence. The coffee turned out to be from a warming pot that had been on for far too long. Rafferty politely took a cup anyway. It couldn't be much worse than the crap the Met served.

Just along from the cafeteria, they stopped in front of a door with a tiny name plate that read "FOR. ENT." which Rafferty assumed was shorthand for Forensic Entomology.

'Come on through. Sorry if the lights are a little harsh. We don't get much daylight down here.'

Blinding white light assaulted Rafferty as soon as she entered the room. Somehow, they'd come through 180 degrees to face the direction of the car park. The only natural light came through a tiny window at almost ceiling height through which Rafferty could see the tyres of the nearest parked car. Not much of a view. No wonder they needed the halogen strip lights that ran the length of the room.

When her eyes adjusted, Rafferty realised that the light was bouncing off hundreds of white boxes, each of which contained a tiny, dead insect mounted on a stick pin. The boxes ran wall-to-wall except underneath the window where there was what appeared to be a filing cabinet.

In the middle of the room were two small desks, a laptop on each, and, besides that, a raised viewing table with yet more lights and an array of magnifying glasses. In the centre, on a raised pedestal as if it were of great importance, was a Petri dish filled with maggots. Live ones.

'Take a seat,' Cowan said, impervious to the wriggling beasts.

As Rafferty sat, she adjusted her chair so the maggots weren't in her eyeline.

'Oh,' Cowan said once she noticed. 'Sorry about that.'

She got up, moved them to the top of the filing cabinet, and sat back down.

'About my joke... Sorry. I spend my days cracking jokes to get through the darkness. I know that can come over as a bit, well, cold.'

Cowan waved her apology off with a smile. 'No biggie. So what number is this if it's not your first? Murder investigation that is?'

Rafferty strained to think. Twenty-odd a year for six years. Maybe more. That wasn't counting the accidental deaths, suicides, and the many death-by-dangerous driving cases she'd attended.

'Over a hundred,' she said. 'But only a dozen serial killers.'

'Ooh, do you think this one's a serial?' Cowan said excitedly.

'Nothing I've seen suggests that.'

With a sigh, Cowan slumped, dejected. 'Then I'd best get to it.'

'If you don't mind.'

What was it with experts meandering through things at a plodding pace this week? She had a killer to catch and he'd already got a heck of a head start.

'As soon as someone dies, they start to decompose. The odours they give off attract insects. The first, true flies of the order Diptera, arrive in minutes.' Cowan pulled one of the tiny square boxes from the wall and pushed it across the table.

Rafferty shuddered. 'I know what a fly looks like. Moving on...'

'A succession of bugs will appear as the body goes through the five stages of decomp – fresh, bloated, decay, post-decay, and dry.'

Left to her own devices, Cowan was clearly going to show every single stage by pulling out the relevant bug and plonking it on the table. Sod that for a game of soldiers. Even though Rafferty thought she knew the answer, she asked the obvious question. 'And our man is?'

'Dry,' Cowan said. 'The bits of him that weren't submerged anyway.'

She produced a folder full of photos from her drawer. Rafferty recognised her victim's bathtub. He'd been human soup, bones poking out above the waterline while the rest of him was submerged in a melting pot of fat and decomposing organs. The bugs had attacked the exposed body parts above the water line much more than the parts below.

A second set of photos showed the side-by-side comparison of the exposed and unexposed bones.

Cowan pointed to the pitted, drier bone. 'The dry stage starts at around day twenty-four after death.'

'So he's been dead about a month?'

'Longer. Among the samples I examined, there are signs of *Piophilidae*, or cheese flies. They tend to arrive around the ninety-day mark normally-'

'Three months?' Rafferty exclaimed.

'Normally,' Cowan repeated, 'but in the heat we've had, it might be a bit quicker. We're early in their cycle so it's not more than that. I'd peg your time of death at somewhere between forty-five and ninety days.'

A month and a half to three months. That was one hell of a window. It also meant that all the efforts to comb the area around The Happy Plaice for CCTV would almost certainly be fruitless: nobody kept footage for that long.

'And there's no way to narrow it down?'

'Not with any reasonable degree of confidence.' Cowan shuffled uncomfortably in her seat. A silence fell between the two. What more was there to be said? Rafferty was about to make her excuses and leave when Cowan smiled.

'Are you sure you don't want to see the rest of the bugs?'

33

INCOGNITO

ONCE WE'D SWAPPED out our rental, we headed back to Puerto Banús. This time, we were just another Audi A9 cruising the streets. Posh, respectable, and totally invisible among the flashier cars parked along the Golden Mile.

We'd swapped our clothes too. Rather than going for Gucci or Prada – both of which I could see from where we'd parked our car – we'd stopped off in Central Málaga at a huge *El Corte Inglés*, a fancy department store a bit like John Lewis, where we'd picked up some good-enough suits in the clearance section.

Again, it was to fit in, not to show off. Now we could cruise along the backstreets of Puerto Banús without drawing attention to ourselves. Unlike the young guys we saw strutting around who were walking peacocks, eager to start a fight just to flex their muscles. Even having Tank with me wouldn't deter them when it was fifteen on two.

And no doubt they were armed too.

'Any thoughts on where to start, Tank?'

He looked at me as if I'd asked him how to build a rocket. Virtually every backstreet in Puerto Banús follows the same theme: big villas surrounded by high walls with a cast-iron security gate and flash cars parked out front.

It makes working out who might be friendly nigh on impossible. Now that we've been out of the game for a few years, we don't even know who's legit and who's on the take. The rich and the criminal co-exist side by side. The unwritten rule about money is simple: don't ask, you might not like the answer.

Since I'd last come here, more of the grunts have moved in. They are the coked-up morons walking down the Mile. At night, they'll be in the clubs. Back in the day, it had been Opium where the Bakowskis hung out getting off their tits on the good stuff. Fine whisky and cocaine, not the fruity cocktails the bars are now advertising.

'Who's here these days?' I asked. 'The Camorra, the Cali Cartel, the Pollokshields, the Aggi Gang?'

Tank nodded. 'Everyone.'

Background, and more practically language, divides the underworld. The Italians didn't hang out with us. We didn't mix with the Latinos. Except when there was business to be done.

The groups have their own bars, their own restaurants, even their own strip clubs. Neither Tank nor I know which groups hang out where so we need to get the lay of the land as fast as possible.

'Okay,' I said. 'We can't sit in the car and watch the world go by. Whoever Tiny turned to had to be someone outside the Syndicate, someone the police wouldn't be watching. We want someone on the fringe. But they'll have to know who Tiny is, ideally owe him a favour, and they'll probably speak one of the languages he does.'

He spoke English, Russian, Ukrainian, and a bit of broken Spanish. Between 'em, those languages are spoken by about a quarter of the planet.

This could take a while.

WE SPENT the better part of a week trawling the bars, listening to accents, trying to pick out anyone with an English or a Ukrainian accent. We'd hung out in a nightclub watching young Russians down vodka like water, sat outside a café listening to Latinos yabbering away in rapid Spanish about "imports", and even – woe is me – visited a strip club where nubile young Polish girls were grinding up against metal poles and middle-aged German drug smugglers were tucking fifty-euro notes into the girls' underwear. Just to be thorough, Tank had taken one of the girls back to the VIP area to "interview her". From what I could hear, she sounded terrified of him.

Eventually, in a restaurant on the sea front, we heard an Irish voice talking in a low hush. Smart. Whispers draw attention, quiet speech doesn't. Except this time.

'There's a fight goin' on down at the poor house,' he said to his friend. 'It'll be grand. My money's on the Russian fella.'

The friend grinned. 'Aye and the Jockey said it'll be no 'olds barred. They'll go 'til one of 'em's unconscious.'

The skin around Tank's eyes crinkled, the thought of watching, or better yet taking part in, a big fight was enough to make him happy. Back in the day, the Syndicate had run a few of these fights. Only outsiders were allowed to take part. No point letting our own boys kill each other.

But that wasn't what interested me. It was the mention of the Jockey. Could it be the guy I'd known all those years ago? If it was then Tiny knew him too. Had he been here back when Tiny went on the lam? If he had then maybe, just maybe, he'd have heard about Tiny coming to town – if he ever had.

One thing bugged me: if Tiny was on the run, he'd have had

slim pickings on who he could have turned to. Anyone too close to him would be watched. Those not in his inner circle wouldn't help. If it were me, I'd want to go to someone I had power over, someone who I could force to do what I wanted. Tiny wouldn't be the guy begging for scraps. He'd be the guy demanding help.

Could someone like the Jockey be in the sweet spot in the middle? He wasn't one of the Syndicate but he'd be friendly with guys who were.

When the Irish boys had moved on, I pulled over the wait-ress and asked where the poor house was. She pointed out across the bay at a pub on the spit. It was hidden behind rows of yachts.

We settled up and headed over. It was ten minutes on foot, traipsing past millions of pounds worth of yachts. I spotted several triple-engine speed boats. There was only one use for those: smuggling. We were in the right place.

A sign out front proudly proclaimed the bar to be *The Pour House*.

That made a lot more sense.

The smell of beer wafted out, mixing hops with whatever was cooking inside. I sniffed the air. I could smell burgers, fish 'n' chips, and even curry. As I lingered in the doorway, wait-resses buzzed to and fro, carrying plates and giant steins full of beer. I waved off the offer of a table and headed towards the bar.

A portly bartender stood wiping down a dusty bar with an even dirtier rag.

'Two pints of Guinness,' I said, 'And a word with the Jockey.'

The bartender arched a curious eyebrow. 'He expecting you?'

'Tell him that it's Auggie Yermak. He'll remember me.'

No reaction to my name. That wasn't unexpected. I'd been out of the game for years after all.

For a guy who resembled a wooden barrel, the barman disappeared out the back faster than I'd have given him credit for. He reappeared after only a minute, flipped up the part of the bar that divided the staff from the public, and beckoned for me to follow him.

'Just you. Your thug stays here.'

I nodded at Tank to say it was okay to sit this one out and traipsed after the bartender. He led me down a narrow, dusty hallway. Halfway down, we had to press ourselves against one wall to let a waitress pass us without putting down her tray. We passed the IN and OUT doors of the kitchen where the smells I'd noticed out front became almost unbearable.

'In there,' he said, jerking his head at a door with no markings.

When I pushed the door open, I found myself walking into a well-appointed office that would've been at home in any corporate setting. Behind a big desk was the Jockey, real name Aled Parry.

He was so engrossed in his newspaper that he hadn't clocked me. Or so I thought. As I stepped towards him, Aled dropped the newspaper. In his right hand was a Smith and Weston pistol which was aimed right at me.

'Not one more step.'

I held up my hands. Aled continued to stare dead ahead as if he couldn't see. I slowly waved one hand. He didn't react. He couldn't see a damned thing. It was only when I looked at the newspaper again that it became apparent it was upside down.

'That's no way to greet an old friend.'

'If Tiny sent you, you're no friend of mine.'

I shook my head. 'Tiny's gone. He's in the wind. Has been for eight years.'

'Like fuck he is,' Aled spat. 'And quit waving your arms, you bell end.'

'You've seen him then.'

Aled laughed. 'Son, I haven't seen a thing since glaucoma got me. Now, you going to explain what you're doing here or do you want to find out how accurate a blind man with a pistol can be?'

'I'm looking for Tiny.'

'You and half of Interpol.'

'Sounds like you know where he might be.'

Aled cocked his head to one side. 'Might have a clue. What's it worth to you?'

'There's ten grand in my car boot with your name on it.'

'Naw, there ain't. Your car's already been searched.'

Shit. I couldn't help but be impressed. We'd walked the last half mile so he'd worked damned fast to trace us... unless he was bluffing.

'See, there's a man after my own heart,' I said. 'Cold, efficient, ruthless. Look, you hate Tiny too. That much is obvious. What'll it take for you to tell me what you know?'

'He stole five hundred g from me. I want it back.'

I whistled. 'You know I don't have that. Yet. If I find him, I'll get you the money.'

He motioned for me to sit down.

'How do I know you'll deliver?'

He had me there. 'You don't,' I said. 'But if you don't tell me, you've got zero chance of getting your money back. And I'll let you keep the ten on account.'

'Let me?'

'Yep,' I said. 'You want the Greco coming down on you for ten grand? I saw the boats out front. Three engines ain't subtle. And don't say you'll kill me. I'm not buying that. Two murders for ten grand or a bit of information for five hundred? You're a businessman, I'm a businessman. Let's do a deal.'

He paused just long enough for it to be awkward and then nodded.

'Alright, deal. I've seen him. Once. It was the week shit hit the fan. He turned up in town looking for money.'

Just as I'd expected. 'And you were the lucky schmuck he picked on?'

Aled nodded. 'You got me there. He turned up, threatened to expose some... proclivities of mine. Said I had 24 hours to find the money or else.'

I shuddered. So the rumours were true. The Jockey was a nonce. I was glad he couldn't see the look of revulsion on my face.

'How'd you pay him?'

'Cash.'

'I figured that. But how'd you find the money if this place isn't that profitable?'

Aled squirmed in his seat. 'Borrowed it, didn't I?'

'And who lent you half a million?'

Another awkward wiggle. 'The Malkhan Mob.'

'You borrowed money from one mobster to pay another. Brave move.'

'You didn't come here to criticise my finances,' Aled said.

'So is that it? You saw him once?' I leant forward as if I was going to get up.

'When he got here, he wasn't himself. He wasn't the cocky *shef* anymore. He was desperate. He had to be to ask me for money. You're not telling me he couldn't have got money from somewhere else.'

He probably had. It's expensive being a fugitive. Money to live. Money for information. Money for protection. It all adds up fast. Especially so for those on the red list. I'd have blackmailed Tiny if he'd come to me while he was on the run.

'You blackmailed him, didn't you?'

Aled paled. 'I... tried.'

A hearty laugh escaped me. This pathetic wastrel couldn't blackmail a schoolboy. 'Then what?'

'Then he told me the money would be every year. That if I'd just given him a gift – of five hundred grand – he'd have fucked off and left me in peace. Now, he sends someone to collect. I thought you were here on his behalf.'

That explained a lot.

'Hang on,' I said. 'What happened to the last guy?'

'He had an accident. Chicken wire around the limbs and torso, then thrown in the Bay of Gibraltar. He'd have been shark food in hours.'

Nice imagery. And a good way to get rid of a body. It wasn't Aled's first rodeo.

'What did Tiny need the money for?'

'Paperwork is my best guess,' Aled said. 'I heard he got into an argument with a guy that makes perfect Russian documents – allegedly on real government kit and with an inside man to make sure official records line up. Only a rumour mind but I'm minded to believe it. The guy's hotel burnt down the week that rumour went around.'

My mind flashed back to the ruins we'd driven past. The hotel I'd stayed at. I remembered that guy. He was part of the Malkhan mob. If Tiny had deliberately crossed them... well, he was a braver man than I.

'When he left, where was he going?'

'Home. That's what he said. Wouldn't tell me more than that.'

Finally, I believed I'd learned everything I could from Aled.

'Thanks for your time,' I said.

The blind man held out a hand. Rather than shake it, I leant forward as if to give him a hug. As I did, I snatched up his own pistol, turned it into his chest, and pulled the trigger.

He slumped over into my embrace.

'Sorry, old-timer. I can't take any chances.'

34

NO MAN'S LAND

IF SHE DIDN'T KNOW BETTER, she'd swear that Brodie was glued to his office chair. He'd texted telling her to come down whenever she got the chance.

'What've you got for me?'

'Let's take a walk,' Brodie said. He stood and shrugged on his sports jacket.

She started to ask why and he held up a finger, just enough so she could see it.

This was weird. He'd never suggested a walk before. She went along with it. The pair of them rode the lift up to ground level in silence before exiting by the Thames-side security door.

He walked briskly, forcing her to speed up almost to the point of jogging, and it was only when they were a couple of blocks away that he fell into lockstep.

'Brodie, you're scaring me.'

'Ash, this shit is weird. It's freakin' me out, lass.'

'What is?'

'You remember Zholnovych?'

'How could I forget?'

'This new guy – Cem Watzinger – is just like him. A ghost.

His identity popped outta nowhere several years ago. Overseas landlord, no tax records, no benefits claims, nada. It's like he exists outside of society.'

'Except,' Rafferty said, 'he lives in north London.'

'Exactly. It's dodgy, lassie. Everything about it. I was searching earlier and my computer cut out. Like it turned off.'

'So?' Her laptop did that occasionally. Didn't techs call it a blue screen of death?

'The timing was off. I restarted. Everything I'd been doing for that session was gone.'

'Session?'

Brodie stopped, looked around furtively, and lowered his voice to barely more than a whisper. 'We have virtual machines that we create for each sensitive investigation. They're self-contained so everything is kept separate.'

That made sense. No digital cross contamination. No viruses.

'What'd you do?'

'I spun up another VM and tried again. Same keywords. Same result. Immediate crash.'

'And?'

'Lassie, someone's tampering with Met Police equipment. I can't search for anything about Cem Watzinger without my kit going down. That's no wee hardware problem.'

The big man wasn't making sense. Who could tamper with the Met's servers? They were the police for God's sake.

Brodie held up his hands. Four fingers down, six up.

'Six?'

'Shh!'

Now she knew he'd lost it. MI6. First Morton and now Mr Sensible himself thought that spies were interfering with his record searches.

'Come on, lassie, think about it!' Brodie said. 'First yer Zholnovych evidence disappears. And all the backups go too. Then this fella pops up, same dodgy crap as last time, and searches fer him crash the Met's system. That's no coincidence.'

It sounded insane. It was insane. The fact that she was even having this conversation, walking past the Korean War Memorial on Victoria Embankment, with one of the Met's most brilliant minds, was mental.

And yet.

Somehow, it made sense.

'Alright,' she said. 'I'll humour you. Why would the Secret Intelligence Service tamper with a misper and a random bathtub murder enquiry?'

'Russia,' Brodie said simply. 'Think aboot it. Zholnovych. That sounds Russian to me. Then this new guy-'

'Who we know literally nothing about.'

'What if he's Russian too?'

Rafferty gave a wan smile. 'You're clutching at straws.'

'The watches he had in his flat. The ones on the inventory. They were Soviet era.'

'You sound utterly insane. Owning a Russian watch doesn't make someone Russian. I'm wearing clothes made in Bangladesh, a watch made in China, and boots made in Italy. That doesn't make me a Bangladeshi-Chinese-Italian.'

His face fell.

'And these earrings?' Rafferty said, brushing back her hair to show off two tiny, bezel-set studs with milgraine edge, 'they're from Paris, so I must be part French too. And fabulous with it.'

'Fine,' Brodie huffed. 'If yer not going to tak' me seriously, I'll get back to work.'

Without a second glance, he sped up, leaving Rafferty trailing in his wake.

And wondering just what the hell was going on.

Was SIS interfering in Met operations?
Or had Brodie gone barking mad?

35

PAYING FOR PROTECTION

NOW WE KNOW how Tiny's funding his retirement in hiding: a good old-fashioned extortion racket.

Clever. It's infinite unlike any stash of cash. Linden hadn't mentioned that as part of the bolt plan. Maybe he hadn't known.

It's not the small fry stuff we'd done as teenagers either. Back then, we'd been the younger kids hired to smash a few windows so the Syndicate could offer the businesses nearby "security services" for a quid a week.

Shocker, we didn't smash their windows up afterwards. They thought the service was great: as soon as they paid, their problems went away.

Before long, there were hundreds of businesses, all paying a few quid a week, just to stop us smashing up their property. Getting paid not to commit crime was the easiest crime of all.

And it gave Tiny the capital he needed to expand.

It was a gateway crime. Like the tri-engine speed boats outside *The Pour House*. They might only be running baccy in from Gib or hash from Morocco now, but sooner or later they'll realise they can use the same trick to run harder stuff for much more money.

'Why you shoot him?' Tank asked as we packed up our stuff in our hotel room in Benalmadena.

I looked at him. 'Why do you care? You're not usually squeamish about that sort of thing.'

He didn't reply. Instead, he stared off into the distance. Distracted. Talk about hypocritical. He'd tortured and killed two men but cared that I put an old man out of his misery?

Truth was I hadn't needed to kill Aled. But I hate loose ends. If word had got around that the Jockey had blabbed, it might get back to Tiny. Much harder to get information out of a corpse.

Aled was so mixed up in smuggling locally that people would assume he'd been killed because of that. Or because he hadn't paid back the Malkhan gangsters he'd been borrowing cash from. They'd never imagine it was an old friend from years ago. People didn't know me. I was in and out of Puerto Banús in less than a week. With all the tourists about, I was a ghost.

Just like Tiny would've been.

He couldn't have afforded to stay. There were too many old friends and even older enemies. Too many rival gangs. People who hated him. People who would've blackmailed him. Even people who would've tried to use him as a bargaining chip with the police. No doubt even the Greco would let a smuggler go if they could nail a bastard like Tiny instead.

'But where to?' I mused aloud. Tank had turned his back on me and was now struggling to get the zip on his case done up. I leant over to help him. 'It's got to be Schengen... or he's got to have snagged yet another ID, a good one. Easy enough to come by around here.'

Tank shrugged. 'Dunno, boss.'

Where would I go in Tiny's shoes? Once he'd got a bit of

cash, he had options. An entire continent to explore and no
compelling reason to be anywhere.

He'd told the Jockey he was going home. Why? Was it just
an off-the-cuff remark? Tiny's usual deadpan sarcasm? Surely,
he'd know that was a terrible idea.

Then again, maybe he was like Zholnovych.

Even Tiny has family. His mother, Ruslana, bless her heart,
lived in a huge house on the outskirts of Odessa. She was in the
game too. Used to run girls from the east all the way to London.

It was mad. Going to Ukraine would have meant more fake
documents, leaving Schengen and the hassle of getting back in
afterwards. And the police would have been watching. It was
risky and the reward wasn't there.

No. Tiny wouldn't have gone home.

Where then? Latin America? Hide out with the Cali cartel
or similar?

Could work. Then again, he's no longer useful to them. I
know he's not in the game. Word would've got round. And
while somewhere without an extradition agreement is sensible,
it's boring. Tiny can't stomach a quiet life watching Netflix and
reading crime novels by the pool. He wants to live.

Then there's the small matter of the elephant in the room:
the war.

Back when Tiny fled Britain, Ukraine was, for the most
part, peaceful. Then Crimea happened. And now... well,
nobody's running drugs in and out of Odessa anymore because
Odessa's been flattened.

'Tiny's aunt,' I said. 'What was her name?'

'Polina?'

'Where'd she live?'

I had a vague feeling she wasn't from Kyiv despite her
accent.

'Lviv,' Tank grunted.

Western Ukraine. Away from the fighting, right near the Polish border. If Ruslana's still alive – and that's a big bloody if as she was old last time we saw her a decade ago – then surely, she'll have gone west, to family.

If Tiny did go "home", the physical place won't exist anymore. But maybe the people still do.

There isn't much to be gained from going to Kyiv but maybe, just maybe, he's gone to Lviv if that's where his family has ended up. Without any better ideas, it seems as good as any.

'Change of plan,' I said. 'It's time to visit the old country.'

36

FACIAL RECONSTRUCTION

THE DEAD MAN was proving to be as much a mystery as Zholnovych. What Brodie had said kept rattling around Rafferty's brain, torturing her. She alternated between thinking it insane one moment and then the least improbable solution the next. Occam's razor.

Like Morton used to say, if she heard hooves, it was more likely their mounted colleagues on horseback than it was an escapee from Regent's Park Zoo.

Except he'd been the one to suggest the zebra last time they'd spoken. It was him who told her that the security services might be involved and to leave it well alone. But it was an itch that she couldn't resist scratching.

Cem Watzinger popped into existence, lived alone in squalor, and appeared to have no job, no ties to the community, and didn't own anything of note except for a box of old watches, all of which were nearly worthless. They weren't Rolexes, Breitlings or OMEGAs, they were Russian, cheap, wind-up wrist watches. He must've simply taken a fancy to them. Or got a bargain. Or maybe they were left in the flat by someone else. The rest of the evidence logged on HOLMES was boring: clothing, a few pounds in cash, and the usual knickknacks that everyone accumulated. There was some trace evidence left to process. Kflom was convinced there was drug residue everywhere and Rafferty wanted to believe it – it fitted with the state of the flat – but the last time she'd relied on his gut, it hadn't exactly gone well.

Science, not speculation, was the way forward. From the work done by the forensic anthropologist, Doctor Lucie Fearn-Wright, they had the skull measurements. Nearly all the bones were there except for a few. That was yet another mystery.

Now, Rafferty waited impatiently outside the office of the Met's lead forensic artist, a short-haired woman with riotous frizzy, purple hair. Her name was Flick something or other. Nearly everyone just knew her as the Crazy Hair Lady.

It was her job to take the science and turn it back into life.

Finally, she let Rafferty in.

'Hiya!' she said cheerfully.

In no mood for chit-chat, Rafferty forced herself to smile. Unlike the office she'd visited at the Natural History Museum, this one was in the eaves of the Met with a sloping ceiling under which there were an array of filing cabinets. Along the longest wall was a huge projector screen. There was a skull displayed on it in 3D.

'That our victim?'

'Yep!' Flick said cheerfully. 'Faithfully reconstructed and rendered for you.'

Solid work but it wasn't much use. If Rafferty had wanted to see what the skull looked like, she'd have headed back down to the morgue to see Fearn-Wright's reconstruction in person.

'I assume you've added more layers than this.'

'Right down to business, eh?' Flick said. 'I like that. Efficient. A woman who knows her own mind.'

Rafferty glared.

'Here we go then, Mrs Grump-a-dump.'

Another glare. 'It's Inspector.'

Flick smiled. 'Alright, Inspector Grump-a-dump.'

Fine. She'd earned that one. Rafferty smiled back.

Flick winked. 'I knew I'd crack you. I always do. You know, there was this one guy last year who-'

'Seriously, Flick, don't test me.'

'Fine,' Flick said, now sulking. Or pretending to at least. If she were, she'd missed her calling as a live stage actor.

'Now who's a grump-a-dump-dink?'

The smile returned. 'Here we go then. We took the skull marks to put down a base layer. From the report by... Kah-flume? Kay-Flow-em?'

'Kflom.'

'Right. Him. His report said the victim's clothes were approx. a thirty-four-inch waist and a thirty-three-inch leg. That tallies with the bones. I've therefore assumed he's reasonably slim for his six-foot-four frame and estimated the tissue depth markers on the face accordingly.'

That seemed fair. Rafferty nodded encouragingly.

A few clicks later, the skull began to morph into a rudimentary face. First, pin-like markers appeared, each with a millimetre depth written on the face of the pin in a tiny font that Rafferty had to squint to read, and then, as the render completed, salmon-coloured flesh rose up to cover them. It was a pudgy, much-too-smooth face but unmistakeably human.

'The next bit is a blend of art and science. We can guess at skin-tone. He's probably Caucasian from the bone measurements so let's give him a light, year-round tan on mid-tone skin.'

Another click, another ripple as the render morphed. Still a pudgy kid's face, but now the salmon flesh was closer to Rafferty's own skin tone.

'Now, we know from Doctor Fearn-Wright's report that he

suffered numerous peri-mortem injuries. He had a hard life. There were healed breaks to the zygomatic, the maxilla, and the nasal bones. Adding those injures to our sim gives us this.'

The skin contorted as if pulled by something within the depths of the skull, ridges forming. The nose twisted a few degrees off-centre.

'Wow.'

Now, they had a bald, eyeless skull.

'It's cool, right?' Flick bounced on the balls of her feet as if to underscore her enthusiasm. 'Just wait for the next bit.'

In quick succession, Flick applied texture to the skin, ruddy with age, a man who'd suffered a lifetime without proper skincare. Then eyes appeared, deep hazel, and a mop of foppish brown hair to match.

'I'm guessing at brown,' Flick said apologetically. 'It's the most common colour. Of course, your man could've been blond, red-headed, maybe even had dark black hair though that's less than one per cent of the population.'

Rafferty pointed at the projector screen. 'You've got the teeth wrong. Those gnashers are perfect.'

'Hold your horses. I'm getting there.'

She switched windows, bringing up photos of the teeth that had been recovered. 'Quite distinctive, aren't they?'

Then, as if by magic, the teeth were rendered onto the skull, yellowed and marked. The recreation still looked off in some way. Maybe it was the hair.

'Can we try trimming that hair? I don't think our man was that coiffed.'

'Uh, okay.'

They spent the next fifteen minutes trying on a variety of hair styles. None looked quite right. In the end, Rafferty asked her to print out the mugshot with short, messy hair. It was the most generic. If they had to guess, they didn't want people to rule someone out based on the hair.

The next job would be to take it back to The Happy Plaice and see if anyone recognised him and could confirm that the victim was the tenant. From there, they might find something concrete, something that would disprove Brodie and get the enquiry back on track before Ayala raked her over the coals for her lack of progress.

Deep down, she knew he'd do that anyway.

37

CROSSING BORDERS

AFTER A QUICK FLIGHT TO WARSAW, we travelled to Lviv by car from Poland.

A nice, young Polish couple had driven us as far as the border. They thought we were returning to volunteer to fight against the Russians. As if. Bloody morons had fallen for our shit without even thinking about it. The combat fatigues? They were from an army surplus store. A close inspection by someone in the know might've given us away but from a distance, they looked pukka. Somehow, they made Tank look even more terrifying than normal.

From the border, we'd hitched a ride with people who really were headed for the frontline, waving them off at Rynok Square with promises to keep in touch – if we made it out alive.

Despite the sunshine and the unreasonably high temperature, the mood was sombre. I'd imagined a bustling, lively market square filled with hawkers and children. In reality, it was quiet, serious, sombre. Nothing like the Ukraine of old.

'It is good to be back,' Tank said. He took a deep breath as if inhaling the sweetest, purest air ever. I nodded nonchalantly. Ukraine had never been my home. I'd grown up in London,

coming here only to visit family, and even then, it was Kyiv or
Odessa, never Lviv. Tank on the other hand walked the streets
with purpose, leading us away from Rynok Square at a route
march. Blue-and-yellow flags hung above us; no balcony
complete without one.

We walked parallel to the tram route towards Ivan Franko
Park. Of course, the elderly Bakowski family had a place here. It
was the Ukrainian equivalent of living on the Upper East Side
in New York or on Sloane Square back home: leafy, posh, and
within spitting distance of the centre of everything. There were
rows of townhouses, built from beautiful red bricks, with neatly
painted doors and well-maintained roofs. This was a million
miles away from the horrors of the front line. Even the people
milling around the park looked posh, much like those in Puerto
Banús, but far less menacing. As I had expected, there were a lot
more men than women about.

We took a seat on a bench in the park with a view of Aunt
Polina's house. 'Coming here.... Did we make a mistake?'

Seeing so many men our age in uniform was beginning to
make me doubt our ability to get out again.

'No worries,' Tank said. 'I have plan.'

Well, that filled me with confidence. Monosyllabic Tank
had a plan. It was like an episode of my favourite childhood
cartoon, Pinky and the Brain with Pinky telling Brain that he'd
sort it.

'What's your plan?'

'First, check house. See who there.'

So far, so good. That much was obvious.

'Then what?' I asked.

'See if Tiny come.'

I hung my head. Tank really was a thick bastard.

'Because Interpol wouldn't have thought to look for one of
Europe's most wanted criminals at his aunt's house.' I pointed at

the window of the house I thought was Polina's. 'That's the place, right?'

'*Tak.*'

The townhouse had three floors, two of which had a small balcony. On the lower of the two, I could see a clothes-horse with washing on it. Women's clothes. No surprise there. The closer I looked, the more obvious it became that there was more than one woman living there. The clothes on the left balcony were smaller with brighter colours and intricate patterns I couldn't quite make out from where I stood while on the right balcony, the clothing was brown and baggy, the sort of thing I would expect to see a babushka wear. I pointed it out to Tank.

'Do you think Tiny's mum moved in with his aunt?'

He shrugged.

I motioned for Tank to follow me towards the big house. 'Say nothing,' I said. 'Just nod along.'

He did.

There was a great big brass knocker on the door. It was so well polished that the sun glinting off it was blinding. By contrast, the door was pitch black, almost like the one in Downing Street that I'd seen on the telly no end of times. Except this one was solid wood, not a terrorist-proof bomb shield. Or so I hoped. I wouldn't put it past Tiny to have provided his relatives with first-rate security.

I knocked.

Solid wood.

Phew.

That meant Tiny was relying on his reputation to keep them safe. A reputation that wouldn't last forever.

A woman answered the door. Despite the warmth, she wore a bright green scarf against a thick, gold puffer jacket. Her hair was thick, frizzy and greying, her skin wrinkled and sallow, but her eyes were crystal blue, sharp, and her expertly manicured nails said this was a woman who still took care of herself. At a guess, I'd put her in her late sixties.

I wasn't going to be able to bullshit her easily. I'd intended to pretend to be at her door to announce Tiny's death, to gauge her reaction and try to work out if she'd seen or heard from him. It wouldn't work. She'd nod along, cry with me even, and then, knowing the Bakowski family, knife me on the way out the front door with an "I knew you were full of shit smile".

Time for plan B.

'Polina,' I said, switching into my rusty Ukrainian. 'I'm a friend of Tiny's and this is-'

'I know Tank,' she said, beaming. 'How are you, boy? When did you enlist?'

Shit. She knew Tank? This wasn't how I'd envisioned this going at all. The hair on the back of my head stood on end. This wasn't right.

'Good,' Tank said. Even when speaking Ukrainian, he was a man of few words. 'Uniform very new.'

'Don't just stand there, come in, come in, before someone sees you.'

She stood back to open the door wide. I hesitated for a moment, wondering what I was getting myself into, and then headed in, Tank right behind me.

Inside, the house was opulent. Beautiful paintings hung from the wall, though I did notice a few gaps where it looked as if even more once hung.

'We shipped the most valuable ones out at the start of the war,' Polina explained. 'Just in case.'

I wondered where to. Lviv was as far away from the front as you could get without leaving the country. I didn't have time to think about it for too long as she soon shepherded us into the living room. Here, there was a fancy-looking sofa, the kind I'd seen when I'd visited Versailles as a kid. That had to be a fake.

'Can I get you boys some *obid*?' she asked. 'I have some left-over *varenniki*.'

My mind flashed back to memories of dumplings of all kinds, stuffed with meat, potatoes, cheese, even mushrooms. I could practically smell the fried onions, taste the sour cream.

Could she be trying to poison us? This wasn't my babushka. This was a woman whose sister raised a psychopath, a woman living in opulence as a result of that. Never, ever trust a Bakowski.

'Yes,' Tank said simply before I could decline.

The next thing I knew, Polina was shuffling in with a tray laden down with bowls of dumplings. It smelled even better than I remembered. She hadn't brought in a bowl for herself. If it were poisoned, that was no bloody surprise.

Unlike me, Tank didn't hesitate to dive in. I waited, pretending to enjoy the smell, and then cautiously copied him. Umami flavours erupted in my mouth, making me lick my lips. Damn, it was good. If I were going to be poisoned, this was how I'd want to go.

When we finished, Polina turned to Tank. 'Now, I know you're not here just for my *varenniki*.'

Before Tank could fuck things up, I jumped in with the first thing that popped into my head. 'There's a man trying to kill Tiny.'

A partial lie. There were two men trying to kill her bastard of a nephew and they were both sitting on the sofa.

She waved at me to carry on.

'He's already killed three of our own.'

This time, she smiled. What the actual fuck?

'What is new?' she said. 'People always try to kill him. No one has succeeded yet.'

I couldn't disagree. We chuckled along with her.

'This time,' I said in a conspiratorial tone, 'they're serious.

They killed two men in witness protection to find him. And another in broad daylight in a bar in Malaga.'

'Those intent on murder are rarely doing it on a whim, no?'

She had a point.

'Tank, what do you think? Is it credible?'

He paused eating just long enough to reply: '*Tak*.'

'And what would you have me do with this information?'

Cagey. She knew where he was.

'Pass it on to him.'

She nodded. 'Very well. If I speak to my nephew, I shall warn him.'

No denial. No pretence that she didn't know where he was. She knew. And now we could follow her right back to him.

As soon as she'd finished speaking, she stood up. Lunchtime was over.

She got up to take the bowls out, turning her back as she left the room. This time, I didn't hesitate. Her handbag was slung by her chair. I walked over to it, pulled a Bluetooth tag from my pocket and hid it inside.

When she came back, she smiled again as if we'd never discussed the attempted murder of her beloved nephew.

'You have room for honey *babka*, yes?'

Now that was an offer we weren't going to turn down.

38

MEMORIES OF MURDER

SHE'D BEEN PUTTING it off and putting it off. Now she had to give Ayala a progress update. Or rather, an update on her lack of progress. No doubt he'd be insufferable as always. As if he could've done better with the scant evidence they had to go on.

The one bit of good news was the facial reconstruction, or eFit, that Flick had mocked up was immediately recognised by the proprietors of The Happy Plaice. Their victim was the man who lived in the pokey flat above the chippy, though they were at pains to stress that the squalid flat had nothing to do with them.

The door to Ayala's office was open as she approached. How unusual. Normally, he kept himself tucked away, doing whatever it was desk-based Detective Chief Inspectors did. To give him his due, the desk jockey approach to crime suited him more than chasing down criminals, and he wasn't the only DCI to hide out in New Scotland Yard scoffing Danish pastries and having endless meetings with upper management.

Then she saw why the door was open. Silverman was perched on the edge of Ayala's desk. Officially the Commissioner of Police of the Metropolis, Silverman was the big boss, the woman trotted out to talk to the press every time there was a new scandal engulfing the Met which was nearly every day. Clearly, today wasn't one of those days: Silverman was smiling.

It didn't last long. The moment she saw Rafferty, she scowled.

'Good morning, ma'am.'

'Inspector Rafferty. I hope you're here to update Chief Inspector Ayala on the Cem Watzinger case.'

'As a matter of fact.'

'Good,' Silverman said, cutting her off. 'I was just saying to Betram that his team has had an enviable success rate this year and it would be a shame for this case to interrupt that run of success.'

It took all Rafferty's might not to roll her eyes. They'd had a run of success because they'd pulled the boring cases over and over again. Not one serial killer. Not one mass-murderer. It had been a bloody boring year.

'No doubt that's thanks to the Chief Inspector's strategic nous, ma'am. As a matter of fact, I was hoping I could borrow his, ahem, enormous brain to help progress the Cem Watzinger case.'

'In that case,' Silverman said, leaping to her feet. 'I'll leave you to it. Bertram, I'll see you at the National Portrait Gallery soirée this evening.'

She swept from the room, leaving Rafferty alone in the doorway.

'Shut the door,' Ayala barked.

After doing so, she walked over to his desk and sat on it in the same fashion that Silverman had eliciting a scowl. 'Comfy,' she said sarcastically before he could kick off. 'But if you don't mind, I think I'll stick to the chair.'

She sat down, muttered that it was much better, and leant back defiantly, daring Ayala to make a scene.

'You'd better have progress, Inspector.'

So formal! As if they hadn't worked side by side for half a decade.

If he wanted to play it that way, it was fine by her.

'Cem Watzinger was found in his bathtub somewhere between six weeks and three months after his death. At Chiswick's insistence, the case was referred to a forensic anthropologist who reassembled the bones and charted all the relevant injures. Shortly before his death Cem Watzinger was tortured with a mix of power tools and blunt force trauma. DNA samples were recovered from his teeth but no matching samples were available and he isn't in IDENT1. After recreating his face using an eFit, his identity was confirmed by his downstairs neighbours.'

'All of which,' Ayala said in a slow drawl, 'I already knew.'

'Coulda stopped me anytime then,' Rafferty said under her breath.

'What was that?'

'I said "I just wanted to recap as I know you're busy all the time now".'

He sneered in disbelief but let her comment slide. 'Why was Watzinger tortured?'

'You'd have to ask the killer that, boss,' Rafferty said. 'As that's not me, I'll decline to answer. Would've been much more convenient if I'd done it, wouldn't it? Slap the cuffs on myself, march myself into detention...'

Not even the hint of a smile. Whatever happened to using humour to get through the day? Had Ayala never had a sense of humour? Had he only laughed to butter Morton up?

'You've taken the eFit around,' he said.

'Like I said, confirmed by the neighbours.'

'Not around the neighbours,' he bit back. 'Have you shown it to any CIs? SOCA? Run it by local uniforms?'

'No, no, and yes,' Rafferty answered in turn.

'Run it by SOCA, today. You know Xander, right?'

There was a glint in Ayala's eye. He knew she knew Alexander Thompson. Xander was a bear of a man with salt-and-pepper hair, a silver-flecked beard to match, and the body of a man half his age. She'd met him in the Met's gym just after she'd started working for Morton, only to be introduced to him properly a few weeks later while working on a murder-for-hire investigation that trod the line between murder enquiry and gangland investigation. Not only did Xander head up investigations into London's criminal underworld, he also ran a huge network of confidential informants, criminals paid to pass evidence, and occasionally unfounded rumours, along to the police.

'Indeed,' Rafferty said simply.

'In fact,' Ayala said, 'I'll be seeing him this evening. AirDrop me your eFit.'

She wanted to grumble that she'd do it herself, that he'd been so hands off until now that she was hardly going to let him crack the case in two seconds flat and take the credit for her donkey work. But it wasn't worth the effort. She pulled out her iPhone, found the PNG version of the eFit, one which was face-on, and clicked AirDrop.

As it transferred, she mulled what he might ask next. She should've thought of running the eFit by Xander. Then again, talking to an ex was never fun.

'Shit!'

Her head jerked upwards. Ayala never swore.

He was staring at the phone as if he'd seen a ghost. Had she AirDropped him the wrong file by accident? For a second, her heart raced as she struggled to think what incriminating evidence might be on her work phone.

'What?' she asked finally.

'There's no need to show this to Xander. I know this man. Knew anyway. He was a CI. Your victim is Nathan Linden.'

39

TAG, YOU'RE IT!

MY RUSE HAD GONE UNDETECTED. Or so it seemed.
The Bluetooth tag I'd hidden in Polina's handbag began moving
not five minutes after we'd left. From a quiet bench a few roads
away from her house, I watched the GPS dot move around the
map. She had to be in a car as it was going too fast for her to be
on foot.

There was no way Polina hadn't been in contact with Tiny.
When we'd said someone was trying to kill him, she'd been flip-
pant, dismissive, amused even. Nobody's that cold-hearted
about death threats to their favourite nephew.

Which meant she knew he was okay. Or thought he was.

'Money, Tank. How much does it take to buy that sort of
townhouse?'

Tank shrugged. 'Fifty, sixty million hryvnia. Maybe more.'

I whistled. That was fast approaching one point five million
pounds. I had no idea Lviv was that pricey. Even with a war on.
Then again, Polina could've bought back when it wasn't so
fancy. I asked Tank how long she'd been there.

'Forever,' he said simply.

What about the furnishings? The old rug, the fancy French-style settee? I'd assumed they were all knockoffs... But what if they weren't? Had I been sitting on a real eighteenth century sofa? Looking at a real Leon Blakst painting?

Fuck.

Normally, I'm better at spotting money. I'm no Brighton knocker-boy but I'd hope I'd spot big money. People pay well for that sort of information. Ten percent of the cut for doing nothing but flagging where the goodies are. That's my sort of crime: let someone else take the risk, cream a bit off the top.

Never mind. I'm not here to rob Polina. Even I don't have the balls to rob a Bakowski. Instead, I want to follow her, see where she goes, who she speaks to. I can't imagine she has a direct line to Tiny – I'm never that lucky, and the police would've found him if it were that easy – but maybe she has a circuitous way to warn him someone wants him dead.

As I watched the GPS dot sped up, heading west on the M11 towards the Polish border.

Could Tiny be in Poland? Is it even in Schengen? Probably.

Only one way to find out: follow her across.

We found an older car parked on a side street, one we could hotwire. While I kept lookout, Tank smashed the window and got the engine running. In less than a minute, we were driving off.

'God, this thing reeks of wet dog.'

Tank grinned at me from behind the wheel. 'I don't mind. I like dogs.'

He sniffed as if enjoying a fine glass of *Château Lafite*.

'Disgusting.'

As we drove, the dot continued to move. By the time we reached the border, it had settled in Medyka.

There was a roadblock on the Ukrainian side of the border. Men dressed in combat fatigues loitered, guns slung over their shoulders.

'Tank, we need to turn back.'

If we didn't, we ran the risk of actually being conscripted. Our uniforms might've fooled a couple of Polish do-gooders, but an experienced border patrol, run by actual soldiers, would suss us out in a heartbeat. Coming this way was a mistake.

Tank grinned at me. 'Coward.'

40

AN OLD FACE

'YOUR VICTIM IS NATHAN LINDEN.'

Ayala's words had reverberated around his office like thunder. Now they echoed around Rafferty's skull. It wasn't a name that Rafferty recognised, but a crash course in Linden's criminal history soon followed.

Contrary to his usual apathy towards being hands-on, Ayala convened a meeting, summoning support staff, experts they'd consulted, and a few faces that Rafferty recognised as members of Xander's Serious Organised Crime team. Thankfully, her ex hadn't yet made an appearance himself.

By the time Ayala walked in with Kieran O'Connor, one of the fiercest prosecutors in the country and the man hotly tipped to become Director of Public Prosecution despite being on Rafferty's side of forty, the room was buzzing. Coffee had been poured, sandwich platters had appeared from nowhere, and Brodie had rigged up the projector so that it could be controlled from the head of the table.

The room hummed with chitchat until Ayala slammed the door shut. He looked around intently as he stalked back to the head of the table.

'Everything said in this meeting must stay in this meeting,' Ayala said. 'Before we begin, Kieran will deal with the formalities of that.'

A stack of papers was passed around the room, each person taking one before passing the stack down the line like students getting a copy of lecture notes. One or two glanced at it and passed the stack along without keeping a copy. When the pile got to Rafferty, her jaw dropped.

'What you have in front of you,' Kieran began, 'is a copy of the Official Secrets Act. Those of you who have already signed need not do so again.'

A hand shot up. 'Why?'

'Is minic a bhris beál duine a shorn.'

Rafferty smiled. Kieran had used the Irish phrase in her company before. It played on the idea that opening your mouth could get you punched on the nose. A bit like an Englishman saying "loose lips sink ships" or "don't run your mouth."

The same person piped up to ask Kieran another question. 'And what the bloody Nora does that mean?'

Kieran smirked. 'I can't reveal that until you sign.'

Slowly, each person signed, their neighbours witnessing it. Nearly an hour was lost to completing the paperwork. Kieran, and another man Rafferty didn't know, checked each in turn before ticking them off the list of attendees. As they did so, those in the room demolished the free sarnies, drained cold cups of coffee, and tried to avoid speculating about what the hell was going on. Only Rafferty had a clue and that was just a name. Finally, when the formalities were satisfied, Ayala called the meeting to order once again.

'My apologies for the secrecy,' he said. 'This is... an unprecedented situation, one which I believe has never occurred in the United Kingdom before. Recently, we began investigating the death of a man you all knew as Cem Watzinger. In reality, the deceased is Nathan Linden.'

This time, the name got an audible reaction, gasps and swearing echoing around the room.

Tentatively, Rafferty raised a hand. 'Sorry, but Linden was before my time. Who was he exactly?'

'Linden was a fence,' Ayala said. 'One we thought was small-time. He owned, with his twin brother Craig, a stall in Camden Lock, selling dodgy jewellery and the like.'

That didn't explain the overreaction.

'It turned out, he was working for Dimitri "Tiny" Bakowski, fencing everything under the sun. Cars, jewels, artwork, you name it. We arrested his brother in connection with a murder enquiry back in 2012. Craig, his younger brother, confessed all, implicating Nathan and they both turned Queen's Evidence against Tiny. Craig was murdered shortly after that.'

'I'm still not following what the big deal is.' Rafferty looked around the room. She wasn't the only one who didn't understand why it mattered. Their dead guy was a criminal and a traitorous one at that. Better a dead criminal than an innocent victim.

It was the lawyer's turn to speak. When he did, his rich, lilting Dublin brogue was somehow serious and charming in equal measure. 'It matters,' he said, 'because when Mr Linden turned Queen's Evidence, he helped bring about the downfall of the entire Bakowski Crime Syndicate. Because of him, two of the three brothers were apprehended while Tiny himself has been on the run ever since. In return, Mr Linden was given protected person status.'

That explained the gasps. Linden was in witness protection.

The prosecutor turned to the dour man next to him: 'Eric, do you want to take over here?'

He nodded. 'The UK Protected Persons Service is complex.

What I can tell you is limited for operational security. Regional protected persons units are in charge of witnesses in their respective areas. The Met has its own. These run under the auspices of the National Crime Agency which provides coordination and practical resources through the Central Bureau.'

Eric paused to take a sip of water. 'This often necessitates giving witnesses new identities, relocating them to different parts of the UK, and furnishing them with a new career, all while balancing their need to be protected against the needs of the communities into which we place them. It is, to be blunt, a balancing act. Clients like Linden, former criminals, are not uncommon. As a non-violent offender, he would have been considered low risk.'

'Then why London?' Rafferty asked. 'Why not... Kendall? Or the Highlands?'

'I can't comment on specifics. All I can say is: think about it. If you weren't British, where would you stand out the least?'

He had a point. London was the melting pot of the UK. Only last weekend, Rafferty had read that ethnically Indian individuals, many of them third or fourth generation Brits, owned more property in London than those who identified as White British. It was one of London's biggest strengths. Linden had grown up here so he didn't have an accent to hide but his file mentioned his mother was Ukrainian and his surname was German so he'd stick out like a sore thumb in rural Wales or the Highlands.

'Nathan Linden was assigned to one of our most experienced handlers. He took well to the programme, forgoing all connections to his former life. This disconnection is one of the guiding principles of the service. Clients cannot, ever, get in contact with those from their old life. We monitor this with the utmost vigilance.'

A man guffawed. He was from SOCA. 'So vigilant,' he said, 'that you let him get himself killed.'

The scowl that Eric shot in the man's direction was so severe that his droopy expression momentarily gave way to pure, unadulterated anger. 'We didn't do anything of the sort. As far as we can tell, Nathan Linden had no contact with his former life. Admittedly, our resources are not infinite, especially when a witness has been safely settled for many years, but we have no intelligence to suggest that Linden's death has anything to do with the Syndicate.'

'Just coincidence then, is it?' The man looked around the room. 'Don't pretend you're not all thinking it. A former gang-banger gets tortured to death and we're supposed to think it's all a happy co-inky-dink that he used to work for Tiny bloody Bakowski? I'd bet my right nut that it's not.'

The tension in the room was thick enough to cut with a knife.

'Only the right one?' Rafferty said, trying to make a joke of it. 'Who'd want that?'

A ripple of laughter echoed. Eric didn't join in. Nor did Ayala.

'Ahem,' Kieran said. 'Back to the nut job at hand...'

This time, a smile tugged at the corner of Ayala's mouth. He was human after all.

'Now, this is likely to complicate your investigation,' Eric continued.

No fucking kidding.

'If you have any questions, feel free to ask.'

Rafferty raised a hand. 'I've got one. We had another strange murder earlier in the year – Elijah Zholnovych. Was he in witness protection too?'

41

THE LONG WAY AROUND

WE HAD to take the long way around. I knew we'd have to get out of Ukraine illegally and I knew where: Hrebenne, a tiny village on the edge of Poland. It was the same crossing Tiny and his mother used to bring girls in from Ukraine to work on the streets of London. While there was a border guard, I knew he'd take a few euros to look the other way.

By the time we got out, the GPS dot had returned to Lviv.

But we know where she's gone to within a few feet. A house on the outskirts of the village of Medyka. On the aerial view on Google Maps, it looks derelict, the roof collapsed and the walls crumbling as if it's been abandoned.

That can't have been coincidence. We tell her Tiny's in danger and she immediately takes an impromptu trip to the middle of nowhere on the Polish side of the border?

We have to go find out.

If it is Tiny... well, he won't have to wait long to find out that the threat to his life is credible.

The drive took an hour and a half. We stuck religiously to the speed limit the whole way to avoid getting pulled over in a stolen car. The last thing I wanted was to have to shoot a traffic cop to stay out of jail.

The village is nestled among the flat, rolling countryside which makes the area the breadbasket of Europe. If Tiny is hiding out here, I can see why. Nobody around for miles.

As Tank drove, I watched my phone's GPS, comparing it to the record of where Polina had stopped.

'A quarter mile or so ahead, up on the left,' I said. 'Give or take.'

From the road, we could see the neatly planted rows of next year's wheat harvest. In the far distance, there was a trio of barns that marked the edge of the farm. If the aerial photos were right, the house Polina had visited was just beyond them.

'Here's the plan. Park up. We'll approach on foot. No point giving whoever lives there a heads up that they've got company.'

'Okay,' Tank said. He pulled over in the middle of the road.

'Not right here, you moron. Look over there, on your right. See that little thicket? Pull in there. Quietly.'

He did. We were now only a couple of hundred yards out, the barns shielding us from view. We sat in the car for a while as I conjured up a plan of attack. The occasional car drove past. Not quite as dead as I'd thought.

I tried Googling to find out who lived there. The Polish government kept a *rejestr ksiąg wieczystych* or land registry, a list of exactly who owned what land. Perfect. I clicked to open it up.

The screen read: "Enter the number of the Land and Mortgage Register". There were three boxes. The first one listed postcode options. That was the easy part. But how the fuck was I supposed to know the parcel number?

An angry red box flashed up: *The Land and Mortgage Register number field must be completed!*

Fuck. This wasn't going to get us anywhere.

'New plan,' I said. 'Knock the door and rush whoever is in there.'

Tank grinned. 'Works for me.'

42

ECHOES OF THE PAST

THE MEETING WAS SWIFTLY ADJOURNED after Rafferty's question. Eric legged it without answering.

Then, via Ayala, the answer came back.

Zholnovych was in the programme. He too had worked for the Syndicate before turning Queen's. It suddenly struck Rafferty that it wasn't really Queen's Evidence anymore, it was King's. That was a strange thought. Then again, he'd testified before Her Maj had passed away.

Whatever it was supposed to be called, the fact Zholnovych was a witness for the state had to be kept strictly need-to-know. Naturally, she'd immediately asked Brodie out for a walk.

'I fookin' knew it,' Brodie said, grinning like an eejit as they walked along the South Bank. 'That's why I couldn't see a damned thing. I ain't going mad, lassie! We've got have a wee bevvie to celebrate.'

'Can't,' Rafferty said with a sad face.

'Not another date, lassie? Those apps, they'll melt ya mind. I met ma missus the old-fashioned way.'

'While drunk?'

'Nae,' he said, his voice deadly serious. 'My father arranged it to secure our allegiance with the Plantagenets. A union of the crowns blessed by the Pope himself.'

'Nice pub was it?'

'Aye. Finest Wetherspoons in all of Glasgow. Pints for a pound fifty and two dinners for six quid.'

Now he was showing his age. Even in the mighty Spoons, things hadn't been that cheap for over a decade.

'Still with her, ya know,' Brodie said. 'Not that I haven't tried to fend her off. Three wee ones'll do that to you.'

'You've got three kids?'

Why hadn't she heard about this before? She'd have loved to play Auntie Ash every once in a while.

'Aye, no. Three stone. That's how much I've put on since we met. I can't run fast enough to escape nae more. She just lassoes me back in.'

She lightly punched his arm. 'You bastard. I can never tell when you're serious.'

'Except when I'm tryin' ta convince you MI6 are covering up a murder, eh?' He grinned and changed the subject. 'So, where's your big date? Nearest Spoons is back at Waterloo so I know you've gone downmarket from there.'

'He's taking me up the Shard.'

'Lassie!' Brodie said, clamping his hands to his ears. 'Ye can't do that before he's even bought you dinner. What'll ya Ma say?'

Hilarious. 'It's Oblix.' Rafferty referred to a fancy bar and restaurant on the thirty-second floor. It was a gorgeous place with sophisticated cocktails and the views to match.

'Smarmy bastard! I've been wanting ta take my missus up there for years. That's nae a first date sorta place.'

It was a bit over the top. She could imagine him turning up with flowers, and jewellery, buying dinner, and then taking her to the theatre which meant one of two things: either she'd stumbled into a Fifty Shades novel and met her billionaire or he was

damned desperate. Knowing her luck, he'd be married or
gay too.

'Oblix isn't a patch on Spoons, though, is it? Just think, one
day you could take her to The Coronet.'

Brodie scowled as if mortally offended. 'Hey, that's a classy
pub, that is. Used to be the Savoy Cinema, ya know.'

'Is that what you tell your wife? That you're taking her to
the Savoy?'

He grinned. 'Aye.'

'You know, I once had a bastard of a date take me to the
Savoy Theatre to see Austentatious.' Rafferty named the West
End show famous for being totally made up on the spot every
night. She had a sneaky suspicion that wasn't totally true, that
there might be a bit of a theme if she'd gone and seen it more
than once, but she hadn't yet had time to test that theory.

'Load of crap, was it?'

'Austentatious was great, but the git spun me a yarn about
the Savoy being built on the site of the former cabbage market.'

Brodie stopped dead in his tracks and then doubled up with
laughter.

'And you fell for that?' Brodie said. 'Lassie, you sure you're a
detective?'

'He was cute, okay. And I'd had a few.'

'When did you realise it was a load o' boloney?'

She hesitated. Fuck it. She'd told him most of the story. May
as well finish it.

'When I tried to share that fact with Morton,' she said, her
voice barely more than a whisper.

Brodie bellowed with laughter. He was absolutely losing it.

'All right, all right. It's not that funny.'

He still couldn't stop himself braying like a hyena, pausing
to draw breath before laughing even harder. He was drawing so

much attention that it was time to pretend she didn't know him at all.

'Must dash. Have a good one, Brodie!'

His intermittent chortles echoed behind her as she strode off into the night.

Then, on the wind, she swore she could hear him say: '*Savoy cabbage market*! Hahahahaha....'.

43

THE FARM

I DIDN'T KNOW what we were going to find in the ruins of the Old Farmhouse.

We walked to within a hundred yards of the place. Parked out front was an ancient Zhiguli in mustard yellow. The paintwork was rusted over and the windscreen was smeared with bird shit. Nobody had driven that thing in years.

The building hadn't fared much better. The roof looked about ready to cave in while the gutters had already sagged. Decrepit was the word for it.

'Tiny's not here,' I said. There was no way the man had gone from living in the biggest bloody penthouse in London, right next to Hyde Park, to slumming it in a remote farmhouse that probably didn't even have running water and reliable electricity, let alone broadband.

The only good thing I could say was that the mobile phone signal worked surprisingly well. I had full bars on 4G. I double-checked the map for the third time. This was definitely the place. Polina had come here straight after our conversation. Why?

'Shall we knock?'

Tank grinned. '*Tak.*'

We kept ourselves low to the ground for the last stretch. The path was thick with plant life so I kept flicking my gaze from the floor to the front door and then over to the window. No signs of life.

When we were nearly there, I motioned for Tank to go ahead. If there was going to be a fight, I'd rather he got hit than me. Silly bastard did as I'd ordered. I held up three fingers. Three. Two. One.

Tank kicked out at the hinges of the door. It was so old that it splintered, rusty iron poking through. Another kick, more wooden shards flew everywhere. Several small bits embedded themselves in my face. I bit my tongue. It stung like buggery, but I couldn't make a noise. Not if there was someone inside.

Despite the fact that he must've taken far more than me, Tank didn't say a word. It was as if he was a machine. He kicked the door a third time. Then a fourth. Finally, it came off the hinges, falling inwards into the house and landing against the floor with a thud that rang out like a gunshot, launching a cloud of dust which obscured our view.

'Go!'

Tank did. He strode in, his arms tensed, ready to fight off anyone lurking inside.

Outside, a bird chirped.

Nothing?

Then, from my left, movement. A flash of silver metal. My brain didn't have time to work out what it was until the assailant closed the gap. He, or she, had appeared out of nowhere.

They were lightning fast.

But Tank was quicker. He threw himself in front of me, his hand seizing the knife wielder's wrist. The knife fell to the floor with a clang. I kicked at it, causing it to scuttle across the floor and out of the way.

The two men – and they were both men – grappled like two bears asserting dominance. Our assailant landed a few blows on Tank, but the bigger man won. Before long, Tank had him pinned up against the wall, his hand against his throat.

I picked up the knife. Now that the shock of the attack was wearing off, I looked around. There were piles of sacks around what was once someone's living room. Heroin. I'd recognise it anywhere. Memories flashed through my mind. I pushed them down. When I glanced at Tank, still pinning his victim against the wall with ease, I could see the desire in his eyes. He'd clocked the heroin too. I'd have to keep an even closer eye on him.

No doubt the sacks of it came in from Afghanistan. Virtually all heroin did. Ukraine wasn't the usual route for the stuff. I'd always heard rumours that it came through Turkey then on either through Greece, through Bulgaria and Romania, or through the Balkans.

Shipping it across the Black Sea was smart. Nobody was looking for smugglers breaking into a warzone. From there, the established routes – like the one Tank and I took to get into Poland – would make it easy to take it west to the main markets of Paris, London, and Munich. Throw in a few million refugees as cover and the job was even easier.

'Good work,' I said to Tank. He was staring down our assailant, his hand still locked around his throat. I motioned for Tank to release his grip just enough to let the man speak.

I turned to the man pinned against the wall and switched to Ukrainian. 'Who are you?'

From his face, I could see he understood. I'd half-expected to have to try and get by in Polish.

'Ol-Oleksander,' he stammered between gasps for air.

'You work for the Bakowskis.'

His eyes went wide. 'I... I work for Miss Polina.'

I raised my eyebrow. *Tiny's aunt* was running heroin into Europe. At her age. Impressive.

'She came to see you.'

'Y-y-es.'

'Why?'

He hesitated. 'She'll kill me.'

'Maybe,' I agreed. 'But you're faced with an obvious choice: be strangled to death here and now, or take your chances against an old woman. I'll give you ten seconds to decide.'

As I began to count down, he cracked.

'She wanted me to take a message when I deliver next shipment.'

Now we were getting somewhere. 'What message?'

'I don't know! It's on ... SD card. My pocket.'

He jerked his head towards the front door we'd kicked in. There was a coat trapped underneath it. I tugged it free, unleashing yet more dust. I sputtered as it came free. The coat was heavy, the kind laden down with many pockets.

'Inside... the... lining.'

A sensible precaution. I picked up a large splinter from the floor and ran it down the inside of the coat, shredding the lining to bits. Out fell a tiny MicroSD card. I'd never have found it if he hadn't admitted that it was there. No doubt whatever message was on it was heavily encrypted. It might even hold a cold wallet. Lots of guys use them, digital wallets, not connected to the net, stuffed with millions of euros in cryptocurrencies. No use without a password mind.

'Where are you supposed to take this?'

'To... London.'

'Where in London?'

He scrunched up his forehead. 'Not know yet. Polina tell me "location will come through three hours before sunset, will be within three hours of ///gifted.brains.helps". She give me security code to identify myself. Tell me contact have same code. Only give to them.'

That sounded exactly like standard Bakowski MO: location at the last minute to avoid an ambush, codes so you knew you were dealing with the right person.

Things never changed.

I opened my phone and pulled up the What3Words app to lookup where ///gifted.brains.helps was. St Paul's Cathedral. Central bloody London. No way was that the meet. It was just a starting point close to home.

Home. Tiny hadn't gone home to Ukraine, to hide out in the bombed-out ruins of Odessa. Nor had he gone to the relative safety of his aunt's home in Lviv. Fucking hell. We'd chased his ghost across most of Europe stopping in Paris, Spain, Ukraine and Poland, and then after all that, he'd bloody well gone back home to London, right back to where we'd damned-well started.

Now we had to do the same.

'Oleks,' I said. 'I need you to make the drop. We're coming with you. If you try anything – a call, a signal, whatever – my friend here will crush your balls and then choke you to death with what's left of them. You understand me.'

He nodded.

'Good. I assume you've got a burner somewhere. I'll be having that. Do exactly what I say and we'll get along just fine.'

44

GUERRILLA GANG WARFARE

THE SIZE of the investigation was set to ramp up immensely. Now that two protected persons, both former members of the Bakowski Syndicate no less, were missing or dead, the "limited" budget had to be expanded to cover a multi-agency taskforce. Gold, silver, and bronze commanders would need to be appointed. Everything the force did was hierarchical, almost military. No doubt Ayala would covet the gold commander job, putting himself in charge of overall strategy. He'd sit at the front of the Strategic Coordinating Group meetings, lording it over all and sundry. Then silver commanders would be appointed for each discipline – firearms, public order and the like. Finally, bronze commanders, at the bottom of the pyramid, would actually carry out that strategy.

It was going to be *huge*. The National Crime Agency couldn't afford for this to go public. If the press found out that "protected persons" weren't really that protected, they'd plaster it all over the front pages and then there'd be no King's Evidence for a generation. Gangsters wouldn't turn against their former *shef* if they thought they'd wind up dead anyway.

Even the fabled super-injunction – the strongest legal prohibition available in the UK – wouldn't help. It'd leak and foreign newspapers would love to take a pot-shot at British policing. With the media involved, these two deaths could massively enhance the power of criminal overlords. It was basic Hobbesian logic: might is right.

The best part was that all the evidence that had glitched or been "lost" before had miraculously been found. UKPPS had promised to make sure it was all delivered to the team by the end of the next working day. The chain of custody was fucked – they would never be able to explain the break in custody to a court without sounding insane – but at least it could be used for investigative purposes. Thank God the UK didn't use the "fruit of the poison tree" logic that their American cousins did. In the USA, all that ill-gotten evidence, and everything that flowed from it, would be completely inadmissible.

Before that could all kick off, Rafferty had to talk to the one man who would know what to do.

Unfortunately, Morton wasn't available.

So she'd have to suck it up and talk to Xander herself.

The last time she'd been to his flat was almost four years ago, but walking up Lamb Conduit Street in Bloomsbury, memories came flooding back. Images of Camden Pale Ale and home-made pies in The Perseverance Pub, of wandering down to Bea's bakery for a morning coffee and a slice of cake, and the many images of the inside of his flat just up from the People's Supermarket. She buzzed at ground level and he immediately let her in. By the time she'd climbed up the stairs, he was waiting for her in his front doorway.

'Ash,' he said. 'I've asked Kieran to join us.'

Twice the size of her own, Xander's flat was so sparsely decorated that it felt bigger still.

He'd repainted. The dark walls and wood panelling were gone as was the lingering smell of cigar smoke. Now, the flat was

Scandi clean, light wood everywhere, and there was enough off-white paint slathered over the walls and ceiling to make the place feel more coffee shop chic than man cave.

'Emma's moved in then.'

Xander grinned. 'That obvious, huh?'

Was that why he'd asked Kieran to join them? To spare her blushes? He needn't have bothered. The lawyer was sitting on one of two identical sofas in the open-plan living room. He had his head buried in his laptop as if concentrating on whatever was on screen rather than eavesdropping.

'Hi Kieran,' Rafferty said.

His head flicked up. For a moment, she thought she saw Facebook on-screen. 'Hi Ash.'

'Drinks!' Xander said. 'Whisky all round?'

'With a drop or two of water,' Rafferty said.

'Rocks for me,' the lawyer grunted.

Xander went off to pour the drinks and Rafferty took a seat on the second sofa. From her seat, she had a view back across to the kitchen where she could see Xander fiddling with the ice maker on the front of his fridge-freezer.

'You're such a heathen, Kieran.'

His gaze snapped up from his laptop. '*What?*'

'A,' Rafferty said, 'asking for a drink on the rocks makes you sound American, not Irish. B, you're supposed to drink it at room temperature.'

Kieran grinned. 'He's only got Bells. Emma's kiboshed the single malt collection, made him get rid of everything. Normally I'd agree with ya, but I can't stand the taste of the blended stuff.'

Her face dropped. What a bitch. 'Oi, Xander! Stick a can of Coke in mine, would you?'

Xander sauntered over grinning. 'He told you then. Sorry, I'm fresh out of Coke.'

He set down three glasses, all filled with more ice than Bells.

'*Sláinte!*' Kieran said as he grabbed his.

She held her nose as she sipped at it. 'What happened to your collection of Macallan? Emma didn't make you give it all away, did she?'

Xander scowled at an oblivious Kieran who'd turned his attention back to his laptop. 'Some bastard won it off me at poker night.'

The lawyer smirked. 'Shouldn't bet what you can't afford to lose. Now, when you two have finished flirting-not-flirting, can we get to work?'

It was as if Xander flipped a switch as soon as he booted up his own laptop. 'As you know, your victims, Elijah Zholnovych and Nathan Linden were members of the Bakowski Crime Syndicate who turned Queen's Evidence. What you won't know is that for the last ten years, I've been heading up Operation Songbird which was set up to investigate the break-up of the Syndicate.'

Rafferty gave a little shrug. 'It doesn't take a genius to realise SOCA would be after Tiny.'

'Well, you didn't know it was Operation Songbird, did you?' Xander pouted. He gestured towards the prosecutor. 'Kieran's here because his department oversaw the witnesses who turned against the Syndicate. Neither of us know the new identities of those witnesses but we have a laundry list of traitors.'

So that was it. Kieran knew which gangsters had turned Queen's because he'd overseen their testimony. That would've included seeing Zholnovych testify. Now those witnesses, under new names, were dropping dead and the rest could be next.

'You think Tiny's back and he's going after the turncoats.'

'*An té a luíonn le madaí, eiroidh sé le dearnaid,*' Kieran muttered.

'Eh?' Xander said.

'He who lays with dogs wakes up with fleas.'

Xander's confused expression melted into an appreciative smile. 'That's one way to say it. We've sunk thousands of man hours into Op Songbird and haven't had a whiff of his whereabouts. We had a tip at one point that he was hiding out at his sister-in-law's holiday home in Bucharest, but that turned out to be complete bollocks. He's managed to vanish without a trace. As far as we can tell, he's touched none of his stashed cash – and we found a few bags of old-style fifties at each of his properties so he wasn't short of the stuff.'

At the mention of old-style notes Rafferty smirked. There was a reason that bank note designs got changed every few years and it wasn't just to piss off the public. Swapping one or two at the bank was a minor inconvenience. Being stuck with millions in unlaundered, dirty, old-style notes was much worse. Every design change was a thorn in the side of organised crime.

'There's an obvious answer to that,' Rafferty said. 'Two people can keep a secret as long as one of them is dead.'

Kieran glared at her. 'You know part of my job involves keeping everything secret, right? It's a nice aphorism but we know the Bakowskis follow their own version of *omertà*.'

The lawyer was referring to the Italian mob's code of silence. Bit rich comparing it to legal professional privilege though. Not that arguing about it would get Rafferty anywhere.

'Fair enough,' she conceded before turning back to Xander. 'Who filled the power vacuum Tiny left behind?'

Xander squirmed awkwardly in his chair. 'That's the thing... Nobody.'

'Eh?'

She'd expected him to name one of the many other criminal groups: the Fitzgeralds, the Checkley Crew, or one of the many international gangs that would've loved to carve up the lucrative London market.

'Things just... carried on. Tiny left and his lieutenants just kept going. The same old faces, the same cons, the same import routes. We've banged up a handful, turned a few more into CIs, but nobody's given us a name. It's like the big organisation peacefully broke down into hundreds of little ones. No power struggles, no competition, not even a gangland territory dispute. Stabbings in places like Lambeth, Wood Green, and Ilford have actually *dropped* for the first time in forever.'

'And that's not just Covid?' Rafferty asked.

Xander shook his head. 'I thought the same but the drop started in 2012 and it's been sustained ever since. Tiny's people aren't killing each other. They're cooperating. It's the Uberisation of criminal gig work. The hit men are still killing. The dealers are still dealing. But nobody's taken Tiny's place at the top as far as we can tell.'

Rafferty sat back, stunned. A gang without a leader? Was that even possible? Surely Tiny had left a gaping power vacuum that his lieutenants would've been clambering over each other to fill. One of them must've wanted to become the next Mr Big.

'I doubted it too,' Xander said as if reading her mind. 'It seems Tiny didn't do things the way other criminal gangs did. His org wasn't structured like a pyramid with orders flowing down and money flowing up. Instead, he seems to have taken a leaf out of the terrorist playbook, setting up silos of isolated operations, each responsible for one job, one task, or one area with no overlap. No doubt people cooperated on things, talked to each other, but Tiny kept a tight rein on information. All over our informants have said the same thing: they operated on a need-to-know basis.'

It was bloody clever. Not only did it stop informants grassing on the whole organisation, it also kept competition within the Syndicate to a minimum.

'But we're not flying completely blind,' Xander said. 'We

know the scope of the Syndicate. It's huge. They've got drugs running up and down county lines, using kids to ferry things about. They're running brothels in all the major cities, often with trafficking victims forced to work in them. We know they've been running extortion rackets from Liverpool to Brighton.'

'It's huge,' Kieran said. 'My team and I are bringing twenty to thirty prosecutions a month against known members of the Syndicate and it's barely scratching the surface. We arrest one lemming and another pops up to take their place before we've even had a bail hearing. The courts are backlogged from the pandemic, criminal defence barristers are striking yet again, and my guys are getting burnt out with frustration.'

What a time to be alive, Rafferty thought. It was typical. The police busted their backsides bringing in the bad guys, risking their necks to do so, and then the lawyers walked out because they wanted to be paid more.

'If it is someone associated with the Syndicate,' she asked, dragging the conversation back to more salient points, 'how do we know who? And how do we find them and stop them? Whoever it is has managed to find – and murder – at least one, probably two protected persons. That shouldn't be possible.'

'It's unheard of,' Kieran said. 'Never before has even one witness in the programme been harmed.'

Rafferty didn't want to suggest the police had a Bakowski mole, but it was the most obvious explanation. 'Inside man?'

'Doubtful,' Kieran said. 'Each witness is assigned a handler who works in isolation just like Tiny's cells. Assuming you're right, that Zholnovych is dead, not just a feckin' misper throwing us off the right track, that would mean that our killer has compromised two separate handlers.'

'And there's no single point of failure? No database? No one lawyer reviewing everything?'

Before Kieran could get angry at another jibe, Xander leapt in. 'No. I'm not privy to every detail but my understanding is that everything is locked down. If there were a systemic issue like that, a single person who could be bribed or blackmailed, then there'd have been a break in the system much sooner. It's been running for decades, hiding witnesses from before Tiny Bakowski was born and it still will after he's dead. If the killer is finding them, it's not through us.'

'Then where does that leave my investigation?' Rafferty mused aloud. 'The killer has done what you're telling me is impossible.'

'First,' Xander said, 'find Elijah Zholnovych. This could all be panic over nought. Second, find out what the hell Linden had going on in his life that could've exposed him. Did he call an ex-lover? Talk to a cousin? Run into a Bakowski member on the street? I'll make enquiries of my CIs, see what word on the street is.'

Kieran drained his whisky. 'And I'll run interference with the press, get you whatever warrants you need, and liaise with UKPPS's in-house counsel to ensure they cooperate as far as they can.'

She'd been ambushed. The pair of them had concocted this plan before she'd even arrived. Not that she blamed them.

'Sounds like you've both got this all figured out,' Rafferty said. 'You guys do the easy bits; I'll go solve two murders. Easy peasy. Unless...'

'Unless what?'

'Unless Elijah Zholnovych disappeared because he's the killer,' Rafferty ventured, almost thinking as she went. 'If he somehow found Linden, either through the programme or by random chance on the streets of London, and then decided to kill him, he could have disappeared and then killed Linden before fleeing into the night.'

The men sat there, staring glumly. Her latest theory was plausible.

'Why, though?' Xander asked. 'If Zholnovych is our man, he's a bloody patient killer. Why wait eight years? And did the two of them even know each other? Sure, they were in the Syndicate but doing totally different gigs. Zholnovych was doing carousel fraud, laundering cash and the like; Linden was fencing stolen goods. The two don't mesh. Can you really imagine a white-collar criminal holding a grudge for eight years and then killing a man? His first violent offence is to torture a man to death? I don't buy it. It's far more likely that Tiny is back and is chasing down those who betrayed him. Mark my words, Tiny Bakowski will be at the end of this investigation. Find him and you'll have your man.'

It seemed they were in agreement. All she had to do was the impossible: work out how the killer was finding protected persons.

Before Tiny Bakowski struck again.

45

BACK TO BLIGHTY

WE TOOK the long way around for a second time, travelling with Oleks across Europe.

As insurance, we found out where he was from, where his family lived, and told him that we have people who will kill them if things don't go to plan. It's a lie. One I hope he hasn't clocked.

We let him put the heroin he'd been planning to transport in the car, and then, halfway home to London, an old friend of ours had liberated it from the boot while we were in a service station. Oleks was none the wiser. I was proud of that one. In one move, I'd solved several problems. Firstly, the heroin wasn't tempting Tank anymore. He'd been glancing longingly at the backpack ever since we'd left the farm. I knew if I gave him half a chance, he'd inject enough to kill himself. Secondly, it made getting through customs a doddle as we weren't smuggling so we wouldn't get caught coming back into Blighty. Thirdly, even with the generous discount I'd given my buyer for the unorthodox pickup, I'd added a hefty chunk of change to my Bitcoin wallet.

Seeing Oleks' reaction when we crossed from Calais to

Folkestone was hilarious. We'd gone through the French border, flashed our passports, and then been waved over by customs. Oleks had turned sheet white.

'Chill, kid, I've bribed the guard.'

I hadn't, of course. Didn't need to. The guard swabbed our car and two more and then took the rag back to test. Odd that. I'd always expected one rag per car. Suppose if it had come up positive, he'd have re-run the test to see which car was carrying drugs or explosives. He waved us through and Oleks looked at me with starry-eyed wonder.

By the time we got to the British border and the familiar welcome sign reminding us to drive on the left, Oleks was my biggest fan. He thought I was a drug-smuggling god.

Once we were back on dry land, it was plain sailing. There wasn't even much traffic. The only delays were the usual queues to get across the Dartford Crossing.

We made it to London six hours ahead of sunset but we hadn't had anything more about the location and wouldn't for at least three or four hours yet. Tank looked over at me as if to ask what to do.

'Keep driving, Tank. We can't wait here. Head up the Romford Road. Chiggs is out of the country so his place'll be empty.'

Chiggs was another Syndicate member. He'd barely joined when Tiny disappeared and it all came crashing down. He'd gone through The Ritual, the same one I had. Except for him, it was fixed so he didn't shoot his mother.

After Tiny's disappearance, Chiggs went freelance, running errands for cash. Eventually, he stumbled onto his current business model: keeping houses empty and renting them out for guys who need somewhere discreet to prep for, or lay low after, a crime. He joked it was a stay at HMP AirBnB. If they ever hear him say that, they'll probably sue.

His safe houses-for-hire are legit so I've used them a couple of times. He lets me keep a key to one of his digs on my keyring. Didn't think I'd need it this soon – I'd intended to use it to lay low after I'd killed Tiny – but needs must.

The other benefit is Chiggs ain't his real name so if Oleks cops it, no harm done. The nickname's from where he grew up: Chigwell.

We parked up outside and I ran in to disable the alarm and raise the garage door. Thank fuck there was space to park. As Tank and Oleks came in, I went back into the house to grab a knife as insurance in case Oleks tried anything. A gun would've been better but if Chiggs had one, it was well hidden. I debated texting him. Nah. Better not to leave a paper trail.

Tank manhandled Oleks into the house. The garage opened into the kitchen. I'd already moved the knife block out of the way when I'd borrowed one. No point leaving the rest on top of the island where anyone could grab one.

'*Zaspokoysya!*' Oleks protested.

Go easy.

'Let him go, Tank. He's not going to cause trouble, are you, Oleks?'

A vigorous headshake. Tank shoved him roughly forwards.

Then again. I hadn't had time to discuss a plan with Tank. Oleks was with us the entire way. We know there's a drop to be made at sunset. It's obviously either money, in the form of a cold wallet, or an encrypted message. I don't dare tamper with the SD card. One wrong move and it'll be wiped and then, even if Oleks does hand it off, we'll have shown our hand.

It won't be Tiny himself at the rendezvous. In all the years I knew him, he never got his hands dirty. Even when we were kids, he'd be the one sitting at the back of the class while his lackeys passed around bags of weed.

We'll have to watch. Shame I don't have another Bluetooth

tag. The old-fashioned way will have to do. Let Oleks make the hand-off, see who turns up to collect it.

And then follow them all the way back to Tiny.

46

THE MET'S FINEST

THE ZHOLNOVYCH CASE made more sense now.

Before going full-on with all and sundry investigating Zhol-novych, massively increasing the chances of a leak to the press, Rafferty decided to return to see Joe Singleton, the man respon-sible for the missing persons enquiry, on the off-chance that he'd made progress despite the interference by the UK Protected Persons Service.

She found him right where he was last time, sitting at his desk, a bored expression on his face. When he caught sight of her, he flashed the barest glimmer of a smile and then turned back to his monitor as if he hadn't seen her.

When she got to his end of the room, he gave another of his trademark sniffs. 'What? No bribe this time? Where's my Wigan Kebab?'

She shook her head. Not this again. 'Joe, it's ten o'clock in the morning. And I've told you, nobody in London sells them. It's literally carb on carb.'

He pretended to be offended. Clearly, he'd missed his calling as a stage actor. 'A,' he said slowly, 'it's always lunchtime somewhere.'

'Alas,' Rafferty interjected, 'not here. Wasabi isn't even open yet.'

Joe glanced at his watch. 'You could come back in a couple of hours.'

'And miss this banter?' Rafferty mocked.

'And b,' he continued as if he hadn't been interrupted, 'it can't be beyond the wit of the Met's finest to buy a pie, buy an oven bottom, and, I don't know, combine the two together somehow?'

'I suppose I could poke a hole in a pie and stuff the roll inside.'

'Do that and you'll never get a favour out of me ever again.'

More faux protest. Joe's stern glare melted into a toothy grin. For a man who was perpetually on desk duty, dealing with nothing but missing persons, the allure of working an actual murder was irresistible.

'Your case has been gnawing at me,' he continued. 'Come on, come on. Follow me.'

He grabbed at the wheels of his wheelchair, reversing away from his desk, then, smooth as butter, turned right through ninety degrees and made a beeline for a security door at the back of the open-plan office. His wheels spun so quickly that by the time Rafferty caught up, she'd almost missed the PIN code he entered into the terminal. If he hadn't had to fumble with holding the security badge around his neck up to head height, she'd have missed it.

'0502? Really?'

Joe glanced back over his shoulder. 'Robert Peel's birthday.'

Brodie would've gone nuts if he'd been there. It was such an obvious code. He'd drilled it into everyone in the Met who'd listen: random, random, random. Any pattern at all and a PIN wasn't much better than a bike lock.

Inside the secure area, there was a series of meeting rooms. They parked themselves inside an empty one and shut the door.

'After you left last time, I tried to forget about Zholnovych. I've dealt with thousands of missing persons but this one... it felt off.'

Rafferty resisted the urge to say "I told you so".

'So I asked around, casually, if anyone had heard of documents disappearing. Nobody had. What're the odds I pull the only case anyone's ever heard of where the missing person's files all go AWOL? Still, I ignored it. Then I heard that all the physical evidence had been "lost" so I spoke to my boss, asked how often that happened. Once or twice. Ever.'

'Those coincidences add up, don't they? They gnaw at you,' Rafferty said. 'I know it did for me.'

'And then I got told, off the record, to drop the investigation. Not in those words. My boss told me there was no budget to investigate. What bloody budget? I'm only spending my time and I can squeeze a few database searches into my hectic schedule easily enough.'

It was like déjà vu. Rafferty got told to kick it to MisPer. MisPer got told to boot it into the long grass.

And Rafferty knew why. But Joe didn't and it wasn't her place to tell him.

'I can sympathise,' she said. 'I've had the same sleepless nights you have.'

'So, I cross-referenced unclaimed bodies in the morgue,' Joe said. 'It's standard practice. We look at hospital admissions, credit card and bank activity, travel card history – Oyster is a goldmine – and then, when all else fails, unidentified bodies are the last resort.'

Dogged policework. The thankless kind at that.

'And?'

'And nothing. Your man's disappeared off the face of the

earth. We've got one mugshot of him from a passport issued two years ago. Nothing before or after that. No interactions with the state that I've got access to. Presumably, he filed tax returns, has a bank account somewhere, but even finding out that stuff requires a warrant.'

'And without any evidence, you can't get a warrant, leaving you spinning your wheels.'

As soon as she'd said it, Rafferty blushed and started to apologise. What a phrase to use around a man in a wheelchair!

'No need,' Joe said. 'It was an innocent slip of the tongue. If it helps, I can insult you a couple of times and then we can call it even. How's that sound, you lanky she-giraffe?'

Rafferty laughed. 'Nobody's ever insulted my height before. Not to my face.'

'Do they normally insult you to your chest instead? You know, I've only ever met one guy taller than you. Two Metre Peter, we called him.'

As soon as he said it, Rafferty's mind raced. Nicknames were a lot like criminal aliases... and poor Joe still didn't know that Elijah Zholnovych was as made up as Two Metre Peter.

UKPPS hadn't released his real identity yet either. Even when they did, she'd signed the Official Secrets Act. She didn't have the real name to share and couldn't tell Joe even if she did.

'Can you do me a favour?' she asked.

'Depends what it is.'

'Run a search for me on a guy called Nathan Linden, see what you can turn up. On the quiet if you don't mind. In particular, can you find out where he might've gone, maybe from his phone records?'

It was a long shot but if she had Nathan Linden's phone logs showing which masts his phone had connected to and the same activity information for Zholnovych's phone, she could see if there was any commonality, any place the two men could've run into each other. If so, then the idea that Nathan Linden had been murdered by Zholnovych would be much more credible. If not, nothing lost.

Joe arched a quizzical eyebrow. 'On the quiet?'

'So quiet that my bosses don't hear about it. If you can do that, there's a Wasabi every day for the next month in it for you.'

'Now that's a deal that's too good to turn down. Leave it with me.'

47

THE CHURCH OF ST PETER

IT WAS a good job I'd taken Oleks' burner phone. In the time we waited, there was a second What3Words code, this time sending us to Whipps Cross Hospital. Our safe house was near enough that I knew we could ignore it. Whoever Oleks was meeting was being exceptionally cautious, slowly moving us to the rendezvous without telling us exactly where it was. I'd have done the same if I'd wanted to avoid an ambush.

The final rendezvous code came in over Signal exactly three hours before the meet:

//curvy.sock.upper

Clever. Like the others, the third code looked like bloody nonsense, but that's the beauty of What3Words. The app divvies the world up into tiny squares, each with a random-looking string of words. When I looked up where the final meet point was, I smiled. I know it well: St Peter's in Aldborough Hatch. Several of the Syndicate's dead, those we didn't kill, are buried there.

It's nice but oddly rural. It's the sharp edge of London where city meets countryside. From where we parked up in the overflow car park of The Dick Turpin pub, just up the road, we could walk to the Tube in ten minutes.

But we're also right next to open fields. It makes this meeting risky. If we stick too close to Oleks, we'll be spotted. And people know us. Tank especially. It's hard to miss a man his size.

Too far though and Oleks could fuck off without us knowing who he handed the SD card to. If I'd had more time, I could've tried to get a dummy SD card, one with a virus on so we could be all cutesy and hand it over and then track who loaded the SD card. That would've been some James Bond shit.

As it is, we have to make do. Tank will have to wait in the car while Oleks goes to the meet. I'll follow from a distance and keep an eye on him.

If I were Tiny's contact, I'd check the bag straight away. As soon as that happens, Oleks will be a dead man. Shame. He seems like a decent kid.

Then Tiny's man will get suspicious. Hopefully, he'll assume Oleks stiffed them. Or someone on Polina's end. Otherwise, he might come looking for us.

Choices, choices. Stick nearby, get a good view, but potentially be seen. Or hang back, stick a mobile with an open phone-line in Oleks' pocket, and try and listen in.

The drop point itself isn't specific. Knowing Tiny, he'll have his man wait on the northern side of the church. It's away from the houses with a good view across the rolling fields to the north. He'll be able to spot Oleks coming.

'It's almost time,' I said. In less than ten minutes the sun would go down. The clouds had turned grey and a light drizzle was coming down. The weather threatened to get worse which would bugger up our visibility. I hoped it wouldn't.

Oleks gave a wan smile. 'This only my second drop. The first, I wait and wait. Then woman take bag and go.'

'Where was that?'

'Brussels.'

Polina really was distributing everywhere. I'd assumed that everything on the streets in Belgium would've come through Amsterdam, Antwerp or Algeciras, not via Lviv.

'You have the phone.'

He nodded. A burner, one of mine. I cleaned everything off it and showed him how to put it on mute, effectively turning it into a one-way radio. We tested it out in the car park, me walking away and listening to Tank and Oleks chatting while the phone was tucked inside his pocket. It worked, but audio quality was a bit shit.

'If they search you-'

'They no search me last time.'

'If they search you,' I repeated, 'say the words "I'm not carrying a gun" so we know.'

Letting Oleks go without us is a huge risk. One we have to take.

He could fuck us over by disappearing. If he hadn't believed my bullshit threat to kill his family anyway. Worse, he could rat us out to whoever his London contact is. If he tries that, we'll have to kill them both.

Twilight was coming.

'Alright,' I said. 'Game time.'

Oleks stumbled out of the car park with his bag. As we'd asked, he headed down the main road as if he'd been waiting in the pub. If his contact wasn't there, he'd meander around the graveyard and wait.

Meanwhile, I looped down through Fairlop Waters Country Park. Nobody would glance twice at a man walking along the footpath in the rain. I paused by the tourist sign to give Oleks enough of a head start. As soon as he started talking to his contact, I'd head out. Tank was listening on conference call from the car so if I needed backup, he was less than ninety-seconds away. The footpath led straight down to the main road, but if I needed to, I could jump the fence of one of the houses on Applegarth Drive and run around through the side passage to get there even quicker. As I waited, the light levels kept dropping. From experience, I knew it would be almost pitch black here before long; my brother and I used to hang out here. He'd smoke weed while I played. That was before Mum died.

I pushed down memories of the past and listened to my phone for Oleks' voice.

The wait seemed to go on forever. In reality, it was only twenty minutes before I heard a faint *pryvit*.

Oleks' voice. Then, in return, a woman's saying hello back. It was older, gravelly, and well-spoken. Definitely a smoker. The accent was pure Kyiv. I began briskly walking along the path. No point running just yet. I'd be there in less than two minutes and there was no point drawing attention to myself if I didn't need to.

'You have it?' The woman's voice. As I strained to listen, it sounded vaguely familiar. Threatening but well spoken. Quite an unusual combination.

'*Tak.* And this,' Oleks said.

I could imagine the scene. He'd have taken the backpack off, the one he thought was full of heroin but which was now full of bags of Tate and Lyle's finest.

The "this" he mentioned had to be the SD card that Polina had dropped off at the farm. We still didn't know what was on it. Probably never would.

'*Dyakuyu tobi.*'

Thank you. She must've taken it from him.

'*Nema za shcho.*' Don't mention it. Oleks' voice.

The next thing I knew, I heard a scream. A guttural,

piercing scream made worse by the tinny audio quality and the fact it lasted only for a split second.

Shit.

Had Oleks killed the woman? Or had she killed him? How?

I broke into a sprint. I knew that Tank would be doing the same.

At the main road, I skidded to a halt as traffic whizzed past. Drivers had put their headlights on and the contrast was blinding against the darkness in the fields. The church across the way was a dim shadow looming large across the road, visible only in short bursts between the traffic.

A car slowed as it approached. Against the full-beam headlights, I couldn't see much. Had Tank caught up with me already?

Then, it braked hard as it stopped on the wrong side of the road. The driver wasn't Tank. I caught a flash of a bald head illuminated by a car going past the other way.

It was over in a split second. A woman – I think it was a woman – opened the rear door on the far right-hand side of the car near the churchyard. It slammed shut a second later and the car sped off.

Then, another car. This time, my side of the road. Tank. He must've been trailing behind the getaway vehicle for a few seconds and not even spotted it.

'Follow that car!' I shouted, gesturing wildly.

He didn't hear me.

'The car,' I repeated. By now, the roar of its engine had become the faintest whine as it sped off.

We were too late.

I shook my head and gestured towards the church. Tank leapt from the driver's seat and led the way across the road, yet another car screeching to a halt in front of us and beeping loudly to underscore their frustration at Tank's parking. Once we were on the other side, I squinted into the darkness.

'Oleks?' I called out.

No reply.

'Let's split up,' I said. 'You take the side near the houses; I'll take the side near the fields.'

As Tank headed off, I carried on searching, looking for any sign of Oleks. The car had stopped almost dead outside. Had the woman been carrying a bag? I tried to replay the moment in my mind. It was all over so fast. I wouldn't have recognised the woman if she'd been my mother let alone a total stranger.

The car then. What did I see? It was an estate, a large one with very bright headlights. A double headlight. There were at least two bulbs. Maybe even three. Like a BMW? I wasn't too sure. Nor did the rear-view lights help much either. I wanted to say there was a big grille on the front but it was so fast I couldn't tell the make or model.

I should've tried harder, even if it was too dark to catch the plates.

'Over here,' Tank called out.

I rushed in the direction of his voice, near the back wall of the church, as far away from the road as possible. Tank was hunched over a gravestone, his enormous bulk blocking out what little moonlight there was illuminating the scene.

'Shove over, Tank.'

He did. Now that he wasn't blocking the light, I could see Oleks, lying on the floor surrounded by a pool of blood. The backpack we'd brought all the way from Poland, the one filled with bags of sugar to replace the heroin I'd flogged in Paris, lay next to him. He'd been stabbed in the thigh, right in the femoral artery. Poor sod would've been dead before he hit the ground. The knife, a small, metal one with a wicked-looking blade, glinted on the floor nearby. As I leant in to get a closer look, I could see where blood had spurted from Oleks' thigh to spray the ground dark red.

Then, almost in slow motion, a light flickered on illuminating the scene before me. The blood looked stickier, red, and somehow even worse than in the dim moonlight. As I twisted to look for the source of the light, my gaze fell on Oleks' face. His eyes were closed. If it weren't for the knife, I'd have sworn he was just sleeping.

I found the source of the light. The church. Someone was in the vestibule.

The side door swung open. Inside I could see a man wearing a dog collar. A man of the cloth.

'Move!' I hissed.

We did. I bolted for the field. Tank went the other way. No doubt he'd made a beeline for the car.

'Stop!' called a man's voice. I assumed it was the vicar.

As if we were going to listen to him.

Did he really want us to stop? If he thought we'd killed Oleks – and it sure as hell must've looked like it from where he was standing – then us stopping wouldn't have ended well.

I ran. And ran. And ran.

When I was sure nobody was following, I made a beeline for the Central Line.

No point calling Tank. I have to assume he's gone back to the safe house.

If he hasn't... well, there's definitely no point calling him if by some miracle the Met have managed to snatch him up already.

No doubt in a few hours, they'll be swarming all over the borough.

That's a problem for tomorrow.

48

ANOTHER DAY, ANOTHER DEATH

THE PREVIOUS DAY'S meeting with Joe was weighing on her mind when Rafferty arrived at work. Another incident room was being set up. Inside, DS Mayberry was pinning documents to a board.

'A-A-Ash?' Mayberry stammered when he saw her.

'What's going on?'

She looked at the board. A printout of a crime scene, this time a church, was in the middle. Around it were a map of the area marked with CCTV and ANPR cameras, a close-up of the victim in situ, and a handful of administrative documents. The Senior Investigating Officer was listed as Detective Chief Inspector Bertram Ayala.

Damn. Ayala had gone himself? She glanced at her phone. No missed messages. Why'd he taken an overnighter? It wasn't like him not to delegate the crap jobs.

'D-Dead guy f-found in Ald-Ald-Aldborough Hatch.'

'Where's that?'

Mayberry pointed at the map. 'N-near Fair-Fair-Fairlop Waters.'

Ilford. East London. Out on the Central Line where the

ancient Hainault Forest divided London from neighbouring Essex.

That explained it. Gang central. From the photos, the victim had been stabbed to death. Garden variety for that part of London.

What it didn't explain was Ayala's involvement. Rafferty shrugged it off. Maybe he knew it was an easy win, a case to cover himself in glory. Or, more optimistically, he was leaving her to crack on with the Linden and Zholnovych investigations.

'When you're done here, can I borrow you?' she asked Mayberry. 'We've had all the missing evidence delivered to the incident room so we've got a busy morning ahead.'

She left Mayberry to set things up, called out for a delivery of coffee and pastries from her favourite French bakery, *Des Rêves et Du Pain*, and then settled in for a busy day of dealing with mountains of paperwork, coordinating with all of the others involved, and, most importantly, reviewing the previously missing evidence that UKPPS had seen fit to intercept.

Now that the cat was out of the bag, they had all the evidence that they should've had months ago. Everything that had been suppressed in Zholnovych's file had reappeared, ready for Rafferty to play catch up and read through the blood spatter analysis, the DNA report, and the results of the gunshot residue test. She started with the latter as it was on the top of the pile.

Rafferty slipped the report from the envelope, the outside of which was marked CONFIDENTIAL: EYES ONLY. Kflom had swabbed the carpet. If a gun had been fired as he'd expected, the tests would be positive for a mix of elements including antimony, barium, silicon, and lead. A positive test meant someone had fired a gun, or, perhaps less likely, set off a firework, nearby shortly before the swab was taken.

No evidence of gunshot residue.

Crap.

Rafferty frowned.

Kflom was wrong.

Wasn't he?

Maybe the GSR test had come back negative because too long had elapsed. Wasn't the rule four to six hours for gunshot residue on a person? How long did it last on carpet? They'd visited the scene on a Wednesday but the victim had been missing, presumed dead, since Monday.

She quickly flicked through the stack of paperwork, looking for the blood spatter analysis report.

'Aha,' she muttered to herself as she found the right envelope. The report was in the same format as the first, a title followed by the usual preamble after which there were black-and-white photos of the scene. Kflom had been certain that it was high-velocity blood spatter, or, in lay parlance, the result of a gunshot. She quickly discarded the preamble pages in favour of the conclusion.

Rafferty skipped over the bumph and scanned down until she saw the conclusion.

Low-velocity blood spatter.

Shit.

Kflom *was* wrong.

Nobody had been shot.

And with that, her case theory went out the window. Now she couldn't prove anyone had been shot or that anyone had died. The evidence was pretty much exactly as Ayala had neatly summarised it all those months ago: a middle-aged man disappeared. Then someone else moved into the house. If it weren't for the fact that they now knew that Elijah Zholnovych was a made-up name, the identity of an unknown protected person, then the case would have been kicked back to Joe to leave on his mountain of low-priority cases to be forgotten until such time as the Met had near-limitless resources and manpower. As if that was ever going to happen.

Raffety turned her attention to the third of the missing reports: DNA analysis of the blood spatter. Again, she raced to find the conclusion first:

Unknown male.

Not the victim. Nor a relative. Nor anyone in the damned system.

How the hell did someone manage to commit a murder without having first been caught for a lesser offence? It was like accelerating from nought to a hundred in the blink of an eye. Unheard of even.

Unless the blood had nothing to do with Zholnovych's death at all. It could've been an innocent cut. Or not so innocent but the unknown man could've been a victim rather than a perpetrator.

It was too much. Rafferty sank forward, putting her forehead down on the desk.

The case theory was already looking weak. Now it looked beyond repair. If it weren't Zholnovych's blood on the floor, then there was no evidence at all that he was dead.

And yet her gut kept screaming otherwise. Two men in witness protection, both former members of the Bakowski Syndicate. That couldn't be a coincidence.

What other information was in the pack? The disappearance had happened so long ago that she no longer had a mental checklist of what she'd hoped to find and what she hadn't yet got around to. That woman in the Angora sweater, Rosie Bray, floated into her mind. Rafferty flicked through looking for any sign of a witness statement from her. Nada. There was one from Fred Albright, but she'd already read that. Odd. Maybe it was only her notes about Bray that made it onto the system. After all, hadn't Bray demanded expenses to voluntarily come down to the station? What a strange woman.

Phone records then? What about those? Another sift through the pile. As she was looking, she remembered her coffee. A quick glance showed it was no longer steaming. She tentatively sipped at it. Freezing.

No sign of the phone records. Rafferty pulled up her phone, dialled Brodie's number, and then, when the call went to voice-mail, left a message asking him to finally carry out all the searches she'd asked for months ago. She needed to know where Zholnovych's phone had been, who he'd called and been called by, who he'd exchanged text messages with, and what data he'd used. No doubt Zholnovych was like everyone else and used Whatsapp or Telegram or some other encrypted app, but with a bit of luck there'd still be location data showing which telephone masts he'd connected to using the phone. That alone could show where he might've gone, who he might've talked to. If she were really lucky, comparing Zholnovych's phone with Linden's would show they'd been in the same place at the same time.

It was the same approach that she'd discussed with Joe. He hadn't had much luck but there was a slim chance that Brodie – who had extensive IT resources, forensic investigation training, and had signed the Official Secrets Act so knew the whole picture – might be able to find something that Joe hadn't. That wasn't to knock poor Joe but this wasn't a fair fight.

Besides, Brodie would probably come back and say they were many months too late. How long did mobile phone opera-tors keep that data for? It wouldn't be forever and the case was now seven months old.

Rafferty got up, strode over to the warming plate where the Met kept a jug of insipid coffee on the boil at all times, and poured herself a fresh cup. As usual, fresh was relative. One sip told her this batch had been on the boil for hours.

An intern. That's what she needed. Someone to fetch coffee, sort papers, and deal with all the crap parts of being in the Met: the endless meetings, the compliance donkeywork, and kissing Ayala's arse.

She grinned and downed the coffee. As much as she hated it, she was her own intern. All the responsibility, none of the freedom, and very little of the credit. That was the lot of any inspector working for a narcissistic career-climbing boss... which was most of them. There had to be good bosses out there – Morton had been brilliant – so why did suck-ups like Ayala get promoted beyond their capabilities?

Whatever.

Back to the pile.

ANPR records. This was a behemoth of a folder.

She cracked it open. The work was comprehensive. In the front was a map of Balham, centred on Zholnovych's home. Each ANPR, or automatic number plate recognition, enabled camera was marked with a CCTV camera symbol.

There were a few about. None were on the cul-de-sac itself which explained the deluge of paperwork. Whoever had compiled this hadn't been able to home in on just one pinch point. That would've been much easier. Instead, they'd cast a wider net, looking at the main roads and all the smaller roads leading to and from the cul-de-sac. There were dozens of possible approach routes, and consequentially, almost as many relevant cameras each of which could have caught someone coming or going from Zholnovych's home.

Talk about a needle in a haystack.

Each camera had a report which listed the registrations of the vehicles that had gone past, the time they did, and the make / colour combination that the DVLA had on file for that reg.

Lots of assumptions in there. First, that the killer, if there was one, had gone past a camera. Looking at the map, Rafferty could see several camera-free routes. A smart criminal could've worked out a route to avoid them – if they could find a resource listing where they were. Sometimes, the locations of cameras were recorded on public maps on Google. Privacy protest groups in particular had a bee in their bonnet about them and would go out of their way to keep abreast of the latest cameras installed, which way they faced, and such.

Second, that the killer had gone past in the timeframe covered by the report. They knew, from Rosie Bray's interview, that a delivery van had gone to the house. Whether or not that van had anything to do with Zholnovych's disappearance was still up in the air. If that van wasn't relevant, Rafferty would have to cast a very wide net which would catch every legitimate resident, visitor, and passer-through.

Sod it. There had to be a digital copy of this. Rafferty fired up her laptop, hopped over to HOLMES and searched through the Zholnovych case file. There was an entire folder marked ANPR now, one dated for earlier in the year which had reappeared as if it had always been on the system.

'Much better,' Rafferty said to an empty incident room.

'W-what is?'

Startled, Rafferty jumped to her feet, catching her coffee cup with her hand as she did.

'Fuck!'

It was a good thing she'd almost finished it and even more lucky the cup was well away from her laptop. A couple of the nearest files soon soaked up the dregs.

'S-sorry,' Mayberry muttered.

She shook her head. 'How long've you been there?'

'J-just a m-minute.'

'Whatever.' Rafferty sat back down and turned her attention back to the screen. There was an HDMI cable in the middle of the table that ran through to the room's projector. She plugged it into her laptop and put the ANPR files on the big screen so Mayberry could see too.

'W-what're we l-looking for?'

'Remember the Zholnovych disappearance?'

He nodded.

'The van that Rosie Bray described. All she remembered was a "white van", so we get to scan through every white van that went within half a mile of the crime scene on the day that Zholnovych disappeared.'

'A-a-alleged crime scene,' Mayberry corrected. 'And a-a-alleged d-disappearance.'

'I see you're still following the letter of the law as laid down by our Great and Bountiful Supervisor.'

He ignored her comment and pulled his own laptop out of his bag. She watched as he opened up a copy of the same Excel files she had on screen.

In silence, they scanned through. Rafferty alternated between the spreadsheet and the DVLA's database.

'A-Ash?'

'Yeah?'

'T-this one.'

Mayberry took a laser point from his pocket at aimed it at the projector screen to highlight a row on the spreadsheet detailing a white Ford transit seen going along Balham High Road. It was, among dozens of such Ford vans, totally unre-markable.

'What about it?'

'It's c-c-cloned.'

That got her attention.

'Show me.' She unplugged the HDMI cable and passed it over so he could hook his own laptop up.

Slowly, he brought up the DVLA's page showing the van's information. It was registered to an electrician up in the commuter village of Cuffley, a good half hour's drive north-east of them.

'And?'

'A-and the p-p-plate was caught on c-camera in W-W-Welwyn less than tw-twenty minutes later.'

Bingo. Cloned plates. There was no way the van could've been in Balham, south London, and then magically made it to Welwyn, a town in Hertfordshire, a mere twenty minutes later.

Someone had taken the plates from a legitimate Ford transit, presumably the one caught on camera in Welwyn and copied them, then put them on a matching model. That made it look like the same van was in two places at once.

'Nice try cloning a van from another county.' Hertfordshire was outside the Met's jurisdiction. Unluckily for criminals, the ANPR database was national and accessible by all of the country's forty-three police forces.

'M-m-maybe stolen?'

No maybe about it. Nobody cloned a plate and used it on their own car or a rental that could be traced back to them.

'Look into that. I want to know when and where it was stolen. With a bit of luck, our killer – and it's looking that way if someone stole and cloned a van just to visit the house, so don't go shouting alleged at me again – will be on camera nicking the van.'

49

REST IN PEACE

FUCK.

Oleks' death wasn't unexpected but I'd never expected it to be so quick.

The drop had to be a botch job: we'd only known where it was at the last minute so there was no time to do anything clever or call in reinforcements.

But for the woman to have killed Oleks so God-damned quickly, without so much as a word in anger or time to taste the product and realise we'd switched it out... that could only mean one thing: she knew.

She knew the drugs weren't in the bag. That's why she'd left it behind. Then, bloody moron that he is, Tank brought it back with him. His bloody addiction – and his inability to think for more than ten seconds at a time – had cost us again. Had he forgotten we'd sold the drugs? Bloody addicts.

We're fucked. A witness saw us with Oleks' corpse. We'd legged it from the scene with evidence.

A total clusterfuck.

And we don't have shit to show for it.

We'd regrouped at Chiggs' safe house. Tank beat me there

as he had the car. No point going straight home if the police thought we'd done it. The bloody vicar. He saw Tank and I running away from a dead body. No doubt by now we're on the Met's radar, or a description of us at least. We'll have to work out what to do about that later. For now, we have one big question to answer: who was the bloody woman? An accomplice of Tiny's, obviously. But how many older women are cold-blooded killers?

'Tell me again, Tank. What exactly did you see?'

'I saw woman. Silver hair. Black car. Then I pull over and you tell me to follow but it too late.'

I rolled my eyes. The last time I'd asked him this, he'd sworn blind it was a silver car and a woman with black hair. I felt like I was watching that stupid Dancing Gorilla skit on YouTube, the one where people are throwing a ball back and forth and it asks you to count how many times they threw it and then asks if you'd noticed the damned gorilla. The first time I saw it, I'd sworn blind that it was all bollocks, until I'd replayed it and seen the dancing gorilla for myself.

The car was, in my memory black, so if Tank had seen something black and something silver, then the woman had silver, or grey, hair. Weird.

'And the plate?' I prompted again.

Tank leant back on the sofa and shut his eyes, squinting as if trying to make out the number plate. 'LB22.... Something something something. I think.'

He sounded unsure.

LB is a London code. Fat lot of good that'd do us. 22 means a car sold between March and August this year. A new, black car registered in London. That narrows it down a bit but nowhere near enough for us to work out who the driver was.

If Tank's right that is.

'Now, timings. You heard the scream when I did.'

Tank nodded.

'Then what?'

'I drove. Fast.'

I pictured it. The car park was maybe five-hundred feet up the road from the church. Two minutes max.

'Then?'

'Then I see car ahead,' Tank said. 'Only notice because is on wrong side of road. I think "idiot". Silly woman, getting in.'

'The black-haired woman getting into the silver car.'

'*Tak.*'

His eyes shot open.

'No!' he said. 'Black car, silver hair woman.'

He was much surer now. But was that just the repetition?

'Then, we go to graveyard. I find Oleks, dead on floor. You come running when I call. Then, priest appear.'

'Vicar,' I corrected. 'Carry on.'

Tank ignored me. 'Priest yell to stop. You run. I run. We come back here.'

'Did you touch the body? Or the knife?'

He sat up, his brows furrowing. 'I... It happen too fast. I grab backpack.'

Great. If Tank left his DNA, or worse, his prints on the murder weapon or on the body, we'll be hard-pressed to explain that no, we didn't kill him, we just set him up for trafficking sugar. What court would believe that?

'I no touch knife,' Tank proclaimed.

He looked at me earnestly. He was telling the truth. Thank fuck for that.

'But why the hell did you grab the backpack?'

'Need take drugs back.'

I bloody knew it. He stole back a backpack full of Tate and Lyle thinking it was his next hit. I suppose it stopped the police realising what went down.

'We'd already sold the drugs, you dumbass.'

'Oh... yeah.'

I want to lash out. To yell. But it won't get me anywhere. Tank wasn't thinking straight. And I still need him, for now. But he's quickly becoming too big a liability. Between the overdose after our trip to The Happy Plaice and this mistake, Tank's addiction has properly derailed our plan.

Another loose end I'll have to deal with. Not that binning a bag full of sugar was going to rouse suspicion.

'Well,' I said finally, 'we'd best hope the meet location was clean.'

By clean, I meant free of CCTV. Normally, the Syndicate was meticulous about handoffs. They had to be in high-traffic areas, ideally on a major A road so that any ANPR evidence would be lost in a mountain of other traffic, but without any CCTV or ANPR covering the location itself, I could see why the mystery woman had chosen the church. Great vantage points, generally no CCTV on church properties, and definitely none at St Peter's, and very few visitors go to a graveyard after sunset. Then there were the very fields I'd legged it across. Nothing but dog walkers around and they don't tend to venture off the path after dark.

'So what we do now?'

'First,' I said, 'we get the petrol cans out of the car. This place is tainted. If the cops are after us, they'll find it sooner or later. We came from here. Then we came back here – and not together either. That's three trips between us. If they find any trace of us on any one of those, they'll be back here in no time.'

Chiggs is gonna kill me. Renting a safe house is one thing. Torching it is a whole 'nother ball game.

Tank looked unfazed. He'd played this game before. Funny how torturing men for a living makes everything else look tame.

'Then?'

'Then we find the woman.'

'How?' he demanded.

I've no idea.

'First things, first. Petrol. We're gonna need this place to go up too quick for the firefighters to save it. What has Chiggs got stored that we need to rescue first?'

Tank shrugged. 'I go look.'

'You do that. I'll go syphon a few parked cars.'

Old school but it beats going to a petrol station and winding up creating another trail of evidence. Fucking amateur hour that. If I've got to clean up, I'll go full scorched earth.

Literally.

50

WAXY

THE SECOND BATCH of files arrived right before the end of the working day. Among them, Rafferty found a few heavily redacted details of Elijah Zholnovych's life.

He'd entered the programme in 2012 with his then-wife, Wasylyna. That was her real name, not the pseudonym that she'd been hidden under. She'd voluntarily left the programme – and presumably her husband – less than eighteen months after going into hiding.

She hadn't been convicted of anything. No criminal record whatsoever.

From what Rafferty could gather, she'd left him and gone straight back to their home town of Ilford. A quick conference call with Brodie had confirmed it. He'd been unable to find a residential address, but she was on HMRC's records as being a PAYE employee of STARLIGHT (Ilford) Ltd.

It wasn't a business Rafferty had heard of. Google showed an address in an unsavoury part of town, sandwiched between a dive bar and a kebab shop. On Streetview, the only visible marker was a brown door with the name of the business stamped on it in subtle, grey lettering.

It didn't take a genius to work out it was a strip club.

After work, Rafferty headed home, showered, and then got dressed up for a big night. She resisted the urge to invite Mayberry or Ayala to go with her. That would've been hilarious. Instead, she headed over to Ilford by Uber at half past eleven. On the way, traffic was slow. A column of smoke rose in the distance. That had to be a *huge* fire.

By the time she arrived, Starlight was guarded by two burly looking bouncers.

'ID, love?'

She smiled. She hadn't been carded in well over a decade.

'I'm almost forty,' she said as she flashed him her driving licence.

The bouncer looked her up and down and then wolf-whistled. 'Love, you could've fooled me.'

He stood aside to let her pass. Inside were stairs. She headed up. As she did, she could've sworn she heard the first bouncer say to the second "Damn girl, that ass" but when she looked behind her, he was staring dead ahead.

At the top of the stairs, the lights turned dim. A kiosk, like an old-fashioned cinema desk, greeted her. A bored-looking woman in her fifties sat behind.

'Welcome to Starlight. Entry's twenty quid.'

Bit steep, Rafferty thought as she delved into her handbag in search of her purse. She pulled out an old-style paper twenty.

The woman tutted disapprovingly. 'Plastic notes only.'

'Err... you take card, right?'

The woman rolled her eyes, glanced at the card machine, and then relented. 'Gimme the old note.'

After handing over the technically out-of-date but still serviceable note, Rafferty headed into the club. To her right were tables set into low-walled booths, a bit like Nando's, except the tables were full of men in their forties and fifties and the food didn't look quite as edible. At the nearest table, a handful of Japanese businessmen were working their way through a bottle of Glenfiddich while a plate of chips, virtually untouched, sat in the middle of the table.

Ahead of Rafferty, at the far end of the club, was a door marked toilets. Beside it was a curtain guarded by a velvet rope. Presumably that was the VIP area.

Then, to her left, the main stage. Right now, a bored-looking girl in her twenties was on it, grinding her crotch against a metal pole that ran from the ceiling to the floor and pretending to enjoy it. The sounds of Def Leppard blared over the sound system.

'Pound in the jar, pound in the jar.'

Rafferty turned one hundred and eighty in the direction of the speaker. Another girl, this one as skimpily dressed as her colleague on the stage, was meandering away from a bar that Rafferty hadn't noticed. She was shaking a pint glass full of pound coins as she moved from man to man, group to group. Each time, the glass grew fuller.

Finally, she reached Rafferty. 'Pound in the jar, love.'

'Err... what?'

'Pound in the jar. That's the price of the show.'

Damn it. She didn't have much change on her.

'ATM over there,' the woman said, jerking her head towards the corner. 'I'll be back.'

Twenty-one pounds and fifty pence later, Rafferty returned with a single note. What a bloody con. A pound fifty to get out her own money. She grudgingly handed it over to the woman who popped it inside her bra and then gave Rafferty a shower of one-pound coins by way of change.

She was about to go and harass the next punter when Rafferty stopped her. 'I'm looking for someone. Wasylyna.'

'Who's asking?'

'I'm an old friend. Her ex-husband is causing trouble again.'

'Right. Well, Waxy's working in the VIP area. You'll have to book a dance. Fifty quid for ten minutes.'

Rafferty scowled.

'It's either that or fuck off.'

'Fine,' Rafferty said. 'Cash only I presume.'

'You got it, babe.'

Another one pound fifty surcharge and fifty quid in actual cash later, Rafferty was shown through to the "VIP" room. Funnily enough, it looked just like the other room except it was smaller and the air was pungent with the smell of spirits and too much air-freshener. Several women were sitting around in booths, just waiting for customers.

An older-looking woman sauntered over. She had platinum-blonde hair, caterpillar-thick eyebrows, and hollow, dead eyes that contrasted against a perfect Hollywood smile. The closer she got, the thicker the smell of cheap whisky became.

'Candy tells me you are here for me. Funny, I do not get many women. Come, come.'

She led Rafferty past yet another curtain until they found themselves in a long corridor with doors on either side. It felt a bit like going to the interrogation suites in the Met, only with the added smells of champagne and vomit instead of just vomit. They went through one of the doors to a small room with a low, round love seat, a pole, and a small speaker. Waxy hit play, blaring Hot in Here out of a tinny, bass-less sound system. At the same time, she hit the button on a timer starting a ten-minute countdown that displayed on a red LED screen.

'Take seat.'

'No thanks,' Rafferty said standing just inside the doorway. 'I'm not here for a dance.'

A panicked look came over Waxy. 'You're a cop.'

Smart lady. Rafferty nodded.

'I am. But I'm not here to cause trouble.'

'Cops. They always say this.'

'Ten minutes. I'm paying you for it and you don't have to dance.'

They locked eyes. Waxy knew the alternative was that Rafferty would slap the cuffs on her and throw her in the cells for prostitution. Nobody could prove that, but it wouldn't stop Rafferty from wasting Waxy's time and getting her in trouble with the club owner.

'Fine, what you want to know?'

'Your ex-husband.'

'Who?' Mock indignation.

'Elijah Zholnovych.'

It was like a secret handshake. Rafferty knew the man's programme name. That was all it took to get Waxy to open up.

The fire in her eyes grew. 'Not ex. Separated. Is not possible to sue for divorce while he in the programme and I am not.'

Huh. That wasn't a problem Rafferty had ever considered. She'd assumed there'd be some sort of sealed court proceedings to deal with that sort of thing. It didn't matter.

'He's dead.'

'No!'

The vehement response, absolute denial, told Rafferty everything. Either Waxy was an Oscar-worthy actress or she had no idea what had happened to her husband in the last few years.

'How?' she demanded. 'His heart? Is how his father died.'

Not the most useful titbit but Rafferty filed it away none-theless.

'That's to be confirmed,' Rafferty said. The clock was ticking so Rafferty steered the conversation back to where she wanted it. 'You left the programme. Why?'

'He bore me. Before, we did things. We travelled. We saw the world. He used to excite me. To make me happy.'

There was a sad smile on her face. That was what she'd missed: the lifestyle of a rich mobster's trophy wife. She wasn't outright saying it, but she might as well have said she loved the money, the drugs, and the danger.

'Then, in the programme,' she continued, 'we do nothing. We stay in. We watch television. No go out. Is no life.'

It sounded miserable. Years of being stuck inside, afraid of your own shadow, unable to enjoy life. It was a life not lived.

'He wasn't violent then?'

'Him?' Waxy scoffed. 'Never. He weak. When I leave him, he cry like little girl. Officers tell me, no go, stay. It no safe. But I do nothing. I come home. Get job here. Live a little.'

Rafferty's gut churned. Something was off about the story. It wasn't that Zholnovych had cried. She wouldn't judge a man for that. She might even buy that he was genuinely non-violent. His work for the Bakowski Syndicate appeared to be that of a paper-pusher, the man who took their ill-gotten gains and ran it through real businesses – like Starlight – to turn it into tax paid, legitimate earnings.

'Just like that?'

Waxy slapped one hand against her thigh. 'Like that. I come home. I get job here.'

'And then-'

Before Rafferty could finish her sentence, the buzzer went. Her ten minutes were up.

'Another ten? For you, forty quid.'

Rafferty shook her head. She hadn't learnt much in ten minutes and doubted twenty would yield much more. Ayala was never going to let her expense any of it. If Starlight were a Bakowski front, Xander would be able to look into that.

She pulled a card from her wallet and held it out. 'If you

hear of anyone asking after your husband, would you let me know?'

Waxy demurred. 'I can't take that.'

No less than Rafferty expected.

'But I can take photo with phone, yes?'

Rafferty nodded. When Waxy had finished taking a photo of, and then handed back, her business card, she was ushered back out of the VIP area. The trip to Starlight hadn't been a complete bust but she somehow felt that she'd missed something.

Perhaps it was just Waxy's manner. Or maybe it was the dead-eyed looks of the other girls. Rafferty made a note to ask Xander if it was still the case that most women doing sex work were victims of trafficking. If it was, she knew the next business to put on his shit list.

She made her way back to her car. There was something off about Ilford, about the club, and about Waxy herself.

And she was going to find out what.

51

WHITE CITY

BEFORE WE'D LEFT, I'd taken the plates off the stolen car so we could put them on someone else's car. That'd send the cops on a royal goose chase.

Then we'd set the timer. A lit cigarette, three matchsticks, paper and a rubber band, the Glendale Special. Simple, but effective. It'd bought us enough time to get well away from the house before the inevitable happened.

I'd arranged a lift with a local minicab firm. They picked us up from the Ilford Exchange, a two- and a-bit mile walk from the house. Far enough to obscure the trail, close enough to be convenient. He'd dropped us off at the Sky Garden and we'd walked to the Tube at Liverpool Street from there.

One quick trip on the Central Line later, we surfaced in White City.

'Remember what I said, okay?'

Tank nodded. Mute as ever.

As well as being famous for what used to be the BBC Television Centre, White City was also home to the largest car dealership in London, probably in all of bloody Europe. I'd typed up a list of the most common car manufacturers on my phone.

Everything from Ford and Volkswagen to Chevrolet and Abarth. We had nearly fifty in total.

The plan was simple: we each take a copy, then go around all the cars looking at recent models and seeing which, if any, jogged our memories. After that, we'd compare notes.

What I hadn't planned on was an incredibly on-it salesman spotting me a mile away despite the vast size of the place. It was so big they'd divided it up into lettered lots, A for Mercedes, B for Lexus, and so on. Each lot had its own warehouse section, its own security guard, and a rat warren of tiny roads connected it all up. There was even an on-site restaurant. Anything to keep the punters from leaving. I should've been able to dodge being collared by a bloody salesman.

'Good morning, sir!'

The salesman looked to be about ten. He was wearing an ill-fitting suit, one of those no-iron shirts that really does need ironing, and a polyester tie. Poor sod probably made less than a tenth than what one of the Syndicate's weed dealers would make. And he had to stand in the pouring rain for it.

'Alright,' I said. Maximum geezer accent today. Proper East End. I didn't want him to remember me, but if he was going to, I'd rather he remember a dodgy accent than anything useful.

'I'm looking for a saloon, something a bit fancy, almost new. Got anything like that? Upmarket, ex-lease sort of thing?'

'What make?'

I knew he'd ask me that. I shrugged. 'I'm flexible. I like something with a big grille on the front and an equally big engine on the inside.'

'A buyer after my own heart!' the kid said. 'And, ballpark, what's your monthly budget?'

Monthly?

Oh yeah. Of course. He wanted to sell me financing. No doubt they made a ton of commission on that.

'I'm a cash buyer.'

His face fell.

'And your budget, sir?'

I hesitated. Whoever had killed Oleks had a fancy car and a driver, just as I'd expect for someone bringing heroin into London. They'd be raking in millions.

'Low six figures,' I said airily. Ironically, I actually could find that sort of cash. Between the money I'd nicked off Tiny years ago and the take from the heroin we'd nicked from Oleks, I was pretty flush.

His eyes lit up again. I could see the pound signs flashing away. A small percentage of a big number was still a big number.

'That buys me a big grille, right?' I said.

'Wow. I think you're the first customer that's ever started with the grille. Okay, we've got a Ford Raptor 4x4 that-'

'Saloon,' I repeated. 'Not a 4x4. Not an estate. Just saloons.'

'Right... Well, Aston Martin? Lexus? Bentley?' He reeled off names faster than I could think.

I shook my head. 'Nothing too flashy. I want comfort, I want style. I don't want it too sporty.'

He paused as if to think. 'Rolls-Royce Phantom?'

Now there was a car I'd have in a heartbeat. Pure, unadulterated class. But I knew it had a super square grille, a giant R, and a huge hood ornament. I shook my head.

'Something a little cheaper.'

He looked around and then pointed to Lot D over the other side of the trunk road. 'BMW? Audi?'

'More like it,' I said.

'Let's go take a look then.'

We started with the Audi, an R8. It was stunning. Sleek lines, a rich sapphire blue, and, as I'd asked, a big bloody grille on front. It was too angular with a honeycomb-like lattice. I wanted something more like a half moon, maybe with up and down lines.

He could tell I wasn't impressed. I tried to describe the shape I wanted.

'Err. What about the G80?'

A Hyundai. When he showed me it, I stopped. It was so close. There was the right grille shape, sort of. This time though, it had a diagonal lattice. Close, but no cigar. It was also much too cheap.

'Another question: what've you got that's bulletproof?'

I may as well as have said we were playing the game "tell me you're a gangster without telling me you're a gangster". Between that and the cash, even the teenager was starting to sniff a rat.

'My boss is an actor, see. I'm just his driver.'

That lie seemed to placate him.

'An actor? What would I have seen him in?'

'Can't say. Privacy and all that.'

He looked crestfallen. 'Oh... okay. Hmm. I can only think of one car on the lot that matches that and it's the boss's own.'

'Damn,' I said. 'Don't suppose we could sneak a peek, maybe take a photo? Ya know, so I can show my boss?'

The kid looked serious. He knew he shouldn't show me it.

'How much do you normally make on a weekday? A few hundred? How about I give you five hundred in cash and you show me the car. Two minutes tops. I won't touch it or anything.'

'Alright. But one look. C'mon, it's parked over by the rare and vintage showroom.'

No doubt that was where they had the best CCTV.

The kid walked me over. A man in his sixties appeared.

'Hi boss, Mr ... Sorry, what was your name again?'

'Yurovsky,' I said without hesitating. I hoped the kid and his boss didn't know shit about Russian history.

'... wanted to see the 1965 Aston Martin DB6 Mark 1. He's an accredited buyer shopping for his boss.'

We were nodded through.

'That, kid, was quick.'

He grinned. 'The DB6 is parked next to his.'

Maybe the kid would go far after all.

The moment I saw the boss's car, I recognised it.

It was the wrong colour. The body was black rather than silver.

But the shape was perfect.

'What is it?'

'That,' the salesboy said, 'is the latest Mercedes-Maybach saloon. A perfect grille, sumptuous interior, and, as standard, it's bulletproof. They start at a quarter mil new, but the waiting list to get one is years long. If your boss is interested, mine might be willing to sell his... but it'd be expensive.'

'How expensive?'

'Let me go find out.'

He disappeared off to find out the price.

While he did, I texted Tank:

Found it.

Now we just have to find the right Mercedes-Maybach.

And learn who the fuck was driving it.

52

THOU SHALT NOT BEAR FALSE WITNESS

AYALA GETTING his hands dirty lasted about as long as an undergrad in Freshers' Week.

The moment it stopped looking like an easy solve, he passed the buck to Rafferty, adding what looked like a gangland stabbing to her already over-piled plate.

At least it was a break from chasing phone records for the Zholnovych case, calling around dentists to see if any of them had a patient with the enamel markings from the Linden corpse, and trying to work out what the hell had happened to the remnants of the Bakowski empire. Xander had been right. Crime before and after Tiny had fled the UK was flat. No extra crimes committed, no drop in crimes committed. It was as if the head had been lopped off but the body kept on walking, zombie like, for the years and years since. It was, as he had said, unheard of.

This case should've been simple, at least as the boss had described it. Rafferty arrived in Aldborough Hatch shortly after the morning commuter rush. It was a cold, blustery day with blue skies and the rolling fields were a sight to behold. From where she parked on the main road, all she could see was the church, the gravestones, and endless, flat rolling fields. Gorgeous.

It was dead peaceful until a chubby vicar in a slightly-too-small frock came barrelling out of nowhere. He was ruddy-faced with windswept receding hair and kind, steely-grey eyes that bored into Rafferty's.

'Inspector Rafferty, I assume?'

She nodded.

'I'm Vicar Victor Hicks. The kids call me Double-V.'

'Do they?'

'Well, no, my congregation is rather more mature than that... but if we had teenagers, I'm sure they would.'

Right. Because they loved to give vicars cool nicknames.

'Well, Double-V, d'ya wanna mosey on down to where the blud got got, fam?'

He looked at her blankly.

'Show me where you found the dead guy.'

'Oh! That. Right this way.'

He skipped down the path, then criss-crossed between gravestones, treading an invisible line between them as if it were a tightrope over lava.

Around the back of the church, the pair came to a halt in front of an old gravestone with very worn font work. In the ground around it, Rafferty could see indentations left by the Met's forensics tent. She looked up and toward the church. No windows visible from here.

When she was happy that she'd seen everything that she needed to, Rafferty produced her notebook and started the interview. 'Okay, Vicar, run me through what happened. I know you've told my colleagues already but-'

Before she could finish, he was off. He bounced up and down as he spoke as if this were the most exciting thing to have ever happened in his church. 'Well, I was in the bath – the

vicarage is attached to the other side of the church, you see –
and then I heard it. A scream. I thought, for a moment, it was
those damned foxes. You know what they're like, yowling away
like a girl screaming in the night. Then I thought, no, that was
too deep, too manly, surely? So I steeled myself, prayed to God
for salvation, and leapt out of the bath, threw on my clothes, and
ran through the church, right across the rectory to that little
door over there.'

The door he indicated was barely visible. There was a
protrusion of rock that marked its place.

'Then what?'

'Then I leant out into the rain and looked. I saw two men,
one hunched over, by this very gravestone. I mustered all my
courage and shouted at them "stop!".'

'And they didn't?'

'No,' the vicar said sadly.

Shocker.

'Then what? Well, one ran away towards the fields. I didn't
see much of him. But the other man, he ran straight past across
the graves. He stood on so many, would you believe it?'

'Would I believe that a knife-wielding lunatic who'd just
killed a man in a graveyard at night would walk across a grave?'

The vicar looked as if he'd been shot. 'Well, when you put it
like that...'

'Carry on, Double-V.'

'Right, well, he was really tall. As wide as a shed. Muscles
like Goliath and ink like a sailor. He moved with such speed
that Hermes himself would've been proud.'

The good vicar had a career in writing if he ever retired
from preaching.

'And?'

'And he ran towards the road, crossed it, and got into his
car.'

Rafferty jotted that down in her notebook too. 'Did you get a plate?'

'No.'

'What kind of car was it?'

'A black one.'

She wanted to throttle him. 'A saloon? An SUV? An estate?'

'The first one, I guess.'

'You guess or you know?'

'I'm not a car person, Inspector. And I was in shock. There was a young man out here bleeding. I only glanced at the car.'

He gestured from the road to the gravestone and back.

'When you looked at the young man, what did you see?'

'He had a knife in his leg. Two cuts, two rips in his jeans. Big, gaping wounds. Like he'd been stabbed once and then the assailant had had another go for good measure. The blood was everywhere. Pints of it spilling down his leg, all over the ground.' That didn't line up with what Ayala had told her. In the brief phone call they'd had, he'd described one stab wound.

Can you show me where on his leg?

The vicar pointed at his own thigh, right where the femoral artery ran. Whoever had stabbed their victim had known what they were doing. He'd have bled out faster than the vicar could get dressed.

'Did the men take anything?'

'No... not that I saw. Why?'

'How far is your bathroom? Can you show me?'

The vicar looked confused, but he did. They walked to the door, he unlocked it with a rusty key hanging around his neck, and then they walked through the vestibule, across to another small door on the far side of the church and then through into the vicarage. The bathroom itself was right at the back.

'That walk took us what, ninety seconds?'

The vicar folded his arms. 'Yes, but we weren't running, were we detective?'

He looked smug.

'No, Double-V, but we were fully dressed. How long do you think it took you to think about the not-fox-screaming sound, get out of the bath, dress, and then run that route back to the graveyard?'

The smug expression melted away. 'Hmm... Three minutes?'

'Right. Now you see why I was asking about the men taking anything. They had at least three minutes to get away after the man screamed. He was stabbed in the femoral so he'd have been dead almost instantly. Why did they hang around?'

Neither of them had the answer.

Rafferty switched tack. 'Were the men covered in blood?'

It was a simple yes/ no question.

'I... I don't know. I didn't see. It was almost pitch black.'

'But you said before that you saw the man's tattoos, didn't you?'

The vicar looked at her sheepishly.

She pulled out her notebook and read his words back to him. 'You said he was "Muscled like Goliath and inked like a sailor", didn't you?'

'Well,' he mumbled, 'there was a bit of light from the full moon...'

Rafferty scoffed. Useless bloody witness.

'Did anyone find blood drips on the ground?'

When he didn't answer, Rafferty stalked off to double check, this time using her phone as a torch. A nick to the femoral would have seen a huge amount of blood loss while the victim's heart was still pumping. Surely, the killers would've been covered in it... unless that was why they'd taken so long?

Could they have taken off their bloody clothes and bagged them?

She imagined Kflom's voice. He'd be telling her to look for the void. It was like the carpet back at the Zholnovych crime scene. If something or someone was in the way of the blood, it would've spurted all over them, not the floor, the moment they'd pulled out the knife. Except the blood spatter on the ground was one continuous, unbroken shape, spurting onto the floor without the telltale void, or gap, to identify where the killer had been standing. The killer hadn't been covered in blood so they didn't have any bloody clothing to get rid of. How the hell did they manage that?

'Is that the route the big man took?'

'I... I guess so.'

'You said you saw him go past, didn't you? Didn't you just say you saw him?'

'Well, yes, I suppose I did...'

The vicar looked at her expectantly as if waiting for the next question. But if he were this unreliable now, he'd be useless in court.

'Would you be willing to sit down with our sketch artist?' Rafferty asked.

Flick would make short work of the vicar. That was one meeting she'd loved to be a fly on the wall for.

'Well, like I said, it was very dark ...'

'But you're willing to try, aren't you?' She smiled at him sweetly.

'Well, yes, if that's what God wishes...'

'Well, Vicar, he does work in mysterious ways.'

Or in your case, she thought, not at all.

53

THE OLD STOMPING GROUNDS

ILFORD HASN'T REALLY CHANGED MUCH.

Sure, some of the shop fronts are new. Ken's Chicken is now the local Na'an Dos and the working man's club is now a Wetherspoons.

But the show-off types still hang out at the Quarry Bank Estate. I used to hang out there back in the nineties. Too cool for school.

'You remember that time Tiny had the fuzz run ragged trying to work out how the heroin kept disappearing from Ilford Police Station's evidence locker?'

Tank shook his head.

'We blackmailed the twat that ran their evidence desk. Tiny told him he'd shagged his missus, filmed it, threatened to share the video with the world unless he handed back any of our gear that got nicked. Worked like a charm.'

The big man howled with laughter. He laughed so hard he couldn't breathe.

The most ridiculous thing was, it wasn't even true. Every-thing with Tiny was smoke and mirrors, lies to coerce people into doing his bidding. He'd once told his own mother there was a bomb in her car just because he'd wanted to borrow it.

Eventually, Tank stopped laughing.

'How hadn't you heard that one?' I asked. 'We used to get away with so much.'

'Still do,' Tank grunted. 'Like burn down house.'

'Like that, yeah.'

The fire had raged for ages. Two of the neighbouring homes had burned down too. I'd had to promise Chiggs that I'd make him whole if his insurance didn't. They probably would. The technique we'd used was brilliant. An actual fire investigator had invented it. His colleagues had spent years discussing the perfect arson and he'd been using it all along, setting fires wherever their conventions went. Clever, if a bit arrogant.

Like driving a Mercedes-Maybach.

It's the sort of thing only the *shef* would do. If I'd tried driving such a flash car back in the day, Tiny would've cut off my left nut for being such a bell end. It draws attention. The Met ain't stupid. If there's a housing estate full of people on bennies and then there're a bunch of Mercs parked outside, they're gonna put two and two together.

Owning a big flash car not only says I'm rich, it says I'm powerful. Like Teflon. The shit just doesn't stick.

That means someone who'd laundered their cash, enough of it to explain the Merc anyway.

If I were them, I'd be keeping the car locked up. No way would I park it on the street. Where in Ilford has secure parking? There really isn't much about, just the usual array of public car parks. I guess the short answer is, I wouldn't park it here.

As we walked around the old estate, I saw flash cars. They were modified boy racers, little GTs with souped up engines and enormous exhausts. Nobody was driving anything worth twenty grand let alone two hundred-odd.

'Kid,' I said, calling over a boy on a bicycle.

'What?'

'I'm looking for someone. Drives a brand-new Mercedes-Maybach. You seen it around here?'

'Who's asking?'

'Matthew Boulton and James Watt.'

I held out a fifty.

'Nah,' he said. 'Not seen one 'round here.'

I snatched the note back.

'Hey!' the kid said, reaching into his pocket for something. A knife maybe?

Sure enough, the glint of a blade appeared. 'The cash is for answering, not knowing the answer.'

I grinned and handed him the note. 'You should be a lawyer, kid.'

'Nah,' he said. 'Lawyers don't get fifty quid for not answering a question.'

I turned to go.

'Hey, mister. I mighta seen one that wasn't around here, ya know, a bit further afield.'

'Where?'

'I'd have to ask my friends Matt and James.'

Bloody kids. They cotton on far too quick. I handed him another.

'Where'd you see the car?'

'What car? I only said I might've. Turns out, I didn't. Nice doing business with ya.'

Before I could I say anything else, he swung his leg over his bicycle and peddled off as fast as lightning.

Little bastard.

54

MUSINGS

HER MICROWAVE DINNER had long since gone cold as Rafferty stared out of the window, watching the city go by. The telly was on, blaring some nonsense about more strikes, more political scandals, and more inclement weather inbound. She switched it off and let her mind drift back to the issue at hand.

If Starlight was a Bakowski operation, Xander hadn't known about it. The moment Brodie had run the Companies House records for the strip club, he'd found that it was owned by a trustee in the Bahamas. Another dead end. The "Person of Significant Control" was supposed to stop shenanigans like that, but it seemed that the regulations simply weren't tight enough. Stooges were paid to put their real names to fake companies, allowing criminals to masquerade as businessmen. It was typical of the way gangs like the Bakowski Syndicate worked, hiding everything with lawyers and paperwork.

UKPPS was just as bad. Like the gangs, they were totally opaque about what they did. It was their company in the Marshall Islands that had leased the Balham house to Elijah Zholnovych. For all Rafferty knew, Starlight could be their strip club. Her contact had vigorously denied it but he would, wouldn't he?

Her contact at MisPer hadn't yet come up with phone records for Nathan Linden. Part of the problem there was that they didn't have his mobile number. No phone had been recovered from the flat and UKPPS hadn't admitted to one either. Joe had, however, found some of the records for Elijah Zholnovych's number which showed bugger all. The mast he'd connected to must have been the one nearest his home. Other than showing he'd ventured as far as his local Tesco Express and Starbucks, there was nothing remarkable among Zholnovych's known movement. There was one big caveat, that the records didn't go back very far, but from what Joe had managed to uncover, the two victims hadn't ever crossed paths.

The "simple" explanation was dead in the water. It was a neat idea, that Zholnovych killed Nathan Linden, one which could've been explained by the two men randomly running into each other by dint of both hiding in London.

But Zholnovych was a non-violent criminal. Waxy had gone so far as to describe her husband as "boring". His house was evidence enough of that. The man had spent his days working on reinforcing the butt impression on his sofa, poring over endless Russian war movies. He didn't strike Rafferty as the kind to suddenly become a killer.

The ANPR evidence backed that up. If he were the killer, it was awfully coincidental that a van matching Rosie Bray's description was in the area with cloned plates on the day of his disappearance. The simplest explanation was that someone in the van had killed Zholnovych, taken his body away in the van, and then disposed of it at an unknown site.

If that same someone then killed Nathan Linden, then it was odds-on they were looking for a killer with links to the Bakowski Syndicate.

It had to be Tiny.

Who else would have reason to take out his turncoat lieutenants? The body in the bathtub had "gang murder" written all over it. Virgin murderers didn't kill so brutally.

But if it were Tiny then why now? And how?

The former was anyone's guess. Interpol had been after Tiny forever and a day. Xander had a whole operation tracking the Syndicate but hadn't seen hide nor hair of him. It was as if he was a shadowy puppet master, pulling the same strings as before but from hiding. How the hell did that happen? He had to be in near-constant contact with his lieutenants and not one of them had leaked anything about his whereabouts.

The latter was equally troubling. Two men, both in witness protection. Assuming Zholnovych was dead rather than AWOL, someone had broken UKPPS's perfect record not once but twice in the span of a few months. That spoke to an intelligent, highly motivated, and well-resourced killer.

Zholnovych had one undeniable chink in his armour: Waxy.

His wife had gone from the programme straight back to the Bakowski heartlands. Hell, she was working in a strip club. Even if Starlight didn't belong to the Syndicate, they'd know that the wife of a traitor had returned. From Xander's description of the breadth of the Syndicate, they would at the very least be extorting Starlight for protection money.

Could Waxy have let something slip that got back to Tiny? She'd have had to have told people something to explain the years she'd been in the programme with her husband. One tiny slip, one mention of Balham, and he'd have been vulnerable.

Then again, he'd been moved, hadn't he? Two years of records were all they had for "Elijah Zholnovych" unless...she was still in contact with her hubby?

She called Brodie.

'Alreet, lass?'

'The misper from months ago, Zholnovych. His wife was in the programme with him. She left. He didn't. Is it possible she could've broken his cover?'

Rafferty could hear Brodie tapping away, the clack of his mechanical keyboard reverberating down the phoneline. When she'd first heard it years ago, she'd mocked him mercilessly for having a keyboard that sounded like a typewriter. Then she'd tried it out and quickly become a Cherry MX Blue convert.

'Hang on, lass,' he said. 'Bear with me.'

'Alright...'

'Your man Zholnovych. His phone records are on the system. Who did that?'

'Joe Singleton over at MisPer.'

Because Brodie hadn't got around to it yet.

'I'd be offended, but he's saved me a job,' Brodie said. 'He's not got much but what I'll do is see if I can find yer woman Waxy's details. If I can cross-reference them, I'll find any contact they might've had after his flit. No doubt UKPPS warned 'em both against it but the poor wee bastard would've been bloody lonely sitting in that house down in Balham on his own.'

'How long?'

'I dinnae know. Depends how smart yer lassie is. Could be an hour. Could be a week.'

'Thanks.'

'Oh, and afore ya go, I pulled the ANPR records for ye church murder. One stolen car in the area. Ye won't like what's happened to it, though, lass.'

'What?'

He told her.

He was right.

She didn't like it.

55

PERSISTENCE

THE CAR WAS DRIVING me mad. That brat who'd robbed us blind was right about one thing: it wasn't in Ilford. If it was, someone would've spotted it.

'It's so annoying, Tank,' I said once we were back home.

'What?'

'Tiny. The car. Everything. How's he done it? We've tracked down two men in witness protection, both hidden with all of the powers of the state. But Tiny Bakowski, the second most wanted man in Europe, has come back to Ilford, bought a fucking Mercedes-Maybach, and resumed trafficking heroin in from Afghanistan, and not a bloody soul has seen hide nor hair of him.'

Tank shrugged at me.

'Dealers. Who do we know that sells smack?'

He reeled off a bunch of nicknames.

'Most of them are in bloody jail, Tank. Who's still out and working the streets?'

Another shrug. Useless.

If I can find one dealer, I can find their source. Then it's a case of following it up the food chain, all the way back to Tiny.

Heroin's the most used drug in the UK. Over a third of all addicts inject or smoke the stuff. Fentanyl is catching up, but skag is the old favourite.

I'd ask around... but given that we'd just stiffed the Syndicate for their whole shipment, it'd draw a lot of attention.

'Alright then, customers. Where're the drug dens?'

'The Ladder?' Tank ventured.

Not a bad shout. The ladder's a weird residential area running between Green Lanes and Wightman Road. To the East is Tottenham, famous for being where the riots started. That'd been a fun night. On the other side is where the posh folk live in places like Crouch End and Muswell Hill. They have money, enough to pay for a heroin addiction.

While not strictly the heart of Bakowski territory, it might not be a bad place to start: close enough to Ilford that dealers could plausibly work for the Syndicate, far enough away that news wouldn't immediately get back to him. I told Tank we had to go.

'You can just order online, no?'

Order online? What the hell was he smoking?

'Where from?'

'Darknet,' Tank grunted. 'Find dealer, send Telegram. You have cash?'

'Err, yeah...'

'Then I sort.'

Tank was going to sort it?

This I'd pay to see.

56

BURN, BABY, BURN

DAMN IT. She'd seen the plume of smoke and thought nothing of it.

The ANPR camera had revealed a stolen car passed along the Aldborough Road a few hours before, and then shortly again after the stabbing.

The same network of cameras had traced the car heading away from the crime scene. It disappeared and, shortly after, a nearby house, one with an attached garage, was set on fire.

Now Rafferty stood looking at the ashes of not one house, but three. The fire had raged out of control quicker than the fire brigade could get there. Even to her untrained eye, she could see that the fire had started in the house in the middle. It had been reduced to little more than a pile of ashes and rubble while the neighbouring houses only had a little of their outer walls left.

'It's arson alright,' Lucien Darville said. 'Easily the most clear-cut case that I've ever seen in my years as a fire investigator.'

That made a refreshing change. Though she hadn't worked with him before, she'd seen Darville's name in the notes for one of the Bakowski murder cases she'd read up on. They'd torched a family home to help cover up a child's murder and it had been Darville who'd been instrumental in proving it.

'How so?'

'The liberal use of accelerants. Someone poured petrol all over the place and then lit it up. I can't give you a steer on the ignition method yet but it seems to have started in the middle of the property and radiated out – see how the centre is the most damaged? It would've gone up quickly-'

'Killing anyone inside,' Rafferty finished for him. 'And given that nobody is inside, that means they used some sort of remote or delayed ignition, doesn't it?'

Darville hesitated and then nodded. 'Probably, but like I said, I can't comment on methodology just yet.'

'Understood,' Rafferty said. 'What about the car? Is the plate still legible?'

She already knew it was the right model. Given that Brodie had tracked a similar car coming within a quarter mile via CCTV, she was convinced that this was the murderers' escape vehicle. But the formalities had to be observed, the boxes ticked. It wasn't just about knowing something, it was proving it in court.

'Afraid not,' Darville said. 'The scene of crime boys will have to pull the VIN.'

The VIN, or Vehicle Identification Number, was a unique identifier stamped on the chassis. Anything short of an inferno and it would still be readable, like a black box for an airplane.

'Right. Thanks.'

When Darville had disappeared off to carry on his work, Rafferty turned her attention back to the devastation in front of her. First thing first, have someone check on the neighbours. It was all too easy to forget the humans. It was a job that Mayberry excelled at. She texted him asking him to take the lead on community management. The likes of Morton and Ayala only saw a problem to solve, a crime to get justice for. That alone wasn't enough. It was the reason she'd had to quit working for Sapphire all those years ago. Any victim was hard to accept, child victims doubly so.

Second, she needed to know where the car had come from. Finding where it had been was a prerequisite for finding who stole it. With a bit of luck, there'd be more camera footage to work with.

Third, she needed to know who the hell her victim was.

She hadn't seen the body in-situ. That had happened before Ayala had kicked the case over to her. From what she'd read of the case notes on HOLMES, her victim was, yet again, totally anonymous. The photo of the scene showed him in jeans, t-shirt, and a jacket. Boring, useless.

At first, she'd assumed the case was, as Ayala had presented it, a gangland stabbing. It was Ilford after all.

But why the anonymity? That smacked of her last two cases. Could she have another missing witness case on her hands?

And if she did, would Ayala believe her?

Belt and braces, she told herself. Think wild thoughts, but only write down concrete details. It wasn't what she knew, or even believed, that mattered. It was what she could prove.

If the body and the burning house were a coincidence then she had to prove that. The VIN on the burnt-out car would be the first step. If it matched the stolen car in the vicinity of the murder, she could assume a connection was likely and put her efforts into tracing the car to find her killer.

If on the other hand, the burnt-out car didn't match the CCTV, she could rule out the house as a secondary crime scene and kick the case over to someone else.

If she assumed her victim was connected to the stolen car then whatever worldly possessions he owned had just gone up in smoke. Another totally anonymous victim. Who the hell was he? Why had he been lurking in a church graveyard after dark? And why had two men driven several hours to ambush him there?

A meeting then. Something planned.

The sheer violence of a stabbing followed by the thorough torching of a house screamed organised crime. Would the Bakowski Syndicate burn down a house on their home turf? Or could one of the dozens of other crime families be trying to assert their dominance?

'Alright, Ash?'

Rafferty turned to see Xander stalking up behind her. Now dressed in a two-piece suit and brown suede shoes, he looked sharp. He was even wearing his "I want to impress somebody" cufflinks. They'd been a Christmas gift she'd given him a few years ago, hand made with hexagon-cut sapphires, black onyx trim, and a diamond accent.

'What's with the rig? You been testifying in court?'

As if he'd bother looking this good for court. She knew he was dressed up for a woman. But why was he here? She hadn't called him. Arson was well outside his purview.

He gave a wan smile. 'Laundry day. This was all I had clean.'

So that was how they were playing it.

As his gaze looked over the burnt-out remains of the house, his baby blue eyes flashed darkly. 'Anyone hurt in there?'

'Thankfully, no. Straight up property damage. Neighbours weren't home and the fire brigade were quick about putting it out. Want to tell me why you care?'

'He's a CI.'

Rafferty perked up. No wonder Xander had come down here himself.

This was getting juicy. A confidential informant's home was

torched? That backed up her gang theory, though it didn't help with knowing whether the arson was connected to the murder.

'Everyone calls him Chiggs,' Xander continued. 'Young bloke, got involved with the Syndicate as a teenager. He knew his days were numbered, wanted out, but you know the Bakowskis-'

'The only way out is death,' Rafferty finished for him.

'Someone's death anyhow,' Xander said. 'If the *shef* goes, the lieutenants often scarper. A few left when Tiny fled. Chiggs was too young to do that. He saw the writing on the wall and when we offered him the chance to avoid jail and earn a few quid, he jumped at it. He's been running these safe houses ever since.'

Rafferty eyed the ashes in front of her. So much for it being safe.

'And telling you who's been using them presumably.'

Xander nodded. 'Yep. But... he didn't tell us anyone was here this week.'

'Then we'd best pull him in for a chat, hadn't we?'

'Arson's a damned good explanation for pulling him in. I'll arrange it. Is there anything else you want from SOCA? I know this one's yours and all...'

Xander Thompson actually acknowledging she was in charge? That was a new one. 'Pull the VIN for me. The burnt-out car has to be the one we caught on ANPR. I need to know where it came from.'

She could do it herself, but then Ayala would have to sign off on it, the paperwork would take ages, and if Xander wanted to do the donkey-work for her, she wasn't going to turn him down.

'Alright. And Ash? Be careful. Must dash – need a word with Lucien.'

Rafferty pointed towards the neighbouring house on their right. 'Think he's around the back there.'

She watched him go, unsure of her next move. The neighbours claimed to have seen nothing so the local canvass was a bust. CCTV ended a good quarter mile away so until they had the VIN, they couldn't definitively match the burned-out car to the ANPR.

Whatever. They'd get that lined up later. For now, the assumption was that Brodie was, as usual, right, and they'd found the killer's car. She'd need to see where else the car had been, work out if it were stolen or not, and then work backwards from there to find the driver. With a bit of luck, one of the ANPR cameras would've caught the driver on camera and then they'd have a mugshot to show the useless vicar.

Rafferty headed back to her car, got in the driver-side and turned on the engine. The screen which showed the police ANPR map hummed to life. Not many cameras in the vicinity. No wonder Brodie hadn't found much after the main roads. Perhaps that was why Chiggs had chosen to set up his "safe" house here in boring suburbia, well away from the madding crowds.

What route would they have driven to get here? Perhaps more importantly, how did they leave? If they'd burnt their only car, they'd have had to leave by public transport. Surely they wouldn't have had the balls to call an Uber from a nearby street? She pulled out her phone and texted Brodie to ask him to check for that sort of thing anyway.

Boris Bike perhaps? There was a stand over by the station. Then there was the Tube itself. Another thing for Brodie to check. If they'd been daft enough to take the Central Line, they'd be on CCTV heading into the station. She texted him again.

Unless the killers had a second car. Then, they'd be looking for a car driving out of the area on ANPR shortly after.

Yet another job for Brodie.

Another text sent.

She was almost beginning to empathise with Ayala. The management side of the job was draining. Between Mayberry, who'd helped canvass the area, Brodie, tasked with every IT-related research query under the sun, and also liaising with Xander, Ayala, Kieran, et al, it was overwhelming.

But Ayala had signed up for this shit and she hadn't. Nor did she get paid anywhere near enough to deal with it. Running even a relatively simple murder meant grid searches, canvasses, CCTV, fingerprinting and collecting the samples from around the scene, taking witness statements, and so much more. The fire had obliterated most of the secondary crime scene in front of her, but that wouldn't stop Purcell, Kflom and their colleagues from swarming all over the place as soon as Darville declared it safe.

Once the VIN had been pulled, the ANPR tracked, and the CCTV evidence reviewed, she'd be in a position to try and find the two men the vicar described. Until then, she had two tasks. Firstly, she wanted to walk to the Tube, noting all the private CCTV cameras on the way so Kieran could subpoena them if necessary.

Then, there was the autopsy to attend and the paperwork to complete. That was before she even thought about dealing with the Nathan Linden murder and the linked Zholnovych disappearance, cases which she'd much rather prioritise over what would no doubt turn out to be a gang stabbing, probably from yet another turf dispute.

Rafferty sighed.

It was going to be a long day.

57

DELIVERY WITH A DIFFERENCE

EVEN THOUGH I knew Tank had the "in" on where to buy, I was gobsmacked by how easy it all was.

Less than an hour after we'd placed our order on the dark-net, a Tesla pulled up outside and a smartly dressed guy in his thirties got out. The guy could've been a teacher or a personal trainer. He opened the boot, revealing one of those insulated bags that delivery drivers use to carry takeaway orders. As he approached, I spotted the familiar branding. It was the same bag the guy who delivers my pizza uses.

Clever.

It was like wearing a high-viz jacket and walking confidently past security. Delivery drivers were everywhere. So long as he wasn't obnoxious, like the motorbike drivers screeching to a halt outside or the cars pumping out music like a rave, nobody would ever pay attention to him.

He knocked on the door so casually that it was obvious he did this all day long. One of those lazy, soft knocks.

'Delivery for-'

Before he could say a word, Tank grabbed him by both arms, yanked him inside and shoved him to the floor. His delivery bag landed beside him with a quiet thud. I passed Tank the rope we'd had waiting by the front door.

As quick as a flash, Tank unfurled it and tied the dealer up tighter than a Gordian knot. He shoved a pair of socks – all we had to hand – into his mouth.

'Get him downstairs,' I ordered. 'And throw me his car keys. I'll move it to the garage.'

Couldn't have the neighbours getting too curious.

58

CAMERAS AND CADAVERS

'A SIMPLE STABBING WITH A SHARP, pointed blade no more than four inches long.'

Rafferty was back in the morgue. This time it wasn't the bloater room nor was Dr Lucie Fearn-Wright in attendance. Instead, she was back in the all-too-familiar confines of Autopsy Room 1 and the dulcet tones of the speaker belonged to Dr Larry Chiswick.

'He'd have bled out in seconds,' Chiswick said.

'Rightio doc, I could've told you that myself. Anything a bit more useful to tell me?'

'The angle suggests your killer was short or perhaps they used an underarm stabbing motion.'

Underarm stabbing? That was a new one.

'Like... a bowler?'

Chiswick looked at her disdainfully. 'Yes, that is one underarm movement.'

He demonstrated using a pair of forceps from his tray table. It looked so clunky, so unnatural. It wasn't the straight jab that came to mind when someone said "stabbing" nor was it the overarm dagger thrust that she'd seen a few times before.

'Why on earth would someone stab underarm?'

He shrugged. 'Element of surprise, perhaps?'

'Maybe,' Rafferty said, unconvinced. Nobody stabbed someone in a less effective way just in case it might throw off the victim or the police. If the victim had lived, he'd have had a chance to fight back.

The doc gestured at the body. 'There aren't any defensive wounds. No skin under the fingernails, no bruising. Your victim didn't see the knife coming quick enough to react.'

That fitted with Rafferty's view. 'How clever does our killer have to be to stab someone in one go and walk away without getting covered in blood?'

'Hmm,' Chiswick mused, 'I'd say pretty wick. First, they'd have to know where the femoral artery is.'

'Remind me?'

'Take your thumb and forefinger, pinch just below your hips.'

She did.

'Now move down 'til your feel a vibration. That's your femoral artery. It runs down to the knee. It's high pressure so like I said, it's a quick death.'

He wasn't wrong. The artery thrummed like the Underground, shaking the skin above it.

'Okay, so the killer could've found that factoid on Google. But how'd they avoid the blood?'

'That bit's harder,' Chiswick said. He stepped towards her. 'Imagine I'm your killer and you're the gent on my table. I stab you in the thigh and pull out the knife. If I stay standing in front of you, I get covered in blood.'

Just like Kflom's void theory. 'So you stab me while continuously moving.'

'Exactly. I pull the knife out as I walk past.'

It meant the killer was right-handed. They'd stabbed Oleks

in his right thigh – the left as they looked at him – and then carried on walking, yanking the knife out as they went.

'And then I throw the knife behind me on the floor as I leave the crime scene.'

It was quick, fluid, and clever, not to mention cold-blooded as hell.

'Is there anything else you've found?'

'Not much, forensically speaking. He's in his late twenties, slim, brown hair, and he's got a tattoo in Cyrillic on his forearm.'

'You kept that quiet. Show me.'

He did. Sure enough, on the underside of the dead man's forearm was ink that read "безстрашний".

'What's it mean?'

'It says "buy your favourite pathologist a coffee and not that Starbucks rubbish either".'

'So you don't know.'

'Haven't a scooby.'

Rafferty whipped out her phone. 'Thank God for Google translate, eh?'

The familiar click sounded as she took a photo of the tattoo and fed it into the app.

'You can translate from a photo?'

She turned the phone to him. '*Bezstrashnyy* or, in English, fearless, intrepid or undaunted.'

The pathologist scanned the phone. He must've spotted the language next to "detect language" because he said in a disbelieving tone: 'In ... Ukrainian? I'd have bet the house it was Polish. I suppose the use of Cyrillic made it dead obvious it couldn't have been... and yet...'

Ukrainian. Again. Her third case linked to the country this year. Were the Bakowskis involved in every damned gangland murder in London?

'Don't bet what you can't afford to lose, doc.'

'Alas,' he said, deadpan, 'a lesson I should've learned when I bet my hair that Morton wouldn't solve the Eleanor Murphy case.'

'Never ever bet against Morton.'

'That,' he said slowly, 'is a lesson I learnt quickly. Except I thought I knew the answer was Polish.'

'Why'd you assume that?'

'Simple,' the doc said, 'his name's on his cards. Oleks Kuleba.'

She shot him a bewildered look. 'He was carrying business cards?'

Why the hell hadn't Ayala told her that? Sabotage? Or ineptitude. The first thing she'd have done when she got to the scene would be to search the victim's pockets. Did that rule out her theory that it was a third witness protection murder?

'Yes, Ash. He was carrying business cards with the job title of Murder Victim.' Chiswick rolled his eyes. 'Bank cards. He had one from PKO – that's Powszechna Kasa Oszczędności Bank Polski Spółka to those not in the know – so I assumed he was Polish. I've taken fingerprints so hopefully that'll let me double check the name.'

'Bit odd,' Rafferty said, 'but I suppose Poland and Ukraine share a border. It's not that hard to imagine someone in the east of Poland being Ukrainian. You got anything else for me?'

'I've taken a few swabs from his clothes and the like. I'll send those off to be processed. Things are running a bit slower than I'd like.'

She nodded. 'Thanks, doc.'

'Good. Next time, show your appreciation with a coffee-'

The sheer gall of it. Chiswick had enough cheek for another arse. But she couldn't blame him for trying. She'd do the same if she thought Ayala wouldn't cop.

'And not Starbucks either,' she said. 'I know you're a Square Mile man.'

'Finally, someone noticed! What gave it away? Was it the mug? Or the t-shirt?'

She grinned as she headed for the door.

Chiswick was a curmudgeonly old git.

But at least he hadn't hit on her.

59

WHEELER DEALERS

OUR DEALER WAS NOW TIED to a chair in my basement, the yellow bulb in the beam above him casting a sinister glow over proceedings. He'd seized up like a deer in a car's headlights, making Tank's job so much easier than usual. A soft drug dealer. What was the world coming to?

The idiot hadn't even been carrying a knife. When Tank had frisked him, all we'd found were his car keys, the heroin we'd ordered on the darknet, a few more bags of other drugs, presumably his next few deliveries, and his wallet.

Next to me, Tank loitered casually. He was holding a power drill and grinning. For a moment, I imagined our dealer seeing it and shitting himself. Then I sniffed the air. He *had* shit himself.

'Whatever you want, it's yours. Take the Tesla if you like.'

'How generous,' I said. 'And we haven't even been properly introduced. I assume The420Guy isn't your real name.'

'It's J-J-Jeremi.'

Tank opened the dealer's wallet, looked at the name on his credit cards to confirm he was telling the truth and nodded.

'Right, Jeremi, this is how things are going to go down. I'm going to ask you a few questions. Answer them, you live. If I think you're lying to me, my friend here uses that drill. *Comprende?*'

He nodded.

'First things first, your heroin.'

As soon as I mentioned it, Tank pulled opened the bag, a smile creeping over his face. Inside was a tiny Ziplock bag full of white powder, identical in style to the stuff we'd stolen from Oleks. It was unusually light in colour meaning it was the good shit, not the black tar that gangbangers peddled to morons.

Tank opened the bag and took a sniff. His smile widened. No smell. It wasn't cut with any of the usual extras: detergent, baking soda, flour, UHT milk, or the like. I'd bet my left nut this was from the same source. I held out my hand expectantly. Tank reluctantly handed it over. There was no way I was letting him hold onto the baggie for more than a few seconds.

'Where'd you get your supply?' I demanded.

He looked at me incredulously. 'The... the darknet?'

'Don't be cute Jeremi. Who delivers it? How? When? What's it cost you?'

Jeremi gulped. 'I pay online. Bitcoin, obvs.'

Tank stepped forward.

'Sorry, sorry,' Jeremi stammered. 'Turn of phrase, that's all.'

'After you've paid, then what happens?'

'They deliver?'

'How?'

'At first, Royal Mail.'

He had to be kidding. They *posted* hard drugs? How on earth didn't they get caught?

'Sometimes, it got intercepted at customs,' Jeremi continued. 'Sometimes, it didn't. Nothing ever came of it except a letter in the post saying my parcel had been seized. No knock at the door, nothing.'

'You said at first.'

'The orders got bigger. I started selling more online. Turns out, people love this quick delivery shit. They'll pay way over the odds to get their fix right now.'

So we had an entrepreneur in the hot seat. 'And the bigger orders weren't delivered by your postie.'

'No,' he said, his eyes leaping from me to Tank and back again.

'You're worried about reprisals,' I said.

He gulped again and then nodded.

'Well, Jeremi, I can't promise your supplier won't kill you. But if you'd like to stay in one piece, you'd best not piss off my friend.'

'Look, I don't know her name but-'

'Her name?' I cut him off. I imagined the woman I'd seen leaving the church. 'Older lady, short, silver hair?'

This time, Jeremi frowned. 'No. Young. Gorgeous lass. Maybe late thirties? Quite tall, dark complexion. She had one hell of a sexy accent – Eastern European, Russian maybe?'

That wasn't the woman I'd seen getting into the car. Damn. I suppose it would've been too much of a coincidence. The kind of criminal who offs a man in cold blood isn't the kind that's stupid enough to drive a half-million-pound car for a garden variety drug drop.

'When you want a delivery, how does that play out?'

'I use Signal to tell her what I want, she sends back a thumbs up, and then I send over the Bitcoin.'

'Then she delivers,' I said. 'Where to? And how quickly?'

'A warehouse in Enfield, down by the William Girling.'

I know the area well. Two reservoirs, one in the north, the King George's Reservoir, and then another just to the south, the William Girling. There are dozens of warehouses around there.

'She usually delivers in a few days.'

Not good enough. 'I want you to message her. Tell her

you're out of stock and need more, that you'll pay a rush fee for delivery tonight.'

'And then you'll let me go?'

'And then the three of us are going to go visit your dealer. Then, it's all over.'

He smiled, the hesitant, faltering kind of smile. Hope mixed with fear.

Tank glared back.

'Don't worry, Jeremi, just do exactly as we say and this time tomorrow, all this will be a distant fucking memory. Now, first things first, what's your phone's pin code?'

60

FALSE ALARMS

RAFFERTY PUT HER FOOT DOWN, running blues and twos all the way to the shout.

The killer's car had been found.

It was parked outside the giant Tesco Superstore in Tottenham in the far corner of the car park, well away from the store's CCTV.

What the driver hadn't counted on was Brodie: he'd been watching the ANPR feeds like a hawk, keeping an eye out for the plates, the right model, or any reports of an abandoned car matching either of those key details. When the car had been flagged as passing a speed camera heading along the A10, he'd sounded the alarm.

Rafferty screeched into the car park to find the Armed Response Vehicle had beaten her to the scene. She spotted a space and pulled in. As she stepped out, a woman yelled at her: 'Oi, you ain't got no kids!'

'Police,' Rafferty yelled back. As she leapt out of the car, she glanced back to see that she had in fact parked in a Parent and Child space. Whoops.

The woman yelled something about wanting to see a

warrant card. As if. Rafferty ignored her and jogged in the direction of the ARV. The driver rolled down his window as she
approached.

'Inspector Rafferty,' she said by way of introduction. 'Any
movement?'

'None,' the man said. 'It's been,' – he glanced at his watch –
'thirty-six minutes since we arrived.'

Damn. Had the car been abandoned? Rafferty pondered
where the killer would've gone if that were the case. Presumably they'd have either nicked another car – in which case, the
owner would've called it in – or they'd legged it on foot.
Where though? The Victoria Line at South Tottenham
maybe?

Before she could look up the nearest public transport on
Citymapper, the driver of the ARV gestured towards the stolen
car. She turned to see a man approaching it, nonchalantly
pushing a trolley full of nappies, food, and a new microwave.

'Hands in the air!'

As the ARV team closed in on their man, Rafferty heard
him yell. He had thrown his hands up, a shocked look on his
face. The man was in his forties with a pot belly. He wore a
smart jumper over a shirt paired with beige chinos and a pair of
walking boots, the combination of which made him look far
more "Dad doing the school run" than "violent killer".

'Easy,' Rafferty said. 'Sir, what's your name?'

'D-Dale Day,' the man stuttered. 'What's going on?'

'Is this your car, Dale?'

He looked at her as if she were insane. Then, equally
confused, he looked at his car.

'No... but yes?'

He squinted at his car in confusion.

'Where's your car key, Dale?'

'My pocket. Right-hand side.'

She smiled at him. 'Okay. Can you very slowly take your keys out for me? You can put your hands down now.'

He did as she asked, his hands trembling as he withdrew his keys and held them up for her to see.

'Now press the unlock button.'

When he did, lights flashed and a beep went off as the car was unlocked.

'What's your number plate, Dale?'

He reeled it off.

As soon as he did, the ARV team groaned. It was the same year and also a London reg, but no dice.

'Right. And the plates on your car...'

He looked at them in confusion. The car was his, the plates were not.

'They're not mine!' Dale protested.

Dale's car was a diversion. The killer had swapped the plates.

'When did you park up here?'

'I don't know... an hour ago.'

She looked at the entrance to the car park where she could see cameras recording number plates. Either Tesco, or one of those private parking companies that some shops hired to run their car parks, was watching who was coming and going so they could enforce the maximum stay. With a bit of luck, Brodie would be able to run down whether the plates were swapped before or after Dale Day parked up.

'And presumably you didn't notice that your plates had been swapped.'

He shook his head. 'When I left home, I just got in my car and drove... I've no reason to look at the plates! I knew where my car was parked. It just never crossed my mind.'

'And where do you live?'

'Crouch End.'

Very posh. 'You park your car on the street?'

He nodded.

A car parked on a backstreet. That made him an easy mark. The killer must've driven from Ilford, swapped the plates either in the car park or in Crouch End, and then buggered off leaving the police chasing their tails. That sort of forensic counter-measure spoke to a sophisticated criminal, one with experience.

Her theory would all need to be confirmed, of course, just in case Dale was an Oscar-worthy actor pulling off a ballsy double bluff.

'I'm afraid you're going to have to come in and make a state-ment, Mr Day.'

'Anything,' he said. 'Anything to help.'

61

THE MIDDLE (WO)MAN

WE WENT two hours beforehand to scope the place out. Unlike the drop with Oleks, we knew exactly when and where the meet would go down which made things miles easier. None of that What3Words bullshit either.

Naturally, we took Jeremi's Tesla to get there. That's what his contact was expecting to see. Luckily for us, the rear windows were tinted so Tank and I sat back and let Jeremi drive the last mile. We probably didn't need to be quite so bloody cautious but after someone had shanked Oleks, I wasn't going to take any chances. It wasn't dark enough to pretend we weren't there, but if the dealer wasn't on it, they might not realise what was up 'til things were too late.

'Time to go, Jeremi,' I nudged when the timer was down to five minutes. We'd parked around the corner to wait. 'And remember, don't try anything cute.'

I don't think he will. He might leg it if he gets the chance. Can't say I'd blame him for that.

The question of what we actually wanted to go down kept running through my mind. If it is the old lady, would we really be able to grab her? Threaten her? Force answers out of her? I couldn't shake the feeling there was something so totally, utterly wrong about it all.

And then I remembered Oleks. The bitch had shanked him without a second thought the moment she'd got close enough. This wasn't some harmless old babushka we were dealing with; it was a cold-blooded killer which begged the question: who the hell was she? And what sort of backup would she have with her? Obviously, she had a driver at the very least. Tank had seen her getting in the back seat after all and someone had to be driving the damned Merc.

Exactly on time, headlights appeared at the junction. A car swung into the little access road that led down towards where we'd parked outside the warehouse. I could see the shape was nothing like the Mercedes-Maybach. It was lower profile, smaller, less sleek, the kind of car a middle-aged mum or dad might drive. Totally plain. As it pulled towards us, it slowed, flashed its headlights, and then stopped thirty or forty feet out.

'This normal?' I prompted.

'Yes,' Jeremi said. 'I get out and nod. She puts the bag on the ground then leaves.'

No physical contact. Smart. It'll make our job harder. But if there's one thing that Tank's good at, it's closing a gap between him and his prey faster than they can react. I've seen it in action dozens of times and every time I'm bloody glad he's on my side. He goes from stock still to holding a victim at knifepoint in seconds.

'Go on then,' I said.

I felt a little bad for Jeremi. But he was going to walk away from this with a bag of drugs which we'd paid for with his Bitcoin. No doubt he'd sell it for a tidy profit.

As I watched he stood in front of the car, lit up by the head-lights which were on full beam. They were so bright that I couldn't see a damned thing. As I squinted, my eyes adjusted just in time to see the passenger-side door swing open and a figure emerge. Whoever it was had to be short. They had a carrier bag which swung as she walked towards Jeremi.

She stopped; the headlights on her car dimmed. And my jaw dropped.

Not because it wasn't the old woman who'd killed Oleks. I'd guessed as much. But the woman in front of me was the last person I'd ever have expected:

Bipa Bakowski.

'Fuck!' I said. 'What the hell is *Tiny's wife* doing here?'

Tank looked at me and then shrugged.

'Right, stay here. Watch from a distance. If shit goes down, move. Got it?'

He nodded, as casual as if I'd just given him my takeaway order. Nothing ever fazed Tank.

Bipa bloody Bakowski. Had she taken over after Tiny fled? Surely not. Everything I could remember about her said she was a follower, a hanger-on, a limpet on Tiny's arms. She'd loved being around the *shef*. Tiny had been the ultimate bad boy. He'd had money, he'd driven fast cars, had the big bloody penthouse looking over Hyde Park. Subtlety was never his bag. And Bipa was no exception. Legs for miles, a few years younger than him, and totally, utterly smitten.

She'd aged well. A few crow's feet, a little less lithe perhaps, but unmistakeably still the trophy wife that Tiny had married. Her head snapped in my direction as I opened the rear passenger-side door and stepped out into the rain.

A flash of fear came over her. The unknown. Then, as I stepped closer, slowly enough to make sure she knew I wasn't about to rush her, her fear turned to surprise. The cute, button nose crinkled into a frown. For a moment, she was as speechless as I'd been but she hadn't had the opportunity to hide behind tinted windows and think things over for a minute.

'You!' she said.

'Me.' I nodded. 'Long time no see, Bipa.'

'What the hell are you doing here?'

I hesitated. Bipa has always been totally loyal to Tiny to the point of obsession. If I pull the usual crap, and threaten her, then she'll clam up and I'll never learn what the hell she's up to. If I try to appeal to her better nature... does she even have one?

It's a risk I'll have to take.

I turned to Jeremi and told him to go wait in the car. He scarpered, glad to be out of harm's way. When he was gone, I took a step towards Bipa and leant forward as if we were old friends catching up after far too long.

'I'm looking for Tiny,' I said confidently.

She shook her head, her expression disbelieving. 'Take a number, join the back of the queue.'

Echoes of Tiny's aunt. The same line: I haven't seen him, honest.

Except this time, Bipa was telling the truth. Her voice was tinged with sadness, a woman grieving her man.

'He's here,' I said slowly, pausing for dramatic effect, 'and someone is trying to kill him.'

The same story. Much easier to keep it consistent if I don't change things up. That way, if she's spoken to Polina, she'll know I was telling everyone the same shit.

'Who this time?'

'A gangster,' I said carefully. 'One who thinks Tiny owes him blood. I know Tiny's back in London, Bipa. Polina told me.'

Her eyes widened further. She wanted to believe me. Then, as quickly as the innocence had surfaced, her expression hardened.

'Bullshit,' she said, her face now a blank mask. Her body language had shifted, she glanced over her shoulder. I could see a man behind the wheel. Her minder. Her Tank.

'I wouldn't believe it either. Ask around. Someone killed a man in the Costa del Sol looking for him. Then they killed a mule called Oleks. They've killed and tortured two of our own too. They won't stop 'til they've found him, Bipa. Help me. I need to get to him before anyone else.'

'My husband is dead. He's been gone for years. If Polina's told you that he's back, she can tell you where.'

Shit. I'd fucked things up bringing Polina into it.

'She doesn't want him back,' I said. 'Not when she's running the show in his place.'

This time, Bipa laughed. 'Polina running the Syndicate? You've lost your mind.'

'Okay, maybe I'm wrong there,' I conceded. 'Think about it. If Tiny's really dead, what's the harm in helping me? I won't find him. He won't be murdered. I'll disappear again as quickly and quietly as I reappeared tonight. But if he's not dead and you know something, tell me because I'll find him. Don't you want to know what's happened to him? To find him if he's still out there?'

She fell silent. I could see a single tear rolling down her cheek, the moonlight making it shine.

'I can't even if I want to. I don't know where he went, you idiot. If I did, I'd have found him a long time ago, wouldn't I?'

Fair point. 'Okay, well, how about I tell you what I know and you listen and tell me if I'm getting anything wrong? No expectations, just chat.'

She didn't immediately object so I took my opportunity and launched into my spiel.

'We know Tiny left London by Eurostar under an assumed name. At Gare du Nord, he ditched his travel identity and headed south under another fake ID. He made it to Puerto Banús where he met up with The Jockey for funds.'

Bipa snorted again. 'That bell end? My husband's financier? As if. But carry on your tall tale.'

'The Jockey spilled the beans to the man hunting him down. He got himself cut open in his own bar using one of his own steak knives.'

A bit of an embellishment. But Bipa was hooked.

'From there, Tiny travelled to Poland. We know he liaised with Polina – we're assuming she gave him money – and now he's come home to London. Another fake identity no doubt.'

'If he's here, where is he?'

I hesitated. Tiny was a creature of comfort. He wouldn't be hiding in a hell-hole like Upper Norwood or have started driving for Uber to pay his way. He'd be living it up.

'That's what I need your help to find out,' I said. But what help did I want? If Tiny wasn't running the Syndicate, who was? And why had they killed Oleks?

'But I'm preaching to the choir here,' I said, chancing my arm again. 'You're running heroin out of Afghanistan, across through Iran into Turkey, and then across the Black Sea into Odessa. That's a ballsy route. Did you come up with that on your own?'

Nobody ran that route. Everything used to come in through Greece, via boat into Italy, or via the Balkans. Adding a sea-crossing and a warzone into the mix ups the danger but makes the new, improved Syndicate unpredictable as hell. It's a plan well above Bipa's paygrade.

'I had help,' Bipa said coyly.

'But not from Tiny.'

'No, not from Tiny.'

An awkward few seconds of silence ensued. I have to steer this conversation back to finding information out, not giving it away.

If it weren't Tiny or Polina, then who? The other brothers, Nicodemus and Pavel, aren't in the picture either. One's still in prison, the other got shanked in a fight behind bars. Not that it matters. She's connected to the car. That means she knows the old woman who killed Oleks.

'Older women are underappreciated, aren't they?' I said.

Her eyes lit up.

She does know Oleks' killer.

'Everyone assumes they're old, incapable, kindly even,' I continued, watching her reaction carefully. 'But women can be hard. They can kill just as easily as men.'

'And they can run things as well as men too,' Bipa said.

So there's a woman in charge. The old lady?

'Then why hasn't she told you where Tiny is?'

'Ruslana would've told me if she knew!'

Finally. Ruslana. Where have I heard that name before? It means lioness. It's a very traditional name, the kind that nobody uses anymore.

Then it hit me:

Tiny's mother.

Fuck.

We stole drugs from Ruslana Bakowski. No wonder she killed Oleks. Stealing drugs from someone like Bipa was one thing. Stealing from the matriarch of the world's biggest crime syndicate was another thing entirely.

'You sure about that?' I teased. 'Think it through. Tiny's back in London and Mummy doesn't know? As if. No doubt she's paying for him to hole up somewhere fancy with hookers and-'

Her fist connected with my face so quickly that all I saw was a blur before my head whipped ninety-degrees to the right. Damn, she was strong.

Loyal to the last too.

I could work with that.

As I massaged my jaw, I tried to look apologetic. 'I deserved that,' I said.

'Tiny would never, ever-'

'Then help me find him. You must know something. If Ruslana is paying his way, there will be a money trail. If we could follow it...'

'There's no money trail,' Bipa said tersely. 'Tiny wasn't stupid. He had funds.'

'If it's the cash he stashed, I know where-'

She was already shaking her head.

'Hawala,' she muttered.

Suddenly everything clicked. Tiny hasn't been looking for stashes of money around warehouses, subsisting off handouts from old friends. That was a means to an end, just the short-term cash to get away from the UK.

He's been using hawala all along. No wonder Tank and I haven't been able to keep up.

Hawala is simple: give money to a hawaladar in one place and pay a fee for their services then collect the money from another hawaladar somewhere else using a password. The hawaladars then settle up among themselves at some indeterminate point in the future, if ever. Tiny's cash wouldn't have physically moved, but he'd have a password, or, from the sounds of it, a long list of passwords, to go and collect the money from other places.

'How long for?' I asked.

'Ages,' she said. 'He'd move money here, stash some there. Nobody except him knew where it all went.'

I smiled. The savvy bastard. He'd sent his money all over the place. Then when he was on the run, he could go collect it and then use the same hawala system to send it wherever he wanted, probably right back to London. Unseen, untraceable passwords as a way to launder huge amounts of cash. It was genius.

If I were in Tiny's shoes, I'd have travelled the world, using my passwords to collect my cash, then sent most of it back to London, get the fake ID sorted, and then come home and live off the dodgy money. Split it out between a few hawaladars to be on the safe side, maybe leave some hidden in case I needed to run again.

'Then he could be here, living right under our noses. Don't you think Tiny would've settled somewhere luxurious?'

My mind flashed back to his pad in Hyde Park: oodles of vast, empty space. It was almost like a show home. I'd joked once it was a show-off home, Tiny's way of saying "You lot can't afford a broom cupboard, but I can afford to keep thousands of square feet empty right in the heart of London". He'd always been a snob like that. A cruel, vindictive snob.

'Then you should look for him in Dubai. Or Tokyo. Or New York. There's no way my husband is back home and hasn't said a peep to me.'

She was so sure of herself. It was almost cruel to break that confidence.

'I suppose you're right,' I said. 'If he contacted you, the police would soon find out, wouldn't they? Then he'd be in jail faster than Jeremi shat his pants. He does, by the way, need that resupply he ordered.'

She kicked the bag in my direction.

'Find him,' she said. 'Find my bastard of a husband. And when you do, tell him that his wife is going to kill him.'

I smiled.

Not if I get there first.

62

JUXTAPOSED CONTROLS

THE VIDEO WAS GRAINY, their faces obscured by light on the car's windshield.

But unmistakeably, there were three people in the car.

The dead man, Oleks Kuleba, was clearly in the driving seat. The other two men were in the back.

Rafferty squinted at the footage, playing the same few seconds of video over and over. She clicked frantically, pausing and unpausing it frame by frame looking for the slightest hint that would tell her who the men in the backseat were. She let out a sigh. It was no use. There was no way to identify the men from the video.

'And this was when?'

'The day of the laddie's death,' Brodie said. 'The car came through the Eurotunnel on Le Shuttle. They're on camera going up the motorway. Then we lose them. I'll keep lookin' o' course, but it'll take time...'

Everything did. But with every passing minute, the two men who had been with Oleks Kuleba the last time they knew he was alive – and probably the same two men the vicar had seen, if Rafferty's gut was right – were getting further and further away.

It was odd. Oleks had come to the UK under his own volition. He'd literally been in the driving seat. Had he suspected that he'd been driving to his own murder? There was a whiff of the Troubles about it: many a man had been whisked across the border to the south and promptly executed without the slightest hint that they were heading for their deaths. That level of brutality spoke volumes about the perpetrators. What on earth had Oleks Kuleba been mixed up in?

'Do we scan passports on the way in? Or is it still old-school?'

If Border Force were still using the glance-and-check method of old, they'd be out of luck. In theory, Rafferty could ask local uniformed officers – the backbone of any real police investigation – to talk to the Border Force official who'd let them through but those officers were so overworked, seeing thousands of people a day, that they'd never recognise the men.

'It's still juxtaposed controls, lassie. Not quite how it used to be, though. Now there are two borders. At Calais, to go through the...'

At her glare, his voice trailed off. He knew she didn't care about the technicalities.

'Aye,' he said. 'They're scanned, so long as yer using a biometric passport. Once by the French, then by our boys.'

'So we've got a record of who's coming and going.'

'UK Border Force do.'

A paper trail. Finally.

Now all she needed was to get a warrant, find out who had entered the UK with Oleks Kuleba and they'd finally have named suspects. She texted Kieran O'Connor to organise the paperwork and then turned back to Brodie. He was already back at work, his fingers flying over the keyboard.

'No need ta ask, lassie,' he said with a grin. 'If there's any sign of the car, I'll find it and join up the dots.'

She nodded her thanks. Knowing the route they'd driven didn't matter too much if the passports could identify the killers. They'd already burnt the car after all.

'Do that. Then I've got another gig for you...'

'What is it, lass?'

'Run the ANPR but bill it to Joe Singleton at MisPer. Ayala's doing his nut over the budget on this and there's no point giving him any ammunition at his next "Fiscal Responsibility Meeting". Were they always a thing? I don't remember Morton ever making me attend one.'

He grinned.

'I think ye will find Ayala made that shit up.'

63

A KNOCK AT THE DOOR

'NOW WHAT?' Tank asked.

We let Jeremi go after our meeting with Bipa. He wouldn't be snitching on us any time soon. Not when his livelihood – and his life – depends on keeping to the Syndicate's code of silence.

Now we have to work out how to break another, equally stringent, code of silence. That of a hawaladar.

Naturally, the money-movers are as secretive as Swiss bankers. I know from Bipa that Tiny's London hawaladar is a guy called Rashee Sanook. I never knew him. The part of the Syndicate I ran was miles away from complicated money laundering, but I know one thing: men with that much money never, ever go anywhere alone.

Sanook's bound to have primo security: guys like Tank, guns, security cameras, and a vetting procedure for new clients so strict, it would make MI5 look like rank amateurs. To get near him, we'll have to be damned good. To cajole private information out of him, we'll have to be even better.

'You ever turned on someone for money?' I asked.

Tank glared. As if.

He'd turn on someone for drugs. I had to search his bedroom

again this morning after we let Jeremi go. Of course he'd managed to nick a few grams. Every now and then I think he's high, but he's been on the gear for so long that he's become an expert at hiding small doses. One of these days, it's going to kill him if I'm not careful.

'Okay,' I said. 'Bribing his security guards won't work. When you were Tiny's muscle-for-hire, when was he most exposed? He must've been alone some time?'

'Women,' Tank grunted.

Plural. Of course. Naturally, that sweaty beast was enjoying what he peddled. The skin game used to be Nico Bakowski's domain. Girls, most of whom thought they were coming to Britain for a better life as cleaners or au pairs, were trafficked in, their passports seized, and then subjected to the carrot and stick approach: free drugs if they did as they were told, the threat of violence if they didn't comply.

'Were you in the room?' I asked.

'I wait outside.'

I'll bet he did. Tiny had a huge penthouse. Private lift, 24/7 security detail, and, on top of that, guys like Tank on an overlapping rota. If Sanook's creaming a small percentage off every transaction, he'll be making serious bank. His security will be even better than Tiny's.

There's simply no way we can walk into Sanook's office and strongarm him the way we'd strongarmed the watchmaker all those months ago.

Nor would we be able to bribe him. He has money and we don't. Not enough of it anyway. An indiscreet hawaladar is a dead hawaladar and Sanook has been in the business for decades.

'We'll have to get him somewhere away from work,' I said. 'Somewhere without the hardcore security detail. He can take people with him but he can't take security cameras and a panic room everywhere.'

But Tank wasn't listening. He was staring towards the front door, his ears pricked like a security dog.

'What is it, boy?' I joked.

He held up a chubby, gnarled finger to his lips. 'Shh.'

I strained to hear what he'd noticed.

An engine?

Several?

'Police,' he said simply.

He didn't move a muscle.

Adrenaline kicked in.

The police? Here? How?

I'd expected them to catch up with me eventually... but that was supposed to be years down the line. I was going to be the guy that killed a mobster. The guy who broke witness protection to take revenge.

Biology fought with logic. I could run. I might even make it. But if I did, I'd look dead guilty.

The best thing to do was to mimic Tank. To stay deadly calm. Surprised even.

'Anything we need to hide, boss?' Tank asked.

I shook my head. Only a fool would keep anything remotely incriminating at his own house. We'd ditched the clothing we'd worn when burning the car – to get rid of any hydrocarbons – and we had no weapons. There was a couple of grand of cash under my bed, easily explained as savings.

'Nope,' I said. 'Let's let 'em in.'

64

DISCREPANCIES

LESS THAN SIX hours after learning about the car coming through the Eurotunnel exit at Folkestone, Rafferty had followed the breadcrumbs to the very end: the last known address of Augustyn Yermak, one of the men in the backseat of the car.

It had been a team effort. Brodie, together with Joe from Missing Persons, had chased down the ANPR data, compared it with the snapshot photos taken, and, eventually, found them.

Their method was simple: he'd looked at the timestamp of each ping on the ANPR cameras, then compared the distance with the time taken. That had been Joe's idea. Eventually, they found a spot of motorway where they'd taken much longer than the speed limit had suggested. After confirming that wasn't down to traffic, Joe and Brodie had surmised that the men had to have stopped off somewhere en route. They had: the Moto Medway service station just off Junction 4 of the M2 where they were caught on CCTV buying pre-packaged sarnies and cans of Coke.

Having Joe play backup to the team had been a stroke of

genius. He was the kind of guy that doggedly checked every single little detail.

He also had an uncanny ability to wheedle information out of people without resorting to a warrant. Perhaps it was his telephone manner or maybe it was his disarmingly honest Lancastrian accent. The service station's manager had succumbed to his charms and handed over the transaction records. They'd bought the sarnies on a credit card which allowed Brodie to work his magic, turning the scant point-of-sale information back into real, actionable intel.

Now here they were, ready to make an "on suspicion of murder" arrest. The whole of the taskforce had wanted in, with the sole exception of Ayala who was managing things from behind his desk.

Xander Thompson had joined them as silver commander, his hand-picked Armed Response Vehicle on-site in case of trouble.

As she watched, her ex barked orders, sending his men to surround the house. It was a mid-terrace, Victorian, and had the smallest patch of grass for a back garden, so the tactical side of things was simple: most of the men, and they were all men, were out front while a handful covered the back door.

It was typical of Xander to have an all-male team. He was the sort of guy who had the Olympic slogan, *Citius, Altius, Fortius*, engraved on a wall-plate and thought that "Faster, Higher, Stronger" meant tall men with big guns. Each wore thick, heavy body armour complete with a camera to record their actions. The footage was the latest mandate handed down from above, designed to keep the Met's reputation. The men hated it: they just wanted to get on with the job and not have to think about every misstep making it into the archives.

Not that she could argue with the team's efficiency. Within

minutes of arrival, they were ready to go. The front man was carrying a Big Red Key to batter the door down.

The second stepped up, warrant in hand. They didn't need one, but belt and braces were the order of the day. Kieran wanted this to be cleaner than a monk's conscience.

'Police! Open up!'

The customary yell. Rafferty could imagine the team at the back bracing for action. Suspects always ran out of the back, straight into the waiting arms of the police.

Except this time.

Instead, the door swung open.

A man with a confused expression looked around, his forehead creasing up with so many lines that he looked like Yoda. He was dressed in a t-shirt and Adidas trousers with tousled, receding brown hair and a smattering of stubble on a weak, pointy chin.

'What on earth is going on?' he demanded.

The team stormed forwards, spinning him around and shoving him to the floor. As they slapped cuffs on him, they recited the caution and then, so casually that it almost seemed like an afterthought, asked if anyone else was in the house.

'My friend – his name's Tank,' the arrestee said.

When Xander nodded, his team went in to clear the property. This was another day at the office for them. The Serious Organised Crime Agency made busts like this day in, day out. And this was an easy one.

Moments later, they had Tank in cuffs too.

Rafferty grinned.

Despite the grainy footage, she was convinced. These were the two men from the Moto Medway CCTV footage. The same men who'd driven into the country with Oleks Kuleba.

They had 'em.

Finally.

65

INTERROGATION

THE INTERVIEW DIDN'T GO AT ALL how Rafferty expected. Normally, the smart ones lawyered up, said nothing, and tried their best not to react at all to questions.

This time, Yermak turned down a lawyer, didn't scream or shout, instead insisting that there must've been some mistake and that, yes, he'd absolutely like to talk in order to clear up the confusion.

Interview Room One was quickly made ready and Rafferty took a seat next to Mayberry. They'd already agreed that, as usual, she'd lead the interview while he took notes and kept an eye out for non-verbal clues.

Once Rafferty had started recording the interview and repeated the caution for the record, she leant back in her seat, surveying her suspect once again.

'Are you sure you don't want to talk to a lawyer?' Rafferty asked. 'If you can't afford one, you can speak to the duty solicitor free of charge.'

The man matched her relaxed body language by leaning back and then he shrugged. 'No point, right? I ain't done nothin'.'

After a momentary pause, she started with the CCTV printouts. As she slid the first one, a grainy low-res screen-grab of the CCTV at Moto Medway service station, across the desk, he reached out to pull it closer.

'Is that you?'

He studied it intently. 'Sure looks like it, yeah. Either that or that poor git cut his face like I did.'

Wrong-footed. Again. Rafferty had expected a denial or, at the very least, a comment about the quality of the photo. She hadn't expected Yermak to pre-empt her first line of attack. He'd inadvertently confirmed it was him as there was no way to make out enough fine detail to spot a few tiny cuts in the photograph.

'How did you hurt yourself?'

'DIY injury,' Yermak said smugly.

Easy to claim, hard to disprove. Yermark was a slippery customer. Rafferty point back at the photo and tried to steer her interview back on track. 'That was taken at a service station in Kent. Have you been there?'

'Sure. Many times. I was there last week.'

Now he was volunteering information? Rafferty cast a side-eye at Mayberry. This was weird. Their suspect was dictating the narrative.

'What were you doing there?'

He shrugged. 'Stopped for a piss and a shit. Might've bought a sarnie. You want a complete log of every time I've been to the bog?'

Cheeky git. Rafferty had to stop herself laughing at the absurdity of it all. Instead, she said: 'Just your movements, not your bowel movements.'

'Well,' he said, shutting his eyes as if struggling to recall a particularly hectic schedule. 'Right now, I'm in a police interview suite. Before I got here, I was at home. When you realise you've got the wrong person, I think I'll go back home. Might swing by Five Guys for a burger and a shake on the way. There's one up at Charring Cross, right?'

'On Friday. Not today.'

'Okay... Breakfast in... how do you pronounce the place – Cool Ong? Kew-Lounge?'

It sounded foreign. French? German?

'Where?'

'In Germany.'

Ah, Cologne. So he'd been abroad.

'What were you doing in West Germany?'

'Stopped for a bit of brekkie. Apfelstrudel, mug of some fruity rubbish they called tea, and a 'nana. Not the freshest pastry to be honest...'

'I don't need your opinion on the quality of your breakfast. Were you alone?'

He shook his head.

'Nah. I was with a couple of friends,' he said. 'My mate Tank and his friend.'

'Oleks Kuleba?'

He gave a shrug. 'If you say so. Sounds about right. Quiet fella.'

'This him?'

Rafferty showed him a second CCTV screen grab, this time from the English border coming into Folkestone.

He nodded.

'How did you know him?'

'Like I said, he was Tank's mate.'

'And you were all travelling together.'

Another nod.

'Where from and where to?'

'Let's see, we picked him up in Poland then we travelled west to come home.'

'But you're not sure about his name. Do you often travel

with people you don't know?'

'That a crime, Inspector?'

Rafferty pursed her lips. Every question was met with another question.

'Just a simple yes/no question,' she said curtly.

'No,' he said. 'Not often.'

'Then why did you do so this time?'

'We picked up Tank's friend while on a road trip. Alex – sorry, Oleks, right? – was heading the same way we were so Tank offered him a lift.'

'From where to where?'

'Poland,' he said simply. 'To here. I know where you're headed with this.'

'Where would that be?'

He paused as if for dramatic effect and then, leant forward and spoke so softly that Rafferty found herself leaning forward as he said: 'I saw the woman who killed him.'

Before Rafferty could speak, there was a rap at the door to the interview suite. She stood.

'Excuse me for a minute. Interview suspended at 13:38.'

She beckoned for Mayberry to come with her and the pair stepped out into the hallway where Ayala was waiting for them.

'That was a shit-show,' Ayala said simply. 'You let him dictate the narrative.'

'I'm handing him the rope he needs to hang himself,' Rafferty shot back. 'He's volunteering specifics. If I have to circle back to deal with contradictions then I will.'

'What's this about a woman? Have we seen any evidence of a woman being involved?'

Rafferty waved a hand dismissively. 'It's all bullshit. We've got him bang to rights. He drove the victim into the country, took the victim to the murder site. He left the knife behind. A witness – the priest – saw them run off from the crime scene.'

Not that their witness struck Rafferty as particularly reliable.

'D-don't forget the b-burning h-house,' Mayberry said.

He had a point, though they had no evidence as to who set the place on fire. Yet. There was overwhelming circumstantial evidence but nothing that would get them a conviction. Yet.

'Any evidence on the knife?'

Rafferty smiled. 'Yep. Prints on the handle. We've probably got some DNA transfer on there too, but no point running an expensive test to look for transfer when the prints will get us the same result in less time and for less money.'

Even Ayala couldn't argue with that. He was as penny-pinching as any DCI she'd ever known. He nodded.

'Then get everything you can from him, run his prints and confirm the match, arrest him, and let the CPS take it from here.'

A murder charge meant virtually no chance of bail. If the CPS signed off on charging Yermak, he'd be held in custody until trial. It was the rare slam-dunk that every detective dreamed of.

'Will do.'

As Rafferty turned back towards the interview suite, Ayala stalked off to watch from the other side of the one-way mirror without so much as a "good job".

She and Mayberry retook their seats and restarted the tape.

'Thanks for waiting.'

As if he had a choice.

'Where were we?' Rafferty asked. 'Ah, the day of Oleks Kuleba's murder. Let's go through it all again. From the Eurotunnel onwards. Just the pertinent details.'

Yermak smirked. 'How do I know what you think is pertinent?'

'Just use your best judgement. If I need more details, I'll ask.'

For the next three hours, interrupted only by a quick loo-break in the middle, Rafferty teased as many specifics as she could from her suspect. He admitted to driving up to Aldbor-ough Hatch with the victim. The story he told – one which nobody would ever believe – was that Kuleba had arranged a date with a woman from the internet.

'How exactly did this go down?'

'He met her on Rate My Ex, ya know, that dodgy dating app where all your exes get to review you and vice versa,' Yermak said cheerfully. 'A self-described "goth" looking for her "'til death do they part".'

'You should write fiction.'

Yermak said nothing. 'Was there a question in there, Inspector Rafferty?'

'Just an observation. Don't you agree it's all a bit far-fetched?'

He tilted his head to one side. 'The truth often is. Reality doesn't have to make sense, Inspector. I can only tell you what I know. He went there. We thought it was far-fetched too so we hung around, had a drink at the pub up the road, and drove by to catch a glimpse of her.'

'In case he got murdered.'

'No,' Yermak said. 'Of course not. In case he got stood up. Or catfished. Either way, he might want a lift. And after driving across Europe hearing all about her, I was curious. You would've been too.'

It was all too neat.

'So you drove by to take a look,' Rafferty echoed, 'and then you saw him get stabbed.'

'Nope, I saw an old woman coming out of the graveyard.

She got into a Merc that was parked on the road right outside the church.'

'An old woman. And you thought she was Oleks' date?'

Yermak shrugged. 'Had to be, didn't it? Nobody else around. Anyway, she got into a car and there was no sign of Oleks.'

'So you went to investigate.'

'Yep. I got out, so did Tank, and then we went to check on Oleks. We saw him lying there, propped up against the gravestone-'

'And then what? You grabbed the knife?'

He shook his head vehemently. 'Never,' he said. 'The priest appeared in the doorway and yelled something. We panicked. We ran.'

'Then what?'

'Then we went home.'

'You didn't think to call the police?'

'Would you have?' he asked. 'You've assumed I'm guilty because I knew the victim and I was in the area. You wouldn't have believed me if I'd called ahead with my side of the story, would you?'

He had a point. It would've sounded just as ridiculous on the phone as it did in person.

'Back to the knife. You said you didn't touch it. Did Tank?'

'No, ma'am.'

Rafferty grinned. 'Then how do you explain the prints?'

'What prints?'

'On the handle of the knife.'

He returned her grin. Smug git. 'Well, detective, I'd say the killer left them there.'

'The old woman who got into the Mercedes?'

He shrugged. 'That'd be my best guess.'

'Then you won't mind if we fingerprint you and Tank.'

'Be my guest.'

Rafferty resisted the urge to scowl.

If this was a big bluff, it was one hell of a gamble.

'Let's do it then.'

NOT ON RECORD

NO MATCH FOUND.

'There must be some sort of mistake,' Rafferty said. 'Run it again?'

Brodie shook his head. 'No mistake, lassie. The prints on the knife aren't in the database.'

'So Yermak and Tank-'

'Aren't ye killers,' Brodie finished for her.

Shit, shit shit.

Ayala was going to go nuts.

THE CAT WITH NINE LIVES

WHAT THE FUCK JUST HAPPENED?

Tank and I strolled out of New Scotland Yard and into a sweet, if bitter cold, night.

'Don't smile, don't say anything, just keep walking,' I said.

No doubt they were watching us.

Hours and hours of interrogation had got them nowhere. Eventually, they must've compared our prints to the knife. Within an hour of that happening, they'd let us go.

'I say nothing. I never talk.'

When we were well away from the police, Tank and I paused overlooking the Thames.

And promptly burst out laughing.

'Well, I never expected that, Tank!' I said under my breath. As I spoke, a cold mist escaped into the night. 'Commit two murders, get arrested for a third we didn't do... and walk out Scot free. Has the Met always been this incompetent?'

He smiled back at me. 'I say nothing to them. I ask for lawyer. By time he come, they let me go.'

Better and better. The police couldn't even compare and contrast our bullshit story. I'd come up with the "woman from the internet" lie days ago. A stupid story, but one that would be almost impossible to disprove. As if Oleks had been catfished and murdered by some old granny. Good luck to the rozzers disproving it, though. Nice goose chase to send 'em on.

'How quick do you reckon they'll work it out?' I asked. They'd know I'd spun them a yarn. They'd want to watch us, no doubt. We were gonna have to be bloody careful tracking down the hawaladar. And even more careful going after Tiny.

'Soon,' he said.

'Then, my friend, we'll just have to be quicker.'

'You got plan?'

'Don't I always?' I said. Of course, I had a damned plan.

I told him.

68

THE ZEBRA STRIKES BACK

CRESTFALLEN, Rafferty retreated to an empty interview suite, shut the door, and collapsed into the chair.

Ayala had made a mistake. They shouldn't have released Yermak and Tank.

She was so damned sure she'd got the perpetrators. They'd come with him into the country, gone with him to the crime scene, and they'd been seen crouched over the body moments after the murder. How much more guilty could they have looked?

Yermak had come across as so sleazy, so obviously involved in something dodgy, that she hadn't thought for a second that he might not be the killer. Now, at Ayala's insistence, they'd had to let their prime suspect go. The risk of being wrong, of being slammed for keeping them under arrest after finding out the knife was used by an unknown third person, had put the fear of God into him. In law it might be the right decision, but she knew it was one they'd regret.

Behind his back, she'd asked Xander to have one of his surveillance teams keep an eye on Yermak in case her gut was right.

Two simple explanations. One, the most plausible: Yermak was telling the truth. There was a murderous granny catfishing men on the Rate My Ex dating app.

No fucking way.

Two, Yermak was the killer but he'd somehow got a knife with someone else's prints on it, then, perhaps wearing gloves, used that knife to kill knowing that the fingerprints wouldn't match his.

That was more like it.

Rafferty sat up and pulled out her phone. If they'd worn gloves, there'd have been fibre transfer from the gloves to the knife. Locard's exchange principle in action. But collecting and processing fibre transfer was slow, it was expensive, and Ayala would never sign off on it in a month of Sundays.

She brought up her phone book, scrolled down to Kflom's number and hit call.

It went straight to answerphone.

'It's Ash. I need a favour. Call me back when you get this.'

69

HAWALADAR

WE'D LAID low at my place for a couple of days after our arrests putting us a week behind schedule. I'd had to assume the police were watching us too. I'd spotted a van in the street marked with an electrician's branding. The police thought they were clever pulling that crap. What they didn't realise was the Syndicate, and presumably every other criminal gang in London, used to keep an eye on the cars parked at or near various police stations. Once I'd walked up past the Quicksilver Patrol Base, a training academy for coppers, to see a dozen vans parked in a line, one unmarked and the rest marked. It wasn't exactly subtle.

Our plan started to come together over a series of long walks, away from the house and away from the Met's prying eyes. They couldn't follow us all day forever. The Met ain't got the budget for that.

Thanks to an old contact still in the game, we found out that the hawaladar lives in Wapping, right on the riverfront, a stone's throw from St Katherine's Docks where Tiny used to moor up. He has the penthouse of a supposedly "secure" building, the kind with fob locks. We could get past that easily enough by tail-gating in.

What we couldn't get past was the lift. A brochure for the building we found online proudly said that the penthouse had its own, private lift. If it were my place, I'd have that lift open into a reinforced entrance hall. That's where I'd put an internal, reinforced security door guarded twenty-four seven.

Unless he does something stupid, or I pay for backup, there's no way we'll be able to storm a hawaladar's home. Short of hiring the Wagner group, it'll be a sure-fire way to end up dead.

That means getting at him while he's in public. Somewhere even his bodyguards, all four of them, won't be able to stop us.

'Where though?' Tank demanded.

That's the million-dollar question. We need to know Sanook's routine: where he goes, when, and who with. Then we need to pick a spot to ambush him.

It'll need to be quiet and have an easy, simple escape route. I want information so at least we aren't trying to make off with a big wad of cash or anything.

Then we'll need to act on that information. Quickly.

There's no doubt that the moment we're out of Sanook's sight, he'll want his revenge. He can't afford not to. His entire business depends on his integrity and his discretion. We'll have become a shiny example that he can't be trusted.

The question isn't if he'll put a hit out on us, it's how quickly. He'll have to work out who we are – not hard for a man with his resources – and then he'll have to work out how much he values damage control. Kill us quickly, quietly, and he can salvage his rep. Botch the job, he'll just draw attention to his own error.

I figure we have a week, tops.

But by then, it won't matter.
Tiny Bakowski will be dead.
And, if I get this wrong, so will we.

70

THE ANCIENT CATFISH

WITH XANDER'S boys watching Yermak, Rafferty turned her attention to the possibility that there was, in fact, an elderly woman out to kill young men who hadn't been in the country long enough to learn how the London Underground map worked.

As absurd as it was, the idea had gained traction with Ayala and Mayberry. During a team meeting shortly after Tank and Yermak were released, they had both been utterly convinced that the knife categorically ruled them out. Neither wanted to entertain Rafferty's suggestion that Yermak had used a second-hand knife.

Now she had to disprove the lunacy.

First, she went back to the priest. Over the phone, he denied any knowledge of seeing an older woman. But, he cautioned, one wouldn't stick out. He had a lot of older, female parishioners as well as a handful of widows that visited their husband's graves at St Peter's to change the fresh flowers, and so older women had become background noise.

After prevailing upon him to agree to do a digital line-up before evening mass to see if he recognised Yermak and Tank, she hung up and headed down to the IT department in search of Brodie.

He buzzed her in when he saw her on the video link, but not before pointing at his own headset several times. She got it – he was on a conference call.

There was nowhere to sit in the long corridor outside so she leant against the wall and took out her phone to distract herself while she waited. Her eye was drawn to the app store. *May as well take a look, right?* she thought as she typed in "Rate My Ex" and proceeded to download the app. When the RME logo appeared on her phone, she opened it up.

A registration page appeared. The first question listed several gender options – male, female, transitioning, nonbinary, none of the above. She clicked male and proceeded to create a fictitious account whose details mirrored that of Oleks Kuleba.

Height? Six foot two. Weight? Average.

Rafferty made a good guess at all the physical questions. It was the preferences that stumped her. What were his likes and dislikes? Did he have "red lines" as the app called it, things he would never entertain in a partner?

She answered all the questions as non-committally as possible to avoid ruling anyone out.

When it came to location, she picked "Poland" where Kuleba was from and where Yermak claimed to have picked him up.

And then had second thoughts.

The whole story reeked of cow manure. If, however, she were to entertain it, what would drive a man to travel the better part of a thousand miles to go on a date? Surely anyone would realise that long-distance would kill things before it started.

A fetish perhaps? Something Kuleba couldn't get at home? Had he grown up in a religious culture and needed to be far away to satiate his appetite without judgement?

Or had he met the woman on the app once he'd arrived in the UK? That would be much more plausible. But it didn't line up with Yermak's spiel at all.

A door creaked nearby and then a shadow fell across her phone.

'Lassie, my brother-in-law is single. He's a right eejit sometimes, but he ain't a bampot.'

Brodie looked down at her, grinning.

'Is this the same one you tried to set me up with before? The one you told me had a really small penis?'

'Aye. That's him. Four-inch Phil, that's what they call him. But don't worry... it smells like a foot.'

Disgusting.

'Or,' Brodie said slyly, 'I know a very nice up-and-coming crime scene investigator who-'

'Hilarious,' she said. 'Do you want to stand in the hallway making awful jokes all day or shall we get some work done?'

'Hallway sounds good ter me,' Brodie said smugly.

She pushed him gently, nudging him towards his office door.

Inside, Brodie's screen already had the Rate My Ex website open.

'You're ahead of me?'

'Mayberry texted, lassie. Said you'd be down lookin' to find out about this wee catfish of yours...'

'And?'

He shook his head. 'Nothin' doing. I cannae find no sign of either yer woman or yer victim.'

'Kuleba isn't on there?'

'I couldnae find him – and I tried ta find him by reverse image search.'

So it was all bollocks.

'Thanks, Brodie,' Rafferty said. 'I owe you one.'

'Dinnae mention it. And aboot Phil...-'
'Not that one.'
'Worth a try.'

MEMBERS ONLY

THE KOH-I-NOOR CLUB is one of London's oldest. Obviously, it's men only. That's not a problem for us.

What is a problem is getting in.

Tank's out. There's no way he'd ever pass for one of London's well-heeled club members. I'm not convinced I will either, but I have to give it a go.

Becoming a member is impossible. To get in, they want you to be proposed and then seconded by existing members, do an interview with their admissions panel, and pay a whopping great joining fee too. It's designed to put people off. It does.

Instead, I'm going to have to go in through the staff entrance.

One cold, wet Thursday, I hung around the back alley outside the kitchen entrance where the bins were. I could see half-eaten lobsters, empty bottles of Petrus, and the remains of Cuban cigars tossed into the bins. Even expensive shit smelt awful after a while.

A white-bibbed waiter emerged at half-past eight, lighting up a cigarette as he stepped out into the night. He looked at me curiously but didn't say anything.

'Busy night?' I said awkwardly.

Bribing people wasn't as easy as I'd expected. Nor would it be cheap. A place like this meant bonanza tips for staff.

'Can I help you with something, *sir*?'

His voice dripped with sarcasm.

'This place – they pay you well?'

'Oh yes, sir. Thousands a night, free use of the corporate jet, and an all-expenses paid trip to Saville Row once a season to get kitted out.'

Sarcasm again. I could work with that.

'How's an easy ten grand sound to you?'

He looked down his nose at me, his nostrils flaring. 'You a cop?'

I burst out laughing. Nobody had ever accused me of working for the rozzers before.

'Nah, this isn't anything illegal or nothing,' I said. 'Here's the thing – one of your members has been avoiding being served with a lawsuit. I've got to give it to him in person for it to be valid. I need to get in, get to him, and I'll be out in two minutes, tops.'

Not a bad lie for something off the cuff. Most people don't know shit about process servers so it was plausible enough. My uncle used to do it, just handing people legal documents and then signing paperwork to say he'd done it. Easy money really.

'And you're going to give me ten grand for that? Just for letting you in and looking the other way?'

I shook my head. 'If only it were that easy eh?'

'What's the catch then?'

'I need to know when he's in the club first. You guys have a membership card, right? It's scanned at the door?'

He nodded so I carried on. 'When you know he's here, you call me. When I get here, you tell me where he is in the club, let me in, and then when it's all done, I'll give you the moolah.'

'I want half upfront.'

'Smart lad,' I said. 'It's a deal.'

~

THREE DAYS LATER, I was back in the alley behind the Koh-i-Noor Club. My new friend opened the door just as I got there.

'He's in the whisky bar upstairs,' he said as he ushered me inside. 'Hang on – your shoes. What size are you?'

I looked down at my feet. What about my shoes? They were black, well-polished, and as boring as shoes got.

'Ten and a half. Why?'

'Stay there.'

He didn't give me much choice.

A minute of awkward lingering later, he returned holding a pair of hideous, shiny brogues.

'Borrowed these from the porter. You're not the first and won't be the last. Where was I? Oh yeah, the bar. Go left at the top of the stairs, second door. Can't miss it. He's in the corner.'

I looked in the direction he was pointing, spotted the stairs, and nodded.

'Nice suit by the way,' he said.

A rental. Under close inspection it wouldn't pass muster. It didn't need to. What was underneath was all I needed. I handed the waiter the envelope containing the second half of his cash, nodded my thanks, and headed up the stairs.

The place was lush. This was real wealth, not drug money. Wood-panelled walls everywhere. Portraits of long dead members, most of them royalty or politicians, hung from the walls. The bastards in here didn't have to hide it. They flaunted it, luxuriated in it. Everyone assumed they were pukka: lawyers and politicians with reputations above reproach. Bet ya if the bastards had grown up in Ilford and fallen in with Tiny's lot –

not that anyone ever had a fucking choice – then they'd have snorted coke, stolen cars, and beaten the shit out of people for money too. These lot just did the coke. I chuckled to myself. We weren't all that different underneath.

Hell, Sanook was living proof this place wasn't on the up.

Halfway up the stairs there was a particularly large painting of Mahatma Ghandi. I wondered what he'd have thought about his image being used in a place like this. Was he into all this opulence? Then again, he was a barrister so maybe he was.

At the top, I turned left as instructed and saw the second door was open. Inside, I could see the bar which carried on the wood-panel theme. A bored bartender was sitting behind the counter deep in conversation with an elderly man opposite him. Behind the bar I could see hundreds of bottles of whisky, rum, and other spirits, plus dozens of jars of cocktail ingredients.

Spotting Sanook was easy. He had the corner table to himself. In front of him there was a copy of The Impartial open to the business section, besides which there was a pot of tea. Even from across the room, he oozed money: Rolex, tick. Fancy cufflinks, tick. Suit that didn't have that polyester-sheen, one that fitted him properly, tick.

Several tables over, I could see four men in suits watching him. They had to be the bodyguards. They eyed me up as I walked into the room. An unfamiliar face in an exclusive private members' club was bound to stick out like a sore thumb.

I made my move. Walking in long, confident strides I made a beeline for Sanook. He looked up at me with a quizzical expression, his eyes darting to his men.

'Mr Sanook,' I said, 'Got a minute? Dimitri Bakowski sent me.'

At the mention of Tiny's name, he nodded and waved off his bodyguards. As they relaxed, Sanook glared, his eyes darting to the bartender as if worried about being seen with me.

'What the hell do you think you're doing?' he hissed. 'If Tiny wants to see me, he knows the rules. This isn't a place for that sort of business-'

I cut him off. 'Don't react to what I'm about to say. Under my jacket, there's a bomb. In my left hand, there's a dead man's switch.'

It was bollocks. My hand was hidden inside my pocket, the "detonator" device I was clutching was a half-eaten pack of mint Polos from my kitchen table. The flashing lights that Sanook would spot on close inspection were, in fact, from a Star Wars Halloween costume. But he had no idea I was bluffing. And he couldn't afford to risk it.

Cool as a cucumber, he nodded. 'You have my attention.'

He'd already acknowledged he knew Tiny so only one question remained: where was he?

'When did you last see Tiny?'

He shrugged. 'Four, five years ago.'

Too easy. Too casual.

'But you know where he is now, don't you?'

'Knowledge is power,' he said. 'And in my game, that's everything.'

'Care to share?'

'You'll regret this.'

He wasn't wrong. I probably would. But so long as I got to Tiny before he got to me, I could deal with that risk.

'We'll see about that. Where is he?'

I looked pointedly at the left hand that was still hidden in my jacket pocket.

'Belgravia,' he hissed. 'Little Russia.'

'Address, now. And his alias.'

He told me. I whistled. The address was right where there were dozens of big, secure embassies.

Sanook added: 'But you'll never get to him. He's playing the oligarch, complete with the bomb-proof security.'

I smiled.

'I got to you, didn't I?'

As I got up, I nodded to his bodyguards before turning back to him.

'If I need anything else, my office will be in touch.'

My pace quickened as I bolted from the room, back down the stairs, and out the fire exit.

'Hey!' a voice called. 'Did you manage to serve him?'

My neck whipped around in the direction of the voice. The waiter I'd bribed lingered in the doorway as if expecting a tip.

'Yep!' I said. 'Thanks. Must dash. Next customer to deal with.'

And I'd better get to Tiny fast.

Before Sanook warns him I'm coming.

72

LITTLE BIRDS

'WHAT AM I LOOKING AT, EXACTLY?'

Perplexed, Rafferty looked from Xander to the screen and back again. He'd marched into New Scotland Yard carrying his laptop and hooked it up to the screen in front of her before playing the grainy CCTV footage she was now reviewing.

There was nothing to it: a man walking along a London street in front of a restaurant of some kind.

'As we agreed, my guys have been watching Augustyn Yermak. This morning, he walked past the front door of the Koh-i-Noor.'

It meant nothing to her.

'Indian takeaway?' she ventured.

He glared at her as if she were being deliberately thick. 'It's one of the oldest and poshest private members' clubs in London. A guy from the East India Company started it in the sixteen hundreds. Francis Drake was a member.'

'I'm still not sure where you're going with this.'

'Your man walked past it at twelve minutes past ten this morning. but he didn't walk past the CCTV of the jewellers

LITTLE BIRDS   337

next door. He walked back past the camera going the other way twenty-six minutes later.'

It suddenly clicked. 'You think he was inside for those twenty-six minutes?'

'Maybe,' Xander said. 'There's a narrow alleyway that runs between the club and the jewellers. It leads around the back to where the club keeps its bins. One way in, one way out.'

'Can you access anything that way? Climb a fence or anything? Perhaps he was testing to see if your guys really were following him? If they'd spooked him...'

Rafferty left her conclusion unsaid. If Yermak had spotted that he was being tailed, hiding out for twenty minutes in an alleyway would be a great way to confirm it.

'My guys don't get caught.'

'Because you trained them and you're Mr Perfect.'

'Look, Ash, I'm doing you a favour here. Your man isn't the calibre of a Koh-i-Noor member. It's the kind of place that oil barons, oligarchs, and hereditary peers hang out. Old money, new money, whatever, the things these guys have in common is money and influence in spades. What use would they have for a low-life like Yermak?'

If Xander was right, that Yermak had gone inside, then he had a point. But it didn't get her any closer to Kuleba's murderer. Unless...

'Can women be members of the Koh-i-Noor?'

Xander paused. 'I don't think so...'

He switched windows, opening up Google Chrome and searching for the club's membership rules. There, in the fine print, it said:

"The Koh-i-Noor has been the preserve of gentlemen for over four centuries. Regrettably, we are not able to consider membership applications from female applicants."

'How the eff do they get away with that?'

Xander gave a wan smile. 'It's a man's world. Still.'

'Then the mystery woman wasn't a member. So Yermak wasn't meeting her.'

'Unless she works there?'

'An elderly woman? You think that's likely?'

'She could be a cleaner.'

She could slap him. 'That's all you think older women are good for? No wonder you're dating that Emma girl. I forgot to ask, did she pass her GCSE resits?'

'Leave off, Ash. I wasn't suggesting anything of the sort. These clubs have bedrooms, they've got bars. They're going to have staff to take care of that sort of thing and it's entirely possible some of those staff are women.'

As if. 'So you're suggesting there's a woman who on Mondays cleans bogs for rich tossers, then on Tuesdays catfishes random Eastern European men and stabs them in graveyards. How exactly did you become the head honcho over at SOCA?'

None of it made sense.

'Do you want me to keep watching Yermak or not? This is an expensive op and my boys – sorry, team – have other priorities. If you're going to dismiss the only lead they've found, it's a massive waste of their time carrying on.'

His tone was far too even. He really would pull the plug. Part of her agreed that it was a waste of time. Going to a private members' club wasn't illegal. But it was strange. Nothing about this case added up. Yermak had been too keen to answer their questions, too quick to offer an insane conspiracy theory by way of explanation. They'd seen no evidence of any crime – yet. And that was what made him so dangerous. If he was involved, he was smart.

'One more week,' Rafferty said. 'If he's involved, we'll know sooner rather than later.'

'Fine. On one condition.'

'Name it.'

'Take the lead seriously. Go check out the club. Deal?'

He offered his hand.

She shook it.

73

THE RED SQUARE

THE OLD LITTLE Russia was in Tottenham, right along the boundary between Haringey, a suburb once described as "the armpit of north London", and Edmonton. I know a few older Russians who still live there. It's still cheap and cheerful unlike the newer Little Russia.

I whistled as Tank and I looked up and down Eaton Square, rows of beautiful houses bedecked with Christmas lights. This isn't Little Russia. This is Little Oligarchdom, the Red Square. It's home to billionaire exiles, the gits who nicked all of Russia's wealth and buggered off to live in the lap of London luxury.

And now Tiny's pretending to be one of them.

According to Sanook, he had rented, under the alias of Kostyantyn Sechin, one of the more modest townhouses. A comedown for the man who'd once owned one of the most prestigious penthouses in London, with a view out over Hyde Park.

The brochure I'd found online for his new digs boasted it was a regency townhouse designed by Thomas Cubit and that it was grade II* listed which, I'd learned from a quick Google, means that it is "of national importance".

Somehow that justifies a price tag of over twenty million

pounds.

Obviously, nobody had paid that much otherwise Tiny wouldn't have been able to rent it. I couldn't see any in the Red Square listed for rent but it had to be in the region of seventy-five grand per calendar month, maybe more.

It's set over five floors, six if the basement counts. If I were Tiny, I'd be making myself at home on the top two, well away from ground level.

I walked past it twice, a camera in hand as if I were a tourist who'd taken a wrong turn coming out of Sloane Square Underground Station. There wasn't a lot to see. Most of the houses had security: CCTV, number pad entry, and, no doubt, reinforced front doors behind which there would be security guards waiting. They wouldn't be Tesco night shift security guards, they'd be ex-military, hard men with quick reflexes, the kind you only fuck around with once before you wind up riddled with lead.

Instead of going with my gut and knocking on the door, demanding justice, and getting myself killed, I waited around until I saw someone emerge from a neighbouring building, one which was home to an embassy.

Damn.

More security.

This is going to be a challenge. I've dealt with security before, but here are secure buildings surrounded by other secure buildings. Between private and governmental security, the whole of Eaton Square is locked down tighter than a nun's arse.

And Tiny would've been warned by now. Sanook would've been in touch before I'd got a hundred yards from the Koh-i-Noor club.

This isn't going to work.

I can't just force my way in.

We'll have to find another way.

74

SISTER ACT

DNA on the knife came back shortly after they'd released Augustyn Yermak.

Rafferty stared at the notification in disgust: *No Direct Match.*

Shit.

Not only was the killer not Yermak, as she'd assumed ever since the prints came back, the killer wasn't any other criminal in the Met's extensive DNA database either.

She clicked through to the detailed breakdown, her mobile pulling up a summary from HOLMES in a mobile-friendly format. She scanned down quickly.

The DNA analysis confirmed that the knife-wielder had indeed been a woman. Just as Yermak had claimed.

Despite advances in DNA analysis, there was no magic profile to look at. Ancestry was still largely guesswork and discerning age wasn't possible either, as much as Kflom kept insisting that it was technically possible to guesstimate from telomere length. Maybe one day.

Before she'd finished reading, Kflom messaged her.

Seen the results?

Yes, she texted back.

We should dig into it more. Heard of Familial Searching? Hotshot company called Eurofins can rank DNA matches to find relatives rather than just who a DNA sample belongs to. Expensive though.

She paused for a split second before asking the obvious question: how expensive?

Kflom showed as typing on her screen. Then his reply appeared: *Dunno. About four grand, I think.*

Interesting. If they couldn't find their suspect, maybe they could find a brother or an uncle who had done time. It was, Rafferty mused, a bit of an ethical quandary. The general rule of thumb was that the database only held the DNA of people who had been arrested. Even that was a low bar: if the charges were dropped, it didn't matter, the DNA remained on file forever. It was a compromise Rafferty's conscience had long since come to terms with.

But did one man getting arrested really mean his entire family lost the privacy they would otherwise enjoy? It struck her as opening a whole can of worms, one that could only be fairly dealt with by including everyone in the database regardless. Doing that would be fair – and it would make her job miles easier.

For once, she was glad it was Ayala that got the promotion to DCI. That meant this decision, and the costs of funding it, fell on his shoulders.

She found him, as always, in his office. As she opened the door, he snatched up his desk phone and proceeded to yabber away as if he were in the middle of an important conference call. He held up a finger to his lips and gestured at the phone as if to tell her he'd be with her in a minute.

The daft bugger went on to make a thing of getting off the phone.

'Sorry to interrupt,' Rafferty said when he finally pretended to hang up. 'I'm sure you're busy so I'll make this quick: we've got an epithelial DNA sample from the knife. No blood. STR analysis says no direct match to anyone in the database.'

'Damn.'

'But,' Rafferty said brightly, 'Kflom and Purcell reckon it's enough to look for a familial match.'

'And?'

'And I need you to sign off on it. We thought there might be ethical concerns given that the sample doesn't belong to an arrestee and so-'

'Ethical concerns?' Ayala mocked. 'Your DNA donor stabbed a man in cold blood.'

Exactly as she'd predicted, he'd taken the contrary view to whatever he thought that she thought and made it much harder to say no to running the test.

'There's also a cost implication,' she said cautiously. 'It's about three grand to run the test.'

A small lie. One she'd easily be able to backtrack from. Three or four. It's an easy mistake to make.

'And the odds that it'll find something?'

Damn.

She hadn't expected that question. Her own Googling had revealed that familial searches resulted in an ID around twenty per cent of the time.

'One in five,' she conceded.

'You want me to throw three thousand pounds at a long shot that your mystery DNA sample belongs to a woman who has a brother, father, or son in the system. Do I have that correct?'

His expression was scathing.

'It's not that unlikely that we'll...'

He shuffled papers on his desk as if he had more important

things to get back to. This was his not-so-subtle way of saying that a meeting was over.

'Look, I know this is a tough case. But I have every confidence you'll crack it. People in this murder investigation team ought to be more than a match for an old woman, wouldn't you agree?'

He might as well have said it outright: crack the case or she didn't belong on the team.

'I suppose so.'

'I suppose so, *sir*.'

THE FOUNDATION

HE WASN'T EVEN in hiding.

Kostyantyn Sechin had a whole life of his own. Tiny hadn't become a recluse, but a *"wealthy Russian philanthropist and founder of the Sechin Foundation"* according to a bio we found online.

'The balls on him,' I said to Tank. 'He fucked off out of the country, blackmailed a bartender to keep himself afloat as he collected his ill-gotten gains, and then came right back here, pretending to be a charitable fucking oligarch.'

As Tank peered over my shoulder at the website of the Sechin Foundation, I noticed the Events section in the scroll bar. What sort of events did a dodgy charity host? I had to click through and find out.

AGM. Boring.

Meeting of the Investment Board. Boring.

Christmas Ball? Now that was a smidge more interesting.

One click later, the lurid details appeared on screen. It was like an Oxford University end-of-year ball on steroids. Ten thousand pounds a plate, bang in the centre of the city, and attended by celebrities, philanthropists, and the most pretentious gits of all, socialites. Lord Toff and Lady Arsewipe would get to enjoy "an evening of hedonism, one-of-a-kind items and experiences up for auction, and some of the finest food available, all for a good cause".

Bleh. A good cause? Even after reading their whole website, I had no idea what the Sechin Foundation actually did. Apparently, the upper classes were happy to shell out cash without knowing the specifics.

How the hell had Tiny pulled that off? He'd managed to return to London and ingratiate himself with the great and the good. The more I thought about it, the more credit I had to give him: of course, the rich and the famous didn't know their host was a retired mob boss.

And, even if they did, he'd have changed his appearance as much as possible. Luckily for us, there was a photo of "Kostyantyn" from last year's ball when he'd given a speech about the importance of "Giving While Living".

The man in my memory was larger than life with a thick head of hair and bulging biceps, his tattoos contrasting with expensive, Italian suits. In his place, there was a balding, slender man with an almost frail look about him. He had thick, rounded designer glasses that covered half his face, and wore the same Penguin-style tuxedo as the other guests. His trademark teardrop tattoo, the mark of a killer, was gone.

If I hadn't known it was Tiny, even I would have walked past him in the street.

'He looks old,' Tank said.

I had to agree. Tiny had gone from punk thirty-something to respectable, sickly forty-something. His hair, what was left of it anyway, was greying badly.

'He's bound to be at this thing, right?'

Tank shrugged.

'He is, trust me,' I said with more confidence than I felt. He had to be there.

The question then was whether we could get in and how tight security would be.

The former came down to money. Ten grand each. That could be a waste. Or the best investment I'd ever made. Tickets appeared to be available by phoning up. Would Tiny be keeping an eye on the guest list, looking over his shoulder for any hint of his past catching up with him? Maybe.

'Security's gonna be tight. Maybe they won't background check their guests – that's a bit mad for a charity dinner – but if this place is chock full of billionaires, they'll all have security. I'm thinking it'll be metal detectors, pat downs, maybe sniffer dogs.'

'No guns then,' Tank said.

'Or knives. If we get caught on the way in, we'll be in the nick before they've got to the toasts.'

'We go check it out?'

'Best idea you've had all day.'

It was also Tank's *only* idea.

~

AN HOUR LATER, we found ourselves outside the enormous skyscraper that was home to the Worshipful Company of Developers and Architects. It wasn't the Ye Old Worlde charm that I'd imagined. Instead, it was a monument to modernism with a glass façade that curved and twisted as it reached skywards.

From the Thames side path out front, I could see the security. There were airport-style scanners looking for drugs, a handful of security guards including one who looked like he should've retired decades ago, and, perhaps most importantly of all, an express, key-operated lift just beyond the security perimeter.

As we watched, groups were searched and batches of them

sent up, around twenty at a time. The lift must've been light-ning fast because no sooner had the doors shut, it zoomed up and up, and then, a minute or two later, it plunged back down to the ground level. I could just imagine the crunch of gears whirring, pulleys spinning, and cables going taut to fling the lift up, up, and away. The engineering required for the lift to work so damned quickly was impressive. Each round trip lasted only a few minutes but oddly the lift was always empty when it came back down: people were only heading up, never down. Was that just the time of day? Or were there multiple lifts so that people took one to get in and another to leave?

I looked around. This was a busy part of central London. The South Bank had the annual Christmas Market on and so was bursting with tourists coming and going, merrily drinking and singing. Security might be tight inside the building, but out here was the usual free-for-all of central London. I could see con men in the distance playing three-card monte with unsus-pecting tourists. No doubt there were dozens of pickpockets hard at working lifting valuables from passers-by too. Some of them might even have worked for the Syndicate once. Now most were working for themselves. There were beggars around too, some in real need, others hamming it up.

'Let's walk the perimeter,' I said to Tank.

It was easier said than done. Other buildings were close by. Unluckily for me, it was a posh enough part of town that rubbish disposal and service entrances were all underground. There was no alleyway to hide in, no back door to bribe my way in through. This was exactly as I'd expected and feared.

'Any ideas?'

'No.'

Go figure.

'Well, we'll think of something.'

I'm nothing if not patient.

Tiny will die.

One way or another.

76

SCHRÖDINGER'S CASE FILE

AT HALF-PAST EIGHT, Joe rolled into his office and began going through his morning routine. Emails, tick. Return phone calls, tick. Order coffee, tick.

Once that was done, he allowed himself half an hour to review what he called The No Hopers. These were his cold mispers, the people who he knew, deep down, would never ever be found.

Among them was Elijah Zholnovych. The nice detective who'd visited him had continued to pester him about Zholnovych despite the lack of evidence. She was convinced his death was linked to at least one, if not two, others.

As he perused the file, one thing jumped out at him: it wasn't so empty anymore.

The "missing" elements had reappeared as if an IT glitch had been resolved. Now, there was a file marked blood spatter analysis complete with photos. Then, more tantalisingly, one marked DNA. Opening it revealed that the blood on the floor, previously dismissed as non-existent, had not only been recovered, it had been sequenced.

Clicking on that sample, however, brought Joe full circle. File not found.

Odd.

The same error again?

He rebooted the system, found the Zholnovych file again, and tried, once more, to access the DNA results.

Not found.

He dialled DI Rafferty and got her voicemail.

'Ashley? It's Joe Singleton from MisPers. There's something strange going on again...'

COMING BACK FROM A MEETING, Rafferty found she had three missed calls: Joe, Kflom, and Kieran, all in quick succession.

She played Joe's message first. As soon as he said "Elijah Zholnovych", she flipped her attention to the HOLMES file. Just as Joe – and, she would learn later, Kieran and Kflom – said, the file had been updated. The UK Protected Persons Service had finally released some, but not all, of the missing evidence. It must've taken them a while to review the security implications of sharing it.

Where Joe had failed was the security tag on the file. He didn't know they were dealing with witness protection. He hadn't signed the Official Secrets Act. All he could see was that there were, in theory, files attached to Zholnovych's case in HOLMES, but he hadn't been cleared to see the results of the DNA test performed on the blood spatter.

It wasn't the victim's at all.

When Rafferty saw the name, her jaw dropped.

She was right.

Ayala had fucked up letting them go.

But not for the Kuleba case.

The man called Tank had been at Elijah Zholnovych's house.

Joe's misper and her exceptionally strange murder investigation were now linked by a common suspect.

What the hell was going on?

77

THE SEVEN PS

PROPER PRIOR PLANNING prevents piss-poor performance. That's what my old man used to tell me.

But he fucked off when I was five so I don't usually follow his advice.

We know where Tiny's going to be in less than a week's time.

Straight away, I'd booked an AirBnB, under a fake name of course, with a view of the tower. Tank and I moved in, taking cash, gear, and several changes of clothes. It was a penthouse apartment, one fit for a king. Parquet floors, a terrace outside to smoke on, floor-to-ceiling windows through which I could see all along the river, my view obscured only by cranes and scaffolding in the distance.

My first thought was a sniper rifle. There's a clear shot right across the Thames. Shoot, pack up, run. A simple, elegant solution that would be perfect if circumstances line up. But I hate waiting for chance. I'd got lucky once in this whole endeavour when Waxy came back into the fold and led me down the path to her ex. I'd had to wait years for that to happen. I'm not going to bugger up my big shot and miss the opportunity to get revenge for what happened all those years ago.

'Tank, how wide d'ya reckon the Thames is here?'

I keep coming back to it over and over, the bloody sniper idea. It's not even a good idea. I just don't have a better one.

He looked over from the sofa where he'd made himself very comfortable. He glanced from the TV over to the river and then back to me.

'Nine hundred feet?'

About 274 metres. Roughly what I'd estimated.

So, the tower's well within sniper range but there are two – no, three – problems. One, I don't know any snipers. Two, there's sod all chance Tiny's going to waltz right in front of the window on this side of the building. Three, virtually every attendee is going to have their own security entourage. The guest list includes actual royalty. No way would they miss a sniper's nest being set up just across the river. The same big, beautiful windows that make it easy to see them work both ways.

'Bomb?' Tank suggested. 'I have Chechen friend. I could go visit – if you give me money?'

The Chechen was famous, or rather infamous, for making small-scale explosives packed with rusty nails and the like. Minimal cost, maximum carnage. Even Tiny didn't deal in that shit.

Besides, giving Tank money, a lot of it, would be a recipe for a disaster. Even if he's serious about the idea, I can't trust him with thousands of pounds.

I pushed that thought down and focussed on the idea of blowing Tiny up. 'Maybe we could fly a bomb in? Drone across the river?'

Might work, but there'd be far too much collateral damage

for my liking. Would the wind stop us flying it over? Or would security see the drone and evacuate?

'No,' he grunted. 'I have idea.'

'Go on then. What is it?'

'Service entrance. Take bomb in. Blow bomb up when we see Tiny go into lift.'

Not a bad idea. If we could channel an explosion into a lift shaft, we'd minimise casualties. Tiny and whoever was with him inside the lift would be killed almost instantly. Still fucking inhumane but a lot less so than a whole party full of people with burns and shrapnel scars.

We'd have to find a way to get a bomb into a secure building. And time it right. Too early, we'd get a bunch of randoms but miss Tiny. Too late, he'd get out unscathed too. Even if we nailed it, the lift shaft itself might insulate him from the blast.

'Won't work,' I said. 'And we'd never get away with it even if it did. Kill one mobster, you're a wanted man. Bomb a building, you're taking his place on Interpol's most wanted list.'

'What then?'

I stared past him. The London skyline, always dominated by big buildings, now also has a mix of cranes and half-built skyscrapers. It's not so much the city that never sleeps, but the city that never stops building. How on earth there's enough demand for all the luxury flats is beyond me. If I hadn't got a council place a decade ago, I'd long since have been priced out.

Those unhappy thoughts kept me occupied as I stared out the window. Tank quickly turned his attention back to his beer and the Arsenal v West Ham derby.

Then it hit me.

With a little tweak, maybe, just maybe, there is a way to pull off the impossible.

It would take balls the size of watermelons and more than a little bit of luck.

But the more I think about it, the more I realise that it could be done.

An explosive end to seal Tiny's fate.

One he'd never, ever see coming.

78

LATE TO THE PARTY

NO WARRANTS WERE necessary so once again, Rafferty raced to put together the muscle required to arrest Tank and Yermak.

The minor bickering she and Xander had had only a few days ago was quickly forgotten as the task force swung into action. The homes of both men were known to the police, their images were on file, and Xander's team had, until mere days ago, been watching their every move. Aside from Yermak's strange visit to the Koh-i-Noor, neither had done anything to warrant suspicion.

Nor had the post-arrest searches that Kflom and Purcell conducted turned up anything. If they were criminals, they were smart enough not to leave behind evidence at home.

They arrived back at Yermak's house at dawn. The plan was identical to last time: get in, arrest him and re-interview both him and Tank, this time about the Zholnovych case. On the other side of town, Mayberry and Ayala were overseeing an identical raid at their other suspect's house.

'Same as before,' Xander said. 'Team at the front, team at the back. We'll knock then ram the door.'

'I know the plan,' Rafferty snapped.

Just like last time, they crept up to the door in near silence. It was dark out and nobody was on blues and twos so there weren't any flashing lights to alert their suspects.

Knock, knock, knock.

Before there was time for anyone to answer, the Big Red Key was employed, smashing into the front door, splintering the wood and causing it to swing inwards, its hinges giving way as it slammed into the brick wall behind.

At the back of the house, the other team did the same, the sound reverberating even from where Rafferty was standing.

The whole place went from silence to yells of "police!" in a matter of seconds as they stormed the property. Then there was silence again. Occasionally, a yell of "clear!" could be heard inside.

Then, the bronze commander, one of the SOCA boys, ducked out the front door and pulled off his blue and black SWAT helmet.

'It's empty,' he called out.

Rafferty swore. She wasn't the only one either. Xander looked as furious as she felt. Maybe, just maybe both suspects were at the other property. She called Mayberry.

'It's c-c-clear here t-too,' he said.

Crap.

They were late to the party. Again.

Only last week, they'd had two suspects under arrest for murder. Now they had solid evidence against at least one of them for a different murder and both men were in the wind.

'Cards? Phones? CCTV?' Xander prompted.

'Brodie's on it. You know if there's the slightest hint of either of them, he'll spot them before anyone else.'

'Then it's time to put out an APB.'

Rafferty nodded. An All-Points Bulletin, or "Be On Look

Out" as some younger, more Americanised officers called it, was a message to every police force in the land to keep an eye out for suspects matching their description.

Somehow she doubted anyone would spot the men before Brodie found them through their digital footprint.

But she'd be happy to be proved wrong.

ODDS AND ENDS

I NEEDED information and I need kit.

The former was easy. Everything I needed was listed online, right there in black and white. For once, I was bloody grateful for British bureaucracy.

Tech on the other hand's harder. I'm running out of cash. Tank and I can't risk going out more than we absolutely have to. We got away with it by the skin of our teeth last time but by now they're bound to have put two and two together. Stupid bloody Tank leaving parts of himself behind at the Zholnovych kidnapping.

We can't go home. I can't touch any legitimate money in the bank.

This is it. My last good chance at getting Tiny.

I have to take it.

In five days' time, this will all be over.

One way or the other.

FOLLOWING IN THEIR FOOTSTEPS

'THERE'S no sign of 'em, lassie. No card activity. No calls. No Oyster tap ins. Nada.'

Typical. The moment Ayala had ordered them released, Tank and Yermak had fled.

'And their last known whereabouts?'

Brodie pointed at the CCTV feed for the building.

'Walking outta here.'

Of course it was.

'How effectively can someone go off-grid?'

'Hard ta say. If they've been planning it fer a while, I'd say months. Ye need cash, shelter, food. People help too if it's fer a while.'

There was a weird sort of parity to it all. Now that Tank was linked by blood evidence to the first victim, they knew that he was linked, somehow, to the witness protection scandal.

Two dead witnesses, both of them connected to the Bakowski Crime Syndicate.

It didn't take a genius to put two and two together and infer that Tank and Yermak had something to do with the Bakowskis too. Except neither had a criminal record.

And nothing suggested that the two of them were smart enough to break witness protection. The big one came over as thick as a bag of rocks, and the other came over as slick but was that enough to beat the best protection the British state could offer?

'This Augustyn Yermak,' Brodie said slowly. 'Suppose yer onto something. Why these men? If Zholnovych and Linden were killed by the same man, and this Tank was at the scene o' the first murder, what connects 'em?'

'Other than the Bakowskis?'

'Yer misunderstandin' me, lassie. Lots of bell ends are in the Syndicate. But why kill these men? And why now?'

It was a thought that had troubled Rafferty already. The two were, as mobsters went, thoroughly unremarkable. Nathan Linden was a run-of-the mill fence, working out of north London and peddling stolen gems, watches, and other goodies. He was the sort of mid-level criminal who would normally get caught for something sooner or later and wind up spending his days in some Cat C prison with other white-collar criminals. Zholnovych on the other hand was more of a mystery. From his utterly pedestrian life in which he watched countless Blu-rays and walked his neighbour's dog every morning, he came across as Mr Boring. He didn't strike Rafferty as a violent criminal either. Had the guy from UKPPS said something about fraud? That sounded more plausible.

'Gotta be personal,' Rafferty said. 'The men weren't working the same cons. A fence and a fraudster wouldn't come into contact with each other day-to-day.'

'But they had to have something in common, reet?'

What did connect the men?

Yermak was intelligent, slick, and confident to the point of arrogance. If he was in the Syndicate, like the two protected persons, he was bound to be in something white collar.

At the other end of the scale, the man nicknamed Tank lived up to it. He was built like a truck, spoke in an almost monosyllabic way, and was clearly the muscle/ enforcer type.

The former was more likely to come into contact with a fence or a con man. But it wasn't his blood at the scene. The link between Augustyn Yermak and Tank arose only from a third, tangentially related case.

Talk about complicated.

And how on earth did Oleks Kuleba fit in?

It had to be something to do with smuggling. He'd come in from Poland by car. Nobody with a legitimate reason to visit the UK would subject themselves to a rideshare to save a few pence. Ryanair flew from Warsaw to London and back for as little as thirty quid. Anyone who couldn't afford that would find London pub prices so shocking that they'd have a heart attack.

Five criminals then.

One missing. Two dead. Two arrested but released.

'It's got to have something to do with Tiny Bakowski,' Rafferty said slowly. 'Could he be out of hiding and getting revenge on those who'd crossed him?'

'Ye thinkin' Tank and Yermak are in cahoots with 'im?'

It made perfect sense. Tiny had the money and the influence to command men like Tank. He enjoyed the ability to operate with impunity as the law hadn't caught up with him yet and, if it did, he was already looking at multiple whole life sentences, so what was one more murder to add to the tally? And he had the brains to break witness protection. Rafferty would've sworn it couldn't be done... but then she'd met Waxy. If the stripper had gone home after a failed marriage, surely the Bakowski Syndicate, even if they didn't own Starlight, would spot that the wife of a traitor had returned to their midst.

Then again... how would Kuleba fit in? He'd been twenty

when someone had murdered him. He'd have been ten when Tiny Bakowski disappeared off the face of the earth.

None of it made sense.

Why had Tank and Yermak gone to Poland if not to fetch Kuleba?

'Brodie, how hard is it to track the route Yermak took?'

The Scot gave a sharp intake of breath. 'What yer askin', lassie, is if ye can track a man takin' a mix o' transport across multiple jurisdictions ... Yeah, we can do that. It'll take a lot o' time and money, though. Why ye askin'?'

'You don't accidentally drive from Poland. They had to drive to Poland... why drive? It's over fifteen hundred miles. Call that a conservative ten pence a mile, that's three hundred-odd quid for the round trip.'

'Before rental fees,' Brodie said. 'We think they left by Eurostar... so they had to rent a car in Paris, Brussels, Lille or Amsterdam. Tha's where I'll start lookin'. We'll need Kieran on-side, mind.'

'How many days were they away for?'

'Dinnae. Couple of weeks?'

'So another five hundred for the rentals. Why spend eight hundred quid to drive a mind-numbingly boring motorway route to Warsaw? What's the advantage?'

'Not flying Ryanair?' Brodie suggested with a cackle. 'I cannae stand it. Las' time I had tae put my legs in the aisle and the poor air hostess tripped over me.'

Rafferty giggled.

'But seriously, lassie, that's no holiday trip. What's yer ex think of the trip?'

Her eyes narrowed. 'Do you have to bring him up?'

'Aye, lassie, I do. Last I heard, he's the head of the Serious Organised Crime Agency and all...'

He was right. The one man who'd know what the hell was

going on out of London would be Xander.

Brodie turned away and tapped at his keyboard. 'I think,' he said slowly, 'he's in his office. His security pass was used half an hour ago. If you run, you might catch him.'

'Gee, thanks.'

'Dinnae mention it, lassie.'

~

BRODIE WAS RIGHT.

Xander was in his office. He was with Kieran when Rafferty knocked on the door.

'Am I interrupting something between you two? I swear you're inseparable these days. Should I be warning Emma and... what's the name of the woman you're seeing these days, Kieran?'

Kieran muttered something that sounded like: 'póg mo thóin.'

She hadn't a scooby what that one meant but it had to be an insult. She grinned as she pulled up a chair. Without waiting to be asked, she leant forward and helped herself to a glass of water from the pitcher on the coffee table.

'Wait, no biscuits. What gives? You on a diet again?'

'Hilarious as always, I see,' Kieran said. 'We were just discussing the men who've turned Queen's Evidence against the Bakowski Syndicate, all sixty-two of 'em.'

Sixty-two. Holy crap. Rafferty had been assuming they were talking about a handful of men, not enough for two professional football teams including subs.

'No surprises,' Xander said, 'But both your victims are on the list. We found them when we were going through the paper copies of the arrest photos for all the witnesses. And no, I'm fresh out of biscuits. No need to keep the tin topped up when the annoying woman that used to pilfer them stopped hanging out in here.'

Touché. Point to Xander.

'I had to get the files from UKPPS,' Kieran said. 'They're hard copy only, and we've got to hand them back after this meeting.'

There was a thick folder on Xander's desk which was open to a mug shot of the man Rafferty knew as Elijah Zholnovych. He passed it over so she could scan through. Apart from the two victims, nobody immediately jumped out at her.

'Are you two looking for things in common between these guys? Or trying to work out who might be next?'

'See,' Xander said, turning to look at Kieran. 'I told you she'd be on the same page.'

'A little o' column A, a little o' column B,' Kieran said. 'But it's not provin' easy. There's feck all in common between 'em. They testified against different people in the gang. Obviously, none of 'em have testified against Tiny yet, though I suspect some would if he were ever found.'

'Then what have you found?'

There was a pause before either of them answered.

'Not much then?' Rafferty said.

'It's a good long list,' Xander protested.

'What're you going to do? Watch sixty-odd men twenty-four-seven?'

She could only imagine the cost of that. The overtime alone would run SOCA into the ground within a month.

'Well, maybe,' Xander said, 'except they're all in the programme and UKPPS won't tell us what their new identities area – and he' – Xander glanced at the lawyer – 'says we can't force them to play nice.'

The great Kieran O'Connor had failed then. A rare occurrence. Nice to know he was human, though. He mumbled something about national security and then averted his gaze.

'It's your lucky day then boys,' Rafferty said. 'I've got a fresh angle to consider. Where did Tank and Yermak go in Europe? There's an international connection here and I'm not seeing it.'

Xander stood up, paced over to the far side of his office, and came back holding a folder full of Interpol Red Notices.

'Number two, Dimitri "Tiny" Bakowski.' He shook his head in disbelief. 'After all this time too. You'd think the criminal underworld would've moved on. But no, Tiny's still top dog. He's managed to go under the radar for so long that I don't think we'll ever find him.'

'Your point?'

'The Syndicate's still going strong. There was a dip in activity, maybe two or three months' worth, after we caught the other two brothers and Tiny fled.'

'And then it bounced right back?' Rafferty said. 'As if nothing had changed?'

'Exactly. I interviewed everyone I could: witnesses, suspects, relatives. We caught a few getting sticky-fingered with pots of money that Tiny had hidden. That's when I knew catching him would be hard. He snaffled money away everywhere: homes of relatives, legitimate businesses he had an interest in, random plots of land he'd bought through trusts.'

'It was a nightmare to track it all down,' Kieran chipped in. 'Biggest Proceeds of Crime Act investigation ever. We seized and auctioned loads of it.'

'And yet he's still in the wind so you can't have found it all,' Rafferty said.

'Exactly,' Xander said. 'So who's helping him? Where's he gone? What money is he using to stay under the radar? Pulling a Lord Lucan takes planning, it takes money, and it takes influence.'

'The where's the bit that interests me,' Rafferty said. She took a sip from her water glass and then inhaled. 'If I'm chasing two men who're killing on Tiny's behalf – and that's a big if – then doesn't it stand to reason that maybe, just maybe, they might've gone to consult with the man himself on their recent road trip around Europe? From what Brodie's been able to uncover, they left on the Eurostar under their real names. In Paris, they rented a car on Yermak's credit card, again not bothering to hide anything. If we can find where that car went, we can work out what the hell they were doing as they worked their way around Europe to pick up Oleks Kuleba and return home to London.'

'It's a good theory, Ash,' Kieran said. 'I'll happily try and help on the legal side of things. It'll be a bit of a challenge especially as we've no idea which countries they went through – yet. Maybe Xander's got some insight on where to start?'

Almost as if he'd been expecting the suggestion, Xander pulled up a map on his computer screen and turned it to face them.

'We know Nico and Pavel tried to flee by boat from Southampton. If they'd succeeded, they'd have landed in Bilbao. Tiny left by Eurostar and arrived in Paris where he vanished. As you both know, Europe is one big, open border thanks to Schengen. Once you're in, it's dead easy to flit around without having to flash papers or leave much of a trail, especially if you're paying your way in cash.'

Rafferty put the folder down and squinted at the map. 'How much money could he have realistically taken with him?'

'Not a lot. Anything over a few grand and he'd have risked being questioned and detained by customs. We know his cards went in a bin in the taxi rank outside King's Cross along with several personal items. He would've known this was his one chance to bolt and he took it.'

He paused as a notification popped up on his phone. Once he'd clicked X to get rid of it, he carried on. 'So he'd have landed in France under a fake identity, one he knew we'd learn about sooner or later, and he'd have had enough cash to eke out a few weeks' existence – if he could cut his lifestyle down to size.'

'You're Tiny, you're going to want to find money. Do you think he stashed money in Paris somewhere?'

Xander shook his head. 'Too obvious. Staying in Paris would risk being seen. He would've known that Interpol would be after him. He'd have wanted to get away quickly, ideally travelling in an erratic, unpredictable pattern until he reached a bolt-hole or friendly face.'

'Where would friendly faces be?'

'Ukraine, I'd have thought. He's got family out there.'

'What about Poland?' Rafferty asked, thinking of Kuleba. 'Has he got any connection with the border towns?'

'Not that I know of,' Xander said. 'But borders are where you smuggle things. Tiny had his grubby paws on everything. The Syndicate bring girls in from Eastern Europe.'

It was a half-formed thought, one Xander seemed tentative to voice. It was vague and easy to discount. Kuleba didn't have any known link with trafficking girls nor, Rafferty imagined, were there many living in rural Poland. Trafficking hubs were far more likely to be in the big cities.

'What about business partners? Tiny sold drugs, right?'

'They'd probably have come in through Amsterdam or southern Spain.'

A lightbulb came on in Rafferty's mind. 'If you were smuggling drugs in, you'd have to keep a goodly amount of cash to pay people with, right?'

Both men nodded.

'And Tiny needed cash...'

'We checked at the time, Ash. I flew to Amsterdam myself

to look. We were on good terms with the authorities there at the time so Kieran was able to get CCTV to analyse for facial matches. Nada.'

'Spain then?'

'It's a big place.'

'You said southern Spain.'

He nodded. 'The Costa del Crime the press call it. It's a big stretch running from Malaga to the rock. Back in its heyday, the police turned a blind eye to where the money came from. Naturally, the criminal gangs flocked there to enjoy their wealth. As you can imagine, it's damned-near impossible to get information out of mobsters at the best of times. On their own turf, that difficulty is increased tenfold.'

Another dead end.

How the hell could they be this close and yet this far?

'What if my two suspects went to Amsterdam or the Costa del Crime? Would that get us any closer to finding Tiny? Could he have holed up in plain sight for the last decade?'

Kieran stroked his beard thoughtfully. 'Contemporary evidence would be useful. Puerto Banús isn't as lawless as it used to be. The gangs are still there, the smuggling still happens, but there's tourism too. Besides, I can't go. The gangs know my face. If I'm spotted, they'll go underground quicker than Mayberry can finish a sentence.'

She glared at him. 'Leave off Mayberry.'

Ignoring the Irishman, she turned to face Xander. 'If I can get Ayala to sign off on it, is it worth getting boots on the ground? Mayberry and I can go while Kieran can play offence from here as we need it.'

'Fat chance of that,' Xander said. 'He's never going to agree.'

'Hey, I'm charming when I want to be.'

'Ten quid says you're wasting your breath.'

Privately, she didn't fancy her odds.

'Deal.'

81

SPECIAL DELIVERY

AMAZON PRIME. Ain't it a miracle?

One prepaid VISA gift card, one brand-spanking new Gmail account, and I was in business. It turns out you can get *everything* online. What we needed were microphones, ones we could connect to the event's sound system. Those were easy enough.

Swanky suits were harder. Tank bought his at M&S. As my "security guard", I figured he could get away with a lot more than me. But when he came home and showed it off, I wasn't convinced. Among the crowd that would be at the party, even bodyguards would be expected to look good. Not much I can do though. A man his size doesn't have many options.

Mine is top-drawer, handcrafted and made to order, just not for me. It's second hand and straight from eBay. The fit isn't quite perfect but it'll be good enough to fool folks for one evening.

As more and more stuff's delivered, my plan's coming together.

Just a few more days and we'll know if it pays off.

82

THE LONG SHADOW

'NO.'

'Why not?'

'Inspector Rafferty, we're not having a discussion about this. You're not going on a jolly to the Costa del Sol.'

Rafferty sulked. 'Fine. You know I've got all that annual leave I haven't-'

Ayala laughed. 'As if.'

'Then what do you want me to do?'

'Find and arrest this Tank fellow, obviously,' Ayala said. 'If you're up to the task of finding Interpol's #2 Most Wanted Man, you can sure as hell find a behemoth of a man you had in custody last week.'

'You mean the man you forced me to let go.'

Ayala glared. 'He didn't commit the Kuleba murder. If you'd done your job properly, you'd have been able to grill him about the Zholnovych case at the same time and we wouldn't even be having this discussion.'

'If UKPPS hadn't interfered, I would have.'

'We're going to have to agree to disagree. Look, I like your theory. The bogeyman Bakowski pulling the strings but you've got no evidence. What if your killer just had a grudge against the men? Or he's acting on his own? As much as you want to invent reasons to hang out with Xander Thompson, there are plenty of reasons to kill that don't involve cold cases from SOCA.'

Catty.

'Then how do you explain the witness protection element, *sir*? This killer has got to two men who were protected by the might of the UK government. They've never ever lost a witness before this and now they're down two.'

'Tory funding cuts?' Ayala joked. 'Seriously, Ash, it's not up to me to explain it. You're talking about one missing person – a case I'm certain I told you not to investigate, I might add.'

Rafferty fumed. Not more than a minute ago, he'd told her she hadn't investigated it properly.

'And one dead man who you can't connect with anything except the witness protection programme.'

'What about Kuleba?'

'Killed by an unknown female suspect,' Ayala said. 'Follow the evidence, Ashley. This isn't a serial killer. It can't be. Like you said, witness protection losing one man is unheard of. Two would be... astronomically unlikely.'

It was the same well of logic she'd been slamming herself into for the entirety of the investigation: she couldn't definitively link the cases. Zholnovych was in the witness protection programme and went missing. Blood evidence put Tank at the scene. Nathan Linden was in the same programme and was found chopped up in his bathtub. Kuleba was murdered and Tank admitted to being there, but DNA exculpated him.

And yet the three had to be linked. Tank linked Kuleba to Zholnovych. Witness protection linked Zholnovych to Nathan Linden. The Bakowski Syndicate linked all three.

But the physical proof wasn't forthcoming.

'What if it is Tiny that's behind it all?'

'Then you'll find that out when you arrest Tank, won't you? Or not. If it's Tiny, his men are generally pretty loyal. You can't give Tank a plea deal on a murder charge so he's going to have no incentive to betray his old master.'

'Which leaves me ...'

'Out of luck. So you'd better hope Tiny isn't involved. If you prove he is, and can't find him, all you're going to do is throw two more unsolved murders on the cold case pile. Worse, you'll be advertising to the criminal underworld that they can act with impunity, killing state witnesses as they please, and we'll be totally powerless to do anything about it. You'll set criminal justice back decades. It'll be like the Italian mob in US before they broke *omertà*.'

This time, Rafferty had to concede that Ayala had a point. There was more at stake here than she'd realised.

'But what if we succeed?'

Ayala's eyes twinkled. He was obviously imagining the glory he'd get if he brought Tiny Bakowski to justice. Half of the mispers in East London were probably old Bakowski murders. If he could close those, he'd go down in history as one of the finest DCIs to have ever graced the halls of the Met. He'd finally surpass their old mentor and get out of Morton's shadow.

And he'd stop another murder before it happened. If Tank and Yermak were hunting Bakowski turncoats, there were dozens more waiting to die.

'Plan for failure first and foremost,' Ayala ordered. 'You've got a small, dedicated taskforce who've all signed the Official Secrets Act. Use nobody outside the team. I want every single one of them on this until you bring Tank in. We know he's not left the ports. Every border guard in the country has seen his photo. Don't call in the media as it'll tip our hand. Instead, work the streets. Talk to every CI we've got. Your man is six foot four and built like a brick outhouse. Someone is going to have seen him.'

'Can we offer a cash reward?'

Ayala hesitated and then nodded.

'How much?'

He pulled out a notepad, scribbled down a number, and slid it across the desk to Rafferty.

She whistled.

If this wouldn't do it, nothing would.

83

CASH IS KING

THE RUMOUR MILL flew into overdrive.

Like the anonymous tip lines that Ayala loved so much, using confidential informants ran the risk of being overloaded with lies told by those looking to make a quick few quid.

Almost as soon as she'd signed off on it, Rafferty had been inundated. Even with SOCA's help sifting through the pile, it was insane. Everyone and his dog claimed to know Yermak and Tank. The most ludicrous tips were discarded while the rest, many hundreds of them, were printed and piled up on the conference table in the incident room.

'So h-h-how do we s-sift these?' Mayberry asked. His gaze was fixed on the pile of printouts in the middle of the room. Satellite piles, organised on-the-fly by Rafferty, had begun to appear around the table.

'First, we ditch everything that mentions Tiny. SOCA hasn't found him in a decade. Any tipsters who are suddenly claiming to know where he is can take a long walk off a short cliff.'

She pointed to the biggest satellite pile. They were the discarded tips, the ones she should just throw in the bin. The only reason she hadn't done so was just in case they turned out to be useful.

'Second, we prioritise tips from current and former Bakowski Syndicate members.'

Mayberry's eyes went wide. 'There are th-th-thousands of them!'

She knew that as well as he did. The largest criminal organisation in the world had a plethora of former, current, and presumably prospective members too. But it was a start.

'Then we want a pile of Polish and Ukrainian speakers. We know that Kuleba was living in Poland and his tattoo suggests he spoke Ukrainian. If, as I suspect, the three cases are linked then language would be a barrier.'

A bit like the *Cosa Nostra* speaking exclusively Italian. The foundations of the Bakowski Syndicate were grounded in family ties, their roots in Kyiv and Lviv. Tips from those who could communicate in their language had a slightly higher chance of being true.

'E-e-easier said than done!'

As they read through, Mayberry's protestations had to be given credence. The theory behind Rafferty's system was good, but in practice they had so little information about their tipsters that they didn't know who'd been in the Syndicate or not. Nor did they know who spoke what languages.

'What about this guy?' Rafferty said, reading one tip aloud. 'Tank was an enforcer, one of the best. If he's involved in something, Tiny Bakowski is involved.'

'That's a b-b-bit like a h-h-horror scope.'

'You mean vague confirmation bias that the reader invests in because they want to?'

He nodded.

'True.'

Rafferty *wanted* Tiny to be behind it so she was quick to

believe it. While Ayala was the prima donna glory hound, it wouldn't hurt her career chances either if they brought the big dog to justice. She just might get her own murder investigation team. Then the tyranny of working for an idiot like Ayala would be over.

They worked in silence for hours, stopping only to grab a couple of dried-out sandwiches from the vending machine in the hallway. By her fourth cup of coffee, Rafferty's attention was beginning to sag. Every now and then, they'd find a tip that looked promising only to find out that it was from a low-level drug dealer or a known liar rather than a Bakowski higher-up that might actually have some insight into what their victims and suspects had in common.

'W-w-what about th-this?' Mayberry asked for the thirtieth time that day.

He slid a piece of paper across the table.

Instead of a rumour, it was a heavily redacted profile of a confidential informant with the code name Slick. A former arms dealer and terrorist, Slick was now allegedly clean. He'd been supplying tip-offs on arms movements to the Serious Organised Crime Agency for years.

'This isn't a tip from the hotline.'

Mayberry shook his head. 'This guy... he s-speaks Polish, Ukrainian and Russian.'

Rafferty glanced at his nationality. 'No, he speaks Chechen. It's a northeast Caucasian language. Russian's Indo-European. Not much mutually intelligibility there.'

'F-further down.'

She scanned down. Sure enough, under skills and assets, Slick was listed as being multilingual. He really did speak all four languages.

'And why are you showing me this?'

'B-b-because he was con-con-convicted for supplying a b-b-bomb to the Bakowskis.'

That got her attention.

The extent of Slick's criminality was undeniable. It spanned three decades running from an early conviction for smuggling drugs into France right through to dealing weapons and bomb-making. The only way he'd avoided a life behind bars was by becoming a confidential informant and bringing down a bigger prize. In short, Slick was ruthless but he'd proven himself reliable.

'And he c-c-called Xander this morning.'

ONE CALL TO XANDER LATER, Rafferty's deskwork was abandoned in favour of going to visit the Chechen. The call was about an enquiry for a bomb. A former Syndicate colleague had contacted him to offer twenty-five grand in cold, hard cash for "enough Semtex to take out an armoured car".

It was the car that got Rafferty's attention. The story that Yermak had peddled only days ago when they'd had him in custody included an insane lie about an older woman in a Merc. Didn't they sell an armour-plated model?

Could it just be a coincidence? Armoured cars were, after all, a common choice for security-conscious travellers.

Then again, this whole investigation had been coincidence and a bomb threat could never be taken lightly.

'Remember, you're here as an observer only,' Xander had cautioned. 'Stay in the van, watch and listen. One of my team will be your escort.'

'Why the hell do I need an escort?' Rafferty demanded.

'Because you're an unarmed bloody detective with no surveillance training, you don't speak Ukrainian, and because this is my confidential informant with information about a case that falls firmly in my jurisdiction.'

Or counter terrorism's, Rafferty wanted to add. She bit her tongue and nodded. Xander had a point. This time, she'd only be a bystander.

'Sit tight and we'll find out if there's any connection to your Merc in no time.'

84

CHECHNYA

TANK WOULDN'T SHUT up about the bomb. The "backup plan" he kept calling it.

Eventually, after days and days of pestering, I gave in. Not because I thought it was a good idea, but because it might keep Tank out of trouble. His addiction had been getting more and more problematic. He was lethargic, unreliable, and a danger to both of us.

So I gave him twenty grand for "the bomb".

That was yesterday.

I know exactly what he'll have done with it. He'll have bought as much heroin as he could find and shot the whole lot of it straight into his arm.

It's what I've been trying to stop happening for years.

But this time I couldn't. If I'd agreed to let him come to the Sechin Ball, he'd have been a liability. Someone at the party is bound to be dealing. That much money in one place would mean drugs *everywhere*.

One hit and Tank would draw security's attention to himself and to me.

So it was better to let him go, hope he shot up somewhere

public, and landed in hospital rather than the morgue which leaves me to finish the job alone.

Me versus Tiny.

It's on.

85

THE LOYALTY TEST

'NOT ONE WORD,' Rafferty said.

She, Ayala, Mayberry and Xander had crammed into the observation room that looked into Interview Room One.

Xander's team had scoped out the Chechen's place of business, lying in wait until the customer appeared, ready to pounce. From what Rafferty had heard over the radio, they'd gone in hard and fast as soon as the team had recognised Tank. He now slouched in a chair, looking more like a man waiting for a dental appointment than a man arrested for trying to buy a bomb.

'That's n-n-not true,' Mayberry objected.

He was right. Tank had eventually said one word.

It was infuriating.

They'd intercepted him as he'd headed into his meeting with the Chechen. On his person, he'd been carrying twenty-five thousand pounds in cash. On the drive back to the Met, they'd hammered him with questions.

They'd asked him to explain it. Nothing.

They'd asked where he was going. Silence.

Where had he been in the last week? No reply.

'It's like getting blood out of a stone,' Xander said. 'I've seen this before. You'll get nothing from him unless you can provoke him somehow, get an emotional response. These guys only break if they're really riled.'

Mr Know-It-All struck again.

'Any suggestions on that front?' Rafferty asked politely.

'What've you got that'll push his buttons? What's he shown any reaction to at all?'

That was the problem. Nothing. They'd accused him of murder. No reaction there. The same when Rafferty asked about the body in the bathtub. What kind of psychopath didn't even react to the idea of a dismembered body? If he were innocent, wouldn't he have looked shocked, revolted even?

She said as much.

'Then we interview him, put the questions to him, get his lack of reply on record,' Xander said.

'We tried. He said nothing. Until we put the tape on.'

'And then what did he say?'

Rafferty smiled. 'He said "lawyer".'

'But he'd declined one, hadn't he?'

He hadn't. He'd ignored the question when they'd offered one. Then, at the last second, he'd asked. A delaying tactic. But why?

'So now what?' Xander said.

'He's finishing up with the duty solicitor right now. I'm pretty sure he's going to refuse to come out of his cell next. That's what I'd do if I wanted to waste time.'

Xander looked sceptical. 'He's not that clever.'

Five minutes later, Rafferty was proved right.

They interviewed him in his cell, the door open and Tank lying on the bed looking up at the ceiling. His solicitor, a forget-table-looking chap in a grey pinstripe suit, perched next to him, awkwardly trying not to sit too far back lest he end up on his client's feet. The lawyer hunched forward, a pen poised in his hand ready to scribble on a pad of yellow legal paper.

Rafferty began the preliminaries, starting the tape, and summarising what had happened so far. When she recapped what Tank was accused of, his lawyer looked horrified but stared at his notepad and carried on scribbling.

'Sir,' Rafferty said. 'May I remind you that, under the laws of England and Wales, inferences can be drawn from silence. That means that when you choose not to say anything, we can infer that you're staying silent for a reason. I'm sure your solicitor has advised you of this.'

Tank turned his head to look at her, unblinking. He said nothing. In the dim cell lighting, he looked pallid, dishevelled, almost like he was going to nod off.

It was a rare criminal that actually managed to say nothing. Most of those who tried to "no comment" their way through a police interview eventually broke down and said something.

More impressively, Tank didn't even bother to say no comment.

'You're a former member of the Bakowski Crime Syndicate, aren't you?'

After each question, Rafferty paused and looked at him for an answer. When none came, she waited a few more seconds. Silence was the most awkward of vacuums and still Tank resisted saying anything.

'You were going to buy a bomb, weren't you?'

Nada.

'And you're murdering men who worked in the Syndicate, aren't you?'

For a second, Rafferty thought she saw Tank's eyebrow lurch a millimetre. He still said nothing. She glanced at Xander out in the hallway. He arched an eyebrow and gave a little shrug.

'You killed Elijah Zholnovych. We found your blood at the scene. Do you deny you were there?'

Nothing.

With great effort, he sat up. Then he leant forward, his head lolloping forward until it was almost resting on his solicitor's shoulder. What the hell? Was he going to sleep?

'I'm sorry, are we boring you?' Rafferty mocked. When he didn't reply, she carried on. 'We have reason to believe you killed Nathan Linden too. Did you?'

Still nothing.

'They were witnesses who'd turned against the Syndicate, weren't they? Men who worked for Tiny Bakowski directly?'

The second half of the question was a reach. She had no idea if they worked for Tiny directly, but it fitted her theory that Tiny was behind all this.

'You're working for Tiny still, aren't you? You're killing these men to exact revenge?'

The only sound from Tank was a raspy exhale. Was he pretending to snore? Or was it simpler than that, a derisive snort? Was she that far off base?

If Tank – and by extension, Yermak – weren't killing on Tiny's behalf, why were they breaking witness protection to commit several murders? And why did they need a bomb for the next one?

So far, they'd managed to catch their victims unaware. The protected witnesses had been in hiding for years. By now, they'd be going about their lives in blissful ignorance.

Unless the boys from UKPPS had told them? Or perhaps they'd moved them?

It dawned on Rafferty that she had no idea how UKPPS handled this sort of security breach. Did they even have a policy? It was a service that operated in a black box, one that prided itself on never having lost a witness before. Could they have come to the same conclusion that she and Mayberry had, that there were another sixty potential victims who'd turned Queen's that now needed to be moved even further afield? Would moving them be the clue that told Yermak and Tank what their identities were?

There was a wheels-within-wheels logic to it all that made her head spin.

She ignored the big picture, grabbed her pen and scribbled. She drew a small arrow towards "Tiny Bakowski" and wrote "puppet master... or victim?".

Then she underlined the latter.

'If you're not working for Tiny Bakowski, are you trying to kill him?'

Almost on cue, Tank began to shake.

Then Rafferty spotted a clamminess about him. He was sweating like an obese man who'd run up the Dune du Pilat in the middle of a heatwave.

Her expression darkened.

He wasn't ignoring her. She'd seen the signs before.

'Shit!' she exclaimed. 'Xander! Call an ambulance. He's going into withdrawal!'

86

CHASING THE GHOST

'IF TINY BAKOWSKI is the intended victim, this changes everything.'

Ayala stood at the head of the conference table. He was in his element as he took credit for months and months of Rafferty's hard work.

Despite their only detainee going into withdrawal in his cell, Ayala looked smug. Tank was still at the Royal London, well out of harm's way. Two uniformed officers were now guarding him around the clock, ready to arrest and charge him with attempting to procure a bomb – if he survived.

The team had been joined by a cabal from across the force: Kieran from the CPS, Xander from SOCA, Eric from UKPPS, and support staff including Brodie, Kflom, Purcell, and a handful more who Rafferty didn't recognise.

'T'anks for that, Captain Obvious,' Kieran said. 'Now we know, I'll nip down the Mags and get ya search warrant for All of Europe. If we comb through all five hundred million people, we'll find one of the most wanted men on the planet in five or six thousand years.'

Brodie sniggered. A glare from Ayala silenced him.

'As you all know, Tiny Bakowski had been in the wind for a decade. He's well-resourced, well-informed, and used to enjoy a network of informants, enforcers, and underworld contacts that span the globe. It is no surprise therefore that he hasn't been caught. If only my predecessor had managed to catch him all those years ago, we'd be in a very different situation.'

A dig at Morton. Ayala really couldn't help himself. Rafferty pursed her lips and just about managed to say nothing.

'This presents a golden opportunity to find him. If these men have been hunting him for years, they will no doubt have come across information that we do not possess. They successfully broke the ring of protection afforded to their victims by UKPPS.'

It was the Eric's turn to frown. Ayala really knew how to make friends.

'And in doing so, they've proved they might have a shot at taking Tiny down. I say we let them.'

Jaws dropped.

'Are you suggesting we let a bomb-maker go?' Rafferty asked.

'Exactly that,' Ayala said. 'The doctors at the Royal London inform me that our detainee has been successfully treated for heroin withdrawal but, with the NHS stretched to breaking point, he's likely to be released later today. I say we follow him back to Yermak and ultimately to Tiny Bakowski. And then,' he added, almost as an afterthought, 'we ensure he gets the help he needs to manage his addiction.'

As if Ayala gave a shit. His grand plan was an enormous gamble. If they messed it up, they'd have let a killer go free at best. At worst, they'd have let a killer go free only for him to commit another murder under their watch within hours of release. Or kill himself with heroin.

'I'm getting déjà vu here,' Rafferty said. 'We've let this guy go once. If we let him go again, won't he just disappear?'

'That's a risk,' Ayala said. 'But one I'm willing to take. We have to look at the big picture here. Losing a pawn like Tank won't stop a criminal mastermind.'

'If he's planning to blow someone up, won't the whole "not having a bomb" thing rather derail that?' Rafferty asked. 'Surely we can get this guy without putting a would-be bomber back on the streets of London?'

'Not in time. You've told me these guys have disappeared one victim, butchered another in a bathtub, and they've been linked to the death of a third man within hours of his arrival in the country. If they're half as dangerous as you say, we have to bring the ringleader in and we need to do it now. Before he kills again.'

Xander shot Rafferty an alarmed look. 'Bertram,' he said slowly, 'are you sure you're not just letting them kill Tiny? I'm all for saving the costs of a trial... but I'd hate for the public to get mixed up in all this.'

The look on Ayala's face was one of glee. 'If Tiny winds up dying because we were forced to let one of his former lieutenants go, that's a death I'm very happy to have on my conscience. This isn't a discussion. As soon as his doctors clear him for release, Tank walks out of the Royal London a free man. I want all hands on deck to watch his every move.'

Rafferty's gut screamed that they'd regret this.

She really hoped, for once, that Ayala was right.

As if.

87

THE FINAL VICTIM

THIS STARTED ALONE ALL those years ago. Me in the warehouse. A horrible life-or-death decision. One I've regretted every day of my life. The day I killed my mother.

My mind flashed back to the moment I realised it had been a real gun, loaded with real bullets. The look my brother had given me. The drugs I'd taken to numb the pain when we'd thrown her into the bunker.

The déjà vu when we'd done the same thing weeks later to bury my brother.

It has to end. Tonight.

My final victim.

Tiny deserves every moment of what's about to happen. And then some.

I'm not going to kill him. *They* are.

The crowd is wealthy, well-dressed, and, if you believe their bullshit, out to raise money for good causes. They've turned out in droves for today's ten-thousand-pounds-a-plate fundraiser, expecting to get a "memorable" dinner and bottomless wine.

They've had the latter. Now's the time for the former.

I walk to the end of the hall where a dais has been set up for the charity auctions and begin to peruse the wares on offer. A once in a lifetime chance to see the Northern Lights from aboard a superyacht? Fuck that shit. Tonight's show is going to be far more unforgettable.

And for most of the crowd, it really will be once in a lifetime.

I check my microphone. One little burst of static, barely audible over the music.

Good. It's working.

Now, I just have to pick my moment.

88

THE CHASE

THE MANHUNT BEGAN within minutes of Tank's release from the Royal London.

Rafferty had emailed her concerns to Ayala just in case it all went tits up. She wanted it in writing that she objected to the farce of a plan.

And then she put her all into making it happen.

Every exit from the hospital was being watched. Between SOCA, UKPPS, Ayala's murder investigation team, and dozens of constables, Tank had no chance of escaping unscathed.

An old trick with taxis was in play. Uniformed officers were circling the building, hoping their suspect would be daft enough to hop in and request a ride straight to the primary crime scene.

Tank didn't fall for that.

Instead, he walked nonchalantly to the Thames. Several times, he toyed with his mobile phone in his pocket. It had been bugged while he was in custody. That was Brodie's doing.

He lit up a cigarette but didn't inhale. A counter surveillance measure, no doubt. He was taking the time to see if he was being followed.

It was like playing a game of chess with a toddler. He was

looking out for Rafferty or Ayala, any obvious police presence. But Xander's team was several steps ahead. The woman with the baby walking past? She worked for Xander. The man selling coffee from a cart? Also one of them.

No officer was used more than once. The choreography would rival even the best West End musical, like a dance in the rain, every actor circling the prey that was Tank.

By the time Tank led them to the flat on the Thames, they knew he'd made several calls. None went through. Instead, they listened to the voicemail in which he promised to be "at the event as soon as he'd changed".

Between the location of the flat, the timing, and Tank emerging dressed in formal evening wear and making a beeline for the bridge to the other side of the Thames, it didn't take a genius for Rafferty to realise he was heading for the Worshipful Company of Developers and Architects.

Their event venue schedule said that tonight was the Sechin Foundation Ball, one of the biggest charity nights of the year, one attended, if Google were to be believed, by most of the Russian expat community in London.

'So,' Xander said as he slipped into the passenger compartment of the taxi she was driving, 'you want to go to the ball with me? Again?'

In his hands were two bags. One suit carrier for him, one dress bag for her. She recognised the dress as one she'd left at his place many moons ago, a Dona Matoshi holographic one-shoulder gown that she'd bought to go to a swanky police do as his plus-one.

It mixed greens, blues, and purple to create a stunning catwalk-worthy look, the kind she rarely dared to try and pull off. She figured it had long-since ended up in a charity shop. He'd even brought jewellery with him, though that definitely wasn't hers.

'Evidence locker?'

'How'd you guess?' he said with a grin.

89

THE LIFE OF THE PARTY

THE UNEASY FEELING in the pit of Rafferty's stomach grew more intense as she and Xander approached the security queue at the foot of the tower.

'Easy,' Xander said under his breath. 'You're crushing my arm.'

She released him a bit. 'Sorry.'

'Ash, security's tight here. Look at it. Everyone is going through a metal detector, a body scanner, and bags are being stored in a cloakroom this side of security. Relax.'

She couldn't. They shuffled through security. When her jewellery set off the metal detector, the guard pulled her to one side.

'Sorry, madam, raise one arm for me please,' he said cheerfully. 'And then the other.'

Once they were through, they were ushered into a lift with a handful of other late arrivals. It whooshed upwards so fast that Rafferty's already strained stomach threatened to throw up.

Then it stopped, the doors pinging open to reveal the poshest party that she'd ever seen. Ice sculptures were on display, one great bear carved from a single block sitting next to a series of ever smaller bears like those dolls that fit inside one another.

'No ice picks on display,' Xander said thoughtfully.

She hadn't even considered ice picks as a murder method.

A waiter swept in front of her, skidding to a halt with a tray full of champagne flutes.

She took one and sipped it as Xander shook his head. The bubbly was to die for: sweet but not too sweet, fruity with a floral note. If this was what posh champers was like, she could see why people drank it. Martini it was not.

'I'm driving,' he said. The waiter swept off with a frown only to return with a glass of water.

'Xander, these people don't drive their own cars. It's the chauffeur-and-chef champagne-and-caviar crowd in the room tonight.'

He scowled and looked around the room. It was a cavernous space, wrapping around a whole floor of the building. The lift had emerged in the centre of the floor, facing north, so that the crowds filled the space all the way around it.

'You go left, I go right?'

She nodded, peeled away from him and made her way through the crowd. There had to be a thousand-odd people here. They were clustered in groups, some small and some large. It was as if it were a gathering of what she called the horsey set. Women with names like Astoria danced with men called Hugo. The chitter-chatter was about holidays in exotic locations, pet racing horses, and the latest acquisitions of art, cars, and fine jewellery. Most were chattering away in English, but a few were speaking Russian. Or at least at Rafferty thought they were.

It wasn't a crowd that Rafferty felt at home in. She'd grown up on a council estate in Peckham before it became trendy. The wealth on one woman's hand here exceeded the lifetime earnings of those she'd grown up with. It was obnoxious.

And yet the crowd were oblivious. They were talking to
their people.

She pushed those thoughts from her mind, concentrating on
the task at hand: finding Yermak. He wouldn't be at home here
either.

The biggest challenge was the dress code. The men in their
evening wear looked so cookie-cutter that even spotting Xander
was now beyond her wit. Every man wore the same thing: a
single-breasted tailcoat, silk lapels, and black trousers with two
lines of braid. Nobody wore buttons either, only studs. The look
was completed with a detachable wing collar and thin white
bow-tie. It was as if the men had all shopped in the same
damned place with not an ounce of personality or colour in the
room.

Nor did it help that their suspect was average height,
average build, with brown hair and eyes. In this crowd, that
made him nearly invisible.

Halfway around her loop, Xander reappeared.

'No luck?' he said.

'None. You checked the gents?'

Xander craned around to look for a sign towards the loos.
He obviously hadn't thought that their man might be hiding out
in a stall, biding his time for whatever was to come.

'I'll do that, you check the kitchens?' He nodded towards
the middle of the room behind the lift. There were two doors
marked "STAFF ONLY", one to go in and the other to come
out. Waiters and waitresses flew through them carrying empty
trays and coming out with new trays laden down with glasses of
champagne, an enormous variety of canapés, and the occasional
special order. It seemed that the guests could have anything
they dreamed of. They need only ask.

As Xander went off to check the toilets, the music paused
and a voice came over the speaker system:

'The silent auction will begin in ten minutes.'

It was a voice she recognised. Somebody famous though she couldn't remember his name. He was an actor of some kind, maybe from one of the soaps?

Ignoring the voice in her head that demanded she try and work out who the speaker was, Rafferty made a beeline for the "IN" door, tucking in behind a red-faced waiter who'd clearly been working too hard.

He spun on the spot just inside. 'Madam, you can't be in here.'

She glanced past him, feigning being tipsy to buy herself time. Three girls were unloading platters from a dumb-waiter and putting them on a table ready to go out the door. No sign of Yermak.

'Sorry, I thought this was the ladies!'

She let herself be led out the other door and back onto the floor. The crowd had begun to coalesce on the side of the room with a view over the river. Some guests were milling around looking at the auction prizes up for grabs. Others were admiring the view. Xander reappeared, his expression one of consternation. He'd obviously found nobody hiding in the toilets.

As the clock ticked down towards the charity auction, two men set up a lectern on a wooden dais. They placed a wooden gavel on top of it ready for the auctioneer to whip the room into a frenzy of charity donations.

Eventually, the actor she'd heard over the speaker system appeared to the cheers of the crowd.

'He's from Eastenders, right?' Xander said.

'How would I know? I don't watch much TV.'

He was about to make a snide comment when the compère motioned for silence.

'My lords, ladies, and gentlemen, pray silence,' he said, his voice growing louder and more enthusiastic with every syllable.

'Tonight, we celebrate the third annual Sechin Foundation Christmas Ball! On offer this evening are some wonderful one-of-a-kind experiences and items that aren't on offer anywhere else. These will be auctioned to raise funds for the Foundation's work in supporting orphans across the Russian diaspora. Before that begins, I think it's only right that we give a hand to the man that started it all. Please give it up for Kostyantyn Sechin!'

Above the crowd a spotlight turned on, focussed on a thin, balding man in a rakish suit that shimmered against a silver-white shirt and purple tie.

'Fuck.'

Besides her, Xander stared, gobstruck.

'That's him, isn't it?' Xander said. 'Tiny fucking Bakowski.'

Just as he said it, the lights flicked off. When they came back on again, a voice came over the speaker. This time, it wasn't the actor who had been compèring. Rafferty recognised it almost immediately: Augustyn Yermak.

'Ladies and gentlemen, your attention please,' the voice said. 'Do not move, do not take out your mobile phones. There is a bomb in the building and if you do not comply with my instructions, I will detonate the bomb and we will all die.'

One woman screamed.

'Bullshit!' one man shouted.

'As proof of this,' Yermak continued, 'I would ask you to direct your attention to the north window. Look on the other side of the river, just east of the Gherkin. In fifteen seconds, I will blow up that building. It's currently unoccupied and nobody will get hurt.'

The lights went out again.

Silence fell. Mentally, Rafferty began to count. She could hear hushed whispers as people counted down, myriad voices all out of time. Some shuffled around, others stared listless and disbelieving. Others were too drunk to realise anything at all was happening. It wouldn't have surprised her if the drunks shouted out "Happy New Year" at the end of the countdown.

'We should do something,' Xander said.

'Like what?' she shot back. 'If he's telling the truth...'

She left the thought unfinished.

'Three, two, one...' Yermak counted down.

Then, it happened.

It was less dramatic at first than Rafferty expected. A loud boom could be heard over the hush in the room. The building they were watching crumpled as if an invisible hand was pulling it down from within. Dust billowed upward and out as it went down. Then, nothing. Where the building had once stood, there was now only a gap with no sign that a skyscraper had ever stood in its place.

'I trust I have your attention.'

The light flicked on, lighting Tiny up.

'The man before you calls himself Kostyantyn Sechin. In reality, he is Tiny Bakowski, mass-murderer, extortionist, and drug-dealer to the world. He has raped, trafficked, and maimed women. He has trained children as his foot soldiers. He has killed hundreds of people.'

There was the briefest of pauses as if the speaker were suffering a lump in his throat.

'I give you all a simple choice. Kill him, here and now. Or I will kill us all. You have sixty seconds to decide.'

Another clock began to tick down.

All hell broke loose. One or two ran for the lift. It didn't work. The power was out. So too went the lights.

Screaming ensued.

'I'm not dying for him!' one man yelled.

Then, around the room, tiny lights flickered to life as people turned their phones into torches, most of them aimed at the dais upon which Tiny stood.

In the space of a few heartbeats, his eyes darted around as Rafferty watched, flicking from fire exit to fire exit, then to the baying mob before he stared, pleadingly, at his security.

The nearest bodyguard looked over at Tiny and then considered the crowd. Rafferty realised that he wasn't a mobster, he was there to protect Nikolai Senchin, Russian philanthropist.

Except Senchin didn't exist.

Tiny did.

And he'd realised he was finally on his own. He began to shuffle towards the nearest fire exit as the crowd drew closer. The mob paused, looking over at the bodyguard.

He shrugged. 'Kill the bastard.'

The crowd descended upon Tiny, a herd stampeding upon its prey. Rafferty and Xander were swept along, buffeted by the split in the crowd as some fought towards the emergency exits and the rest stormed Tiny Bakowski.

Mangled cries went up as the first boot went in. Rafferty couldn't see anything in the darkness. But she could hear everything. Screaming, shouting, swearing.

Then, a minute later, the lights came back on.

There, in the centre of the floor, bloodied and battered, was a body.

Tiny Bakowski was dead.

GUILTY CONSCIENCE

MOB BOSS MAULED BY ANGRY MOB

By Hamish Porter for The Impartial

An unprecedented murder put paid to Interpol's #2 Most Wanted Man late last night when a crowd of posh partygoers were coerced into murdering him by a man who threatened them all with a bomb.

In an Impartial exclusive interview, one anonymous attendee said she feared for her life.

'It was sheer bedlam,' the woman said. 'One minute we were drinking, the next a voice told us there was a bomb in the building. The lights went out and we couldn't take the lift down. Then, he proved he had a bomb by blowing up a skyscraper across the way. That was when everyone lost it.'

Sources at the Met revealed to The Impartial that there was, in fact, no bomb.

The killer had used the borough council's demolition schedules to time his audacious murder, persuading the crowd that he was responsible for what was actually a carefully controlled implosion carried out under the auspices of the London Borough of Tower Hamlets to make way for a new development.

The victim, mob boss Tiny Bakowski, was found dead by two police detectives who attended the party. When asked for comment, Ms Ashley Rafferty and Mr Alexander Thompson of the Met would only say that a suspect was quickly taken into custody having barricaded himself into the media room on the floor below. A Met spokesman said that charges of incitement to murder, among others, would be brought in due course.

Questions are being raised in Parliament today as to the culpability of the crowd. Newly promoted Minister for Justice Donna Morfett told a packed College Green this morning that "mob rule is never the answer" before promising that "all those involved will be brought to justice". It remains to be seen how exactly the Met will discern the culpability of the attendees when it is unclear who attacked Mr Bakowski and how to handle over a thousand potential suspects.

Angrily, Ruslana threw her copy of The Impartial on the floor. Not only had those two idiots who'd stolen her shipment got away, her baby boy was dead. The idiots would pay in prison. Nowhere in the justice system was safe for them. Before they even made it to a trial, someone would take up her offer of a bounty. A hundred thousand pounds apiece for the men who'd conspired to murder her boy. They had to pay the ultimate price.

So too would the police.

It was their fault for not stopping it.

Two of them were there in the crowd: Rafferty and Thompson. Their photos were plastered all over the news which hailed them as the heroes who'd caught the "Bakowski Killer".

Ruslana sneered.

Rafferty and Thompson wouldn't have long to celebrate.

They were dead people walking.

ALSO BY SEAN CAMPBELL

The DCI Morton series:

Dead on Demand (DCI Morton #1)

Cleaver Square (DCI Morton #2)

Ten Guilty Men (DCI Morton #3)

The Patient Killer (DCI Morton #4)

Missing Persons (DCI Morton #5)

The Evolution of a Serial Killer (DCI Morton #6)

Christmas Can Be Murder (*a novella*)

My Hands Are Tied (DCI Morton #7)

STANDALONE TITLES

The Grifter (*with Ali Gunn*)

To find out more visit www.DCIMorton.com

Printed in Great Britain
by Amazon

24307624R00233